BLOOD TRACKS

BLOOD TRACKS

A Tess Grey Thriller

Matt Hilton

This first world edition published 2015
in Great Britain and 2016 in the USA by
SEVERN HOUSE PUBLISHERS LTD of
19 Cedar Road, Sutton, Surrey, England, SM2 5DA.
Trade paperback edition first published
in Great Britain and the USA 2016 by
SEVERN HOUSE PUBLISHERS LTD

British Library Cataloguing in Publication Data

Hilton, Matt, 1966- author.
  Blood tracks.
  1. Women private investigators–Fiction. 2. Suspense
fiction.
  I. Title
  823.9'2-dc23

ISBN-13: 978-0-7278-8567-8 (cased)
ISBN-13: 978-1-84751-676-3 (trade paper)
ISBN-13: 978-1-78010-733-2 (e-book)

All Severn House titles are printed on acid-free paper.

Severn House Publishers support the Forest Stewardship Council™ [FSC™],
the leading international forest certification organisation.
All our titles that are printed on FSC certified paper carry the FSC logo.

MIX
Paper from
responsible sources
FSC® C013056

Typeset by Palimpsest Book Production Ltd.,
Falkirk, Stirlingshire, Scotland.
Printed and bound in Great Britain by
TJ International, Padstow, Cornwall.

For Denise

ONE

The rain-fragmented neon above the roadside bar danced like wildfire over the shingles. It was an artistic image, and one Mitch Delaney felt sure would be wasted on the patrons inside. They were outlaw bikers and beyond the fading tattoos on their bodies didn't give a damn for imagery or art, the wonders of nature, or anything much else for that matter, apart from how full their shot glasses were and how quickly they could empty them again. They were ignorant scum. Violent criminals. The antithesis of what Mitch actually stood for.

Despite the rain, and the buffeting wind blowing off the Harraseeket River, Mitch had stepped outside for a smoke, standing away from the parked motorcycles, under a tree that offered meagre protection from the elements. He'd no patience for bullshit and those inside were full of it: he had to get outside for a calming smoke or his frustration might explode, and with it his cover. Was that such a bad thing? If the game was up, he could go back to his real life, and associate with decent human beings for a change. Hell, instead of the snatched phone calls he did these days, he could spend physical quality time with his wife and son, without the ever-present fear of discovery bringing danger to their door. Why was he even still here, he'd wondered, when his conduit to Sower had already booked? He knew why. He had to maintain his cover in case Crawford Wynne decided to get in touch with the gang. It was imperative that Wynne was traced: if Mitch's real identity came out, no way would Wynne contact him. Except to tell him to go to hell. The long months he'd spent winning Wynne's trust would've been wasted, and he shouldn't swill all his hard work down the drain because he couldn't abide the company he must keep. Enduring his enforced separation from Jenny and his five-year-old son, Jacob, was difficult without him failing in his duty too. The sacrifice they'd all made had to be valued. It would be worthless if he walked away now. Do your duty, Mitch, he berated himself. To your family and your goddamn badge. Have a smoke, chill out, then get your ass back inside where it serves a purpose.

His lighter took half a dozen attempts to set a spark to his cigarette, and he inhaled deeply of it while staring at the bar, the collar of his leather jacket up, his back to the inclement weather. Between the heavier squalls and droplets as thick as his finger the rain came as a turgid mist, and it was through those shifting curtains that he watched the writhing neon and his imagination painted pictures of hellish flame.

He was trapped by the portent of the scene, and the crunch of boots on the crushed-seashell parking lot didn't register in his mind.

He was yanked backwards, and a gloved hand clamped down on his mouth, sealing in his shout of surprise. He was spun, a gloved fist crashing against his jaw. He couldn't tell how many assailants he was up against, but there was more than one. An arm looped round his throat, squeezing the breath from him, even as another man drove a punch into his gut. When he was violently forced down, he was so stunned he'd no fight left in him. Lucidity disintegrated in a series of strobing flashes and pain. He felt his back impact with the ground, boots beating a tattoo against the side of his skull and neck. A coppery wash flooded his mouth, and splinters of enamel from his broken teeth were gritty on his lips. A dull impact sent a scarlet flash exploding across his brain.

Again a boot found the side of his head, and all Mitch could hope for was blessed incomprehension.

His prayer must have been answered, because when he snapped to he was no longer on his back, being beaten mercilessly. Within him he had a deep sense of passing time, and a long uncomfortable journey, perhaps in the rear of a van where his abductors had space to beat him unconscious again each time he'd began surfacing from oblivion.

He was upright, supported, his body numb.

His eyelids were gummy, and it was a huge effort to prise them apart.

His tongue worked in his mouth, a fat slug probing the

edges of his broken teeth. He pushed fragments from between his mashed lips, felt the warm dribble of saliva splash on the chilled flesh of his chest.

Why was he naked?

Where am I?

He forced his eyes to focus.

Brushed steel. Cold light.

Hospital?

No, he'd heard rumours of this place.

Was this *the Greek's boat*?

Panic swelled his lungs, and he reared back, hoping with every ounce of his being that he was wrong about his location.

He saw a long steel table laden with tools, brushed steel cladding on the walls, and a tiled floor with a central gutter. He moaned. He was not wrong.

Why had he been brought to the boat? Had Sower discovered his true identity?

Get away from here, his mind screamed, *get away now!*

He tried. He bucked and flailed, but he was going nowhere.

Glancing down, he found his bared chest with its bluing tattoos, the pale white skin of his thighs, his hairy shins and bare feet. His skin was marbled with blood. His toes had clawed streaks through the dark blood pooling on the tiles, and in the gutter he stood astride. His arms were stretched cross-wise, thick straps of Velcro holding him to a metal pole as tightly as any forged chain. The pole was suspended on a pulley system overhead.

A curse broke from his lips in a spatter of blood-flecked spit.

'You are awake. Good, I'd hate for you to miss the best part, Delaney.' The voice came from behind him. Mitch didn't need to see the speaker to guess to whom it belonged. He recognized the accented sibilance of it, and the ice that it thrust through his heart.

'Why are you doing this to me, Hector?' Mitch struggled at his bonds.

A rubbery squeak assailed his ears.

Dirty yellow filled his vision.

A face leaned in close to his, ugly, twisted in a grin. The

cheeks and forehead were knotty with old scar tissue, as if
the face had gone through a windshield, or been too close to
a detonating grenade. Hector's eyes were still and depthless.

'Before we proceed,' said his tormentor, 'I'll give you one
chance to make things easier on yourself. This I promise. You
will die, Delaney, but it's up to you in how much pain.
Comprende? Where is Crawford Wynne?'

What? This wasn't about his true identity; it was about
Wynne? Mitch didn't know if he should be relieved, because
the shift in focus didn't change his predicament.

'Wynne?' he said, playing up his confusion. 'I . . . I haven't
seen Wynne for weeks.'

'But you do know where he is.'

'I haven't talked with him in—'

A gloved hand slashed across Mitch's face, the dimpled
rubber almost tearing off his left eyelid. He held his head
aside, shuddering, fighting the pain while also expecting
another blow. Tears blinded him.

Hector tilted his head to meet Mitch's eyes anyway. 'Do
not lie to me. I understand that lying comes as second nature
to your kind, but do not do it to *me!*'

'I'm not lying!'

'And neither have you spoken to Wynne.' Hector grunted
and walked away, his thick rubberized coat creaking. He leaned
over the steel table, deliberating over the tools arranged on it.
He picked up a saw and ran his gaze along the serrated edge.

Mitch fought his bonds, in as pointless a battle as before.

When he returned Hector was holding a knife, testing its
balance point on his gloved palm. Folding his hand around
the grip, he pointed the tip past Mitch. 'Come, my friends.
Don't be so squeamish. Hold Delaney for me. This is such a
delicate task I'd hate to slip and miss his tiny *pene*.'

The scuff of feet on the tiles spoke of others in the room,
most definitely those that had snatched Mitch and delivered
him here. But none came forward. One of the nervous watchers
wheezed out a mirthless laugh at Hector's disparaging remark.

Mitch craned to see who bore witness to his torture.
Indistinct forms gathered at the end of the room, but his
watering vision couldn't make out detail. He didn't need to

see clearly to suspect who was there. 'For God's sake! How can you watch him do this to me? We're supposed to be fucking friends!'

'Forget about them. You need only pay attention to me,' said Hector. 'Besides, you have no hope of finding friends here. Only pain.'

The knife slid an inch into Mitch's side. He cried out, but that wasn't enough to satisfy Hector. His torturer twisted the blade, cutting down in a sawing motion to a point above his hip, and now Mitch shrieked.

The blade was withdrawn and blood flooded down Mitch's thigh. He gagged, barely able to catch his breath.

'I will ask again, Delaney. Where is Crawford Wynne?'

His mind had almost closed down, but words jumped from Mitch's throat. 'I don't know where he is! Why won't you believe me?'

'I do not trust your word. You swore loyalty to Alberto, but you were quick to betray him when bargaining with the DA. How can I believe anything from a dog willing to bite the hand of its master?'

Hector had failed to make him as a cop, but in his eyes it made him an informant. In the twisted mind of the criminal the latter was probably worse. 'I didn't betray Mr Sower,' Mitch croaked. 'Please . . . don't do this . . . I swear to you.'

Hector shook his head. 'Something troubles me about you, Delaney. You and Wynne were taken in for questioning. You were both potential material witnesses, and yet you were both freed. Alberto is locked in a cell, while his dogs walk around off their leashes. If you didn't bargain for your freedom then there was another reason you were released. Is there something you'd like to come clean about?'

Should he admit to being an undercover detective? That he'd infiltrated Sower's group via a side-door route through Crawford Wynne? He could lie and claim he was only concerned with bringing Wynne to trial for his crimes, that he had no interest in Sower's activities. Was Sower's torturer *really* prepared to kill a cop? To do so would ignite a shitstorm of retribution. The entire law-enforcement community wouldn't rest until they brought down Sower's empire, and was harming him worth that? Except somehow he felt that Albert Sower was the type who'd relish the fight, even if it were vicariously through this knife-wielding monster. And he feared that such an admission would only incite the sadist to immediate action. No. He had to try another way, divert attention from him. It hurt his cop's moral sense of duty to point Hector at another victim, but he was also a family man, and wanted to see his loved ones again. To do so he'd give them Wynne. But he had to make it sound convincing.

'It wasn't me who made a bargain,' he said. 'But you're right about us being freed. It bothered me too when we were cut loose, it felt too easy, too convenient. Now that you mention it . . . well, it had to be Wynne who made a deal. Right? They must've released me so it didn't look suspicious when he walked. It's probably why he disappeared. But not me, Hector. I stayed. I've nothing to hide because I didn't betray anyone.'

Hector placed a gloved fingertip to Mitch's lips, halting his breathless rush of words. 'So as well as betraying Alberto, Wynne also betrayed you? If that's true then you should help me find him. Tell me where to find Wynne.'

'That's the thing. I don't know where he is.'

'But you have your suspicions.'

Mitch thought hard, and his mind swept the length of a continent away. Jesus, why hadn't he thought about it sooner? If he had then he wouldn't have had to remain undercover, and he wouldn't be here now. 'Louisiana! You should try looking for him in New Orleans. That's where Wynne comes from. Maybe he has run home.'

'Maybe?' The knife dug into Mitch's sternum, steel grating against bone, drilling a way through his chest.

Mitch screeched. He jerked frantically at his bonds and the knife tip withdrew.

Fighting for breath, Mitch shuddered. 'You said . . . if I told you the truth . . . you'd make it easier on me . . .'

'You should have told the truth sooner. You suspected Wynne was in Louisiana, yet you chose to stall. I don't need to honour a promise made to a dishonourable dog like you. Come,' Hector snapped at the onlookers, and all pretence at humour had disappeared. 'Keep this whining dog still.'

This time he was obeyed. Hands gripped Mitch's shoulders, fingers digging into his skin to hold him in place. The man in the yellow coat grasped Mitch's genitals, squeezing them mercilessly. His other hand guided the blade between Mitch's thighs.

'Oh, God! Don't . . . don't do this, Hector!'

Unmoved by the plea, Hector gazed steadily into Mitch's face. 'Do you know where Alberto and I come from?'

'Ye . . . yes.'

'In Bolivia there is a punishment for dogs that bite their masters. Their sex organs are removed and fed back to them. Then their heads are cut off and displayed so the pack understands what will happen if they also choose to turn on their masters.' The warning was meant for everyone in the room, but the next was directed solely at Mitch. 'Crawford Wynne must learn this lesson, and you must serve as my messenger.'

He knew what was coming, and the inevitability of it clenched Mitch's insides as tightly as the fist constricting his genitals. Eyes screwed tight, Mitch made one last desperate attempt at escape, twisting manically in the grip of his captors, and he was almost thankful when he pulled free of the grasping hand. His relief was short-lived.

White fire shot through his core.

He heard the torrent of blood splashing on the floor, and pouring into the gutter and his eyes started open, dreading the truth but desperate to see.

Hector opened his hand, displaying what he held.

Mitch's mouth opened to scream.

Hector's hand slapped over it, and the proof of his emasculation was forced between Mitch's teeth.

Gagging, trying to spit out the choking flesh, Mitch grew frantic. He flopped and twisted and kicked and more blood gouted over the yellow slicker. His mutilator stared, while forcing his gloved hand harder against Mitch's mouth and nostrils. Hector wouldn't relinquish his hold until Mitch swallowed. He aimed an order at the men holding Mitch. 'One of you bring me that upholsterer's gun from the table.'

TWO

The blade had cut exceptionally deep.

The scar on her wrist was pink against her skin, not exactly vivid, but noticeable to someone with an eye for detail. Usually when an observer noticed the scar they formed a wrong opinion of Tess Grey. Most people didn't mention the healing wound, but they considered it, and what it meant about her as a person. Ordinarily she wouldn't give a damn what they thought, or their incorrect assumption of how her wrist had been cut so deeply, but it was different when it was a prospective employer. She turned over her hand and discreetly pulled down the cuff of her jacket sleeve with the other. Opposite her, the woman noticed Tess's discomfort, but didn't comment.

They were sitting in the smartly dressed woman's office on Baxter Boulevard, near Belmeade Park, in Portland, Maine, from where Tess looked out across Black Cove. The office was typical of what Tess expected of an attorney, but with a better view. The woman wasn't a lawyer; she worked on behalf of a specialist inquiry firm, headed by Richard Jackson. Tess had heard of Jackson, a former Special Agent in Charge who'd run the local FBI field office for years, and current specialist investigator, but didn't know his second-in-command. In earlier days the woman would have been termed a private investigator, but she hadn't introduced herself as such. She'd given her name as Mrs Emma Clancy, and her title as Assistant Inquiry Agent to the Attorney's Office. In return Tess had offered only her name and the innocuous tag of genealogist – perhaps she should've given a more highfalutin title along the lines of Historical Familial Researcher and Examiner and met Clancy's smile. Let's face it, she'd thought, we're both private dicks; you have a nicer office, nicer clothes, and a view to die for, but we both do the same kind of scut work.

They had shaken hands in perfunctory manner, then Clancy

waved her to take a seat. In that brief interaction Clancy's glance had gone to Tess's wrist, and her summation had pulled at the corners of her mouth. Tess folded her left hand over her right, placing them in her lap.

'Thank you for coming, Miss Grey,' said Clancy as she sat. She smoothed her skirt over her thighs. 'I hope this meeting proves productive for us both.'

'I hope I can be of assistance to you.'

Clancy consulted a sheet of paper on her desk. Tess doubted she needed to refresh her memory, and that the checking of her notes was simply an unconscious trait. 'You come to us highly recommended,' Clancy said, and nodded to herself.

'I do? Who was it that recommended me?' Tess was surprised when she'd received a call from Clancy's office requesting her attendance, and wondered why she'd come to the woman's attention.

Clancy thought about her reply, but elected to keep her source confidential. 'You were a law-enforcement officer prior to your current position, right?'

'I was with the Cumberland County Sheriff's Office right here in town,' Tess confirmed.

'I've heard that you were good at your job, and would likely have progressed through the ranks had you not left. And yet you're now working in the private investigations industry as a genealogist.'

Clancy was pushing for an admission that Tess's previous job had been too tough to handle and she'd taken extreme measures to get out. If she were any kind of investigator, Clancy should know the real reason for Tess leaving her law-enforcement career behind. Clancy knew, Tess was certain. She didn't feel a need to go over it now, though there was a point she wanted to make. 'I didn't leave. I was forced out. Thankfully I had another skill-set to fall back on. I majored in history and cultural anthropology at Husson University. It makes sense that I use my education to pay for me in my current occupation.'

'Your background makes you the ideal candidate for the task we have in mind,' Clancy said. 'Your law-enforcement and genealogical experience should stand you in good stead.'

Tess didn't know how best to answer; instead she simply waited.

Clancy pushed a file across the desk. 'Inside you'll find details of the person we're hoping to trace. His name is Crawford Wynne, born July seventh, nineteen sixty-nine in New Orleans, all the other details you will require are in his personal file: I'll also have a digital version of the file supplied to you once we agree terms. We believe Wynne is now residing in Louisiana, but all our previous efforts at locating him have come up empty.'

'You want *me* to go to Louisiana?'

'Is travel a problem?'

'No. But why do you not use an investigator down there to locate him?'

'We have, but as I said, without success. The benefit in using an investigator local to the area is one of familiarity, but it also comes with a drawback: out of sight, out of mind. We haven't much faith in the level of service we've received for our fee. Reports from the investigations company we engaged have been less than encouraging, and we can't guarantee that any other company down there will offer a higher level of service. It's why I was tasked with finding someone here in Maine who can offer a more personal service; someone prepared to work diligently on our behalf. Like I said, you've been highly recommended, and judging by your previous successes I have full confidence in your abilities.'

As a sergeant with Cumberland County Sheriff's Office, Tess had distinguished herself, her tough go-get-'em attitude winning her the kind of respect only given grudgingly on both sides of the law-enforcement fence. It was as Clancy had mentioned, before her career with CCSO ended she was poised to rise through the ranks but her climb was based on hard work and commitment, not through manipulation or the internal politics that usually came into play. In regards to her genealogical career path Tess's previous successes weren't huge, but yes, she'd given her full, undivided attention to each case she'd taken on since leaving the Sheriff's Department. The fact that her jobs had been few and hardly taxing of her abilities was beside the point. A dozen times she'd fully satisfied her clients and their glowing testimonials took pride of place on her company website. The jobs she'd undertaken were varied, from compiling family trees through locating beneficiaries of inheritances, and on one occasion tracking down a match for an adopted child in dire need of a bone-marrow transplant. She guessed that Clancy's confidence was based primarily on when Tess carried a badge and gun.

'I take it you've asked Louisiana law enforcement for assistance in locating Wynne?' Tess said.

Clancy laughed through her nose. 'You were a deputy sheriff; you know how these things work. Wynne – despite his criminal tendencies – is not a suspect in the case we're working on, otherwise the FBI would go after him. He's more valuable to us a witness for the prosecution. If a warrant had been sworn for his arrest, the police would indeed act on our behalf, but they aren't going out of their way to trace him as a witness. I expect our request for assistance is still sitting ignored in a fax machine somewhere.'

Tess knew exactly what Clancy meant. There were more important things for a police officer to be getting on with than chasing down possible witnesses on behalf of a prosecutor's office out of their jurisdiction.

Clancy said, 'We're offering an attractive reimbursement package for your time and expertise, and will of course cover all accrued expenses during your investigation.' She shrugged. 'I appreciate you're unfamiliar with Louisiana, and might feel a little out of your depth alone down there. If you wish to hire a local guide then we'll foot those expenses too.'

Tess could use some of those promised expenses up front. Not that she'd admit it, but the income earned from previous cases had already disappeared into the black hole of her empty bank account. She wasn't fully destitute yet, but with no other promise of income on the horizon she desperately needed this job. Her mother had offered her money, not a loan but a gift, but Tess turned it down. Accepting the cash bailout would be tantamount to admitting defeat, and her mother would've won another small victory against her. Securing employment with Clancy's firm wouldn't only balance the books; it would also knock the perpetual frown of dismay off her mother's brow.

She mustn't come over too needy, though a veiled hint concerning her lack of funds might not go amiss. 'Shall I leave the travel and accommodation booking to your office?'

'We can handle that for you, Miss Grey.' Clancy offered a smile that said she suspected Tess was almost bankrupt, but it wasn't without a touch of sympathy. Tess thought that Clancy was counting on Tess's desperation to ensure a service above and beyond what they'd received from previous investigators. Clancy passed a small plastic wallet across the desk. 'It's a company credit card. You can charge your ongoing expenses to it as necessary. If you need to use it for your personal use, payment can be deducted from your fee at completion of the contract.'

Tess resisted opening the wallet and inspecting the credit card. One thing that was certain; it appeared she'd got the job, and there was no way she was going to turn it down. 'I think now would be a good time to tell you how much I—'

'We'll pay a set fee that we believe will be more than to your satisfaction,' Clancy butted in. 'We require you to trace Crawford Wynne, subpoena him as a material witness if necessary, and get him back here as quickly as possible. Your fee is based upon your success, Miss Grey, and we have confidence in you upholding your end. In fact,' she said as if making an executive decision, 'get him back here within the week and you'll earn a bonus of twenty per cent on top. Are these terms agreeable?'

Hell yes, Tess thought. Instead she said, 'I really should ask about your set fee first . . .'

'Of course.' Clancy flicked open the file, turning it so that Tess could read the draft contract on the first page. Tess swallowed hard when spotting the fee. There was an extra zero at the end she hadn't expected.

'As you can tell,' Clancy went on, 'it's important that Crawford Wynne be located, and we're prepared to pay handsomely for his retrieval. But it must be within the week. There's an upcoming court hearing and it's imperative that bail is denied. Without Wynne's testimony there's little hope of that happening. We cannot afford for this criminal to be back on the streets.'

'Then I'll do everything I can to bring back Wynne in time,' Tess pledged.

Clancy's smile became fixed. 'Before you sign the contract I must warn you. Crawford Wynne is not a nice person. While he was here in Maine, he spoke to us about his employer's criminal activities, and he had no recourse but flee back home to Louisiana for fear of retribution. He might not be eager to return with you.'

'You want me to kidnap him and drag him back to Maine?' Tess laughed at her own joke.

Clancy didn't laugh. 'I should also warn you Wynne might not be the only one who doesn't want him here. You should familiarize yourself with the information I've supplied. It makes for stomach-churning reading at times, but it's best you're forewarned.' Clancy studied Tess. 'You don't appear overly concerned by that suggestion.'

'I didn't leave the Sheriff's Department because I was afraid,' Tess stated.

'No,' Clancy said, 'you didn't. But in this instance it might serve you to be cautious. Have you heard the name Alberto Suarez?'

The name was familiar but Tess couldn't bring a face to mind.

'You might have read about his recent arrest,' Clancy went on. 'Though you might have heard of him under a different name: Albert Sower?'

'The drugs guy?' Sower's arrest had made the news weeks ago, but Tess hadn't given it too much notice, too busy with her own life to follow the updates. When she was still with the Sheriff's Department Sower's name had been mentioned on occasion too, but not through any active cases she'd been involved in.

'I think that description is an understatement, but yes. Alongside the FBI, the State Attorney's Office is currently compiling a case against Sower as the head of an organized crime syndicate responsible for bringing illegal narcotics into Maine, direct from his homeland of Bolivia. His group is suspected of transporting drugs across the Canadian border and through some of the smaller ports on the coastline. But those are the least of the crimes they're responsible for.

Corruption, blackmail, possession of illegal firearms, violence, rape, murder, the list is not exhaustive.' Clancy tapped the open file with a manicured fingernail. 'The charges against Sower will mean nothing if we don't have witnesses on the stand. Five of those we'd already secured have gone missing, presumed dead. Someone, we believe, is picking off witnesses, and dealing with them in an uncompromising manner, and sadly the media have gotten hold of the story and have run with it. Because of that we're having trouble reassuring other potential witnesses of their safety. When you do find Wynne, tell him we're prepared to offer leniency from prosecution and witness protection in return for his testimony. If he refuses, then subpoena him and have local law enforcement detain him and we'll arrange his carriage back here.'

'I can do that.'

'I'm sure you can. But before you commit to this you should take a look at the photographs of the one victim we did find. If those pictures don't change your mind, then they might help motivate your search. Even if the sickening manner of his death doesn't shock you, then his identity will. Mitchel Delaney was an undercover narcotics officer working out of Bangor.'

Clancy had kept that denouement to last because it was indeed motivation: there was a full task force investigating Delaney's murder but Tess would still want to do her bit to avenge a fellow law-enforcement officer. She did, but she'd have accepted the task whomever the victim was. More than she required the promised money, she needed to regain her self-worth, and prove to the naysayers – chief of whom was her mother – that they'd been wrong about her.

'You can count on me, Mrs Clancy,' she promised.

'Then call me Emma. If we're going to be working together, we needn't be so formal, need we?'

Clancy assured her that everything Tess needed to get started was contained within the file she'd been supplied, and anything requiring clarification she could glean from the end of a phone. With a promise to have her assistant, Monica Perry, begin booking travel arrangements to New Orleans, Clancy passed over her personal cell number. 'I'd appreciate daily progress updates and that's the best number to reach me on.'

'No problem,' Tess said, and scrawled her signature on the contract of employment. Her handwriting was spidery, partly through barely subdued anticipation, partly through the injury to her wrist that affected her dexterity.

She left the office in a daze, the warnings ringing in her mind, but Clancy's parting shot had had the desired effect of motivating her. She should be concerned that she'd taken on something beyond her abilities, and admit to being concerned by the possibility of running foul of Albert Sower's people during her pursuit of Crawford Wynne. When she'd the resources of the Sheriff's Department behind her she'd have happily taken on anything Sower could throw at her. Could she say the same now? But she wasn't fearful. No. She was angry on behalf of Delaney, having learned he'd left behind a grieving widow and young son. She was equally angry for the others suspected of falling victim in order that Albert Sower evade incarceration; they might have been criminals, but nobody should suffer as Delaney had. Even Crawford Wynne – by anyone's standards a bad man – deserved better than mutilation at the hands of a depraved killer. She'd pledged to find Wynne, bring him back, save him from similar brutal torture, and they were promises she was determined to uphold.

Outside she turned towards Belmeade Park, pondering her first move. Clancy was probably correct: down in Louisiana she might be out of her depth in more ways than one. But she wasn't going to let anything stop her. She was sure she could engage the help she needed, and who to go to for it.

She took out her cell phone and called her brother Alex, walking head down as she spoke into the phone. She didn't notice the car parked on Baxter Boulevard opposite Clancy's office, or the undue attention its occupants paid her. The fair-haired man in the front passenger seat took out his cell phone and hit a number. Tess didn't hear the corresponding ring of a phone in the office she'd just left.

THREE

C harley's Auto Shop, a squat cinder-block building with a tin roof, sitting on the corner of a Portland street, stank of hot rubber and engine oil. Old oil, degraded, the air gritty with it. It was an aroma that took Tess back in memory, way back to when she was a small child, watching from the rough bench in his workshop as her grandfather tinkered with his boat's outboard motor. It was a happy smell, though it had no right to be. The metallic clanks and knocks, the hiss of pneumatics, had no real place in her memory, but they were fitting all the same.

An elderly man, his legs bowed like a sailor's, was working under the hood of a classic Ford Mustang. It was a muscle car, a genuine car of distinction, unlike the gas-saving Prius she'd parked outside. Tess allowed her gaze to trail along the car's masculine lines, and she nodded in appreciation. It wasn't with any knowledge of automobiles, or even a wish to own a classic like it, just that the car embodied earlier times, as did the smell of perished oil. She could imagine her grandfather driving a car just like it, back when he'd been a Homicide cop in NYC. Back before he was shot dead by a punk cranked up on LSD after her grandfather walked in on a convenience-store robbery. Her grandfather's life in exchange for a few dollars and a handful of Hershey bars scooped up as the armed robber fled the scene.

The old man adjusted an inspection lamp, aiming its phosphorus glow below the hood, leaned in for a closer look, then fiddled with something in the guts of the engine. He *tsk'd* under his breath, then stood and scratched under his shirt collar. A thatch of white hair poked out, but his neck was pink from the razor, his hair beginning again after the shaved demarcation zone as bristly silver fuzz.

Tess waited to be noticed. But the mechanic looked again at the engine, grumbling in puzzlement. She purposefully scuffed her shoe on the floor. Between the other bangs and clanks the soft scrape was almost inaudible, but the man's hearing was tuned to the unusual. He turned as if alarmed, and stood there looking at her, breathing heavily.

'Sorry, I didn't mean to startle you,' Tess said.

The mechanic scratched his neck again, and his face crimped up in a bunch of lines around his pale-blue eyes. 'I wasn't startled. You just aren't what I was expecting to see, that's all. Can I do something for you, ma'am? Problem with your vehicle?'

'I'm actually looking for someone, a guy, and was told he might be here.'

'Well, a pretty young thing like you, I wish it was me you'd come calling on.' He smiled in that genial way, face crinkling, to show he was kidding. 'Who is the lucky fella?'

'I was told to ask for Mister Po.'

'*Mister* Po?' Laugher crackled in his throat, threatening to erupt as a cough any moment.

Tess didn't know what to say. When first she'd heard the name 'Mister Po' she'd fleetingly pictured the Chinese master from that old TV programme about Shaolin monks. Not Grasshopper but the guy with ping-pong balls for eyes.

'Are you a Fed?' He didn't sound judgemental, and Tess guessed it was her tailored trouser-suit, buttoned-down blouse, and sensible shoes that gave the old mechanic the impression.

'No, sir. My name's Teresa Grey. I'm not a law-enforcement officer, but I won't lie to you, I am an investigator of sorts, and there's a case I'm looking into that, uh, Mister Po might be able to help me with.'

The mechanic laughed again. He dislodged the phlegm in his throat this time, and reached for an oily rag, with which he discreetly covered his mouth. 'Mister Po, huh? Don't start calling him that or he'll be getting way above his station an' he's already a royal pain in the ass.' He threw the rag in a steel drum that doubled as a trashcan. Then, chuckling, his hand fluttering like a bird's wing, he said, 'Hold on there, ma'am, and I'll go see if *Mistuh Po* is taking callers this fine day.'

Tess smiled as the genial mechanic walked away. He even swayed like a sailor walking the deck of a galleon on the rolling waves. He called out a loud 'Yo!' and rapped on the doorframe of an office cubicle in the back of the garage. The office was formed of two partition walls set at a right angle to the original brickwork. There was no roof. The door was in the front wall, as well as a large window. The glass was the colour of cigarette tar, and almost opaque. Beyond the stained glass a shadow stirred.

'Someone's here to see you, Po. You in or not?'

Tess smiled at the mechanic's question. It wasn't as if she couldn't hear a reply.

'If it's a cop or revenue man tell 'em I'm out of state and you've no idea when I'll be back.'

'It's a young lady,' said the mechanic, his tone loaded with promise.

'Does she have a kid with her that looks anything like me?'

'Nope. Just her.' The mechanic turned to wink at Tess. 'An' she's a looker.'

'Good. You can show her in.'

The old man waved Tess forward, and opened the door for her, sweeping an arm in invitation. Tess smiled at his graciousness, even if it was all a bit of fun. The mechanic winked again, then ambled away. Tess stood in the doorway.

'Come in. Take a seat.'

The instruction might have sounded terse, except the voice was languid. It was a match for the man reclining in a battered old office chair with his feet propped on the edge of his desk, his ankles crossed, hands folded at his middle. He wore a faded blue denim shirt, denim jeans, black laced-up boots. On first impression his lined face and angular frame hinted at someone with an over-active metabolism, at someone who was never at rest, jerky and jittery in his movements. But to Tess his pose and wide smile were more reminiscent of an old alligator kicking back in the sun while it digested a large meal. Tess moved into the cramped space between the desk and the window. A wooden chair was set kitty-corner to the desk, piled high with automobile magazines and paperwork, stained, as was everything else, with grimy fingerprints.

'Clear yourself a space, ma'am,' said the man. 'Just throw those papers on the floor there.'

'It's OK, I don't mind standing.' The truth was, she didn't

fancy sitting cooped in that corner like a chicken in a shack. Plus, her suit had just come from the dry cleaners and she wanted no reason to send it back so soon.

'Suit yourself.' The man didn't move. Only his turquoise eyes did, making a cool sweep over her before returning and meeting her gaze. He waited for her to say something.

Tess leaned forward and extended her hand. 'Teresa Grey.'

'A name like yours must win you some snarky remarks,' he said, while checking out the shape of her hand. His gaze lingered for the briefest moment on the pale ring of skin on her third finger, then longer on the scar on her wrist, and she knew he was more astute than his laidback nature belied.

Tess had heard all the jokes before: 'Ain't trees green?' and other such glib comments. She did not deign to answer, only raised the corner of her mouth in an indolent smile. The man returned the smile and said, 'Where I come from the trees really are grey.'

'Talking of names,' Tess said, 'I find yours a little unusual, if you don't mind me saying so. Why Mister Po?'

'Charley out there already said you should drop the "mister",' he said. 'It's just "Po".'

'Like the horror writer?'

'Quoth the raven, "Nevermore",' he said, but didn't elucidate. Finally the man unfolded his hands and stretched to meet her fingers. His knuckles were ingrained with the ever-present oil, his fingers and palm rough with calluses, but his grip was surprisingly light. 'I'm Nicolas Villere. Po just happens to be a nickname. "P", "O", there's no "E" in the spelling.'

'Po? Oh, like that panda that does kung fu?'

He released her hand and while she straightened up, he settled back into his previous pose, frowning at her. He probably wasn't familiar with the cartoon character she'd referred to and was wondering if he should be insulted. He came to a decision and laughed under his breath, though it was a humourless sound. 'When I first arrived here from Louisiana, some of the folks 'round here named me Po'boy. It was meant as a slur on my Acadian heritage. Well, ma'am, I showed them I was nobody's boy.'

'You'd prefer if I called you Nicolas, or Mr Villere?'

'My friends call me Po.' He shrugged. 'Depends on your reason for coming looking for me.'

Tess was unsure how to answer. Oh, she knew why she'd sought him out; she just wasn't positive he was the right person for what she had in mind.

'I'm an investigator,' she began.

Po nodded. 'So I heard you telling Charley. Thin walls. But you also said you weren't law enforcement. What kind of investigator are we talking about, Miss Grey? You one of those private eyes like I've seen in the movies?'

Tess chuckled to herself. 'Nothing like that, I'm afraid. I'm only a genealogist.'

'You look into family trees and stuff, huh?'

'I do. But there's more to my job than that.'

'Oh, yeah?' He didn't sound impressed.

'Family trees work both ways, Mister, uh, Po. Sometimes my services are required when clients seek their descendants as well as their ancestors.'

'I can see how that might work. Paternity cases, beneficiaries of inheritances, stuff like that?'

'Yes, stuff like that.'

'Tell me I've been left a bunch of cash in someone's will, won't you?'

'I'm afraid not, Po.'

'Then why are looking for me? My joke about kids was just that. I don't have any illegitimate children.'

'Not that you know about.'

For the first time Tess noticed a flicker of agitation go through Po, but it didn't extend beyond the turning down of his mouth.

'Relax. I was only joking too.'

Po studied her a moment longer, before finally unhooking his heels and sitting upright. 'So? You going to tell me what you want, or do I have to keep guessing?'

'I was told you might be able to help me,' said Tess.

'If you've a problem with a car, I can help. Don't know why you'd come to me otherwise.'

'It isn't for your superlative expertise with automobiles,' Tess said.

Po didn't say a word. He waited. He was good at waiting, Tess guessed. Now she thought of the Edgar Allan Poe poem he'd quoted earlier, and how it aptly suited him: 'And the raven, never flitting, still is sitting, still is sitting . . .'

'I need someone to accompany me to Louisiana, someone who knows the land and the people down there.' Now Tess waited, but her only reward was a minor shift of Po's shoulders. 'I urgently need to locate someone. That's why I need your expertise, Po.'

'I haven't been home in a dozen years. Why me? Why not just employ a guide down there?'

The partition walls were thin, and the cubicle had no roof. Anyone could listen in, and she was certain that Charley the mechanic had an ear cocked in her direction. He'd heard the scuff of her shoe over the tumult of the auto shop, and she was sure he'd hear every word she said now. Then again, Charley probably already knew about Po's past, so why worry?

'I need more than a tour guide,' Tess said, 'I need someone who can also act as my bodyguard if necessary.'

'You must have me confused with Kevin Costner.' Po stood. He towered over her, despite the desk between them. Standing there like that, his sinewy forearms folded across his chest, his rangy build reminded Tess more of Clint Eastwood, back when he was Philo Beddoe, and knocking down all-comers in the bareknuckle ring.

'When I say "bodyguard" I use the term loosely. I only need someone who can watch my back: I'm not asking you to take a bullet for me.'

'I'm just a mechanic. A grease monkey.'

'I heard you learned your trade at Angola,' she said. 'Among other things.'

'You seem to have heard a lot of things about a man whose real name you didn't even know.' He nodded his head slowly, but with him there probably was no other way. Not unless he was riled. 'I was a mechanic before I went to the Farm; learned the trade from my daddy. While I was inside, I pulled some time in the tractor-repair shop, and bagged manure for the Range Herd group.' He grunted. 'Apparently my TABE results weren't high enough to sit in on the automotive technology classes, so unless you want me to fine-tune a John Deere or shovel shit, I'm not sure what "other things" you're referring to.'

Tess guessed he referred to the Test of Adult Basic Education inmates of Louisiana State Penitentiary undertook so they could attend various vocational studies while incarcerated there, and thought that he was lying. Despite his laconic manner, she believed he was sharp as a razor. Anyone who could quote Poe had a more than basic education, whether or not he'd had regular schooling. He'd been wasted at Angola – or the Farm – if he'd served his time working agriculture and looking after the sixteen hundred head of cattle. Then again, he did put her in mind of a rodeo cowboy, so maybe there was something in his white lie. 'I heard you were the go-to man when things got tough down there.'

He unfolded his arms and they hung low and loose by his sides. There were tattoos on his forearms that his rolled sleeves failed to cover. She didn't believe they were prison tats, like she'd seen on other ex-cons. 'I'm sorry,' he said. 'I think you came to the wrong man. I can't help you, Miss Grey.'

'Tess.'

'Tess?'

'That's what my friends call me.'

'So we're friends now?' Po's mouth quirked up again.

'I wouldn't go that far yet, but I'd like to hire you. We'll be spending some time together. I think it'd be best if we start off on the correct foot. Getting our names right feels like a start.'

'Despite what you think you've learned about me, you don't know a thing. Perhaps I'm not the kind of man you want to spend any length of time with.'

'So tell me. I heard you did twelve years in one of the most secure prisons in the nation. I assume it wasn't for stealing hubcaps.'

His eyes crinkled. He was still, but behind the facade his brain was working furiously, trying to decide how much to divulge.

'There's no point in keeping secrets, Po. Now that I know your name it'd be easy for me to check you out. Come clean so there are no surprises between us?'

'Fair enough. But in return I want to hear the story behind that cut to your wrist.'

Tess frowned. How she'd been scarred had nothing to do with her reason for employing Po, and she sure as hell wasn't going to tell her story to a stranger. 'That's my private business.'

'So's *my* goddamn life. That's the deal, Tess Grey. No secrets between us, right?'

There'd always be secrets. Tess had actually mentioned no surprises, and that was a completely different issue. 'I want reassurances. I'm not interested in hiring some crazy rapist, or mad axeman,' Tess said.

'I can assure you I'm neither,' Po said, and his delivery had become even slower. 'But how do you feel about spending time with a convicted killer?'

'You murdered a man?'

'I didn't get fifteen years for stealing hubcaps.' He held up a finger to waylay her next question. 'I did twelve. Three years reduced for good behaviour. Got paroled out and came here. I was lucky I had a job to come to. Charley's a good man.'

'Why did you murder this man?'

'He killed my father.'

For a moment Po held her gaze, seeking reproof. There was none. Given the opportunity Tess would like to have had her day with the junkie who shot her grandfather. He died of a drug overdose before justice could catch up with him.

'Your sentence was reduced because of good behaviour?'

'Model inmate.'

'Yet I heard that you earned quite a reputation while you were at the Farm.'

'Angola's a brutal place. Some things you have to do just to stay alive.' He nodded to himself. 'While I was there I killed another man. Self-defence. He tried to stick me in the eye with a shiv.'

'He was trying to kill you? Why?'

'I'd killed his brother. Family feuds run and run where I come from.'

'He was the brother of the man who murdered your father,' Tess said, getting the tale straight in her head.

'Isn't that what I just said? There are two surviving brothers; they probably want their go at me. Kind of a reason I haven't been home in a dozen years, and have no plans to the contrary.'

Tess doubted that Po was fearful of retribution. But it was as he'd pointed out; feuds ran deep in the south. If those brothers tried to get revenge for their kin Po would have to kill them, sending him back to Angola for the rest of his years. Or he'd die. Whether that was by lethal injection or under the guns of those brothers, she could appreciate why he didn't want to court such destiny by returning to Louisiana.

Tess nodded in decision. 'Well, I'm sorry I wasted your time, Po. I'll have to find someone else. I couldn't possibly put you in such an untenable position by asking you to go back.'

She held his gaze, allowing the sarcasm of her words to sink in. When he'd got the message she turned to leave.

'Hold on.' Po came round the desk, placing one long arm up against the doorframe, effectively blocking her way out. Tess had to look up to meet his face. So close up she could smell his sweat and cologne, and feel his warmth. She could also see a crisscross pattern of puckered scars on his inner forearm. Defensive cuts from fighting off the knifeman trying to blind him. Hemmed in by a self-confessed killer she should've been intimidated. But she wasn't.

'Having second thoughts?' she asked.

'No. You'll have to try harder if you expect me to haul my ass back to the bayous.'

She shook her head. 'What's the point? You're obviously not the kind of person I'm looking for.'

'Are you calling me a coward?' He bristled, his back tightening. Then he tilted his gaze down at her hand. 'I'm not the one with the slashed wrist.'

Tess lifted her hand, blinked at it. Under the subdued lighting the strip of scarred flesh was barely discernible. But like most who noticed her injury, Po had drawn the wrong conclusion. She felt like smacking the son of a bitch in the face.

Tess dropped her hand by her side. 'You know nothing about me.'

'So you expect me to take you at face value, huh? Little Miss-goddamn-Prissy! In the space of minutes you've inferred that I could be a rapist, an axeman, and a coward. So how do I know you're not some stuck-up flaky bitch who's going to make my life hell?'

'You don't. But that doesn't matter. Forget about it, Po, because now you'll never know.' Tess pushed under his armpit and out the door. Charley was bent under the hood of the muscle car. He glanced up, and she wasn't sure if his expression of reproof was for her or the engine he was working on. But then he flicked a glance over her shoulder and she knew it was aimed at Po. The old mechanic's mouth formed a tight line as he went back to his tinkering.

'You can't leave.'

Po's words caught Tess mid-stride. She turned abruptly and glared at him. 'You can't stop me.'

'We had a deal,' Po said.

'What deal? There was no deal.'

'I told you my terms and you went forward with the negotiations. That makes a deal in my opinion. You owe me an explanation.'

'I owe you nothing. I'm leaving, I haven't time for this crap.'

'Time's something I have plenty of,' Po said, and walked forward. 'But enough of it's been wasted here. Come on, there's a diner across the way. Let me buy you a coffee and you can tell your story. Then you might want to fill me in on a few more details about who you're searching for.'

FOUR

'I didn't lie to you earlier,' said Tess as she sat opposite Po in a booth of a family diner a block from Charley's Auto Shop. The diner was busy, the morning rush on, people aiming to grab and go on their way to work. 'But seeing as we're playing "show and tell" I might as well get it out there. No surprises, right? I'm not with law enforcement. I used to be a sheriff's deputy, but now I'm not, and haven't been for the best part of two years.'

Po lounged in his seat, one long arm on the table, his fingers incessantly turning his mug of black coffee as if engaged in some formal tea ceremony. 'Funny, isn't it? I was a con. Now I'm an ex-con, and will be for the rest of my days. Is it the same for cops? You're never anything but?'

'There's probably something in that,' Tess admitted. 'It wasn't my idea to give up on my career, that decision was forced on me, and looking back I can see why, even if it was against my wishes. I'm not exactly bitter, but I regret what happened to end my spell upholding the family tradition.'

'Your father was a cop?'

'Yes. And his father before him.' She didn't feel the need to share all of her family history, and felt she'd said enough for now. But Po's silence coaxed more from her. 'My grand-father was an NYPD detective, my dad a patrolman on the same big-city streets before he relocated our entire family here to Portland, where he took a job with the Sheriff's Office. Dad worked his way up the ladder to Chief Deputy Sheriff. Y'know, I'm certain he'd have made Sheriff in the upcoming elections if bowel cancer hadn't taken him.'

'I heard about him,' Po said. 'That'd be Michael Grey? The cancer took him young.'

Tess sipped her coffee. It was strong, almost to the point where it tasted burnt, but that could have been the ashes of loss swilling around in her mouth. She wondered why she was being so forthright with this man she'd barely met – an ex-con and self-confessed murderer no less – but his steady gaze held hers and was almost hypnotic. 'Fifty-three. Way too young.'

'It's a terrible thing to lose a parent,' said Po, and she wondered at his tone. Someone of his background probably had no love of cops, and the untimely death of a chief deputy was nothing to cry about. But maybe she was wrong and he really felt for her having lost his own father. Some cancers were no less a killer than a redneck with a gun.

Tess offered a tight-lipped smile. 'I've two brothers, Michael Jnr and Alex, both of them older than me. They preceded me into law enforcement; both of them are still serving. Michael married a girl from Ohio, and followed her to Dayton. He took a position with the State Troopers out there, while Alex has stayed here in Maine with Portland PD.'

'You served here too?'

'I did. It's how I knew who to go to when looking for a ne'er-do-well like you.'

Po didn't rise to the bait; he continued eyeing her, turning his cup. Finally he lined up the handle so it pointed towards her. It was a cue for her to continue her story.

'I was never expected to follow my brothers into law enforcement.' Tess gave a grunt of mirth. 'You should've seen the disappointment in my mom's eyes the day I announced I'd enrolled. She thought I should put my college education to better use than wrangling belligerent drunks and abusive husbands. I guess she hoped I'd become a librarian, or maybe a historical tour guide or something safe like it.'

'She was afraid for you,' Po pointed out.

'That's exactly what was wrong. I used to wonder why she was so proud of her boys, when the thought of her baby girl following her menfolk into uniform curdled her gut. Yes, it was definitely fear that informed my mom's opinion, fear that I'd be killed in the line of duty, the way my grandfather was. She wasn't as worried about Michael or Alex's welfare.'

'Or she didn't show it so openly,' Po corrected.

Tess sipped her coffee again. Now it didn't taste as bad. 'Ironically Mom's reluctance to give her blessing only spurred me on: I was determined to prove her fears were unfounded, that

I could be as good a cop as any of the male Greys before me.'
To some extent Tess had, attaining the rank of corporal then
sergeant in quick succession, and she'd had her eye on senior
officer promotion to lieutenant soon after. But that was when
her mother's fears were almost realized. 'The best-laid plans
of mice and men, and all that jazz,' she said.

'Plans are like laws,' Po said. 'Sometimes they're best
broken. Occasionally things work out for the better that way.'

'Now you sound just like my mom,' Tess laughed bitterly.

'She sounds like a wise woman.'

'Now you definitely sound just like her.' Tess's laughter had
curtailed. 'She said she knew no good would come of me
joining up. Pity she didn't gaze deeper into her crystal ball
and see how things would actually turn out.'

'I take it you mean bad?'

'Very bad . . .' She halted. He'd almost prised private details
of her life from her. There was no benefit in telling Po her
story. He was a stranger, and a convicted criminal. She didn't
owe him her life story, and when she walked away she
didn't want him to know any of the intimate details. Hell,
she wasn't even sure why she'd accepted his offer of coffee,
other than he'd practically steered her to the diner by force of
will. She told herself that she'd accompanied him so that she
could walk out on him on her terms; proving who was stronger.
The man was infuriating and the sooner she saw the back of
him the better. Except, well, she wasn't exactly sure that was
the truth. She desperately needed this job, and the timescale
was slim and getting shorter by the second. Sower's bail
hearing was looming: could she afford the time to find another
guide? And who was to say she'd find anyone less annoying?
As much as it aggrieved her to admit it, she needed Po.

Around them the bustle of the morning crowd continued, the
waitresses still took orders and shouted out prepared drinks.
The coffee machines steamed and hissed. Chairs scraped and the
murmur of conversation was incessant. But to Tess it was as if
a veil of silence fell over them. Across from her Po waited.

Ah, hell, she decided, why not? Her woeful demise was in
the public record, if he wanted to find it out. If he wasn't
interested, then he wouldn't bother looking, so where was the

harm? Perhaps he'd see her differently if she hinted that she wasn't the 'stuck-up flaky bitch' he thought. Or perhaps it'd assure him that she was. Whatever. 'You're not the only one who has killed a man,' she said, sitting back, her fingernails tapping the table as she waited for his reaction.

He turned the handle of his cup toward himself. He fed one of his callused fingers through the too-small handle, raised the cup to his lips. He didn't drink, just watched her through the steam. Finally he said, 'Sometimes cops kill criminals. It happens.'

'Yeah,' Tess said, 'they do.'

Except the man she shot wasn't a criminal.

'Criminals also kill cops,' he said, as if it somehow balanced out the universe.

Her thoughts went immediately to Mitch Delaney's horrific fate, and then and there decided that everything hung on how Po responded to her next words. 'And you think that's right?'

'It's just the way it is,' he said. 'Don't know about the rights or wrongs of it; I guess each case has to be taken on its merits.' Again he waited, prompting for more. But she wasn't playing his game anymore. She stood up.

'You're leaving?'

'I need to get moving. It's obvious you've formed an opinion of me that you don't like. I can't see things working out between us.' Tess started by him.

'Nuh-uh.' Po closed his fingers over her wrist. 'We aren't finished yet.'

'We're finished.' Tess jerked her hand out of his grip, but she didn't stride away as intended. She glared at him, conscious that others in the diner were glancing their way. She snorted, sat down again. 'Look, Po, I get it. You have a right to know what you're getting into, but you don't need to hear my life story to form a judgment about me. You've spotted the injury to my wrist, decided I'm weak, and if that's your opinion then *fuck you!*' Now was the time to storm out. But she didn't, she waited and she resented the fact that she needed this man's help so much. It didn't help when he only offered a lazy smile. 'Ah, hell, I'm tired of these games. Stop toying with me: do you want this goddamn job or not?'

'Maybe a trip home wouldn't be so bad,' he concurred. 'Especially on someone else's ticket.'

Tess exhaled sharply. But she forced herself to relax. 'It isn't a vacation I'm offering. You'll be working for me, and there's no time or place for personal agendas. Do you understand?'

'I understand,' he said, but not whether he agreed to the terms.

'OK, so we're good?'

'We're good,' he said. 'How soon do you plan on leaving?'

'You don't want to know how much I'm paying?'

'The money's not important. As long as I'm not out of pocket then I guess I'm still earning.'

His comment gave Tess pause. How could he admit that payment wasn't important after she'd just warned him against pursuing a personal agenda? Maybe that wasn't it, though. Maybe he wasn't as altruistic as everyone else she'd ever known, or more likely he was toying with her again, still enjoying his little power play. Whatever, she'd no time for games. Whether or not he needed the money she did, and wasting time here wasn't how to earn it. 'OK, let's get going.'

'So soon?'

'You might want to grab a change of clothes. We could be gone a few days.'

'Don't I get to know who it is we're looking for first?'

'We've wasted enough time already,' Tess said, deciding it was time to show exactly who was in charge. 'You can stay here and finish your coffee, but if you want this job, you can learn what you need on the way.'

FIVE

Enduring one thousand four hundred and forty-five miles on an airplane from Portland International Jetport to Louis Armstrong International, New Orleans, was Po's idea of a personal nightmare. He told Tess so, and offered to drive them, but she couldn't spare the two or three days a road trip would take, not with the clock ticking against them. It wasn't that Po feared flying – Tess thought it was more a fear of crashing – but that there was something totally unnatural to him concerning the notion of speeding five hundred miles per hour through space, entombed in a metal cigar with two highly flammable gas tanks strapped to the sides. Tess had cajoled him aboard, pointing out that – statistically – air flight was far safer than driving. Po said he'd rather not end up a statistic, but he relented. No, he endured. Most of the time they were in flight, he sat silently, eyes closed, hands gripping the armrests on his chair. Tess attempted to engage him in conversation, but it was as if he thought that by opening his mouth he might disrupt the plane's aerodynamic integrity, so he kept it firmly shut – most of the time. It didn't help that they hit stormy weather over Virginia and the ride became bumpy. Po didn't strike her as a religious man, but he suddenly found the power of prayer, if she read the silent writhing of his lips correctly. She found his aversion to flying surprising. He'd admitted to killing two men, and had survived twelve years in one of the nation's most brutal prisons, and looked like a man who'd spit in the face of the devil himself, and yet he was a sweating, shaking wreck when it came to boarding a plane. Perhaps it was because he didn't feel in control of his own fate; he was the type to fight, and what chance was there of doing that if plummeting to earth from thirty thousand feet? Phobias were illogical fears, so what could she say? Show her a spider and she'd run a mile shrieking, and yet she'd never felt afraid of any human antagonist. Actually, that wasn't entirely true. Otherwise, why would she have gone looking for a companion like Po? Simple: the person responsible for the brutality performed on Mitchel Delaney demanded a degree of fear from anyone with sense.

While Po sweated through the flight, she felt chilly, and it had nothing to do with the air conditioning that Po had turned to full. Once they were airborne and the seat belt light extinguished, she'd pulled out her iPad and gone over her case notes for probably the tenth time. Thankfully she had the window seat, while Po blocked any view from those in the seats opposite, so it was unlikely anyone would accidentally spot what was displayed on the screen, and be shocked by its vulgarity. Actually, the image wasn't so much vulgar as debased. The picture she studied now was one taken during an autopsy, and displayed the lower half of a male murder victim. To anyone the bristling hairs, and the thickly muscled legs, should identify the corpse's gender, because there was no clue in the genitals. More aptly, there was no hint in the area where the genitals once were. Mitchel Delaney had been worse than emasculated: his penis and testicles had been cut away, leaving only a gaping wound from his exposed pubis bone and deep between his legs. Tess knew from other details obtained from the ME's report that those missing parts had been forced down Delaney's throat, the violence of the act the actual cause of death. Such had been Mitch's brutal treatment, his jaw had dislocated as he fought against his murderer, and abrasions on his tongue and the roof of his mouth indicated that some kind of tool had forced the dismembered parts down inside his trachea. Afterwards, Delaney's lips had been stitched together with steel staples; his murderer was determined those parts stayed where all his efforts had placed them.

'Are you looking at those damn photographs again?' Po sounded strained. He worked his mouth, swallowing a build-up of saliva.

Tess swiped the photo off screen, but it was a wasted attempt at hiding the horrible picture. Po had already seen it: Tess had showed him it, and others from the autopsy report, when she'd explained what her job entailed and why it was so important that Crawford Wynne be returned to Maine. She hoped to gauge

Po's reaction to the depravity before he committed to acting as her guide in the Deep South. He'd squinted at that particular photograph, sucked air through his teeth, and said, 'Is that what was on the cards for your ex if he didn't book out?' His comment shouldn't have been funny, but his delivery had elicited a laugh from her, before she realized she hadn't even mentioned Jim Neely to him yet and she'd clamped down again. But he'd wangled details about her ex-fiancé from her soon enough.

If she didn't know otherwise, she'd believe Po had been a cop in his former life. He had that way of eliciting information invaluable to the best of detectives; teasing forth the answers he sought via indirect and seemingly unrelated questions, paired with periods of silence the interviewee felt compelled to fill. While waiting at the boarding gate he'd brought coffee and sat next to her. He held hers out, but in a way that she had to reach for it, and as he passed it over he touched the pale skin on her finger.

'You lose something, Tess?'

'No,' she said, eyeing him steadily. 'I threw the damn thing away.'

Po sniffed, sitting back in his chair as if uninterested.

Tess looked at her hand, frowning.

'Something to do with your injury?' Po said.

'Kind of, I guess. But I don't want to talk about it.'

Po kept his peace.

'OK. So I used to be engaged. But now I'm not. Are you satisfied?'

'If I'm accompanying you to Louisiana it's best that there's no jealous boyfriend lurking in the wings,' Po said. 'We don't want our relationship to be misconstrued.'

She was a pretty, educated, and groomed young woman; he was fifteen years her senior, a rugged, unkempt man with oil under his fingernails, an ex-con. Who'd confuse their association for anything but a professional one? Unexpectedly the very notion caused a flutter in her stomach.

'Don't flatter yourself,' she said a tad too forcefully.

'People usually wear an engagement ring on their left hand,' Po said, unperturbed by her spikey response. 'Why was it on your right? You a rebel at heart?'

Tess held up her left hand, wiggling the ring finger. 'I was saving this exclusively for a wedding band. Looks like it keeps its exclusivity for a while yet.'

'So there's no new guy in your life?'

'Why? If you're thinking of proposing . . . don't.'

'Never crossed my mind.'

Tess shook her head. Her right foot bounced up and down, and she fought to control it. She checked the boarding information above the gate, and there was still time to kill.

'So your ex was a jerk?'

'You've got that right, and then some.'

'He left you?'

'Give me some credit.'

'You said it was "kind of" due to your injury?'

'You're freakin' persistent, aren't you?'

'Just trying to keep my mind off flying.'

'Jesus, the sooner we're on the plane the better.' Her foot still bounced. She forced it flat, concentrated on her coffee. Her foot began jumping again. 'OK! Why the hell not?' She held out her damaged wrist. 'When Jim showed up at hospital he tried to lay a guilt trip on me, said something like if I'd stayed with him like I should've, things wouldn't have ended up the way they did. Asshole! If they hadn't already cut it off when I went to surgery, I'd have taken off his engagement ring and thrown it at him then and there.'

'There was nothing else close at hand, huh?' Po said. 'Shame there wasn't a used bedpan to throw at him.'

Despite herself she wheezed out a laugh. But she sobered quickly. 'We didn't break up immediately. Not until after I left law enforcement. The final straw came when I caught him apologizing about me to some of his friends. Jim was actually ashamed of me; being connected to me cramped his style, I guess. Things hadn't been that great between us before, but when I heard how shallow he was I told him we were over. Because he'd replaced my original ring, I got to do what I wanted to when I was in hospital. I slung his ring at him and told him to get out of my life.'

Apparently Po had learned all he needed for the time being. He slipped back into silence, to Tess's relief. She was glad he hadn't pushed for the full story, because refusal would have most likely offended.

She now regretted being so open, because one-sided her tale sounded as if she was the flaky bitch he'd assumed. Also she felt embarrassed that he'd caught her looking again at the autopsy pictures, in case her interest was misconstrued as an unhealthy fascination with the macabre.

'I'm just going through my notes again,' she said, feeling that she should explain her interest as more than morbid curiosity. Not that she needed reminding, but those pictures of Mitchel Delaney's horrendous torture served as the motivation Emma Clancy promised.

'Why don't you just do some online shopping? Look for some nice Jimmy Choo shoes or something?' Po grumbled.

'That's so demeaning,' she said. 'Do you realize how sexist you sound?'

He shrugged, nonplussed. 'At least bring up some nice pictures of cute puppies and kittens like other girls do. Here am I trying to keep my mind off being mangled in a plane crash and the first thing I see on opening my eyes is *that*.'

'You don't strike me as a puppies and kittens kind of guy.'

'Huh, you're right. I couldn't eat a full one.' Po's eyes slipped shut. He leaned back in his seat, his fingers digging into the armrests, but she noted that for the first time a smile had edged its way on to his thin lips.

'How can you even see what I'm looking at from over there?' She was in the window seat, Po at the aisle, an empty seat between them. The angle would make things difficult, even if he had his eyes open.

'I don't need to see to know what you're looking at.'

'You psychic, Po?'

'Nope. I hear you constantly clucking your tongue against the roof of your mouth. Don't you know you do that when you're deep in thought? You sound like a goddamn woodchuck.'

Tess was aware of her habit. And it was perturbing to learn that Po had picked up on it so soon; he was paying more attention than he was letting on, and she wasn't sure she was comfortable with that.

The engine roar diminished.

Po sat upright in his seat, sweat forming like a row of pearls on his top lip. 'What's wrong?'

'Nothing's wrong,' Tess reassured him. 'We're starting our descent, that's all.'

'They glide the goddamn plane in?'

'No, they just have to lose some speed. For God's sake, chill out.'

'You do this all the time? Fly? You know what all the weird sounds mean?'

'I fly occasionally, but there's something I've learned to do when something out of the norm happens.' She nodded at the prim young woman walking along the aisle. 'Watch the flight attendants. If they look concerned, then you know it's time to put you head between your knees . . .'

'. . . And kiss your ass goodbye,' Po finished. He grunted at where his knees were pressed to the back of the seat in front of his. 'There's no chance of me doing that. Do they design these seats for midgets?'

'You know why they tell you to take up the brace position, right? It's so your neck snaps on impact. Saves any suffering when the plane becomes an inferno.'

'Jesus . . .'

Tess grinned. But she soon grew guilty about adding to his discomfort. Her seat was spacious, the curve of the window and the absence of a passenger in the centre seat allowing her more space than usual. But she could imagine how uncomfortable the ride was for someone of Po's gangling frame. He'd taken the far seat so he could extend one leg into the aisle, but he hadn't had much opportunity for that what with the flight attendants pushing trolleys to and fro, and passengers making the return trip to the toilets a few rows behind them. She guessed his bones would be aching for freedom.

The seat belt signs illuminated and the captain's voice came over the intercom. His tone was conversational, chirpy, but so low in volume Tess couldn't make out one in three words. It didn't matter; she knew the routine. She packed away her iPad and cinched her lap belt. She didn't have to remind Po to belt up, he hadn't once loosened his the entire flight. A buzz of anticipation went through their fellow passengers, a mixture of excitement and agitation making its way through the cabin like a wave. Itching butts moved in seats, and heads swivelled for the overhead baggage compartments as people plotted to grab and run the instant the doors were opened. Tess never understood the majority's need to be first off a plane, as their haste wouldn't see them progress much further than those who took their own darn time. All airports were run on the same system: hurry up and wait. It gave her deep satisfaction after ambling through the process to find her bags were first off the conveyor belt in baggage reclaim, while those who'd pushed and shoved their way to the same point had a longer wait for theirs to arrive. She wondered how Po would react when they landed: maybe he'd run for the doors too, or make like the Pope and kiss the tarmac once they were back on terra firma. She laughed at that image, and avoided catching Po's quizzical glance.

'Someone's happy at least,' he grunted.

'I'm keen to get moving,' she told him. 'Won't be long 'til we're on the ground now.'

'Good,' he said. 'I ain't flying back. Once this is done with I'm putting it down to experience. A bad one.'

'Once we've found Wynne I'll get him back to Maine. If you choose to drive or take a train home, so be it.'

'I'm not too keen on trains either.'

'You don't seem too keen on much.'

He looked at her, and his turquoise eyes narrowed. Tess looked away quickly, as if she was more interested in the view as they came in to land.

The pilot set them down at Louis Armstrong International without turning the plane into a rolling fireball, then taxied to the gate. As soon as the seat belt lights dimmed there was a rush of humanity as they began tugging bags from the overhead compartments, and squeezing into the aisle. Po sat. Tess glanced at him, and his look of incredulity at how close a large woman's backside jiggled to his face was a picture. He averted his gaze, his fingers working in and out, but Tess knew it wasn't with a desire to grab the proffered flesh, but perhaps to shove it aside. A tall guy in a linen jacket elbowed his way past the woman, glancing once at Tess before forging a way down the packed aisle to greet a fellow traveller. Impatient idiot! Why the hell couldn't he wait until they were off the plane? As the doors opened and passengers began filing out, Po visibly relaxed – for the first time since the boarding gate back in Portland. 'Jeez,' he sighed. 'There's something I dislike more than flying, and that's goddamn landing.'

They left the plane, Po pleasantly thanking the stewardess for her attentiveness, and walked up the tunnel. Po limped slightly, but it was due to stiffness and not an old injury. Tess toted her bags, leading Po towards baggage reclaim. She'd brought only one suitcase and Po also travelled light. He'd stuffed some clothing and toiletries into a canvas holdall, and Tess couldn't help a smug grin when their bags were some of the first off the belt. They headed out the arrivals lounge and Tess searched the overhead signs for the rental-car booths.

'Meet you outside,' Po said.

'You dislike airports that much, huh?'

'I need a cigarette,' he corrected her.

'I didn't realize you smoked.'

'Is that a problem?'

'They're your lungs you're poisoning. Knock yourself out.'

'I'm not a slave to nicotine, but there are times when I need one. Now's one of those times.' Po waved without waiting and headed for the exit door. Tess watched him go, noting there was more alacrity to his pace than she'd grown used to. He really did need a cigarette after enduring those hours of hell.

She turned, seeking directions. A man was staring at her, and he was a beat too slow in averting his gaze. He was almost as tall as Po, but broader. He wore a linen jacket over a buttoned shirt and jeans. Not bad looking, if you discounted the slick of sweat on his face. Tess thought she recognized him from their flight, another New Englander out of place in the balmy south, and realized it was the man so eager to disembark with his friend he'd shoved his way past their fellow passengers. The man walked away, and Tess waited for him to glance back at her. But he didn't, and in seconds she'd forgotten about his intense scrutiny.

She hit the Hertz counter and collected the keys to the vehicle arranged on her behalf by Clancy's assistant. Outside she found Po leaning up against a support column, blowing blue smoke at the heavens. Immediately the wet blanket of humidity enfolded her, and Tess felt her lungs hitch. Hell, it was so hot down here in the south. Perspiration began gathering in the small of her back before she'd lugged her bags over to Po. He nodded without a word as she held up the rental-car keys.

'Want to drive?' she offered.

'Driving's one thing I am keen on,' Po said.

SIX

'Hmm. Not exactly the kind of wheels I'm used to.' Po had hidden his dissatisfaction well, but once they were on the road and rolling west he'd made it clear that the rental car didn't elicit the road warrior in his soul. He called the minivan an 'old lady's car', a 'piece of crap', a 'tin bucket', and other names less savoury and all delivered under his breath.

'It will get us where we're going, and isn't likely to attract any unwanted attention,' Tess pointed out.

'They couldn't even rent you an American vehicle?'

'I didn't ask.'

'Wish I'd gone to the rental booth with you now.'

Tess thought the Honda Odyssey was a good vehicle. It was spacious and comfortable, plenty of room for their luggage in back, and thought it might be fun to drive. But she daren't say so; not following Po's assertion that it was an old lady's car.

'And how old is this model? Should've asked for a new car, this has to be seven or eight years old, right?' Po went on, muttering something else under his breath.

'I think I preferred it on the airplane where you hardly spoke,' Tess told him.

Po jutted out his bottom jaw. 'So ignore me. I'm not used to having a passenger along for the ride. I'm just venting for venting's sake.' He tapped his hands on the steering wheel.

'OK, Po, take a deep breath and relax,' Tess said.

He exhaled in a short blast.

'Better?'

'That's me good now.' His lips quirked. 'No more complaining about this goddamn chicken shack on wheels.'

Since leaving the airport they'd followed the I-10 through the bayous to the shore of Lake Pontchartrain, before heading across country for Baton Rouge. It was her first time in

Louisiana, and to Tess it was an alien landscape compared to the forested hills and rocky coves she was used to in Maine. The cobalt sky, turquoise waters, the panoply of vibrant colours and myriad shades of the landscape evoked a response in her that was at once warm and fuzzy. A little sunshine on her face was a good thing. It was hard to imagine that not long ago Hurricane Katrina devastated much of the land nearby, and the upheaval had had a profound effect on the people hereabouts. Katrina was one reason they were heading for Baton Rouge instead of New Orleans, because Crawford Wynne was allegedly one of approximately two hundred thousand residents displaced by the mega-storm. Occasionally she spotted hints of the catastrophe, seeing the sagging rooftops of abandoned dwellings among the trees, old rusted husks of cars left to wallow in the mud, but near the interstate the land had been mostly cleared of the wreckage.

'Is it still as bad in New Orleans?' she wondered aloud.

'Is what as bad?'

'The aftermath of the floods.'

'There's been rebuilding work done, the levees have been shored up, but I guess it's still as bad for some.' Po's eyebrows lowered. 'I guess it was bad for the poor folks beforehand and hasn't got any better since.'

'Why'd they stay? Why not move when the others did?'

'I guess there's no place like home.'

This time there was a trace of melancholy in his voice, and Tess wondered what kind of mild torture she'd placed on Po by asking him to return to the land of his birth. His words told her he missed his home desperately. Up north in Maine, he possibly felt as dispossessed as those whose homes had been washed away in the storm.

'Did you grow up in New Orleans?' Tess hadn't thought to ask before.

'Nope. New Iberia.' Po nodded back over his left shoulder, giving her a general direction, but that was all he offered.

'Did your folks move inland after Katrina?'

'My folks?'

'You said your father was murdered, but you never mentioned your mom, or any siblings.'

Po shrugged. 'I'm the last of the Villeres. There's that other bunch they named the street for, but my kin? I'm not much to look at but I'm all that's left.'

'Oh.' Awkward. Tess had assumed that Po's mother was still alive. He'd never mentioned her, but it now stood to reason that she'd passed. Otherwise would he have stayed away as long? Because of the manner in which he'd avenged his father's death he struck her as a person who held family loyalty above all else and wouldn't have abandoned his mother if she were in danger from a feuding family.

'How well do you know Baton Rouge?' she said to change the subject.

'I knew it a long time ago. Not sure what we'll find now. I hear it's grown some since last I was in town, what with all the refugees settling there.'

Set on bluffs north of the coastal plains, Baton Rouge was generally spared the flooding that communities lower in the delta suffered, but it wasn't totally immune to the effects of high winds and hurricanes. In 2008 Hurricane Gustav struck the city, with winds topping one hundred miles per hour, enough force to pull down power lines, topple trees, and tear shingles from rooftops, and killing more than a hundred and fifty people, but in comparison to the cataclysm that struck New Orleans it was seen more as a troublesome breeze by those who'd been displaced three years earlier. Most of those two hundred thousand inhabitants had not returned to New Orleans, and now Crawford Wynne was lost among them.

'Finding Wynne isn't going to be an easy task, is it?' she said.

'Nope. Particularly if he's got news of what's happening to his old buddies and doesn't wish to be found.'

Po was right. If Wynne thought he might be next on the murderer's list, he'd make sure nobody could find him, and losing himself among displaced multitudes would simply be a start. Tess's normal lines of inquiry might prove useless in locating him, but that was another reason why she'd asked Po to accompany her: he'd be able to open doors that would stay resolutely shut to her.

Approaching South Baton Rouge, they got off the interstate

onto county roads, skirting most of the outlying suburbs, and passing instead through industrialized areas dominated by petrochemical factories, and then, at a place signed as St Gabriel, Tess saw the mighty Mississippi River for the first time. Here the river was slow moving, about eight hundred yards wide, and pretty damn impressive. Some people referred to the Missouri River as the Big Muddy, but the same could be said of this part of the Mississippi because here the water was brown with silt, sluggish, flat, though she knew it was deep enough that it could support large ships and tankers, as she spotted more than one forging upstream to port. She even fancied that she could smell the river – it was mildly unpleasant, like spoiling garbage – but with the windows up and the A/C on full blast to counter the humidity, she might've been imagining it. Po appeared untroubled by the smell. Discreetly she lowered her chin and sniffed, dreading she was more in need of a shower than she first assumed. Suddenly she was looking forward to reaching their hotel and freshening up.

Po had already set the coordinates in the satnav, but Tess delved in her purse and took out some folded sheets of paper given to her by Monica Perry, Emma Clancy's assistant. They were printed details showing the hotel, its location, and a booking reference number. 'Do you know where Nicholson Drive is?'

Po kept his attention to the road. 'We're on it. But it runs away into town before we need to get off. The hotel's on Aztec, right?'

'Yeah, Aztec Street, off Nicholson.'

'Uh-huh. I know where that is.'

'I just wondered, because you paid no attention to the satnav when it told you to continue on the I-ten earlier.'

'Those things don't always think logically. Or maybe they're too logical. They don't have common sense, or a memory for a shortcut the way I do.' Po flicked long fingers at the dash-mounted device. 'See, it isn't complaining now. After trying to get me to do a U-turn, it has now realized that I was right all along.'

'It'd have been much easier if you'd followed directions in the first place,' Tess pointed out.

'I got us here, didn't I?'

'Yeah, OK,' Tess acquiesced reluctantly. 'I suppose you did. Just try not to look so goddamn smug about it.'

When she looked at him he offered a smile, and she felt a tug at the corners of her own lips.

Po's eyes sparkled with victory, and it wasn't at winning the argument. He caught her gaze and held it. Tess felt those sparks of light jump and she blinked, looking down quickly, concentrating on the paperwork in her hands. It was diversion enough, and Po found his own, now keenly watching the road signs. Evidently Baton Rouge wasn't as familiar to him as it had once been.

'Your client didn't exactly roll out the red carpet,' Po said as he finally turned the Odyssey into the parking lot of a small nondescript hotel, one of a budget chain.

'We can't complain. This hotel was chosen for anonymity; I couldn't exactly demand five stars and a spa.' Tess looked at the hotel, noting the faded signage over the doorway, the doorframes that were blistering paint, and tried not to show dissatisfaction. 'First impressions might be doing it an injustice.'

'Yeah,' he agreed, without elucidating, and she wondered whose first impression of whom he really referred to.

'We don't know what it's like inside yet,' she added.

'Call me a pessimist,' Po said, as he shut off the engine and unsnapped his seat belt, 'but it suits me down to the ground. Five stars and a spa? Hell, if we'd turned up at one of those hotels you'd have seen me running a mile.'

The hotel wasn't as bad as first impressions promised. Tess had to be honest: her room was clean, comfortable, and roomy, and what more did she need. Wi-Fi came free, and she had a desk on which she could set up her laptop, iPad, and phone. There was room enough to spread out the notes in the file that Clancy had supplied. It was an office away from home, and one she'd get good use of. But only after she'd showered.

Next door, through the thin walls, she heard Po bumping around, and then the sound of jetting water. Po had prioritized as she had. Tess felt her cheeks flush when realizing she was picturing the ex-con undressing for the shower and enjoying what she'd conjured. Hell, what was she thinking? Keep your mind on your job, she scolded. Po's an annoying son of a bitch, arrogant as hell, and where's the attraction in that? She was still raw from her relationship breakdown with Jim Neely, and discounting a date that had gone no further than a couple of beers with an old colleague from the Sheriff's Department, she hadn't thought about re-energizing her love life. Po was almost old enough to be her father, and he was unkempt and had oil ingrained in his knuckles. Not the kind of man who'd ever caught her eye before, let alone her imagination. But then, she had to admit; Po's rugged exterior, his languidness, and his old-fashioned mannerisms had their own appeal. She switched on her own shower, and as an afterthought turned the temperature to cold.

SEVEN

A rap on the door roused Tess. She sat up on the hotel bed, momentarily fuddled by sleep and alarmed to find herself in an unfamiliar place. She blinked, noted the sheaf of papers scattered across the bed beside her, and finally understood she'd drifted off while perusing her notes.

The knock came again, delivered by a single knuckle, not insistent.

'Yeah?' Her voice croaked, and her tongue was sandpaper against the roof of her mouth.

'Wondered if you wanted to grab some supper?'

Muffled as it was, Po's voice was instantly recognizable.

'Uh, yeah, uh, what time is it?' Tess scratched for her cell phone to check, but Po beat her to it.

'It's just after seven.'

Tess had no idea how long she'd slept. Not long, but it had been deeply. It was the damn humidity. Even with the air conditioning on, the atmosphere in her room was treacle-thick. After showering she'd dressed in jeans and a T-shirt. Both were damp with sweat, wrinkled from sleep. 'Can you give me a few minutes?'

'F'sure,' said Po.

'I need to change. But I'll meet you down in the lobby?'

'Sure thing. Could do with a cigarette.'

Po must have wandered away, but she didn't hear his progress on the carpeted hallway floor.

She scraped together her notes and dumped the papers inside the file. A mirror above the desk caught her reflection. Uh-oh. Not good. Her eyes were puffy and her hair frizzy. Maybe Po could smoke a couple of cigarettes while she got herself ready.

Turning on the shower again, she ensured it was hot this time. She showered quickly, but washed and rinsed her hair twice before she was happy. The supplied hairdryer was near to useless but she persevered, and got her fair hair looking almost presentable if not dry. Having brushed her teeth, she pulled on her T-shirt and jeans and slipped on a pair of pumps. Her hair was still damp, her clothing rumpled, but so what? Her attire would pass. After a spritz of perfume, she grabbed her purse, knocked off the lights, and locked the door behind her.

Po wasn't in the lobby, he was outside, propped against the wall adjacent to the exit. He was dressed in Levi's and a jean jacket over a black shirt. Ordinarily the double denim look didn't work for Tess, but on Po it looked right. He stood with one boot heel and his shoulders braced against the wall, a cigarette drooping from his mouth. On noticing her, Po went to pinch off his cigarette.

'Finish your smoke,' Tess said. 'I really don't care.'

There was somebody out there mutilating people with a knife, and that concerned her more than passively inhaling Po's smoke. Her first day in Louisiana hadn't exactly been productive. She owed Emma Clancy a phone call, but what exactly could she report? She was certain Clancy – and Richard Jackson, her boss – expected more for their bucks than their investigator sleeping the afternoon away and filling her belly.

'Hungry?' Po asked.

'Starving. But have we time for this?'

'We need to eat. There's a place up the block I've heard good things about from the receptionist.' Without waiting, Po sauntered off. He tossed his finished cigarette in a storm drain, then gestured up the street to a delicatessen. 'They do coffee and sandwiches. Maybe they'll rustle up one o' those po'boys you've heard such good things about.' He was laying on the accent thick, then his mouth turned up at one side. 'Unless you got finer tastes?'

Po winked, turned away and left her standing. Had Po just flirted with her? She shook her head in disbelief, then hurried to match his pace.

They ordered food and drinks, took a seat at one of the available tables in back of the deli beneath a ceiling fan. Tess was grateful for the wash of cool air. She discreetly dabbed a bead of sweat trickling down her cheek with a napkin. In contrast Po was untroubled by the wet heat, cool as ever. People from the subtropics must have different blood to New Englanders, she thought.

'Did you sleep?' Po asked.

'Does it show?'

Po didn't comment. He picked at a pulled-pork sandwich filled with rice, coleslaw, and chopped cucumber, liberally coated with barbecue sauce. 'While you were napping I made a few calls,' he finally said.

'You did?' Tess had been caught mid-bite of her own turkey sandwich.

'Uh-huh. I put out a few feelers with some old contacts.'

Annoyance nipped the skin between her shoulder blades, and she pushed aside her sandwich. She felt guilty enough that she'd slept most of the afternoon, and his announcement didn't alleviate it. He was here to protect her, not lead the damn investigation. He should've checked with her first before going ahead like that. She assumed that those feelers Po was talking about was to guys he'd known in Angola. OK, she concurred after a moment, it made sense. Crawford Wynne was also an ex-con and probably moved in similar circles to those Po met at the Farm, so maybe she shouldn't take issue. 'OK. Did you learn anything useful?'

'Too early, but they're going to ask around and get back to me. I think we've plenty time to eat our supper before we get a lead.' His eyes sparkled on the final word, as if enjoying playing detective. 'Good?'

'I need you on the ball like that,' Tess said, and gave him a steady look, 'but in future you should run any ideas by me first.'

'I wasn't seeking approval. I meant your sandwich. Is it good?'

She stared at him, miffed by his disregard and flippant attitude, but she wasn't going to rise to the bait. He was testing the boundaries of their relationship, and she wouldn't give him the pleasure of seeing her rattled. She picked the sandwich up. It came in a soft dough bap almost as long and thick as her forearm, bulging with sliced turkey and a mass of salad, again dripping with sauce. 'I'm in danger of getting fat,' she said. 'Mind you, the rate I'm melting, I'll be a puddle on the floor before the evening's out.'

Po chuckled. 'Yeah, I forgot how damn hot it gets down here in the summer. We'll acclimatize soon.'

He didn't appear in need of acclimatizing, but now they were on the subject, Tess could feel a warm trickle down the small of her back and she shifted uncomfortably. Her skin prickled as if her clothing was woven from horsehair. Somehow being under the ceiling fan was making her feel worse, not better. She picked up her napkin again and mopped her brow. She used the damp tissue as a pointer. 'Aren't you worried that by calling those contacts you're advertising your presence here?'

'Not worried,' he said. 'If it happens, it happens. I agreed to accompany you here and knew what the consequences might be.' Po sat back in his seat and held her gaze: for the first time he appeared serious. 'If the Chatards come looking for me, I don't want you getting involved. You take a back seat, right?'

'Chatards? Tell me that isn't an Acadian swear word,' Tess quipped.

Po's eyes grew diamond-hard. 'It's the family I'm at odds with.'

'Yeah, I got that. But here's the thing, Po: if you've got my back, then I've got yours. There'll be no taking a back seat from me.' Tess wafted the napkin. 'Before you start getting all chivalrous and treating me like the fairer sex, don't forget old-fashioned behaviour like that is deemed sexist in some parts. I used to be a deputy, remember, and am not about to run away when the going gets tough.'

Po squeezed out a smile. 'It's exactly because you were a deputy that you shouldn't stick around. I don't want you bearing witness to what I might have to do.'

How did she answer that proclamation? She stared back at Po. He watched her for a beat, then gave a subtle nod, and bent back to his sandwich.

Her appetite had diminished. She pushed aside the sandwich and reached for her coffee. It wasn't half bad for being served in a paper cup. 'I'll get on to some ideas I've been thinking about,' Tess said. 'Once we get back to the hotel.'

'They can wait, right? I've asked to meet up with an old friend later. He might prove helpful.'

'Who is it?'

'Guy called Pinky. I think you'll like him.'

'With a name like Pinky, what's not to like?' Tess took another sip of coffee, but then pushed it aside. 'I'm done. And the stuff I planned can wait. Do you think Pinky can really help?'

'He won't lead us to Wynne, but there are other things he can help with.'

'The Chatards?'

Po didn't reply. He stood, apparently finished with his food also. 'You want to walk? It's a good ways.'

'In this heat?' She flipped the napkin on the table and stood. 'To the Batmobile, Robin.'

'Is that what we're calling the chicken shack on wheels now?' Po asked. 'I suppose it does help with my street cred.'

They walked back to the hotel, Po taking the opportunity to smoke. He matched his long-legged gait to her shorter steps, for which Tess was grateful. Her clothes were chafing, even her pumps had conspired to rub her toes raw in spots. Maybe those cold New England winters weren't so bad after all, she thought. She trudged listless and miserable.

As they approached the hotel she wondered if she had time for another shower. Surely three times in one evening wasn't overkill in this cloying humidity. But that was as far as the thought went. Po grunted something, bringing up her head.

'Who's that?' she asked.

'Beats me.'

A man was hunched beside their Honda, one hand cupped against the driver's window to see inside the dim interior. Next he checked the door handle, but it was locked.

'Wait here,' Po said.

'Like hell!'

They hurried towards the lot, and some sense made the man glimpse back. He straightened. He was almost as tall as Po, but broader across the chest and shoulders. His face was hidden in shadows from the peak of a ball cap.

'Help you, podnuh?' Po called as they strode towards him.

The man turned briskly and headed in the opposite direction.

'Hey! I'm talking to you,' Po snapped.

The man kept going. He hopped over a low wall at the edge of the parking lot and lurched inside a car waiting for him at the kerb. A driver already had the engine running. Tess began jogging as the car pulled away along Aztec. Po tried to halt her. 'They're gone.'

'I'm trying to get their licence number,' Tess said without slowing.

'Knock yourself out. But you'll be wasting your time.'

Tess stalled. He was right. What was she going to do, even if by some miracle she could zoom in her vision enough to catch the licence-plate number? Report the men to the police for being nosy? The one in the lot hadn't done anything but look, after all. But what exactly had been his interest in their rental?

'Probably looking to steal something,' Po suggested.

Luckily they'd taken all their belongings inside the hotel earlier. There was nothing, excluding the satnav and CD player, that the sneak thief could have stolen had he gained entry to the Honda. Po was right. The men in the car were probably opportunistic thieves preying on inattentive tourists. They would regularly prowl around vehicles in hotel parking lots checking what they could snatch. They should report the incident to the local police, before someone else's car was broken into, but Tess knew how much attention the complaint would receive, little or nothing. She shrugged, and walked back to Po. She chewed at her bottom lip.

'Let it go. We've more important things to be getting on with.' Po took out the keys and hit the fob to unlock the doors.

EIGHT

I f ever there was a human equivalent of a slug, then Pinky was it. He was hugely obese, so much so that his little pointed head sank into the flesh of his shoulders, his chest and middle one long thick tube that seamlessly became equally tubular legs. His arms were inordinately thin by comparison, and it was only after checking her first impressions that Tess felt mildly embarrassed. Earlier she'd cautioned Po for his outmoded attitudes, and there was she casting ugly aspersions on a man obviously troubled by some horrible medical disorder.

Despite his nickname, Pinky Leclerc was black. He was lounging in a booth, a small table before him on which sat three empty beer glasses, and one on its way. Po had obviously spoken with him on the phone earlier, but the man's small currant eyes sparkled when Po led the way across the bar towards him. He held out his arms, his fingers writhing with excitement. As hard as she tried, Tess thought again about slugs, and now squirming maggots as his digits wiggled. And Po was certain she'd like him?

'As I live and breathe! Nicolas Villere back home where he belongs!' Pinky's voice was high-pitched with unrestrained emotion. He was genuinely delighted to see Po sauntering towards him. Tess noticed Po's shoulders tighten at the loud announcement, but he didn't comment. Pinky struggled to free himself from behind the table.

'Don't get up, Pinky,' Po said.

'Don't get up? I haven't seen my old friend in a dozen years and I'm not allowed to give him a hug, me?' Pinky waved off the instruction and pushed aside the table. He made it up to one foot, but by then Po had reached him. Po leaned in and gave his friend a manly hug around one shoulder. Pinky beamed, his tiny eyes sparkling in the dim light as he patted Po's back.

They exchanged welcomes while Tess stood with her hands clasped at her middle. Other patrons of the bar were watching

the show of affection in bemused silence. Po finally turned
from Pinky and waved her forward. 'Pinky, this is my friend
Tess.'

'Charmed,' Pinky said, reaching out a hand for hers.

His touch was warm and dry, not icky, as she'd feared.

'Nice to meet you,' Tess said, and found she meant it.

'What's a lovely young woman like you doing with an old
wrinkly like him?' Pinky beamed his love at Po despite the
taunt.

'We're not that kind of friends,' Tess said coolly, and caught
a tug at the corners of Po's mouth.

'Come, come, sit down, please. You can sit here, lovely
Tess.' Pinky patted the bench to his right. Po slipped into the
booth to his left. Pinky waved grandiosely at the barman.
'Some beers over here?'

'Please, just iced water for me,' Tess said.

'I'll still take a beer,' Po added for clarity and the barman
nodded.

Pinky shifted his bulk around. He looked directly at Tess,
slipped his hand into hers and said, 'I have to admit, I was
surprised to hear from Nicolas when he called me today. I
thought that your powers of persuasion must be very high to
get him back home, but now that I see you I can understand
why he'd follow you anywhere.'

'Ignore him, Tess. He's a shameless flirt.'

'Flirt? *Moi?*' Pinky's right hand went to his chest, then
fluttered in the air. 'Nicolas Villere, if you've got it, share it
around I say, me.'

The man's speech patterns were unusual, and Tess wondered
how much of it was affected for show. She wasn't sure, but
she suspected that Pinky was a homosexual, or was sexually
androgynous, whatever, she didn't find his flirting threatening
in any way. In fact, his campness was oddly endearing. He
was the flipside to Po's irascible machismo. The old adage
that opposites attract was often true, but she had to wonder
what had brought these two completely different types together
in friendship. Actually, she suspected that she knew exactly.

The barman delivered their drinks to the table. Once he'd
left, Po said, 'Did you source the things I asked for?'

'Directly to the point as ever, eh, Nicolas? You aren't going to ask about my health, my work, my love life first?'

Po picked up his beer. 'You haven't held down an honest job in twenty years, and we don't have time in one evening for you to relate your sexual exploits. How you feeling, Pinky?'

'All the better for seeing you,' Pinky grinned.

'So now that we've caught up, did you source the things I asked for?'

'Now hold on there, cowboy!' Pinky patted Po's knee. 'I can see that the lovely Tess is burning to ask how a prima donna like me knows a prime hunk of beef like you. Am I right, my dear?'

Tess grinned as Po squirmed. 'I must admit: the thought has crossed my mind.'

'Why, we were bunk mates!'

'Cell mates,' Po corrected. 'There's a distinction.'

Pinky flapped his right hand. 'Don't believe him, Tess. There were plenty of times we cuddled up on cold nights.'

Po shook his head.

'Am I lying? Oh, how scandalous of me.' Pinky peeled with laughter.

'You're not lying, just misrepresenting the facts,' Po said. 'There were times when I hugged you, when you needed a shoulder to cry on.'

'That is a fact for which I'm eternally grateful, me.' Suddenly Pinky's expression firmed and he leaned towards Tess again. 'If it wasn't for Nicolas, I would not have survived the Farm. It was hell on earth for a man of my delicate nature. If the animals hadn't got me, I'm sure I would have done for myself. But Nicolas rode to my rescue on more than one occasion like the gallant knight he is, him.'

Po shrugged off the extravagant compliment.

'Black, gay, and physically incapacitated,' Pinky went on, 'I was meat to those seeking easy prey, and trust me, Miss Tess, there were plenty of carnivores among the Farm animals. He can deny it all he wants, but that rough-looking brute masquerading as Nicolas Villere is a saint among men, my guardian angel, him.'

Tess appraised Po, and it was obvious he was uncomfortable with the praise, but Pinky had confirmed something to her. For all he was a person with a tainted history, one capable of brutal retribution, Po was also loyal and protective. But this was coming from another man who'd spent time in prison, so should she trust Pinky's assessment?

'Did you get the guns like I asked?' Po pushed.

'Whoa! Wait on! Guns?' Tess's voice came out as a hiss.

Po blinked slowly. 'You do know what we might be up against here, don't you, Tess?'

'I know . . . but *guns*?'

Pinky looked from one to the other. 'I sense a little friction. I'm not sure how to answer now, me.'

'Hopefully in the affirmative,' Po said. Then to Tess, 'They're for self-defence only. I'm not going to go on a shooting rampage, if that's what's concerning you.'

'We're neither of us licensed to carry a sidearm,' Tess reminded him. 'What you're suggesting is illegal.'

'Do you think those we might go up against will be carrying *legal* firearms?'

'That's beside the point,' Tess argued.

'How? Tess, you looked at those photographs enough times. Hasn't it crossed your mind that if we're looking for Crawford Wynne, then those responsible for the murders are looking too? Somebody's cleaning up for Albert Sower. Do you really want to cross paths with them unarmed?' Po rested his case, taking a sip of his beer to show he was done talking. Tess wasn't.

'I'm neither naive nor an idiot,' Tess said, 'but neither am I prepared to break the law. If things get out of hand then we call for backup from the local police, we don't get into a damn shoot-out.' Tess knew there was always the possibility that they might collide with someone also seeking Wynne. But she hadn't planned on the sort of retaliatory action Po suggested. The last time she'd actively held a gun, things hadn't ended well for her. Unconsciously she flexed her wrist, rubbing at it with her other hand. But Po must have caught the surreptitious action, because he decided he wasn't finished after all. 'If you aren't happy about packing, then I'll do it for both of us.'

'I'd rather not,' Tess said, but a stab of caution went through her. 'But, hell, I guess we're in this together.' She shrugged. 'I told you I had your back and meant it.'

Pinky grinned expansively. 'Nicolas, stand aside, I think I've just fallen in love all over again, me.'

NINE

The following morning found Tess and Po on Gardere Lane, a couple of miles from their hotel in South Baton Rouge. Before travelling there, Tess had Googled the news feeds about the street and now wished she hadn't. Gardere Lane was a crime hotspot, and though new houses and condos were springing up nearby, ancient apartments that defined suburban blight dominated parts of the street. The neighbourhood was predominantly black, and Tess doubted that a man of Crawford Wynne's social and political beliefs could make the place home. He'd last minutes at most if any of the residents got a glimpse of the racist tattoos he wore on his body, one of them prominently on his face. Crime was rife on Gardere, but hardly surprising. How did people live like this, she thought, without following their most base instincts? She was being unfair, though. There would be good, law-abiding people stuck in the same rut here, unable to move on, making do with what they had. She recalled Po's sage words when they'd talked about the hurricanes that had pushed many of New Orleans' residents north to the state capital. 'I guess it was bad for the poor folks beforehand and hasn't got any better since.'

Kids were in the street, some on bikes. Sneakers, board shorts, and tank tops seemed the uniform of choice. Those that wore baggy jeans did so with plenty of boxer short showing in back. There were older people too, sitting on walk-up steps to the second-floor apartments A gaggle of young mothers stood gossiping, with their toddlers at their feet. The gossiping was animated, lots of laughter ringing out and arms gesticulating for emphasis. Vehicles parked in front of the apartments were brightly coloured, some sporting bespoke paint jobs, some with souped-up engines and huge exhaust pipes. The cars were anomalous to the scene: belonging to people with more money than their living arrangements suggested. Their

Honda Odyssey stood out because it was so ordinary. Already they'd caught a few suspicious glances, and on one occasion a kid had ridden directly up to Tess's window and stared into her face, deciding whether or not to send out an alarm. Tess had squeezed out a smile at him, and he'd smirked but ridden off without further drama.

Po found a turning and pulled the Honda down a side street. It dead-ended, facing an expanse of coarse grass and weeds where an apartment block had been demolished. There was still housing to each side, and Po searched for an indication they'd found the correct address. 'That looks like the place,' he said, with a nod for the apartment block to their left. It was similar to the other houses they'd seen on Gardere Lane, with a central stairway allowing access to the rooms on the top floor.

'I'm beginning to think this isn't a very good idea,' Tess said. 'I'm not sure we're going to be welcomed with open arms.'

'You can stay in the car if you prefer, but I think coming with me is the safer option.' Po turned off the engine.

During her law-enforcement career, Tess had grown used to patrolling areas equally as poor and rundown, possibly as dangerous, but being thousands of miles away and without the armour of a badge and uniform was an entirely different ball game, though she wouldn't let that stop her. 'I've no intention of staying in the car.'

'We should be OK. Pinky vouched for us with this guy; I trust Pinky.'

'Then let's do it.'

Po adjusted his shoulder holster, concealing it beneath his jacket, but ensuring the butt was in easy reach. The gun was an S&W automatic, with its serial numbers filed off. Pinky swore the gun hadn't been used during the commissioning of a crime, and was as clean as they'd find in Louisiana, but Tess doubted it. She had a similarly 'clean' gun – hers a Glock 19 – in her purse. Hopefully they would have no need of the firepower, but then again . . .

The man they'd come to speak with was called Trey Robinson. Pinky had assured them that if anyone in Red Stick knew Crawford Wynne, it would be he. How and why Robinson would know was beside the point, and Tess didn't feel the need to ask. Crawford Wynne was the archetypical redneck white supremacist, and Trey Robinson the leader of a black gang. The popular saying 'keep your friends close and your enemies closer still' had never rung truer.

'Maybe we should leave our guns in the car,' Tess suggested.

'No way,' said Po.

'They'll probably take them off us before we get close to Robinson.'

Po had also spotted the two men standing in the stairwell. They didn't openly show their weapons, but they'd be packing. After all they were there to block unwelcome access to the apartments on the upper floor. Both men were young, black, and wearing shades, despite being set back in the gloom.

'No they won't.' There was an edge to Po's voice that sent a thrill up Tess's spine. Once over she had welcomed the buzz of adrenalin in her veins, but now she wasn't as enamoured. Po looked over at her. 'Pinky called ahead, made the introductions. We're expected.'

'I know that, but . . .'

Po was already sliding out of the car. 'Follow my lead, and don't say anything unless I give you a nod.'

'Yes, sir,' Tess hissed. 'Hell, sometimes I forget who's working for who here.'

'This is what you're paying me for, remember? My expertise.'

Tess held up her palms. 'OK. You're right. I'll be the obedient little woman and keep quiet.'

She was rewarded by a smile that showed an eye tooth, the equivalent of a smirk from Po.

'Just stop acting like an ass,' she said, 'and remember who's in charge.'

Po had already forgotten. He was on his way to Robinson's house. Tess got out the car and followed. Her pumps sucked at the hot tarmac underfoot.

The guards stepped out to bar progress.

'We're expected,' Po told them.

Both men lifted the fronts of their shirts displaying the butts of handguns. It was a show of force but also an unspoken question. 'I'm packing,' Po told them. He didn't expose his gun. 'So is my friend. But we aren't here for trouble. Trey's expecting us.'

'Ya leave your guns here wid us,' said one of the men.

'No. We don't. Go get Trey and I'll tell him the same.'

The second guard lifted his sunglasses to inspect Tess. 'Hollywood cracker bitch ain't goin' in.'

'She's with me, she stays with me.'

'Then you stay outside, bra,' said the first man.

Tess tried not to be offended, but could feel her temperature rising. Her face was reddening and there was nothing she could do about it.

'That's right, ho. Get some colour in yo cheeks,' laughed the second man.

'Enough with the racist bullshit,' Po said, 'and go tell Trey I'm here.'

'Racist bullshit? Now that's rich coming from a white man.'

The educated voice hadn't come from either of the gangsters but from above them. Tess followed the voice to its source and saw a third black man leaning over the railings. He had his forearms crossed, one over the other, dripping gold from his wrists and fingers. He was a handsome guy, fine-boned features, hair oiled and woven into cornrows. He spoke with more culture than his lackeys. He was smiling, and it looked like genuine humour flashing in his eyes.

'Are you Trey Robinson?' Po asked.

'You're Nicolas Villere.'

Po moved past the guards and Tess went to follow. The second guy, who'd since lowered his shades, interjected. 'Ya look like a Fed to me.' He sniffed an inch from her hair. 'Ya smell like a Fed to me.'

Tess was tempted to knee him where it hurt, but restrained herself. 'Who says I'm not?'

Po had paused on the steps, watching. But Tess didn't need his assistance to deal with a punk like this.

'If I were a Fed, I'd have you face down on the ground with cuffs on, and an entire TAC team storming those stairs. Instead, I'll just ask you nicely: are you going to let me by or do you wish to try me?' Tess eyed the young man and didn't flinch. 'Well?'

The guy grinned. 'I like ya. Fo' a tight-assed cracker ho, I mean.'

'I like you too,' Tess said, smiling overly sweet. Then she shoved a palm into his shoulder and pushed him aside. 'But not that much.'

The guy thought it the best fun he'd had in ages. He laughed, almost as uproariously as his friend, who now began shoving him too. Above them Trey Robinson shook his head in bemusement at the antics.

'You can't get quality staff these days,' he remarked as Po approached him across the landing.

'Maybe you're just in the wrong business.'

Robinson nodded at Po's wisdom. But he wasn't ready to change his ways. 'Then who would you come to when looking for some Klan peckerhead like Crawford Wynne?'

Air leaked between Po's teeth. Tess joined her companion, standing facing Robinson, who was yet to relinquish his position. Leaning on the railings he could survey his domain. It didn't amount to much when all that faced them was the rental car and the front of similar buildings opposite.

'Can you help us?' Tess asked. 'Or are we all wasting each other's time here?'

Po's mouth puckered at one side and she caught his sidelong glance.

Robinson called down to his friends, speaking in a swift patois that was lost on Tess. There was no anger or recrimination in Robinson's tone, and his buddies only laughed, stopped their messing about, and showed some semblance of order again as they returned to their positions.

'Pinky Leclerc warned me you were a cute one,' Robinson said as he finally turned to appraise his visitors. Tess wasn't sure if he was referring to her looks or her attitude. Neither description offended. But she knew not to take the man's pleasant nature at face value; you didn't get to rule the streets in this kind of neighbourhood by being nice.

'I take it there's no love lost between y'all?' Po said.

'Crawford Wynne is beneath my notice. He's a piece of

crap not worth my time or effort.' Robinson nodded his head, as if in contemplation. 'But I owe Pinky, and Pinky says he owes you, Nicolas Villere. So I asked around on your behalf. Wynne hangs with some biker trash down in the bayous, running Charley and whores between New Orleans and Lafayette. You're a coonass; I'm looking at you and thinking you know your way around those bayous.'

Po didn't react, though Tess took Robinson's remark as an off-hand insult.

'You know Morgan City, Nicolas Villere?' Robinson went on.

'I know it.'

'The Cottonmouths have a clubhouse down there. Some shit-hole off Railroad Avenue near the waterway.' Robinson ruminated. 'Those good ol' boys tried to move in to South Baton Rouge. I didn't allow it. You get me?'

'I get you,' Po said.

'Give those motherfuckers my best regards, why don't you, Nicolas Villere.'

Without another word, Robinson walked away. They were dismissed. But they'd learned what they'd come for and no amount of questions would gain them anything else of use. Po tilted his head. *Let's go.* Tess again followed, like the obedient little woman as promised, all the while shooting daggers at Po's wide shoulders, then for good measure at the two guards. The one who'd got too close earlier now kept his distance, but it didn't deter him from grabbing his groin and lolling out his tongue. 'Very attractive,' she told him. 'I just bet the girls fall over themselves to get at you.'

'They do, but I'd make time for you, ho,' the gangster said. 'C'mon over here and let me taste some a dat white booty, let me suck da head off it.'

'Leave it,' Po said. His words weren't solely for Tess.

The black guy and his friend found the situation uproariously funny again, and began slapping shoulders. Their talk was now too fast and singsong for Tess to follow, but the vocal one made his intentions obvious by again grasping his groin and giving it an over-exaggerated wag in her direction.

'Leave it,' Po said again, but this time only for her ears.

'Men are such assholes.' Tess included Po in her estimation.

'Some more than others,' said Po. 'Come on, there's no good can come of hanging around here any longer.'

As they approached the Honda, Po held out the keys. 'You can drive.'

'You can drop the act now, Po. I don't have to play the dumb wench any longer.'

Po blinked at her as he fished his cell phone from a pocket. 'I wasn't acting, I was asking. I need to speak with Pinky as a matter of urgency.'

'What's up?'

'Not sure yet, but I don't trust that asshole Robinson one little bit.'

'Really?'

'Really.'

When they were back in the car and moving again, away from Gardere Lane, Tess said, 'You think Robinson's sending us on a wild-goose chase?'

'No. I think he set us on the right path, but that isn't it. Didn't you notice how he kept repeating my name, emphasizing it even?'

'I thought that was just him being facetious.'

'Hopefully that's it, but I don't think so. It's like he was letting me know he knew who I was – beyond Pinky's friend, I mean. Like my name was familiar to him.'

'You had a name in Angola,' she reminded him. 'Maybe that's where he heard it.'

'Yeah,' he said, but didn't expound. Instead he began tapping in Pinky's number. Tess watched him in her peripheral vision, while also steering the car back towards the intersection with Nicholson Drive. Had she paid more attention to her mirrors she might have noticed the car pull out of the lot of a meat market and fall in behind them. She might have recognized it as the same car that sped away from their hotel the evening before.

TEN

This felt like cop work to Tess, and she had to admit she'd missed it. If left to her latest techniques she'd have run Internet searches on Crawford Wynne's relatives, and from there tracked them to current addresses by the local censuses, and other avenues she had access to, then followed the breadcrumbs of Wynne's trail until she located him. But this old-fashioned method of knocking on doors and pulling in favours was more appealing to her sense of adventure, and was very much the process she'd followed as a sheriff's deputy. Though working as a genealogist had served to keep her mind active, it was a safe and formulaic activity, and didn't fully satisfy her the way real detective work had. It was great to get back on the front line. OK, so she'd been peeved that she'd to play second fiddle to Po, but admittedly they had sniffed out Wynne's location faster than her genealogist's route would have, but hadn't that always been the case? She doubted Emma Clancy hired her for her expertise in compiling family trees, but because she was experienced in dealing with the kind of people who could lead her to Wynne, and this was a case in point. When she phoned Clancy she could report that they had a good lead to follow, and by this time tomorrow might even have gotten an eyeball on her elusive witness.

Interestingly it appeared that cops and ex-cons shared similar methods. She looked over at Po to tell him so, but his face was serious. He'd just gotten off the phone to Pinky, and she hadn't followed their conversation too easily. Now that Po was back in his native Louisiana he'd fallen into a speech pattern foreign to her, one that was dominated by clipped terms of 'dis', 'dat', and 'd'other'. She felt he'd deliberately phrased his speech so she didn't follow everything that was discussed, and Pinky had responded in kind.

'Everything all right?' she asked.

Po frowned. 'Been better.'

'Why, what's going on?'

He pondered for a moment before deciding she needed to be in on what he'd learned. 'Apparently there's a price on my head.'

'Those Chatards?'

'Yeah, Pinky said there's a bounty out on me, couple of thousand dollars.' Po snorted. 'Kind of insulting when you think about it. But to a punk a couple thou is big money. Plenty of them will look to cash in.'

'And you think Trey Robinson's the type to claim the bounty?'

'For all his Elleshyew education he's still a street punk, a gangbanger. So yeah, I wouldn't put it past him to try to get his hands on that money.'

It took a moment for Tess to realize that Po was referring to LSU – Louisiana State University – and that his education didn't make Robinson any less a gangster. 'He didn't try when he had you right there in front of him.'

'Why risk a shoot-out? He knew we were armed and wouldn't go down easy. Two thousand dollars wasn't worth risking his ass for. But it's no risk if he set us up with a phone call after. Pinky said this bounty is payable for information leading to my capture. What are the bets that Trey's on the line to one of the Chatards this instant?'

'We can't be certain of that.'

'F'sure.' Po shrugged his shoulders. 'If it happens, it happens. If it doesn't, well it's not worth worrying about.'

Ahead of them the traffic had stalled. Tess slowed the Honda, then brought it to a halt. Behind them more traffic began to build up, a bronze-coloured saloon edging in close to their rear fender, with other vehicles lining up behind it.

'We should go directly to – where was it Trey said? Morgan City? If we go and check out the clubhouse he mentioned we can be there and gone before the Chatards arrive.'

Po grunted. 'My thoughts exactly. Tess . . .'

She looked at him.

'I'm not afraid of the Chatards. In fact, part of me wants to go seek them out and put an end to this, but it's not right that you're caught in the middle of my troubles.' He rubbed a hand over his mouth, and she heard the rasp of whiskers against his palm. 'You should wait at the hotel and I'll go on down there myself.'

'Nuh-uh. We go together.'

'Reckoned you'd say that.'

'So why mention it at all?'

'Don't want you saying after that I dragged you to hell with me, that's all.'

'Hmmm? Reverse psychology? Works every time.'

'I gave you the option to wait at the hotel,' he said.

'Knowing fine well I'd refuse.' Tess offered a flicker of a smile. 'I'm coming, let's leave things at that, shall we?'

Folding his arms across his chest, Po relaxed into the seat, satisfied at the outcome.

Ahead of them the traffic still wasn't moving.

'Accident, you think?' Tess wondered.

'Just traffic congestion. I guess Baton Rouge regularly comes to a standstill like this. It did when I was here last, and if anything there are more cars on the roads these days. We'll just have to sit it out.'

Tess fiddled with the blowers, directing cool air at her face. She squinted, blinked, feeling grit from the adjusted air vent sting her eyes. She poked at her eyelid with a thumbnail, muttering softly. A mote of grit – perhaps a boulder – irritated beyond belief. Her eye watered, and she blinked again to dislodge the dirt and tears. Frustrated, she adjusted the rear-view mirror to check where the irritant was. Instead, she met another set of eyes staring back at her in the mirror. Tess screwed her weeping eye, concentrating harder with the other. She noted her watcher's reaction, and it was as blatant as the last few times she'd spotted him. He ducked.

'It's *him*,' Tess whispered harshly, as if the man in the car behind theirs could hear.

'What?' Po squinted at her.

'I think it's that guy from the airport.' Tess stared into the rear-view again, but the man had deliberately averted his face.

'Which guy?' Po twisted round. 'You didn't mention any guy.'

'No. Don't look, he'll . . .'

'Son of a bitch! It's the same car that asshole took off in last night,' Po said, and didn't care if he was caught looking.

Tess peeked again in the mirror. 'Who do you think he is?'

'No idea,' said Po, already unclipping his seat belt, 'but I'm going to find out.'

'Wait, maybe we should—'

Too late. Po was out of the door and striding towards the bronze-coloured car. Tess was caught in flux. She craned round to watch, still conscious of being in control of their car. Then she spotted the second guy, sitting in the passenger seat alongside the watcher. Hurriedly, she switched off the engine, and clambered to unclip her belt.

She expected strong words and recrimination, pointed fingers and challenges. Not what happened next.

The driver hit the gas and the car shot forward, ramming the Honda just as Tess was getting out. She spilled onto the asphalt, her left elbow taking the impact and sending a blast of agony through her body. Stunned, she rolled onto her back, and good job that she did. The lunatic at the wheel revved, ramming the Honda forward, and its back wheels missed Tess by a hair. The Honda smashed into the car in front. Distantly Tess heard shouting. She'd never heard his voice raised and it took a moment to understand it was Po shouting at those in the car. Tess scrambled to rise. Her back collided with another stalled vehicle, and she glanced round to see a startled woman blinking at her, her mouth wide in a soundless cry of alarm. Ignoring the woman, Tess looked for Po.

He aimed a kick at their watchers' car. It was a futile act. The driver had thrown it into reverse and aimed it at an angle at a gap in the traffic. The sound of crumpling metal was harsh as the car impacted the side of a panel van and pushed the larger vehicle aside. There was a narrow gap now in the stalled traffic and the driver went for it, speeding backwards. Po looked tempted to draw his sidearm, but to do so would bring trouble from local law enforcement they couldn't afford. Instead he began jogging after the furiously reversing car.

'Po! Leave them!'

Tess stumbled around their crumpled Honda, cupping her

abused elbow in her opposite palm. There was an opening between the Honda and the next car in line, the road surface strewn with broken glass and plastic. The scream of the reversing car's engine was loud, and again she heard Po holler. He was wasting his breath. Whoever they were, their watchers weren't about to give up. Another crashing detonation sounded, and Tess peered over the roofs of cars to where they were forcing their way through another space too narrow for safe passage.

Unbelievably, Po launched himself on the hood of the moving car, and hammered the windshield with his palm. Tess raced towards him, more concerned about Po's welfare than halting a getaway. 'Po!' she yelled again. 'Just let them go.'

Po scrambled higher on the hood, grabbing at the roofline for stability. The car swerved, punched through the breach and found a way on to a rumble strip allowing access for highway maintenance vehicles beneath a nearby underpass. The driver hit the brakes, and Po slid up and part way on to the roof. The car was then wrenched in a tight turn, and with no possibility of fighting the centrifugal force, Po was cast aside and he rolled across the asphalt. The breath caught in Tess's throat, but then Po popped up, his jaw flexing, and he took three enraged lurches after the car. But it was out of reach. Again she watched his hand go for the butt of his gun.

'No. Don't.' Tess jogged towards him.

Po's breathing was ragged. His eyes sparked with unrestrained fury. But he nodded and his hand slipped by his side. Tess saw blood on his knuckles, a bright red slash that drew her gaze.

'You're hurt.'

'Not as much as those assholes are going to be when I catch up with them.' Po stalked past her, and she was sure he was about to jump inside the Honda and give chase. She ran after him and caught at his elbow.

'Wait. Don't do anything stupid.'

'It's a bit late for that,' he said, and he was right.

'OK, then don't do anything else. There's no possible way to catch them now, and no real need.' She tapped her head to emphasize a point. 'I got their number this time.'

'You think that'll do any good?' Po scanned around. Other

drivers and passengers were out of their vehicles now. All bewildered, some angry, as they babbled about the madness they'd witnessed. Some turned to Po and Tess for answers. She knew that when the police arrived, they'd be the centre of even more attention. Jesus, what were they going to tell the cops?

'Best we get our guns out of sight,' Po suggested sotto voce.

'I knew that carrying them was a bad idea,' Tess said. 'Anyway, it doesn't look like you need a goddamn gun. What were all those John McClane antics back there?'

'Who's John McClane?'

'You're kidding me, right? *Die Hard*, and about a thousand sequels.'

'Now if you'd said John Wayne I might've known who you were talking about.'

'What planet have you been on all these years?' Tess asked, then immediately regretted it. Oh, yeah, Po had missed most of those 90s action movies while locked up in Angola. Still, there'd been plenty of sequels in the meantime, as recently as a year or two back, so Po must know who the actor Bruce Willis was. Only when she caught a sly grin as he turned away did she realize he was having fun with her. The son of a bitch was distracting her, taking her mind off his insane pursuit of the maniacs in the car and the possible trouble they'd just gotten in with Baton Rouge PD.

ELEVEN

'They made the first goddamn move,' Po reminded Tess as he guided their car south for Morgan City. He gripped the steering wheel with force, as if there was a need to hold the car together. But that wasn't it. Although the Honda had caught the brunt of two solid collisions, both front and rear, the damage had proven mostly cosmetic and didn't impede its mechanical integrity. Po was still pissed that their watchers escaped, and that despite all his attempts to halt them Tess wasn't happy with him.

'If you hadn't confronted them things would've been different.' By 'different' Tess meant 'without violence'.

'Different doesn't always mean for the better,' Po responded.

'You're right. It could have been much worse.'

'Only for those assholes.'

'No, Po, innocent bystanders could've been hurt,' she snapped. 'You were reckless and out of control back there.'

'I showed those fuckers not to mess with *you*; isn't that why I'm supposed to be here?'

'No. I'm here to find Crawford Wynne, and you're here to help me, not spoil my chances. For all we know those guys might've led us to Wynne, but that's not going to happen now. We should've played things cool, watched, assessed, we might've learned something useful.'

'And how do you suppose they would've led us to Wynne?' he demanded. 'You said you spotted one of them at the airport. They followed us here, and were still following us 'til I frightened them off, not the other goddamn way around.'

Tess fumed. He had a point, but he'd also made discovering why they were being followed more difficult. She frowned at him; his face was set in stone. He wasn't about to admit he was wrong, but neither was she. Just whom had she aligned herself to? OK, she'd learned of Po's record and understood he had the capacity for shocking violence, but she hadn't expected it to explode like that. Its suddenness had stunned her, no doubt about it, forcing her to recall the last time she'd been caught up in a vicious encounter and its repercussions on her life since. She'd put off returning to the field too long, but maybe for good reason. Fleetingly she considered that she'd made a mistake in accepting this job, that she wasn't ready to return to her old life, and Po's rash actions had forced her to face reality. But anger quickly tamped the notion down. Nothing was going to derail her from her assignment, certainly not Po's hot-headedness. It was time to make that clear.

'We were lucky to get away with our part in that mess,' she said. 'Don't do anything as stupid again and I'll let it slide.'

'I won't make a promise I can't keep.' Before she could bite, Po changed the subject. 'That was good work back there, and quick thinking by you. Having an ex-cop as a partner has its advantages, f'sure. If it were only me back there, I bet I'd've been hauled off to jail.'

Was his off-handed compliment a way of making amends? His choice of word when describing their relationship was interesting. Suddenly they were 'partners', not employer and employee? She decided to let the turn of phrase go for what it was, choosing instead to accept the unspoken thanks.

Tess had informed the rental company of the 'accident' and requested a replacement vehicle, but to collect it from Hertz's Baton Rouge compound added undue delay. To beat word of Po's presence in Morgan City reaching the Chatard family, they couldn't spare the time. Clearing things up with the responding police officers had eaten enough into their day, but they'd come out of it clean. Witnesses at the scene pointed blame for the chaos at the mysterious men in the car that fled the scene. Po's over-exuberant actions were forgiven when he explained he was trying to stop the enraged driver from ramming any more vehicles – and possibly injuring someone – by uselessly trying to grab the keys out of the ignition. His hood-surfing escapade was down to circumstance, Po claimed, where it was a choice between leaping on the car and being run down. Some of the bystanders watched him as if he was a dangerous beast while others were filled with adoration. Once they ran his details and discovered he had a criminal record, the cops eyed him suspiciously, but he'd no outstanding warrants against him, and no fresh charges were laid. Even though there was much she held back, and some details she delivered as outright lies, Tess's past as a sheriff's deputy won them both some professional courtesy. On Tess's part, it was a spontaneous decision to keep the car's licence number secret, as was neglecting to mention that the men had been following them since their arrival in Louisiana – perhaps even before that. Admitting to the cops that she – or perhaps Po – was the target of the men would cause complications that would jeopardize her assignment. The general consensus was that frustrated and overheated, the driver had snapped when confronted by the traffic delay, and had taken uncompromising measures to escape the bottleneck. Sweating like a hog, Tess was happy to go along with the conjecture for appearance's sake.

Afterwards they'd briefly returned to their hotel, grabbed their necessaries, and got back on the road. Tess had waited until Baton Rouge was diminishing in their rear-view mirror before raising the subject of Po's recklessness, and it had simmered since. Both of them were now apparently growing tired of the bickering.

'How's your elbow?' Po asked, changing the subject again.

'Sore, but it will be fine.' Actually her elbow throbbed, and she expected it to bruise, but she'd escaped serious injury. She checked his knuckles. They were grazed, but the bleeding had stopped – it was a superficial injury too. 'Were you seriously trying to punch your way through that windshield?'

Po flicked a glance at her. Silence.

'Crazy,' she said.

'It was down to circumstance.' He shrugged. 'It happened. Now let it slide like you said, why don't you?'

'Even if you managed to smash the windshield, what were you going to do then? Were you going to haul those guys out by their hair or what?'

'I was trying to get answers. They sure as hell didn't want to give them.' Po looked across at her, and his features softened a little, along with his tone. 'Why do you think they were so desperate to get away?'

It was obvious to Tess that the watchers were involved in

a way she didn't fully understand yet, but she'd admit it was worrying. Those men had been on the same flight out of Portland. That meant that they were on to her from the get go, and knew exactly why she was in Louisiana. Her first thought was that Emma Clancy perhaps wasn't as confident about her abilities as she'd first claimed and had sent other investigators on the same trail. But if that were the case, she hardly expected investigators to react the way those guys had. Twice they'd been spotted in suspicious circumstances; twice they'd fled, the latter time employing extreme measures to get away. There was only one reason Tess could think of. 'They're on Albert Sower's payroll.'

'F'sure.'

Tess ran her hands through her hair, ignoring how tacky it felt. 'Do you think those were the men responsible for doing away with the other witnesses?'

Po's mouth twitched in conclusion. 'They're not the killers.'

'How can you be certain?'

'Because the people responsible for the injuries in those pictures wouldn't have run from us.' Po checked his mirrors. He'd been doing it regularly since leaving Baton Rouge. 'Those guys are looking for Wynne, but they'll hand him off to someone else to deal with. Not that they can find him now; not since I chased them off.'

'They could always ask Trey Robinson where we've gone: it's apparent they were nearby when we met with Trey, they didn't just happen on to us when we were on our way back to the hotel.'

'Robinson won't speak to them.'

'He spoke with us,' Tess said.

'Only because Pinky vouched for us. If they go in cold, they'll get stamped on.'

'Trey Robinson is small potatoes when compared to Albert Sower,' she reminded him.

'There's a big difference, though. Sower's in prison, Robinson isn't. A man at his liberty is more dangerous than one guiding things from behind bars.'

'Tell that to Albert Sower,' she said.

'If those guys show their faces on Gardere Lane, especially

if they start throwing their weight around, I can guarantee the outcome, and it won't be rosy for them.'

'You're putting a lot of faith in those bozos guarding Trey. They were a joke.'

'No,' Po corrected. 'They were *joking*. They were being nice because Pinky told them to be nice. If we'd gone in there under any other circumstances we wouldn't have come out alive. Believe me.'

He was possibly exaggerating, but what could she say? If Robinson had turned nasty there would have been little she or Po could have done about it. Although they'd only seen the three gangbangers, it was obvious that there'd be others they hadn't spotted: they'd probably been observed all the way in and out of the neighbourhood. Trey Robinson was an asshole, but he was no fool. He only had to give a sign and their day would have ended badly. Thankfully Pinky Leclerc carried influence with the gang boss, and probably because he was the one supplying him with weapons. But what if Sower also had his equivalent of Pinky in Baton Rouge, someone who could vouch for Sower's men too? It was as Po had worried earlier: Trey Robinson wasn't above claiming the bounty on his head. Maybe that wasn't the extent of how far he was ready to betray them.

Po seemed to have the ability of reading her during her times of quiet reflection. He drummed his fingertips on the steering wheel, drawing her attention. 'If they have a way in with Robinson, then so be it. If it happens, it happens,' he said, and it sounded as if that was a credo of his. 'It just means that we need to get to Wynne before they do. We're on the way, they aren't, so let's just try and maintain our lead, shall we?' He put his foot down, and the Honda sped up, though not to his satisfaction. He grunted. 'That's if grandma's grocery go-getter makes it to Morgan City this century.'

As Po concentrated on driving, Tess took out her phone. She should call Clancy and tell her what had happened. But to do that would guarantee a response where the police would be called, and Tess preferred the opportunity to find Wynne first. Of course, it was only supposition that those men were working on Sower's behalf, and she might have misread their involvement and they weren't after Crawford Wynne. But why else would they be following her? More importantly, how did they know to follow her to Louisiana? Other than her brother Alex, those in Emma Clancy's office, and Po's friend Charley, who knew about her travel arrangements in advance? Had Po mentioned her plans to someone and the news had found its way back to Sower's people? She doubted it, there had been no time, but she had no other theory. Until she knew for certain, she needn't inform Clancy about them, although assistance in tracing who those men were would be helpful. Instead of calling Clancy she composed a text message and included the licence-plate number she'd earlier committed to memory, asking for ownership details. Clancy would have immediate access routes to the DMV whereas Tess might struggle to get the information while they were on the move. As far as Clancy need know, checking the licence number was only one of many breadcrumbs that Tess was following.

While she waited for a reply, Tess nursed her sore elbow, and watched the scenery flow by. Po had sunk back into silence mode, but that suited Tess for the time being.

Moss-hung trees and water dominated the landscape. The sky was pale blue, low clouds barely thicker than mist hanging over the swamplands. The sun was directly ahead, and Tess pulled down her visor to avoid squinting. A pelican made lazy flaps of its wings, skating inches above a waterway, its reflection almost its conjoined twin on the glassy surface. It was an idyllic scene.

'Beautiful,' she said under her breath.

'Until you step on a gator,' Po said.

The trees, saw grass, and lily pads hid more than lurking alligators. There were communities out there in the bayous, and she assumed some of the people living in the swamps were dirt poor. She thought that Po – or more correctly Nicolas Villere – had grown up in one such small community. He hadn't said, but she guessed his upbringing hadn't been a bed of roses. He'd shared no detail about why his father fell foul of the Chatard family, only that he'd been murdered for his trouble, but she'd learned that his dad was all he'd had. It didn't surprise her that Po had responded in the

uncompromising way he had, taking the fight back to the
Chatards. So why was she stunned by the way he'd gone at
those assholes in the car? She should remember just who
– and what – he was, and show him some wary respect.
She'd asked her brother Alex to recommend someone to
accompany her, and he'd pointed her at Po. Alex had
suspected the kind of mess she might be stepping in and had
chosen Po because of it. In this swamp country she should
be thankful that she had her own snapping gator.

But should she?

Alex barely knew of Po beyond his nickname and reputation. What if her brother had made a big mistake in sending
her to him, and Po – an ex-con, and possibly current criminal
– was involved in some way with Albert Sower? What if those
men in the car were actually friends of Po, and his over-reaction
to chasing them off was an act so she didn't suspect they were
working with him? She recalled last night how he'd tried to
deter her from getting a close look at their car, then acted as
if there was nothing to worry about after they fled. What if
Sower had got to Po in some way and he was working with
those men, sticking close to Tess until she led them all to their
target?

No. That was nuts. Surely she wasn't as naive to be fooled
so easily? She caught a sidelong glance from Po.

'Something wrong?' he asked.

She shook her head. Thought about the promise he'd made
to watch her back, and in turn hers to watch his. Thoughts
like those she'd accused him of weren't conducive to forming
the bond of trust they required.

'I'm sorry,' she sighed.

'What did you do wrong?'

'The way I spoke to you earlier; I'd no right doing that.'
Tess experienced another twinge in her elbow. 'Who knows
what might've happened if you hadn't chased those lunatics
off. I should be thanking you, not getting on your case.'

He laughed. 'That was you getting on my case? Hell, you
should hear Charley at the auto shop; he reams me out a new
butthole on a daily basis. To hear him you'd think I was the
hired hand and not the other way around.'

'Oh? I thought he was in charge.' Charley's name was above the door, after all.

'It's my place. I put in the money when it was going down with the financial crash a few years back. Charley stayed on: he manages the shop for me, and he does a damn good job. But, ha, sometimes he forgets who's really the boss.' He spoke fondly of the old mechanic. Charley was possibly the nearest thing to family that Po had. 'I'm surprised you didn't realize when I didn't have to beg the old coot for time off to accompany you.'

Tess finally understood something about him: Po also sometimes forgot who was really the boss; maybe that was just his way. 'I assumed you were just a loose hand he could do without,' she said.

Po grinned. 'Well, there is that.'

The elevated levee highway took them alongside Lake Verret, with the Atchafalaya River to their right, and the Intracoastal Waterway to the left. Along the route various establishments had sprung up to cater for travellers, and Tess could have had her pick of a *boudain*, which was a Cajun rice dish stuffed in a sausage skin, gumbo, a Po'boy sandwich, or a daiquiri, dependent on her taste. Sadly she wasn't hungry. They also passed a funeral home, offering coffins for sale: hopefully they wouldn't need those.

Soon the levee highway was bordered by Flat Lake and Lake Palourde and it was only a short hop into Morgan City, which was a rather grand name for a community of its relatively small size when compared to Baton Rouge or New Orleans.

Po had programmed their destination into the satnav device. It directed them into town, past shopping malls and chain hotels to the intersection with Route 182. They followed the route, which was again resplendent with fast-food outlets, then a right turn that took them a few blocks towards Railroad Avenue. The satnav announced they'd reached their destination, but Po had only requested a central location on the avenue so they'd a short drive to go yet. Instinctively Po turned left, heading for the hinterlands of the town. Some distance along it they came to an underpass, where the avenue split and paralleled the rail tracks it was named for. The business establishments now primarily catered to marine and power engineering, and there were a few auto shops not unlike Charley's back in Portland. Sitting in a crumbling asphalt lot, through which weeds sprouted, was a faded wooden shack with a tin roof. The doors and windows had been boarded up. Po pulled the Honda into the lot.

'This is it?' Tess said, her voice laden with incredulity.

'No. Take a look over there, across the tracks.'

On the opposite side of the railway was a second spur of the road. Two hundred yards along it, Tess spotted another lot, this one surrounded by a tall chain-link fence. Within the fence was a single-storey building, again wooden with a tin roof, but in a better state of repair. Outside the building she could see a handful of motorcycles, and two pickup trucks. There were no signs or decals to announce it was home to the Cottonmouths MCC, but she didn't require them.

Dust devils played across the tracks.

A speedboat whined along the Intracoastal Waterway, its outboard motor working hard as it pushed upstream, but from where they sat they had no view of its progress. Birds squawked and wheeled in the sky and one of them offered a fishy deposit that splattered down the Honda's windshield. 'Hopefully that's a good omen,' Po said.

Tess spuriously eyed the bird crap dribbling down the windshield. How could getting crapped on by a bird be good luck? Strange superstition, she thought.

'How do you want to play things?' Po finally ventured.

'You could always run in, smash all the windows, and drag Wynne out by the hair.' She offered a wry twist of her mouth. 'That's supposing he's even inside.'

'He probably isn't. But we have to find out.' Po unbuckled his belt and got out the car. He opened the back door, felt under the seats, and drew out their guns – hastily concealed there before the police arrived at the scene of the crash at Baton Rouge. He handed Tess's Glock between the front seats, and she hurriedly inspected it before shoving it away in her purse. Leaning inside the Honda, Po disdained the shoulder holster this time and merely pushed his gun into his waistband and covered it with his shirt. 'You ready, Tess?'

'We're just going to walk on over there?'

'Yes, unless you want those hard-asses laughing at us when we drive this chicken shack through the gates.' He nodded towards the motorcycle clubhouse. 'I don't see too many minivans in that lot.'

'What if we need a quick getaway?'

'And you'd rely on this heap?'

'Fair point.' Tess got out the Honda, adjusting her sticky clothing with a quick shrug and dance. She slung her purse over her shoulder, in easy reach should the need to delve inside for her gun arise. Birds still wheeled and squawked, and Tess dodged away before her clothing earned decorations she could do without. *Good luck, my ass.*

They crossed the railway tracks. Tess could smell the heat. It wasn't damp as before, but gritty and tasted like creosote on her tongue. Beads of sweat rolled from under her hairline and trickled down her cheeks. She swiped at them distractedly. By comparison, Po walked as though untroubled. It was a front. There was tenseness in his frame she hadn't noted before. He was checking for observers, expecting ambush, and preparing for the worst.

TWELVE

Tess had never been in the clubhouse of a motorcycle gang before. She'd watched plenty movies and TV shows, and read a number of accounts in novels and such, and knew what to expect: hairy men in leather vests, loud music, flowing alcohol, ribald humour and bursts of spontaneous aggression. But on entering the establishment, her bubble of expectancy burst, and she wasn't sure how she felt about that. Going into a potentially dangerous snake pit, she was on edge, prepared, and meeting this innocuous sight threw her off-kilter.

Instead of the clichéd scene, she found herself standing in a short foyer in front of an elderly woman sitting at a desk. Beyond the woman, a set of double doors were wedged open to allow some air through to a room reminiscent of a high-school classroom with tables and chairs set out in rows. A corkboard was chock-full of flyers and posters for upcoming events and rallies. There was a bar, but it was a small podium in one corner, currently unstaffed, and with cloths over the pumps. Two men played checkers at a table while a third observed them, leaning in to study each move. They were hairy, bearded types, but right now more studious-looking than outlaws. None of them was Crawford Wynne. Tess looked at Po but he offered nothing. Had they found the correct place? Po had based his assumption on the motorcycles in the parking lot, but this was nothing like any clubhouse Tess had heard of. Even the name didn't inspire the same visceral response as other gang names did. Most sounded aggressive, or subversive at least. The Cottonmouths sounded wussy, until she recalled that the cottonmouth – also known as the water moccasin – was the most dangerous venomous viper in these parts.

The woman glimpsed up at them.

She was no Hell's Angel, just a regular woman dressed in

a baggy T-shirt and pale grey slacks. Her hair was dyed copper, but the grey was showing at the roots. She was wearing spectacles, and her lipstick required reapplication. She smiled at them.

'Can I help y'all?'

After a flicker of curiosity for Tess, she'd directed her question at Po. He looked the type to be at home astride a Harley Davidson. But this time, Tess pushed in front of Po, and extending her hand to the woman she said, 'Hopefully you can help.'

The woman accepted Tess's handshake, and her fingers felt cool and leathery.

'I'm Tess, and this is my friend Hank.' It wasn't a good idea to mention Po's real name, and it was the first name that came to mind. 'We're not even sure if we're at the correct place. This is the HQ for the local motorcycle fanciers, right?'

The old woman frowned slightly at Tess's description, but she nodded. 'Yes, honey, it is. I'm Marnie Ross, club secretary. There something I can do for you?'

Tess made a show of looking around before settling her gaze on Marnie again. 'We thought we might be able to take a tour, maybe see a few of the club members' motorcycles.' She touched her chest. 'As you can probably tell, I'm no aficionado, but my friend Hank is a huge Harley fan. A club member, and a mutual friend from up north, told us that we could stop by and take a look at your cycles while we are in town.' Tess feigned embarrassment. 'Mind you, that was a few months ago now. We're not even sure he's still a member of your club.'

Marnie pursed her lips. 'Most of our members are out, as you can probably tell. We have a charity ride scheduled for later today and they're out at the rally point getting ready.'

Tess turned to Po. 'Man, did we choose the wrong day, Hank. Isn't that just typical, though? I told you we should've called ahead first.'

'And I told you I lost his number.' Po rose to the part admirably, playing the dumb boyfriend to a T. 'But he told me he could be found here most days.'

Tess threw up her hands, turning back to Marnie wearing

an exasperated look. 'I don't suppose you can help us get in touch, could you? Hank has lost the number and we have no home address for him. Does Crawford Wynne come in most days like he promised?'

A tremor passed behind the woman's features. 'Crawford Wynne's your friend, huh?' She turned and looked at the three men playing checkers in the back room. Tess worried that the game was up and that Marnie would call the men through to throw them out. Instead, the old woman leaned forward and lowered her voice. She patted the air with her long, dry fingers for emphasis. 'Wynne isn't a name mentioned with much fondness round here, honey. And it surprises me that you'd be his friend.'

'Well,' said Tess, reading the situation, 'he's not exactly a friend, just an acquaintance of Hank's.' She leaned in conspiratorially. 'Personally I found Wynne a bit of a creep, but Hank thinks he's OK. Mind you, Hank isn't the best judge when it comes to his friends. I take it Wynne has made himself unwelcome here?'

'That would be an understatement.' Marnie fired a dour look at Po for his stupidity. 'If you want my advice, miss, I'd steer well clear of him *and* his sort.'

'If it were down to me, I'd be happy if I never saw him again. But Hank was looking forward to catching up with his old buddy. You don't happen to have any idea where we might find him, maybe you've an address or cell number we can try?'

Marnie sat back in her chair. Her head shook as she considered. Coming to a decision she pulled open a desk drawer and hauled out a large ledger. In this enlightened age most people kept their records on a computer: the ledger was anachronistic, a dog-eared thing frayed along the edges, with Post-it notes stuck in the top to mark some of the pages. She opened it like a preacher laying a Bible on a pulpit. She licked a finger to turn leaves. After a quick sift of the yellowed pages she looked up, shook her head again, but this time in the negative. 'I don't have Wynne's address. Say's here he was staying with Ron Edgerton, but I can't imagine he'll be welcome at Ron's place now.'

'Had a falling out?'

'And some. Ron caught Wynne with his wife, Celia, and there was a huge bust-up. Their dispute spilled over right here a month ago and they had to be pulled apart by the other boys. Most of them took Ron's part and hustled Wynne outside. I didn't see, but Wynne was sent packing – if you catch my meaning?' Marnie didn't elaborate, but didn't have to. There had been some old-fashioned retribution laid on by the Cottonmouths. 'I'm doubting that Wynne left a forwarding address with Ron or Celia, 'specially seeing as they've patched things up between them now.'

Tess mopped her brow with her fingertips, unconscious of the motion. Po brushed against her as leaned over the desk. 'You said "most of them",' he said to Marnie.

'Huh?'

'Most of them took Ron's part. Somebody didn't.'

Tess was impressed, though mildly irritated. She was the details person and she'd missed the obvious, whereas Po had been right on it. Marnie shrugged slim shoulders with barely any effect on her oversized T-shirt. 'There were a few of the boys thought Ron was overreacting.' She made a face that said she disagreed strongly with the rebels. 'You think maybe one of them stayed in touch with Wynne? Possibly.'

'Can you put us in touch with any of them?' Tess asked hopefully.

Marnie exhaled through her nostrils. She leaned back, meeting first Po's gaze, then Tess's. 'I wasn't entrusted with my chair position for being green.' Marnie took off her spectacles, and cleaned the lenses on the tail of her shirt. Placing the glasses back on, she eyed Tess spuriously. 'I know y'all ain't friends of Crawford Wynne. Hell, girl, you're the corn-fed type he'd eat for breakfast, and I don't think ol' Hank there would take too kindly to that kinda behaviour. There's some other reason y'all are looking for Wynne and I can't imagine it's a good one.'

The old woman had apparently been around the block a few times and wasn't as gullible as Tess hoped. The game was up, then. It was time to go for broke and tell the truth, but again Po interjected. 'He owes me money. Wasn't sure you'd tell us where to find him if you owed Wynne any loyalty. But I can see now that you don't regard him too highly.'

'Must be a lot of money to warrant a trip all the way here to Morgan City.' Marnie sneered to show she wasn't buying Po's explanation either.

'It's not so much the cash that counts, it's the principle,' Po said without missing a beat. 'Wynne owes me and I intend to make him pay.'

Marnie grinned. 'Now we're getting somewhere.' But then she held up a finger, and Tess noted that the polish was in need of reapplication as urgently as her lipstick. 'If you've a personal beef with Crawford Wynne, then that's your business. But this here club is *my responsibility*. I don't want you bringing trouble to its door, not when I've tried so hard to clean up its image. These days the Cottonmouth MCC is a charitable institution and we ain't losing our licence for nobody.'

'So point us in the right direction,' Po said, 'and we'll go away. You won't see or hear from us again.'

Marnie squinted behind her spectacles, cocking her head like a quizzical dog. A tiny rainbow flared off an oily smear she'd missed cleaning off the right lens. She glanced back at the trio playing checkers, and not a one of them returned the look. She leaned forward, flipping pages in the ledger. Then tapped a chipped nail on one name. 'Jerome Benoit. You might try him.'

'Thanks,' Po said, 'an address would be helpful, though.'

'I'm not giving you his home address, but you could try speaking with him in person. He's along with the others getting ready for the charity rally. You'll find the club massing on Pine and Lakewood, readying for a ride to raise funds for Teche Regional.'

'How will we recognize him?' Tess wondered.

'He'll be riding the trike, the only three-wheeler in the group. But if he doesn't happen to be astride it, look for the good-looking boy, looks like that *Pretty Woman* actor. But I'll warn you up front,' Marnie said with a sour grin. 'That boy ain't no officer or a gentleman.'

'Noted,' Po said.

Marnie held up a warning finger. 'And I'll also remind you: the Cottonmouths are doing a charitable rally for the sick children, y'hear? I don't want to hear of any mess or fuss when you talk to Jerome.'

'I'll keep things nice and quiet, under the radar,' Po pledged.

THIRTEEN

The air shifted, and bars of light flickered, and without looking up from her work, Marnie Ross knew someone had entered the clubhouse, even before she heard the faint squeak of the hinge as the door was released behind them. Her first thought was that the couple had returned to prod her for more information on goddamn Crawford Wynne. She'd warned that she wanted no mess or fuss from them, and already they'd come back to bother her again. What part of *fuss* didn't they understand?

The door opened again, and shadow was cast over her desk in the foyer. Only then did she glance up, hoping to see that ignoring them had done the trick and sent them off without troubling her a second time. But instead of the cowboy and the corn-fed girl, she found a different couple staring down at her. It was two men, one fair-haired, and the other one darker. They were dressed in shirts and sports jackets, over trousers, but to her the image didn't fit: they looked like they'd dressed for the occasion, to form a false impression, and their disguises said more about them than the tough set of their jaws. They were detectives, or they were rivals from another outlaw biker outfit. Neither impression sweated her. She'd dealt with cops and punks in the past and likely would again in the future. She peered at them sourly over the rims of her glasses, waiting for them to announce their intentions.

The blond man swept a disdainful glance over her, before stepping aside and checking out the view inside the clubhouse. Back there a trio of the boys was bickering in good humour over a game of checkers. The blond took an uninvited step past Marnie's desk and she held up a hand. 'I'm sorry,' she said, 'but who are y'all?'

The blond ignored her, moving to the doorway for a better view of the club. The darker guy stepped closer to her desk, and he pulled the ledger towards him that she'd earlier checked for Ron Edgerton's details, but had neglected to return to its drawer. Marnie snapped a hand down on it, caring a damn that her chipped nails almost raked skin from his fingers. He jerked his hand away, folding his fingers into a fist.

'You don't get to touch that without a warrant, son,' Marnie snapped.

She expected him to badge her, start throwing around the weight of officialdom. He didn't. He swore, and he wasn't kind about her age or her looks. Marnie rocked back in her seat.

'You ain't the police, right? Trust me, son, I can see right through you. I've been cussed at by cops before and they make a darn better job of it than you.'

The man looked momentarily taken aback, and that suited Marnie. Place him on his back foot and she'd already started the process of deflating his bubble. To further disarm him, she ignored him, turning instead to the blond. 'You! You've no right going back there. Unless you want to pay your subs and join the club, it's for *members only.*'

The blond eyed her as if she was something he'd tracked inside on his shoe. He approached her, stood over her. 'We're only taking a look around. There a problem with that?'

'My problem is that this is a private club,' Marnie stated. 'You do know the meaning of the term?'

Ignoring the remark, the blond sniffed. He looked at his pal. 'Doesn't look as if he's here.'

'No,' said the dark-haired man.

'Y'all are looking for Crawford Wynne, right?' said Marnie, and she made his name sound like shit. 'Just like the couple that just left are.'

The two glanced at each other, but didn't elect to answer. They didn't have to. It was apparent that Wynne had attracted trouble, but that didn't surprise her: that man carried trouble like stink on a mangy dog.

'Did you tell those others where Wynne is?' asked the blond.

'Nope. And I'm not telling y'all either,' she said. 'Now. There's the door. Don't let it hit you on the ass on the way out.'

Again the two shared a glance, but this time Marnie

wondered if she'd gone too far. They weren't put off by her spikey attitude.

'We should get Hector,' the dark-haired man suggested.

'We should,' said the blond, then directed his next words at Marnie, 'I'm sure he'll get you talking.'

Marnie crossed her arms beneath her breasts. 'Fetch whoever you want, honey. I've friends I can call too. Henry! Jimmy! I could do with y'all through here. There's a coupla bozos refusing to leave.'

In the clubroom, the two guys set aside their checkers game, scraping back their chairs and standing. The third man also moved to join them. They were all big, muscled, tattooed, and wearing leather vests and denim jeans. Their faces were set with dire promises of violence, and they bunched their fists in anticipation.

The blond and the dark-haired man looked at each other but didn't retreat. They smiled in anticipation, but it was because they'd seen another man appear through a doorway at the back of the room. Marnie followed their gazes and spotted him though, and indignation jolted her out of her seat. 'Hey! How did you get in there?'

Her words turned the trio of bikers in their tracks.

The man named Hector kept coming, and he was only feet from them before he allowed a knife to slip from his sleeve and he palmed the handle.

If Hector's intention in showing the weapon was only to motivate answers, Marnie would never know, because the Cottonmouth trio responded the way they would if confronted by a rival gang member: they switched to full testosterone mode. They went from gentle lambs enjoying their board game to angry bears. The air was split by curses, and the aggressive posturing of overheated bodies. The biker called Henry Thibodaux slapped his hands on his chest, then threw out his cupped palms, curling his fingers, challenging Hector to try it.

Hector complied, but he didn't go for the big guy confronting him, he made a strange swooping motion of his upper torso, crabbed sideways and jabbed out with the blade. It went under James le Boeuf's chin, stabbing upward through the hairy skin of his throat, and Marnie was positive she saw a glint of steel in Jimmy's open mouth as it opened in shock. Hector withdrew the blade, snicking it down, and a line of blood spattered the floor. Jimmy's hands went to his throat and mouth, and he staggered aside. It was a drama of seconds. When Hector turned to Henry, the big guy had lost his will for a fight and he backpedalled away. The third Cottonmouth charged for the far corner, and the exit door where Hector had entered.

Marnie was horrified by the fleeing biker's display of cowardice, and she screeched out a cry. If she'd a gun she might have shot him in the back herself, but she didn't have to. Beside her the blond pulled out a revolver, and he took a wild shot at the man. The round hit wood somewhere near him, and the biker bent suddenly at the waist, and practically threw himself for the door. He crashed through it out of sight, and out of Marnie's immediate concern.

Jimmy was on the floor now, making muffled squeaks as he tried to stem the blood pouring out of him. Henry was still backpedalling from Hector, who came on with no emotion in his dull gaze. His dead eyes, and the surety of their promise of uncompromising violence, were enough for Henry. He spun and looked for an escape, but there was nowhere to go but through the two men and Marnie, who was hemmed between them. Rather them than the maniac with the blade. He hollered and came at a full charge, shoving desks and chairs aside. Maybe he intended scooping up Marnie as he barrelled through, but again she would never know. The blond shot at Henry. This close there was no missing. The bullet struck him under the sternum, and Henry crashed face down, arms reaching almost to their feet. He didn't attempt a heroic crawl for them, because all life had fled as the bullet destroyed his heart.

Marnie's mouth dropped open.

She was cold, even the inside of her mouth felt icy.

She was no newcomer to violence. Hell, she'd run with the Cottonmouth MCC back when they were feared outlaw bikers, and had witnessed dozens of knifings, shoot-outs, and brawls, often taking part in them when she was younger and ramped up on amphetamines and coke. But as age caught up, and sensibilities changed, and other avenues presented where the club could funnel funds without the need for violence, she'd been disconnected from that turbulent world. Having raw-edged viciousness present like this was like being doused in icy water one second then set aflame with gasoline the next. Her mind reeled.

When the dark-haired man grabbed her collar and yanked her forward, scalding heat finally washed through her. She could feel her face burning. Her eyes were too dry.

'Why did you shoot him?'

Hector's words were for the blond.

'He was coming for us, I had to stop him,' said the blond, and his tone said he feared his scarred companion.

'I would have stopped him,' Hector stated, and he lifted his knife. There was not a drop of Jimmy's blood on it.

'You get *her* still,' said the blond, with a jerk of his revolver towards Marnie.

'But I do not get the time to fully enjoy her.' Hector aimed the blade at the far door. 'One of them got away. He'll bring the police here. I told you, no shooting. *Ustedes los norteamericanos*: you watch too many fucking cowboy movies.'

'Sorry, man,' the blond said.

Hector sniffed away the apology, then stepped over the recumbent form of Henry, and stood with his gargoyle face inches from Marnie's.

'Tell me where to find Crawford Wynne.' He set the tip of his knife against her left cheek. 'Unless you want me to cut out your eyes? *Dime, vieja mujerzuela.*'

She didn't require a translation to understand the urgency of his demand. Marnie pointed, and the blond grabbed the ledger from her desk. He jammed it into Marnie's hands. 'Quick about it,' he snapped.

Shaking, struggling with the pages, she finally found what she was looking for. 'Here,' she indicated a name. 'He's staying with Jerome Benoit, right here in Morgan City. I . . . I don't have Benoit's address, but I'm . . . I'm sure you can easily find out where he is.'

'The others that came looking for Wynne, you told them this also?' Hector asked.

Marnie nodded, her head down. She clutched the ledger to her chest as if it would stop whatever was coming.

'Then time is shorter than I thought.' Hector's head swivelled towards the blond man. 'Shooting that fool might have been the right thing to do after all. Now. You may as well shoot her. As much as I'd like to I won't waste any more of my time on the *puta*.'

Hector walked away.

The blond lifted his gun, but he paused.

It wasn't because he was loath to shoot her, Marnie understood.

'Better let her go,' he said to his pal, who still held Marnie's collar. 'Unless you want covered in her brains?'

Marnie moaned.

'You really want to do this?' the dark-haired man asked.

Blondie took a quick glance at Henry and the blood pooling round him.

'I've already crossed that line,' he said, then winked at Marnie. 'As my buddy Hector would say: *Adiós, puta.*'

FOURTEEN

The Cottonmouth MCC had massed at the intersection of Pine Street and Lakewood Drive, for easy access to the I-90, which they planned taking over the Atchafalaya River to Berwick, then on up to New Iberia. There were upward of forty motorcycles, plus two support vans decorated with the club decals, and strewn with banners denoting the fund-raising rally. There were also upward of forty riders, plus pillion passengers, and others solely on foot, toting plastic collection buckets. Passers-by and well-wishers had also gathered to see off the convoy, and there was a general air of carnival about the proceedings. The tough image of a motorcycle gang was leavened by joviality, face paint, and even fancy dress costumes. Po wasn't buying it; despite Marnie's assurance that the Cottonmouths were now good ol' boys raising funds for charities, he knew it was all a public front to divert the cops from what they got up to in their private time. Charitable institutes didn't make deadly enemies of the likes of Trey Robinson by shaking collection tins.

Marnie's description of Jerome Benoit didn't help, because he didn't look like the actor Marnie had alluded to, dressed as an ape and waving a huge inflatable plastic banana. But Marnie had been correct when stating he'd be the only one riding a three-wheeler. Tess commented on the Honda Goldwing's aesthetic beauty, but Po was nonplussed. 'Those things are fit only for ageing baby boomers with weak knees and swollen ankles,' he snipped.

They stood at the fringes of the parked convoy, watching while men and women in leathers and denim prepared for the reasonably short trip. They were inconspicuous enough, and twice already Tess had dropped coins into buckets rattled under their noses, so to the Cottonmouths they were simply a pair of onlookers like all the rest. Some of those that had come to see off the rally mingled with the motorcyclists, and they could have too, but Po had urged caution. He was waiting to get Benoit alone but until now he'd been ensconced firmly at the centre of the high japes and had attracted a crowd of his own. He hooted and danced on his trike, bopping passers-by over their heads with the banana, orchestrating laughter from the audience.

'He's got to be melting inside that costume,' Tess noted. Without a heavy fur coat she felt as if she were smouldering under the afternoon sun. Benoit was now standing on the seat of his Goldwing, the banana wedged between his thighs, wagging it up and down like a huge phallus.

'Marnie was right about him; that isn't the behaviour becoming an officer or a gentleman.' Po folded his arms across his chest and continued to watch Benoit's lewd antics. It took a moment before others in the MCC noted what Benoit was up to, and a moment or so longer for them to act. An older guy with a shaved head and drooping white moustache headed over and waved Benoit down off the trike. Benoit wiggled his hips, making the inflatable dance, eliciting a round of laughter from the crowd, but the older guy wasn't amused. He jerked his head, stabbing a hand at one of the parked vans. Benoit plucked out the banana, bowed for the audience, but then he hopped down and strode for the van. As he walked he pulled off the ape mask, and shook out glistening black hair that hung over his fur-clad shoulders. He did have Hollywood good looks, though his nose was large and slightly off centre. As soon as he was on the move away from the gathered audience, Po went forward. Caught out, Tess wavered a second longer before following. He looked back at her, shook his head gently. Tess slowed, then halted. Po strode into Benoit's path and held out a hand. Benoit threw back his head, spraying drops of perspiration. Po asked him something, but it was lost beneath the babble of the crowd.

Benoit jabbered something and made to walk past, but Po's hand on his chest held him in place. More words passed, Benoit shaking his head in denial.

Tess watched the younger man frown, then shake his head again, this time with some anger. She still couldn't hear what passed between them, but Benoit didn't look ready to make friendly conversation. He nudged past Po and headed for the nearest panel van. Po wasn't going to be ignored though. He went after Benoit, grabbed the back of the ape suit, clamped his other hand over his mouth to stifle argument, and manhandled the biker to the open van doors.

Unbelievable, Tess thought, as Po forced Benoit into the van and climbed inside with him. Po leaned out, winked at Tess, and then pulled the doors shut. Some people nearby had noticed Po loading Benoit in the van, but accepted it all as part of the show, as if Po was playing the role of the bad-taste police. They shook their heads in amusement, then walked away. Good job too, because in the next moment the van rocked wildly from side to side, and something thudded against the nearest side panel causing it to ring hollowly. Tess made out a fresh dint in the panel, and it was suspiciously shaped like Benoit's large nose. 'Oh no,' she moaned under her breath.

There was another dull ring from within the van, followed by a series of sharper bangs. The van rocked on its suspension again. The conversation from within was muffled and one-sided. It ended with a low cry of pain. Silence. Tess took an involuntary step in the van's direction, but thought better of it. She looked around, checking if anyone had noticed the commotion. The carnival atmosphere prevailed, although she spotted one woman dressed in club tags squinting over. Maybe the sounds of moans and creaking suspension could regularly be heard from that van, because the woman suddenly smiled wryly to herself and turned away. She wandered off, rattling her collection bucket. Tess waited, and was relieved when the back doors finally opened and Po stepped out. She had no view of the interior, and fleetingly wondered if Benoit was unconscious, or worse. But after a second or two the younger man also clambered out of the van. He looked shaky, a little flushed, and his nose appeared more swollen than before and twin trails of blood smeared his top lip, but otherwise he was unhurt. He wiped at his nose and mouth with the front of the gorilla costume, while staring balefully at Po's back as the rangy ex-con strode towards her.

'What happened?' she urged Po.

'I'll reveal all as soon as we're on the move. Let's go before Monkey Nuts decides to shout a few of his buddies over.'

'I take it that asking him nicely didn't occur to you?'

'I did ask him nicely at first, you saw me,' said Po. 'But Benoit doesn't understand the concept of being nice. So I had to ask in a way that would get through to him.'

'By bashing in the questions with the wall of the van?'

'It worked.'

They headed for the Honda, and only as they drove away did Po add, 'I got a lead on Wynne, but we'll have to be quick. Once Benoit shakes off the cobwebs he'll get on the phone to warn his buddy we're coming.'

'I hope he's not far off, it won't take Benoit long.'

'He'll have to find a working cell first.' Po dropped a phone he'd taken from the biker out of the window and it smashed into tinkling components along the asphalt behind them. 'Besides, we're not far off Benoit's digs. That's where Wynne is supposedly holed up.' He told Tess an address on Union Street and she moved to punch it into the satnav.

'Relax,' he said, 'I know where Union Street is.'

Their journey took them back across town and over Railroad Avenue, though at its opposite end to the Cottonmouth club-house. At the intersection the traffic was stalled by a number of police cruisers racing to an emergency call along Railroad. They had their lights and sirens on and responded in numbers.

'I wonder what that's all about,' Tess said.

'Nothing to do with us,' Po replied. 'If Benoit chose to report his assault then the cops are headed in the wrong direction.'

Once the fleet of responding police cruisers disappeared the traffic got moving again, and Po flicked a cursory glance at Tess. The delay might prove more than an encumbrance in their journey time. 'Maybe I should have knocked out Benoit's lights. Chances are he'll have got to a phone by now.'

Tess grimaced. She couldn't advocate violence, but perhaps this time her volatile companion was right. If Crawford Wynne received a warning they were coming he might take off before she was able to press the subpoena notice into his hands. Even afterwards he might not comply and what then? Did she give

Po the go ahead to knock out Wynne too, so they could hogtie him and drag him back to Maine?

Po steered the Honda onto Union, and began checking house numbers.

'How positive are you that Benoit gave you the correct address?' Tess said.

'He wasn't in a lying frame of mind,' Po assured her, 'not when I twisted his arm up his back. He went over the address a couple times to make sure I had all the details. Check it out.'

He'd drawn the rental to a halt opposite a wood frame house perched on cinder blocks. It was dilapidated, with trash on the strip of dusty grass that passed as a front lawn. The frame of a motorcycle missing its wheels and seat was part embedded in the dirt. The bench seat from an old gas-guzzler had been set against the front of the house and around it was a scattering of empty bottles and flattened beer cans. Holes in the walls were plugged with wadded paper, and looked suspiciously like bullet holes, as if the home had once been the target of a drive-by shooting. The number on the mailbox corresponded with the number twisted at pain from Jerome Benoit. It was getting to mid-afternoon, but a light was on behind drawn blinds in what Tess took to be the living room. No tell-tale shadows moved beyond the grimy blinds, though.

'Do you think he has left already?' Tess asked.

'Only one way to find out.' Po got out the car. 'Keep that pistol in reach, I'm not sure Wynne's going to be overly happy to see us.'

Reaching into her purse, Tess adjusted the butt of the Glock so she could draw it if necessary. Her wrist ached, but she wondered if the pain was psychosomatic. She flexed her hand as she got out the car and walked round to join Po who stood peering across the street at the decrepit house.

When she was a sheriff's deputy Tess had attended many similar dwellings, seeking to speak with homeowners who might be victims, witnesses, or in fact felons, and there'd always been a method of approach. Usually she had back up if the situation was deemed dangerous, and other deputies would take positions to cover all exit ports. She knew that on most occasions a nervous or desperate individual would try to escape from a rear door or window, and often it was the officer there who grabbed them. She contemplated sending Po to cover the back of the house, but he'd already made his own plan and began striding for the front. Anxiety trickled through her, and she wavered. One of them should cover the back, but the image of a coked-up lunatic flashed across her vision. He came at her with his huge knife glistening, already casting rivulets of blood in the air as he slashed at her. Biting down hard on the image, Tess hurried after Po, following him up the front steps.

Po glanced at her, lines puckering his brow.

'You OK, Tess?' he asked.

'Sure. I'm fine,' she lied.

'You look . . . nervous,' he said, and she was sure he was about to say 'afraid'.

'I'm fine,' she said again, and a tad harsher, 'don't forget I've done this a thousand times.'

'You're sure? If you prefer I'll go in and speak with Wynne first.'

'I told you I'm fine. How many damn times do I have to repeat myself? Don't forget, if he refuses to come with us I have to be the one to subpoena him.'

Her statement was untrue; either of them could serve the legal summons. What she really meant was that she had to do it, because beyond proving to anyone else she could still do her job, she must first prove it to herself.

'Suit yourself,' Po said and this time his gaze lingered. 'It's just that you don't look yourself.'

Under his scrutiny Tess found holding a brave face difficult, but she managed.

'OK then,' Po finally said, balling his fist to knock on the door.

FIFTEEN

The shrivelled *boudin* stank like shit, and even looked like a desiccated turd to Crawford Wynne. But it was all he'd found approaching edible while rooting in the refrigerator, so he sliced it up and dumped it in the pot with the *étouffée* leftovers from Jerome Benoit's lunch before his buddy had headed out in that ridiculous ape outfit to the equally ridiculous charity rally. Shit, they were supposed to be fucking outlaw bikers, not bleeding-heart bucket-shakers. Benoit had asked Wynne to accompany him, despite the fact he was as welcome as a fart in a space suit anywhere the Cottonmouth MCC were these days. Fuck 'em. They were a bunch of limp dicks, and he was sorry he'd ever hooked back up with his old crew after skipping out of Maine. Back in the day the Cottonmouths were feared, now they were laughable, and his politics didn't sit well with their bright new image. They were running scared from a bunch of niggers up in Baton Rouge instead of showing the spearchuckers the meaning of respect. Only one way to do that and it was to stamp down on their necks. Hard. At least Sower's gang had the balls to admit they were criminals and weren't afraid to show it. They didn't hide behind false facades – all that patting disabled kids on the heads that the Cottonmouths got up to was enough to make him barf – and he'd heard on the grapevine that Sower's gang were actually stepping up their activities since the big man himself had been taken in by the law, making things very difficult for those hoping to keep Sower behind bars. Shit, if it weren't for the fact his head could end up on a stake outside Casa Sower, he'd have loved to be in on the action.

The fuck had he been thinking?

That was the problem, he hadn't been thinking straight. When the Emergency Services Unit, a locked and loaded tactical team, had grabbed Albert Sower in a morning raid, Wynne had to admit that he'd panicked. He'd already served a stretch in the Maine State Prison at Warren and had no wish to return, and had taken the alternative instead. He spoke with some tight-assed bitch called Clancy, an investigator working for the DA's office. He'd made all the right noises, pledged his assistance as a concerned witness, and then – at first opportunity – lit out for the South. In his head it was the right thing to do: he'd no intention of going state's evidence against Sower, but some of his buddies might not see things that way. They were known for hitting first, asking questions later, then, only as a final resort coming to a fair judgement. Up until a few weeks ago he'd kept in touch with his old biker pal, Mitch Delaney, but things had gone cold at that end. He hoped that Mitch had lit out – as others in the gang apparently had – and not actually made the mistake of turning fink. Do that and Wynne himself would happily cut up Mitch's face next time he saw him. Loyalty to your crew was important to Wynne, and there was nothing worse than a rat. It's why it pained him so much that the Cottonmouths had turned against him. For fuck sake, he'd only rolled with one of the skanks that took up the bitch seat on Ron Edgerton's Harley. Where was the crime in that? They were supposed to be a brotherhood, one for all and all for one, and in his mind that meant that the sisters were fair game. Goddamn liberals, they'd be adding PC after their MCC moniker next, the politically correct assholes.

At least Benoit was still a swinging dick. He'd backed Wynne in the fistfight that broke out at the clubhouse, only because he had a gripe with Edgerton, the guy claiming ownership over the woman, but that was still something. He'd allowed Wynne to crash at his place, and they'd even talked about forming their own breakaway faction of the Cottonmouths, maybe adding a tag of their own: The REAL Cottonmouth MCC. Benoit had gone off to the rally to catch the ears of a few of the guys they might recruit. Wynne had wished him luck, but he didn't hold much hope. Benoit was as skilled at diplomacy as he was at cooking. And if the sour *étouffée* were anything to go by then their gang would remain a duo for some time.

Ah, who was he to complain about Benoit's lack of culinary

skills? Wynne knew his limitations: he would burn water if left to his own devices.

He rattled the pan on the hob and set a heat under it, reminding himself to regularly stir the slop before it coagulated into something resembling a Texas field pancake. Immediately he ignored his own advice and slumped in a chair at the kitchen table, pushing aside spoiling dishes from a previous meal of dirty rice. While he waited for his late breakfast to warm he idly scratched at the tattoo on his face. It was an unconscious trait. Sometimes he forgot about the ink, and even he was occasionally surprised when catching his reflected image. The tattoo was a brand that didn't fit with the new improved Cottonmouths, not when Nazi symbolism sat badly with fund-raisers. He wondered if his tattoo was the real reason a fight was picked with him, him poking the woman just the excuse that his old pals had found to oust him from the club. If he'd a choice in the matter he'd cover the tat – it made him too identifiable in any crime – but he couldn't grow a beard for shit, and now he'd lost so much hair up top he'd taken a razor to the rest of it. Why cultivate on your chin what grows naturally on your ass?

He brayed at his own wisdom, the sound a phlegmy crackle in his throat. He hawked up and spat on the nearest plate, making a silent bet it wouldn't affect the rank taste of the rice if he fed it back to Benoit for his supper. He laughed again, planning on playing the prank on his buddy. He'd delight in telling him the secret ingredient afterwards. Benoit would see the joke: after all, this was the guy who ate the contents of an ashtray on a five-dollar bet.

There was a rattle and thud at the back door.

Jesus! Speaking of the devil. Benoit was back sooner than expected. Wynne thought of transferring the rice to the concoction in the pan and inviting Benoit to share his breakfast instead. He reached for the fouled plate, and only then wondered why the fuck Benoit had come in by the back door. Probably forgot his key. But why force the door when he knew Wynne was inside? A prickle of warning went through him, and he began to rise. His butt had barely cleared the seat when he sat down heavily again. The gun aimed at his head enforced his reaction.

'He's in here,' said the fair-headed man behind the gun.

Wynne squinted at the guy, and it took him a moment to recognize the clean-cut face.

Wynne grinned, began to stand a second time. 'Hey? What you doin' all the way down here, Wel—'

The gun slapped up against his jaw, and it was as much out of surprise as it was the blunt impact that sat him down again.

'Whathafugg?' he mumbled through his bruised lips. He tasted blood in the back of his mouth.

Another familiar figure entered the room, but any relief at spotting a friendly face was buried under the growing agony in his mouth. Wynne probed at a cracked tooth with his tongue while blinking up at his old friends.

'Jesus,' said the dark-haired man as he glanced around the less than salubrious kitchen. 'We'd have saved ourselves some trouble if we'd thought to look for a cockroach in the sewer. This is some shithole you've scurried to, Wynne.'

Dabbing his mouth with his sleeve, Wynne said, 'If you'd have let me know you were looking I'd've given you directions. What the fuck is this all about, guys?'

The blond jerked his head at the door. 'Hector will explain all.'

Wynne tried to struggle up, his heels skidding in the grime on the floor as he pushed back in the seat. 'Hector? *He's* here? Now wait up a goddamn minute . . .'

Before he could say another word, Wynne was grabbed and held in his seat, the gun pressed against his neck, fingers digging deep into his scalp. A third man announced his arrival by rapping his knuckles on the door jamb. He ignored Wynne, instead casting his gaze over the unsavoury room.

'Something's burning,' Hector declared.

The dark-haired man grabbed Wynne's food off the hob and dumped it in the sink alongside other unwashed pans and crockery. As an afterthought he clicked off the heat.

'You should have let it burn,' Hector said. 'The smoke would've camouflaged the stench of this place. Wynne, it does not surprise me that you live like a dog cowering in its own filth.'

Wynne wasn't a coward, but he was under no illusion why

Hector and the others had followed him to Morgan City, or what that meant for him. 'Jesus, Hector, I don't know what you've been told but it isn't the truth. You know I'd never turn on Albert, right? I was just talking shit, stringing the cops along, keeping the door open so I could slip away.'

'Huh,' said Hector, unimpressed. 'So you are to be forgiven for running away? That is a disloyalty in itself.'

'No. You don't understand. I ran so the bastards couldn't use me, so I couldn't be forced into saying anything against Albert. They were pressing me into making a deposition, but I told them fuck all then got outta there.'

'You make a weak argument, Wynne. Running away is abandonment. Abandonment is betrayal. Betrayal is unforgiveable.'

'No, man. I'd have come back. All you had to do was say the word and I'd've come running.' Wynne looked up at the gunman, then across at the dark-haired man. 'Come on, dude. Jacky Boy! You know me. I wouldn't turn on you guys.'

'Don't kid yourself, Wynne,' said Jacky Boy. 'I know you all right. I know you'd cut your own mother's throat if she didn't suck your dick hard enough. As far as you were ever concerned, it was all about you, *dude*. You ran to save your own ass, and that's all.'

Hector indicated that Wynne stand. When he wasn't quick enough, the gunman stuck the muzzle under his chin. 'Get up.'

Wynne stood, and he was turned around on tiptoes.

Hector eyed him, as if weighing up a prize turkey in a butcher's shop window.

'What shall I do with you?' he wondered aloud.

A runnel of sweat ran down the side of Wynne's face, but he daren't wipe it away. He felt it drip down his shirt collar.

In another room a telephone started ringing.

Hector turned his head fractionally, listening to the distant tinkle as if guessing what it meant. Returning his attention to Wynne he'd come to a decision. But it wasn't a case of 'saved by the bell' for Wynne.

'I was going to punish you here, leave you propped on the front porch. But your other pursuers are dogged. They will be here soon, and as much as I look forward to meeting them in person it will impede on the time I have with you. I've travelled far to find you, Wynne, and am not going to spoil my enjoyment now. Come, and you can be thankful that I give you one last opportunity to serve Alberto.'

Wynne almost went to his knees, but he was shoved forward. Jacky Boy grabbed his arm, while the fair-haired man prodded him in the spine with the gun. Wynne turned to look back at Hector. 'Jesus, thank you! Thank you, Hector! I . . . I thought you'd kill me for sure. Thanks for giving me another chance. I'll do . . .'

Hector shook his head.

'I didn't say I would spare you.' Hector turned up the side of his mouth. 'You will serve as notice to those who might choose to follow.'

He was bundled out the door, just as a vehicle pulled up opposite the house. The gun to the back of his head demanded silence, but there was no way Wynne could holler for help, because at Hector's words he had almost swallowed his tongue.

SIXTEEN

P o knocked again.

There was no response. No sound of movement. No shifting of the shadows behind the blinds. He shared a glance with Tess, and she felt her mouth tighten. 'We should check around the back,' she said, but didn't follow the suggestion with action. She stood slightly behind Po, and his presence was reassuring. When did she originally begin feeling this way, unsure of her own ability to do her job? No. She was no longer a cop. These days she was only a private citizen, and she had no right to be standing on the porch of a desperate man's home about to take away his liberty. Why in God's name had she even accepted this task?

Because she had to.

Not just for the remuneration that admittedly she needed badly, but also for her wellbeing and state of mind. She had been forced out of her career, and more than anything wanted to prove to the naysayers, of whom both her mother and Jim Neely rated highly, that she was still capable of performing. She'd signed up to protect and serve, and it wasn't through her own fault that that duty had been snatched from her. Helping put Albert Sower behind bars was the kind of validation she required. To do that she must bring back Crawford Wynne, whose testimony would send Sower down permanently.

OK. Get a grip, girl, and get on with your job. She edged away from Po, leaning to peek through a narrow gap between the blinds and window frame. She saw a slither of a room as uncared for as the house and yard. No person was visible. She moved the other way and this time checked a kitchen window. The light was off inside, but enough daylight was available to make out a ramshackle table and ladder-backed chair. An empty plate sat neglected on the table, and flies bounced off and on it in search of morsels. She looked back at Po.

'He isn't here,' she mouthed.

'Or he's hiding,' Po replied.

'I should go around the back.'

'No. Wait up.' Po reached for the door handle. It twisted in his grip and the door fell open an inch. Po raised his eyebrows.

'What are you doing?' Tess hurried to his side.

'Taking a look.'

'You can't. It'd be breaking and entering.'

'I haven't broken anything. The door was unlocked and open like this when we found it.' Po offered a conspiratorial smile. 'Don't say that wasn't a line you used when you were a cop.'

'We have no right to go inside.'

'I probably had no right bashing up Benoit's face either, but I did. C'mon, Tess. Do you want to get this done or not?'

'Yes.'

'So throw away your goddamn rulebook, will ya?' Po pushed open the door, allowing it to swing naturally on loose hinges. A waft of hot, stale air rode over them. Sickly sweet, it made saliva flood Tess's mouth, and she forced down a retch.

'What is that stench?'

'That's the aroma of bachelorhood,' Po said wryly. The stink was an accumulation of unwashed laundry, spoiling food, spilled beer, sweat, and vomit. It was the smell of the drunk tank at most police stations and one that Tess was familiar with.

'Hello.' Po's voice was barely discernible as he announced them. 'Hello. Crawford Wynne?'

No reply was forthcoming.

From somewhere inside the house there was a ticking noise. Unlike the sound of a clock these ticks were intermittent.

Tess's attention went to the kitchen. The ticks were coming from there, like someone knocking a slim metal bar against steel plate. From where she stood in the open vestibule she could see that nobody lurked in the dingy kitchen, though. Po had gone left to check the sitting room. He returned within seconds. 'Not there.'

Tess moved into the kitchen, seeking a pantry or cellar door. It was unlikely the house had a basement, but there might be a crawl space, as the house was raised above street level on cinder blocks – a precaution against flash-flooding of the nearby river. While she checked, Po searched two bedrooms he'd discovered at the back of the house.

The horrible stench was worse in the kitchen, unsurprisingly. Dirty dishes and discarded take-out boxes were strewn about the work surfaces. The plate on the table and the rank leftovers on it continued to attract flies. Tess ignored everything else, and moved towards a door in the back left corner. As she edged closer she listened intently, but all that sounded was another loud tick. It was off to her right so she disregarded it. She fed a hand into her purse and wrapped her fingers around the butt of the Glock, then reached for the door handle with her free hand. 'Hello? Anyone in there?'

No reply, but what did she really expect?

Her fingers wavered over the door handle, unsure of what she should do next. Her guts clenched.

Before her nerve failed she pulled open the door, sliding the gun half out of her purse.

Whoever had designed the house had gone for space-saving measures rather than convenience. The door off the kitchen opened directly into a tiny bathroom with a shower stall, WC, and pedestal sink all cramped into no more than six-by-six feet. Handy for drunken bachelors, she thought. They could sit on the toilet and vomit in the sink without having to move between either. The shower stall was empty, apart from an empty shampoo bottle abandoned in one corner. The window was tight shut. Tess reversed into the kitchen.

Tick!

From deeper in the house she heard Po moving around. By his lack of alacrity she assumed his search had come up blank too. She turned and surveyed the kitchen, looking for clues as to where Crawford Wynne had gone.

Tick!

What the hell was that noise?

She tested the air, and thought she detected gas.

Tensing, she prepared to bolt. But what were the chances of outrunning an exploding gas main?

Tick!

Allowing pinched air to hiss from her throat Tess moved for the cooking range. Holding a palm over one of the ceramic rings she felt warmth rising off it in waves. The ticking was the cooling of the appliance. Not long ago someone had warmed something to eat. She checked and found a pan resting in the sink alongside a number of piled dishes and cutlery. The pan contained some steaming brown sludge she didn't care to identify, but it was apparent that Crawford Wynne was no accomplished chef. The burnt muck was the source of the gassy stink, she realized with some relief, not a ruptured gas pipe. Having spoiled his lunch, had Wynne left the house to find something to eat and they'd missed him by a few minutes at most? Damn typical, she thought.

Her attention was drawn to the table. Not what was upon it, but down at the floor where the ladder-backed chair was shoved aside. The legs of the table had been forced a few inches to one side as well, clean tracks in the dirt showing the action had been recent. Maybe Wynne had been sitting at the table and realized his food was burning and had leapt up to grab the pan off the hob. That'd explain the sign of disturbance, except she wasn't convinced. She opened her mouth to hail Po, but he beat her to it.

'Tess. You should come and see this.'

She took a last look around the kitchen, then headed through the vestibule. Po waved her towards a door at the rear of the sitting room. The door was shut. She nodded at the kitchen. 'Signs of a disturbance back there,' she said.

'They're not the only ones.' Po indicated the door lock. At first glance there was nothing evidently wrong with the lock, but on closer inspection she saw that the retainer was twisted out of its holder in the doorframe. Fresh splinters of wood and dust lay on the floor, showing that the door had been recently forced inward. That door had been shoulder-charged, but on the way out whoever was responsible for the forced entry had taken the time to close the door behind them. It was probably the same person who'd lifted the pan off the hob to avoid the house burning down. She doubted that those were the actions of Crawford Wynne.

Po pointed at a splotch on the floor. It was only one of

many drips and stains, but this one was fresh. It was a glob of saliva, and it was tinged red. Someone had spat a bloody mouthful on the floor, and this she did believe was the work of Wynne.

'They got to him before us,' Po announced.

'We can't be certain of that,' Tess replied, but she knew the truth. And Po knew that she knew it.

'How'd they make it to him before us?' he asked.

Tess had no idea.

And she was momentarily lost as to what to do, or where to go, next. She grew aware that she was still clutching the butt of her Glock. She withdrew her hand, rubbed it over her face. She caught the waft of gun oil and stopped what she was doing, and searched for a tissue in her pocket.

'We should get out of here,' Po announced.

'We should call the police,' Tess said.

'Yeah.'

Except she didn't.

Po took the tissue from her.

She watched as Po wiped down the door handle. 'Did you touch anything?'

She thought of the hot hob. She had held her hand over it only. 'The bathroom door handle.'

Without comment Po walked away and she followed to the kitchen. As he wiped down the door handle she again studied the table, and also took another lingering look at the pan of food discarded in the sink. 'Wynne was sitting here when they entered the house,' she said. 'He was preparing some lunch: the hob was cooling when I checked. He wasn't that shocked when they forced their way inside, so maybe he thought it was Benoit; maybe they don't respect things like door handles too much and Wynne was used to his pal making a noisy entrance. It was only when they came in here that he tried to get up. See here,' she indicated the scuff marks on the floor, 'and the pan in the sink? I think there was more than one man who came for him, possibly even three or more.'

It would take a single man with a gun to control him, and to quickly flip the pan off the hob into the sink, but it was more likely that Wynne's abductor had assistance. A more likely scenario was that two men controlled him, keeping him seated, while a third person handled the hot pan, knocked off the power and such. Judging by the bloody saliva near the back door Wynne had been struck in the mouth to help keep him subdued.

'There were two in the car earlier,' Po said. 'But it's as I said back then; I think they'd hand Wynne over to a third man, a professional. You're probably right and the three of them came for Wynne together.'

'But how'd they know where to look?'

'Remember those cop cars we saw screaming up Railroad Avenue?'

'Aw, hell! They forced a location from Marnie or those others at the clubhouse. But how could they know to look there? Do you think Trey Robinson gave them the heads up after all?'

'No. Not Trey. There'd be nothing in it for him. Not if he wanted to earn the bounty from the Chatards for my head.' Po was already heading for the front door. He again used the tissue to wipe down the handle to remove his prints, then handed back the tissue. Tess took it from him and shoved it away in a pocket. Po went off the porch and across the shabby front yard shaking his head and muttering to himself.

Tess had an idea what he was up to when he crouched down alongside their rental and began rummaging.

'Son of a bitch,' she sighed. Last night when they'd disturbed the guy beside their car in the hotel parking lot, he'd noticed them returning and made it look like he was attempting to gain entrance to the car. He hadn't been. He was covering for the fact that they'd surprised him as he planted a tracking device on the undercarriage of the Honda. Proof of the point was when Po straightened and held out a small black box in his palm. 'This explains how they knew where to find us at Robinson's place in Baton Rouge, and how they followed us to the Cottonmouths' clubhouse. Tricky bastards.'

He was probably right, Tess decided, but it didn't explain why they knew to follow her from Maine in the first place. Somebody had sent them after her, and considering the shortlist of people who knew her destination it didn't make this discovery feel like a success.

'Let me take a look at that,' she said.

Po tossed her the tracking device. It wasn't amazingly sophisticated, but these days it didn't have to be. You could probably pick up transponders like it at any branch of Radio Shack. Regardless, it had done its job. Tess cursed under her breath. There was she hoping to prove herself by bringing in Wynne and she'd been outwitted by simple technology.

'Don't go busting your balls over it,' Po said, taking back the device and turning it over in his hands. 'I was fooled too.'

'That doesn't help, Po. I should've known better. Hell, if I'd've given it more thought I'd have realized that the guy was up to more than trying to steal our freakin' CD player. They planted a tracker on us so that we'd lead them to Wynne.'

'Hunh. Yeah. But they got the hop on us by cutting out the middleman. While we wasted time going to Benoit, they came directly. I guess when they spoke with Marnie they weren't as nice about it as we were.'

'Do you think they hurt her?' Her question was rhetorical, because there was no doubt.

'And those others in the chess league,' Po added. 'Those cops weren't responding in numbers like that because a few harsh words were thrown around.'

Tess threw back her head, hands over her face. A groan of frustration welled in her and she struggled to hold it in. Those people died because she'd fucked up again.

Po's hand rested on her lower back. 'C'mon, there's nothing we can do about it now. Let's get out of here, OK?'

He steered her to the Honda. But before he could start the engine Tess leaned forward and placed her face in her hands.

'You do realize that we'll be implicated in this, don't you? Once the cops follow up and find Wynne missing, Benoit will talk. He'll tell them how interested you were in finding Wynne, and how you forced Wynne's location from him. The cops will assume you were also the one responsible for hurting Marnie and the others.' Tess spoke in a monotone, her hands partially muffling her words. She finally lowered them, raised her head and blinked back tears. They weren't tears of regret, but anger. 'We need to put this right before it explodes in our faces.'

'You want to go to the cops and explain ourselves? OK, then let's do it.' Po's words surprised Tess.

'We should,' she added, but was again reticent.

Po rubbed his palm across the back of his neck. 'If you think that's the correct thing to do, then I'm happy to go along with your decision. But . . .'

'But what?'

'But that means we'll be cut out of any further investigation. There's no way we'll find Wynne then and we'll probably get booted back to Maine with our tails between our legs.'

Tess shrugged. 'You get paid whatever the outcome.'

'I didn't come here for the money,' Po reminded her. 'Neither did you, I'm betting.'

Tess lifted her damaged wrist, rubbing it distractedly with her opposite thumb, and the motion wasn't lost on Po.

'You've a point to prove to yourself, huh?'

Tess's mouth pinched, but she met his gaze. He'd pushed for these answers before, and she'd always refused to share them. Back then he didn't have the right to know the intimate details of her downfall, but after this, well . . . perhaps an explanation was owed.

'I've a point to prove to *everyone*,' she admitted reluctantly, but once that was said, her story came more easily.

There was a storm coming over, having swept down from Canada to dump upward of fifteen inches of snow across New Hampshire and the southern tip of Maine. Portlanders were used to inclement weather fronts, but this one – so early in the season – had caught some people napping. It wasn't so much the snow as the driving wind that forced it almost vertically in blinding flurries, causing whiteout blizzard conditions. Anyone with an ounce of brain had found a warm spot indoors, but there were others not so wise, and some that had no option but brave the storm. Residents trying to drive home found that the going was worse than tough, and some abandoned their vehicles. Those that didn't leave their trucks and cars got stuck in drifts, slewed off road, or ran into abandoned vehicles in their path. That nobody was killed in any of the numerous collisions was a miracle.

Bad weather could be the law-enforcement officer's friend. A cold snap or torrential or sustained downpour forced the bad guys off the streets, and there was a definite dip in the crime statistics for the duration of most storms. Usually a sheriff's deputy could park their cruiser out of the way, settle in for a quiet night, and hope the bad spell lasted to the end of their shift. Perhaps they'd answer a call to a domestic disturbance – people forced together who really shouldn't be in each other's company for more than a minute or so – or to a brawl at one of the bars, but that was about all. Thieves, muggers, and robbers: most preferred calmer conditions under which they'd ply their trades.

That night was different, and anything but a quiet one for the emergency services. Cumberland County Sheriff's Office logged more calls for assistance than it had any other night that year. It was a case of all hands to the pumps, and even some of the deputies on opposite rotation were called in to assist. Sergeant Teresa Grey was enjoying dinner at Hugo's on Middle Street, having already tried the panko-crusted day-boat scallops, and about to tuck into the restaurant's renowned bittersweet chocolate cake served with peanut-butter ice cream, when she received a call from the dispatcher on her cell phone. Sitting opposite her, Jim Neely, her fiancé, rolled his eyes, and reached for a napkin to dab his lips. He knew as resolutely as Sergeant Grey that their cosy night together was over.

'It'll be this goddamn weather,' Jim predicted, with a lolling eye toward the nearest window. It was as if an orange blanket had been draped over the restaurant, the white wall of snow catching and holding the dim glow of the exterior lights.

Tess apologized with a roll of her own eyes. 'I'm sorry, Jim. Duty calls.'

'Yeah,' he muttered. 'But isn't that just typical?'

Hugo's was situated at the top of Portland's Old Port, a once humble family eatery that had evolved dramatically over the last few decades to a point where it now enjoyed national attention for its fine cuisine and innovative menu. Resplendent with soft leather seating, wrought iron and red birch furniture, bespoke china, and hand-stitched menus, it was a place of opulence someone on a sergeant's pay grade rarely got to enjoy. Dinner was Jim's treat, and he'd been looking forward to a treat in kind from Tess afterwards.

'They're sending a car for me.' Tess stood, looking forlornly at the untouched sweet just served to their table. 'Maybe you should leave your car here, Jim. It sounds as if the streets are bad tonight.'

'I'll follow you out,' Jim said with little enthusiasm.

'No. Finish your dinner. I wish I could stay with you but . . .'

'Yeah, you already said. Duty calls.'

Jim was disappointed, but he needn't be so surly about it. When he'd first began dating a deputy he had to understand that her job came first, their relationship afterwards. Since she'd been promoted through corporal, and then to sergeant, the constraints on their personal time had only grown tighter. Nevertheless she was sorry about having to leave. She really did want to taste that chocolate cake and ice cream.

Jim peered out of the windows, pure hatred on his face for the storm. When he turned to look up at her, his hatred barely slipped.

Tess touched him on his hand. 'I'm sorry, Jim. We'll do this again another time. 'Kay?'

His face grew less pinched, and his eyes softened a little. 'What're the chances of you getting home tonight?'

'Slim to nil,' Tess said, offering a regretful shrug.

'So there's no chance of waking up beside you in the morning?'

Tess would have promised to do her best to get home before he had to be up for work, but it would have rung false. Instead she patted him again on the hand and turned for the door. She didn't as much as offer a peck on his cheek, but then again neither did he.

A sheriff's department cruiser rolled up within minutes, and Tess got in alongside a young black guy she knew, Arlin Porter, who was wearing a thick parka over his dark brown CCSO uniform shirt and cream trousers. His Smokey Bear-style hat was protected by plastic, but lay on the console between them.

'D'you believe this storm, Sarge?' Arlin asked.

'It's bad,' Tess agreed.

'This night can only get worse.'

Arlin Porter had no idea how right his prediction would prove.

Ordinarily a drive from Middle Street to the Sheriff's Office on County Way should take five to ten minutes. It took Arlin the better part of twenty minutes to negotiate the stalled and abandoned traffic on Spring Street and High Street. Once they hit Park Avenue the going was a little easier, until they met a jam outside the Portland Ice Arena, where a bus had skidded on the wet snow and blocked the road in both directions. Sheriff's deputies already on the scene had funnelled the traffic along side streets as best they could, but the snow made them treacherous and Arlin had to negotiate another two collisions on Congress Street before they reached their destination. Things, Tess thought, would have been much easier if she'd worn her uniform to dinner at Hugo's.

She kept a spare uniform in her locker, and once she'd dressed, and collected her sidearm and equipment belt, she took Arlin's lead and donned a parka and fitted her hat with a plastic cover. She took her kit bag and a pair of thick gloves to the cruiser where Arlin waited for her. She would ride with him that night, an extra pair of hands rather than carry out her usual supervisory role.

'Calls are stacking up, Sarge,' Arlin informed her before she'd even settled in.

'Pick one, and let's go.'

Arlin called up the dispatcher, and a harried voice announced that Fire Department paramedics on a call to an address at Holyoke Wharf had requested police backup. The Portland Police Department was as busy as the other emergency services, and could CCSO respond until they had a unit free? Portland Police Department had jurisdictional responsibility for the city, while CCSO patrolled the fourteen towns in Cumberland County that didn't have their own police resource, responding to emergency calls, and enforcing criminal and traffic laws. But it wasn't unknown for the sheriff's deputies to pitch in and help when required of the PPD.

'You know our motto,' Tess said to Arlin.

'First to serve,' Arlin quoted back at her as he hit the lights and sirens.

They made better time on Route 1 around the old harbour front. Snow was still falling but the wind had dropped marginally. Still, the wipers could barely keep the windshield clear, and outside the large wet drifting flakes reflected their gumball lights. Tess felt she was at the centre of a kaleidoscope. As they approached Holyoke Wharf, they looked for the first-response crew in need of assistance. Arlin spotted the PFD ambulance parked adjacent to the wharf, its rear doors open, but there was no sign of the paramedics. He pulled alongside the red and white truck, tyres squeaking on the drifting snow. Arlin informed the dispatcher they were on scene, while Tess was already getting out the car. It was slippery underfoot.

Across the way a gas station's lights beckoned. She saw two paramedics hunched over a man lying at the rear of an old station wagon. Heart attack, she assumed, if the driver was as ancient as his car. She began walking, heard the clunk of the cruiser's door as Arlin followed.

As they approached, one of the paramedics looked up at them. Snow had accumulated on his hair and shoulders, but he seemed oblivious to it. The second medic was female. A short woman like Tess, but a bit older at perhaps thirty-five. She too was covered in snow, but took a moment to bat it off her hair and her eyelids as she greeted them. She didn't bring them to speed on their casualty, but aimed a shaking finger at the gas station. 'In there!'

'What's happening?' Tess asked, following the medic's gesture.

'Two guys, trying to rob the convenience store,' the medic said breathlessly, but she had already turned back to her patient.

Tess looked for Arlin; saw the deputy drawing his sidearm. She held out a hand, forestalling him. 'Are they armed?' she asked the medics, trying to spot any wounds on the victim lying on the gurney between them.

'Yes,' the woman said, 'but I'm not sure what with. We pulled in to grab some snacks, and came across this guy lying here. He has bleeding to his head, and looks to have been knocked down. I saw two Caucasian males inside, they were hollering at the cashier. That's when we called for backup.'

Tess drew her sidearm. 'Can you move the victim?'
The male medic nodded sharply.
'Good. Try to get clear in case there's any shooting.'
'We haven't seen a gun,' said the woman.
It didn't mean the robbers were unarmed. Neither did it mean that the deputies wouldn't be forced to discharge their weapons. The last Tess wanted was for any innocents to be caught in the line of fire. She told Arlin to call it in and request extra patrols. But that night she didn't trust anyone to reach them quickly enough. It was down to her and Arlin to work with the cards they'd been dealt. Through her own radio she heard Arlin's voice, rattling off a brief update and request for assistance. She heard 'A-ffirmative' responses, but it would be minutes before the first patrols arrived at the scene. Protocol dictated that she set up a safe perimeter, wait for assistance. From within the convenience store there was a loud bang. Not a gun, but something crashing to the floor. It was followed by a man's bellow, then a cry of pain. She started for the door. Without question, Arlin moved alongside her, before he fanned out to the right, trying to get a view through the front window. He shook his head, dislodging snow from his hat, but it was because he could see nothing of the suspects. Tess crouched as she approached the entrance. It was automated and slid open. Tess ducked around the doorframe, a quick scan, before withdrawing. She looked at Arlin, who'd moved up beside her. 'Cover me,' she said unnecessarily.
She went inside, rushing to the corner of a shelved unit containing the usual motorists' supplies. She poked her head around the next corner and immediately saw three men struggling beyond the counter. The two robbers had vaulted the cashier's desk to get at the cash. The attendant was a slim Chinese man, and though he was outweighed and outnumbered he wasn't for going down without a fight. He was no Bruce Lee though. He clung to both men, scrambling to pull a bag from one of them, while holding back the hands of the other with swipes of his left arm. He screeched incessantly, as if the money they'd grabbed had come from his own wallet. The three of them crashed down behind the counter, shouts and curses ringing out.

'Sheriff's deputies,' Tess hollered. 'Put down your weapons.'
Her order didn't elicit a lessening in the racket.

'Sheriff's deputies!' She followed her words this time,
moving fast along the aisle towards the counter. She held out
her gun, finger trembling on the trigger guard. Arlin moved
too, although he approached the fight via the other side of the
aisle. He also called out for compliance.

A figure broke free of the melee and vaulted the counter.

'Get down! Get down!' Arlin hollered at the man. The guy
was tall, skinny, his face covered by a scarf hastily wound
round his head. In the tussle it had been pulled askew and
covered one of his manic eyes. He wore a heavy chequered
coat, jeans, and boots. In one hand was a small cotton sack.
In the other a large hunting knife. 'Drop your weapon, drop
your weapon!' Arlin yelled.

The man shouted something, his words muffled by the scarf,
and he ducked away from Arlin, directly into the aisle where
Tess was. She opened her mouth to bark out the warning
that protocol demanded, but the man swiped at her with the
knife. Tess jerked away, but the blade ripped into the cuff of
her parka, snapping her hand to one side, and Tess's gun
went off.

Inside the store the sound was tremendous. Tess's ears
rang, and she barely heard the shout of warning from Arlin
as the tall guy kicked at her. He got her good, right under
the breastbone, and she sank to her knees. The man cut at
her again. She got her gun hand up, so it saved her throat,
but she felt the cold fire of the blade go through her wrist
and her gun clattered to the floor. The man brought back the
knife, ready to plunge it again into her. Tess was defenceless
against it. She howled, a mixture of frustration and fear.
Through her mind's eye danced her mother's face. 'I told
you so!'

Boom!

Arlin's bullet took the robber in the side of the head. The
scarf danced loose as he fell. So did parts of his jaw. He
landed flat on the floor alongside Tess. She reached for his
fallen knife, to throw it clear. That's when her hand flopped
uselessly back on itself, held to the wrist only by a strip of

meat. Blood gouted from her severed wrist, cut almost through from one side to the other. Tess blacked out and didn't know another thing. Not until much later, waking from surgery.

'Everything just happened so fast,' she told Po as they sat in the Honda, parked on a patch of decaying gravel alongside a small church. The boughs of a spreading oak dappled the sunlight on the windshield. Unconsciously Tess flexed her fingers, trying to rid herself of the psychosomatic pain her recollections had ignited. 'If I'd shot him when I had the chance, then . . .'

Without asking permission, Po reached across and took her right hand in his. He turned it over, and again she thought those rough fingers should not be capable of such a delicate touch. His index finger traced the risen scar tissue on her wrist, following it from the inner wrist joint almost to the radial artery. He turned over her hand and there was a similar scar on the other side, although this one was barely noticeable. 'He almost took off your goddamn hand!'

'Yes. He cut through the joint, severing tendons and veins. His knife nicked the radial artery too. The surgeons saved my hand, but . . . well,' she paused, her eyes fogging, as she curled up her fingers: they trembled. 'I underwent microsurgery, and months of rehab, but I struggle with any intricate tasks now. I've lost all dexterity in my fingers. I couldn't thread a needle to save my life.'

'Me neither,' Po said, 'and I didn't have my hand chopped off.'

Tess thought of the defensive cuts on his forearms: a shiv couldn't deliver the chopping force of the huge hunting knife her attacker was armed with. But it could have easily put out his eyes or punctured the arteries in his throat if he hadn't got his arms in the way. He'd killed his attacker, and Tess could only wonder how he'd managed to do so. Her injury – or the shock of it – had thrown her into unconsciousness in a heartbeat.

'You once admitted killing a man,' Po went on. 'But now I hear the full story it was actually your deputy. What did you call him? Arlin, wasn't it?'

'Arlin shot my attacker, yes. He also arrested the second robber, who I hear came out with his hands up.'

'Ah. That stray shot you got off?'

Tess felt glass in her throat. She nodded, but didn't say.

Her bullet had cut through the counter and ended up lodged in the Chinese clerk's chest. After all his heroism the man had been slain by friendly fire.

'So what was your reason for leaving the Sheriff's Department: the shooting or your injury?'

'A bit of both. Although I was exonerated of any wrong doing, and that it was proven my gun went off as an accidental discharge while trying to defend myself, an innocent man had still died. Officially I was off the hook, but it wasn't a popular decision with everyone.'

Po nodded sagely. 'I recall hearing something about you in the news, and you were getting the shitty end of the stick. I didn't give it much thought at the time, but yeah.'

'My case attracted some anti-law enforcement lobbying. Quite a crowd gathered outside the Sheriff's Office demanding my dismissal, and things grew ugly. If this were anywhere other than Portland it would probably have ended up in a riot. My legal advisers encouraged me to lodge my resignation, as an all-round goodwill gesture.'

'You did that?'

'I'm not a complete idiot. That'd feel too much like admitting it was my fault. No. I waited, but my injury meant I was no longer fit for active service. I didn't want to steer a desk from the office so ultimately I was pensioned out on medical grounds. It didn't satisfy the lobbyists, but to hell with them. They should walk a mile in a cop's shoes before they start criticizing.'

'So the clerk died, huh? Unlucky.'

'He died immediately; my bullet got him in the heart,' Tess dipped her head, allowing her a moment to hide her glassy eyes. 'I was hospitalized for weeks. And for what? Two hundred and twenty-seven bucks. Not even a fucking handful of Hershey bars!'

Po squinted at her final remark, and she realized she hadn't shared the finer details of her grandfather's ignominious end.

She didn't explain, just waved her comment aside. 'The old man the paramedics took away? He survived. Apparently the robbers tried to roll him at the gas pumps, and when all he had was a twenty-dollar bill for gas they hit him over the head and left him for dead. With such small pickings they turned their attention on the convenience store.'

'Desperados,' Po said. 'Or assholes.'

'A bit of both,' Tess said, echoing her earlier words. She suddenly realized that Po was still holding her hand. It had grown comfortable there in his palm, but perhaps the gesture was more intimate than either of them intended. She drew it away.

Po wasn't finished. 'You told me you caught Jim Neely apologizing about you to some friends: it was because of what happened, right? And he was ashamed of you? What a jerk!'

'Seeing the back of him was the only good thing to come out of the worst night of my life.' She laughed bitterly. 'Everything else I lost I'd've liked to have held on to.'

'So completing this case is about making amends, right, restoring your reputation? Kind of make or break? Well, if you want to go to the police then so be it, it's probably the right thing to do. But if you'd rather throw away that rulebook, like I said, and go after Wynne's abductors, well . . . I've still got your back.'

'Oh, believe me, I want to go after them, but there's a problem: I don't know where to start.'

Po held up the transponder. 'Now they've got Wynne, they might give up on us. But I don't see it. We've both seen two of the guys working for Sower, so in some respects that now makes *us* witnesses. You know what happened to all the others, right?'

'They'll come after us.' The prospect should have terrified her. She straightened, turning to look Po directly in the eyes. 'Good. Let them come. We might be able to salvage this case if we can take one of them in.'

SEVENTEEN

Tess and Po were back on the road, and they'd little to say to each other as they privately ruminated over their latest discoveries.

Much of their theory concerning Wynne's disappearance was based on supposition, but it gave Tess focus after being beaten to the punch, and Wynne snatched from under her nose. Of course, even the fact that Wynne was missing was based on assumption, but it seemed highly probable. He hadn't left the house bleeding without reason, and he hadn't been responsible for breaking his way out of the back door midway through preparing lunch either. It appeared that more than one person had forced Wynne from the premises, and he'd been bundled out of sight through the backyard and along a narrow alley towards the grounds of the church they'd checked out. Presumably the parking lot alongside the church was where his abductors had left their vehicle while they came upon Benoit's house from behind. Droplets of blood on the crumbling asphalt showed that Wynne hadn't stopped bleeding before he was forced inside the vehicle and driven away. From the church grounds to wherever, Tess had no clue where next, but she was certain that at that time Wynne was still alive. How long he'd keep breathing was hard to tell. She had to also assume that once he'd been forced to the car and there was no further need for mobility, his abductors might well have finished him off.

Was there still time to save Crawford Wynne's life?

Doubtful.

Calling the police wouldn't help him either, because where would anyone look? It was a defeatist attitude, but also a pragmatic one. When considering Mitch Delaney's murder, no mercy had been shown. The slaying was brutal, and also punishment, and Tess had to force down the images she conjured of what Wynne must be suffering right now.

Visualizing Wynne's fate made her nauseous. He was a criminal, a racist, a thug, but he was still a human being: no one deserved to die like that.

Po sat stoically behind the wheel. His profile was more aquiline than usual, his nose more pronounced, but that might be because of the way he chewed at his lower lip. She couldn't tell if he was thinking about Wynne, plotting their next move, or mulling over what he'd just learned about her. In hindsight, exposing her past as fully as she had was probably a bad idea, and she wished she could take everything back. He'd caught her when she was emotional, sickened by having missed Wynne by a whisker, and discovering the horrible truth that they'd been played ever since leaving Maine. Had Po gone in for the kill when she was vulnerable and open to manipulation? The slick son of a bitch had even held her hand to coax her story from her.

She closed her eyes, exhaling wearily.

What if she was wrong about Po's motives and was doing him a disservice by thinking the worst of him? Maybe, she considered, having learned the truth about her, he was revaluating his original opinion of her, the way she was of him. Initially she'd found him frustrating and annoying, his pigheadedness and contrition rubbing her up at every turn, but now, after she'd bared herself so fully, it was as if she'd earned some respect from him. Well, if she had to be honest, his willingness to remain at her side had also won him some respect in return.

'Where'd you put the transponder?' Tess asked, breaking her train of thought.

'Glove compartment.'

'Switched off?'

'On. I thought it best we didn't let those assholes know we'd found it.' He finally glanced at her. 'You do still want them to come after us, right?'

'I know it's a big risk, but yeah. My first instinct was to destroy the tracker, but I'm glad I didn't. It's evidence that we were being used. And it might bring them to us.'

'If it's either of the two we've already seen I'm not worried. What if it's the other guy?'

'Then all the better,' Tess said. 'If we can capture him, it would probably break the case wide open.'

'Except he might not be as easily captured.'

In her mind's eye Tess again conjured the shocking violence the killer was capable of. Closing her eyes didn't help. She shook her head, then reached for her purse where she'd dumped it on the back seat. Pulling it into her lap, she delved inside, feeling the cold metal of the gun, but that wasn't what she was looking for. She lifted out her cell.

'Calling Emma Clancy?' Po asked.

'I'm still putting off my next update; there's something I want to check before I speak with her.' She didn't ring a number, but brought up the browser application instead, opening the website of the *Daily Review* – a local news agency. Already the first hasty reports were coming in from the scene at the Cottonmouths' clubhouse. The reports were sketchy but – yes – shootings had been reported to the local PD. There were no details concerning the number or identities of the fatalities, but it didn't take much imagination to piece the facts together. 'Oh, man,' she moaned.

'Not good news, then?'

'The worst.'

Po exhaled deeply through his nostrils, but that was as far as his show of regret went. Perhaps he'd grown inured to violence while incarcerated at the Farm. When she was a deputy, Tess had dealt with violent death, and like most cops she'd formed an ability to compartmentalize the horror and shock most people experienced, but she had to admit it had been a while, and the deaths of Marnie and the others weighed heavily. She didn't doubt that the fundraising Cottonmouths were far from the paragons of virtue Marnie made them out to be, but still . . .

'Their deaths aren't your burden to carry,' Po warned. 'Let it go, Tess, or it'll eat you up. The only ones responsible for their deaths are Sower's punks. Let it go, OK.'

Tess's vision grew blurry. 'Sower's people followed us to the clubhouse; they wouldn't have gone there otherwise. Those people would still be alive.'

'You can't say that. They're resourceful, they would've

probably tracked down Wynne themselves, and the outcome would most likely have been the same. Instead of blaming yourself, use your anger for something else. Let's focus it on taking down these sons of bitches before they hurt anyone else.'

She used her sleeve to mop her eyes. Po was right. Tears and recrimination wouldn't help. After the Chinese clerk died in the convenience-store shoot-out, they hadn't helped then. Circumstance was a bitch, and not something she could change. As a reminder of that simple truth she studied her scarred wrist. Her fingertips tingled.

'How do you suggest we do that?' she finally asked.

'I'm not sure yet. One thing's for certain, we need to get on the front foot again.' He had steered the Honda out of Morgan City, and they were back on the levee between Lake Palourde and the Atchafalaya River retracing their route back to Baton Rouge. 'You left your stuff locked up at the hotel, right? We followed my methods to get here,' he went on, 'and it's done us little good. I'm thinking it's time that you worked some of your wizardry and gave us a lead as to who exactly we're dealing with. You up to that?'

'You expect me to do what the police have been unable to?' Tess shook her head in remorse.

'Yes I do. We've a starting point they hadn't.' Po gave her a quick nod. 'Has Clancy replied to your text yet?'

Clancy hadn't replied yet, though Tess hadn't given it much thought since hitting the send button. Perhaps Clancy wasn't the texting type, and was waiting until they spoke in person before offering the information she'd asked for.

'You don't think they'd be as stupid as using their own vehicle? It's likely that it's a rental; I don't know how they knew where we were coming, but after they followed us from Portland I think they picked up a car at New Orleans the way we did.'

'Uh-huh,' Po said. 'But did they expect us to spot them, and check them out? Those guys didn't come over as the most professional to me. They could've made an amateur's mistake when hiring the car and used their genuine details.'

'That's hoping for a lot.'

'That's the thing with most criminals. They're not the geniuses they'd like us to believe.' Po grunted deep in his chest. 'Even I got caught, remember?'

Tess laughed at his frankness.

She caught a sly grin from her companion, and realized he'd intentionally lightened the mood.

'I guess it's one lead to follow. I might be able to come up with something else too. You know that the principle behind plotting family trees is similar to how cops collate known criminal accomplices, right? Perhaps if I follow similar threads I can pinpoint who's doing Sower's dirty work.' She took in a deep breath, steeling herself now that she had a plan in mind. It felt good to have direction, even if it might not play out. She took out her cell again: now was as good a time as ever to get started. But one look at the screen told her that the detective work would have to wait. Now that they were back out in the bayous cell coverage was poor, and her Internet service was non-existent and would probably remain that way until they returned to civilization.

EIGHTEEN

'You seriously believe that bars and steel doors will keep me from you?' Albert Sower clenched his fingers, released them slowly, as if mentally testing the strength of his constraints, and then sneered at their ineffectiveness. 'All I need do is point my finger at you and . . . well, I'll leave you to form that picture inside your own pretty head.'

Emma Clancy didn't respond to Albert Sower's threat. She sat opposite him in a secure interview room at Maine State Prison, controlling her revulsion for him through the knowledge that, yes, she did believe he was securely locked up, and if she had any say in the matter he'd never walk free again. She folded her hands in her lap, crossed her legs, and watched him while he smiled at her silent insolence. His smile was a mask; she suspected he was raging inside.

If she'd met him on the street, with no knowledge of the crimes he was responsible for, she might've found his wavy dark hair, tanned complexion, and startling black eyes attractive. For a man in his early forties he had a good body, lithe and strong, tall for a man of his heritage, and where his forearms emerged from the sleeves of his shirt they were muscular, as were his manicured fingers. They were the kind of arms some women would like to be embraced by, but Emma was under no illusion: those arms were more likely to beat and crush than hug tenderly. His fingers were the kind that fit tightly around throats. She knew that if she wasn't careful he could easily reach across and throttle the life from her, and had noted the flexing of his fingers each time he wished to make a point. Thankfully his hands were shackled to the table top that separated them.

Throughout her career as a private investigator, and latterly working for Richard Jackson on behalf of the DA's office, she'd met bad people, but she'd also met decent folk caught up in bad situations, so had always cautioned herself against making snap judgement concerning their nature, but with

Albert Sower her first instinct had been correct. The man was evil. There was no lesser description for him, and she suspected he knew it and revelled in the fact. He'd been counselled against speaking to her by his defence team because it might affect the outcome of his upcoming bail hearing, but it was apparent now that he'd agreed to the meeting because it fed his malicious intent to spread terror and taking pleasure in his ability to do so. He didn't expect his second hearing to be any different from the first, so why be concerned about adversely affecting the outcome? As far as learning anything important she could use against him, she'd drawn a blank. Emma had been on the end of a barrage of sly insults and now he was resorting to making threats.

He eyed her wedding ring, aiming an index finger at it.

'If you think you're safe from my reach, you should think again, Mrs Clancy. Haven't you heard: my enemies swear I'm a ghost, I can walk through walls and locked doors, I can enter your bedroom when you're sleeping and can spirit you away from the arms of your husband.'

He'd have an impossible task doing that, considering she was separated from her estranged husband by the breadth of a continent; he'd moved to Los Angeles with his mistress pending finalization of their acrimonious divorce. But Emma wasn't about to divulge her private life to him, not when it could be used as ammunition against her. Instead she said, 'I don't believe in ghosts.'

'It doesn't matter what you believe, as long as it is this: the personification of my will can come for you at any time, wherever you are. All I need do is direct it.'

'Threatening me isn't helping your case, Mr Sower.' Emma glanced at a corrections officer waiting near the door. The guard stood with his hands clasped over his belt buckle, his shoulders rigid, seemingly aloof to the proceedings as he deliberately stared into space. He might deny overhearing their interaction, but it wasn't the guard that Emma referred to. The room came equipped with CCTV and audio surveillance. 'I should remind you that everything is on record, and can be presented in evidence against you in court.'

'I won't make it to court. Not if there's nobody left to

present a case against me.' He touched his extended fingers to the sides of his head and his gaze grew diamond-hard. 'My will is strong, Mrs Clancy, *and* directed.'

'Is that an admission, Mr Sower? Would you like to admit to your part in the disappearance of certain key witnesses? Is there something you'd like to put on record regarding the murder of Mitchel Delaney?'

Sower sat forward, his manacled wrists extended over the table, presenting his palms to her. Despite understanding she was playing into his game, she watched as he fisted his left hand – miming grasping something – while with the other hand he made a cutting motion. He flicked his left hand upward, and snatched at the air with his teeth. Next he smacked his lips. 'Mmm, delicious,' he said.

Emma shook her head, before catching herself. The last thing she should do was react to his goading, but he was disgusting. He sat back, smug in the knowledge he'd won a rise out of her.

'I should remind you that I haven't been charged with murder.' Sower smiled. 'If I had my case would now be in the hands of the Attorney-General and not underlings of the lowly *District* Attorney.'

'You might think that you're untouchable,' she said, 'but you're not. I know what you've done, and will present witnesses to stand against you, and you will be tried and found guilty for murder alongside all your other crimes.'

'Witnesses? Ah, you're referring to our man in the Deep South?' Sower was careful not to directly mention any names, but he noted the minuscule squinting of Clancy's eyes when he could only be referring to Crawford Wynne. 'I wouldn't hedge your bets on him: right about now I expect he will be growing very tight-lipped.'

'Would you care to explain what you mean by that?'

'I think you're already clear on my meaning.' Again he leaned over the table, but this time he lowered his head and muffled his words into his cupped palms so neither the CCTV nor audio recordings would be admissible. 'I warned you about the personification of my will: it beat your bloodhound to our quarry.'

If what he claimed was true, then Tess Grey had failed to find Wynne before Sower's killer had. But Emma couldn't be certain that Sower was stating a fact, or if this was just another of his nasty manipulations he enjoyed. How could he even know she'd sent someone to find and bring back Wynne in the first place? Oh, it was easy enough: if drugs, alcohol, and weapons could be smuggled inside a supposedly secure prison then word could. But it troubled her that information known only to a select few had found its way to Sower.

She'd have liked to push him for his source, but he'd already lounged back again, and raised his eyebrows, waiting her reaction. If she did, she'd only confirm she was rattled that someone close to her or Tess was feeding information to him. She wouldn't give him the satisfaction.

Apparently Sower was attempting to lead her down a certain path, as evidenced by his next words. 'How highly do you value loyalty, Mrs Clancy?'

'Loyalty is generally overrated,' she said, 'and can't be relied on, except maybe from a pet dog. You should know this when you consider how many of your people were prepared to turn against you. Oh, wait,' she clicked her fingers for emphasis – 'that was before you had them murdered.'

Sower grinned, but deigned not to answer the accusation. 'You make the very point I was about to. You can only guarantee loyalty through two things: fear and greed. You don't appear frightened by me, so what is your price?'

'Are you attempting to bribe me?' Emma pitched her voice so the microphones would easily pick it up.

'I'm only posing a hypothetical question. What would it take for you to put aside your animosity toward me?'

'There isn't a figure large enough. I've always thought that hate is a strong word, but it's nothing to what I think of you.'

'Admirable,' Sower said. 'And it makes me reconsider what I thought of you.'

'I don't want your admiration.'

'Oh, it's not that, Mrs Clancy. I just realized that – for all that you hide it well – you are frightened of me.'

Emma shook her head, and now she offered a smile of her own. 'You're wrong, and about more than me being frightened.

You said that only fear and greed guarantee loyalty, but there's a third thing. Mutual respect. But I don't expect you to understand that, not when you've no respect for anyone but yourself. And talking of respect, I've too much self-respect to give in to either fear of you or any promise of reward.'

'Such a shame,' he said. 'The latter would have been beneficial to us both, but the subject is academic now. Sadly, for you, that leaves single recourse.'

Sower erupted from his seat, barking out a wordless sound, and Emma startled back, almost spilling from her chair. She quickly stood and retreated, and she could kick herself for doing so. If he'd thrown his weight forward he might've grasped her, but that was never his intention. At his post by the door, the stunned corrections officer grabbed at a canister of Mace on his belt, but there was no need of the incapacitant spray. Sower had already sat down again, and a self-satisfied grin built on his wide lips. Inducing fear was always his favoured tactic and Emma's wide eyes and the throbbing pulse in her throat pleased the bastard no end.

'So now you're trying for cheap shots?' Emma sneered. 'If that's the case I won't bother wasting any more time here.'

'That suits me fine, I find your company tiresome and am ready to return to my cell.'

Emma looked at the uniformed guard. 'You heard him: it's time to put the dog back in its kennel.'

'There is one last thing I'd like to mention,' said Sower, and she should have ignored him and left the room, but she faced him, her arms crossed over her chest. Sower lowered his brows at her, and pouted his bottom lip, mocking her petulance.

'Well?' Emma snapped.

'I just thought I might remind you: it's a long drive back to Portland,' Sower said. 'Be careful, Mrs Clancy. Horrible things can happen to lone women drivers on such journeys. But I can see you're such a brave soul, afraid of nothing, so you *should* feel safe enough.'

'I'll let you know next time I see you,' she said, 'in court.'

Out of the interview room, she marched away, Sower's disparaging laughter ringing in her ears.

Having left the prison, Emma followed Atlantic Highway south, past Sherman Lake, and on to the stretch approaching Davis Island and the bridge over the Sheepscot River to the town of Wiscasset beyond. The route was familiar to her, having travelled back and forth to Warren on a number of occasions in the past few weeks, and she drove on automatic, her mind distracted by the recent events in the interview room. Other road users were few and far between, though it wasn't always the case. Through a drizzle of rain, and the spray kicked up by its tyres, she could see the lights of a semi-trailer a quarter mile ahead, and in her rear-view the headlights of a vehicle equally distant behind. She paid neither vehicle much more than passing attention as she pushed on for Portland.

Her mind was still on Albert Sower.

The judge had denied Sower's first bond application, deeming him a flight risk, and also that he posed a danger to potential prosecution witnesses, but with the imminent collapse of the case against him he might in fact get to walk free. She had to find someone willing to face him, and had laid much faith in Tess Grey bringing back Crawford Wynne. Without Wynne's testimony, the case would go nowhere and not only would a bail hearing be pointless, Sower would be released through lack of any evidence in the charges laid. During previous cases against him Sower had a track record of witness intimidation, and others suspected of involvement in his organization. Whenever Sower's name came up witnesses had the habit of withdrawing their statements, even some police officers were susceptible to falling foul of his scare tactics and deliberately sabotaging prosecution evidence against the gangster. Emma had to admit that she was nervous, though she'd never admit it to him, so how could she blame anyone else for being fearful?

Initially held at Knox County Jail, Sower had been relocated to the special management unit at Maine State Prison at Warren. The SMU was the only facility trusted with controlling the behaviour of the unruly and violent prisoner. In some respects his treatment was unprecedented, being held pending trial and considered innocent until proven guilty. But Sower had attained designations that set him within the remit of incarceration in an SMU. He ticked various boxes being a threat to others, an escape risk, and a man prone to untelegraphed bursts of violence. Ironically he also fit neatly into the category of a prisoner at risk of harm. If he were placed in the general population, he wouldn't last more than a day or two before his fellow inmates got to him. Emma would be happy to learn that Sower had been stabbed to death in the shower, but that was on a purely personal level. Professionally she hoped he made court, because she wanted all of his despicable crimes laid against him, so the world would learn how much of a monster he was. It would be delightful, and a huge relief, when he was sentenced to a cell for the rest of his miserable days. Sower was making things difficult for the realization of her dream though, and wasn't making any secret of it with all his crazy talk of 'personification of his will'. He was obviously talking about how he could influence murder by proxy.

She could deny it all she wished, but the evil bastard had placed a nugget of anxiety in her, disturbing her in a way she found alien. She wasn't one to stop for hitchhikers, but generally it was through a lack of regard for their predicament, not that a passenger might turn out to be a weirdo or serial killer. But as she drove the first few miles from the prison, she watched the verges for strangers, and more than once her mind played tricks, forming lurking silhouettes out of the bushes. Hell, what was she afraid of? It wasn't as if one of Sower's people would be waiting to leap on the roof of her car like the maniac in a slasher movie. She doubted even that anyone could get off a clear shot at her with a gun, not while she moved at speed through showering rain. She tried to force down the fear of ambush, seeing Sower's parting shot as a last-ditch attempt at rattling her. Fuck him, she wouldn't allow him the satisfaction of terrorizing her. But it was easier said than done. Her mind still strayed to the sides of the road, when she should be concentrating on driving.

Red flared up ahead, turning the rainfall bloody, but she missed it, her attention on the deep shadows beneath the canopy of trees to her right. Her car swept on, and she had travelled another four hundred yards or more before squinting at the blurred image beyond her windshield. Her mind didn't process what she saw, and she'd gone another hundred yards before a warning switch flicked in her mind, and she trod on the brake pedal. The brakes bit, but the tyres found little traction, aquaplaning on the film of standing water on the asphalt. Her breath caught in her throat as she fought the wheel. The back of her car began to slide. Training kicked in a second later, and she released the brakes, steering into the skid, then once the car was heading in a straight line again, she pumped the brake pedal, bringing it to a controlled stop. She'd avoided a collision with the rear of the jack-knifed semi-trailer by little more than a car's length. She slumped back in her seat, feeling a cold shudder pass through her.

Horrible things can happen to lone women drivers on such journeys. Albert Sower's warning had almost proven portentous. Hell, there was no need of crazed attackers when the road conditions and other users could so easily end her life. What the hell had the driver been thinking, coming to halt like that and leaving his truck straddling the route? Perhaps he'd hit an animal, or there was an obstruction up ahead. Emma buzzed open her window and craned out. The rain had grown heavier in the last few seconds, and the wind whipped it against her forehead. She squinted, trying to see. Her wing mirror blazed with light from the vehicle approaching from the rear, making seeing impossible. She ducked back inside, powering up the window, peering instead through the dappled windshield, before her wipers streaked the view again.

A figure materialized out of the mist to the left of the truck. It was a man, judging by his size, but it was added to by a hood on his parka coat. The figure held up a hand, waving at her, as if that was enough of an explanation for his impromptu stop, then he bent as if to inspect a tyre on the freight trailer. Maybe he'd caught a flat or the tyre had blown out. Not something she could assist with. She looked for a way around, but the tractor unit was turned toward the opposite lane. To edge by she'd be forced on to the shoulder, and in this weather she expected it to be so soft her car would sink to the axles in mud. On the other side was a metal barrier, preventing vehicles from plunging down an embankment to a tributary of the nearby Sheepscot River. Damn it, but it appeared she was going to be held up until the semi-trailer got rolling again. Immediately she began plotting an alternative route, and decided she could backtrack, and perhaps pick up a different road out of Newcastle, the last town she'd driven through. But the only road she could think of would take her miles out of her way, and by the time she circumnavigated the river to Wiscasset this obstruction could have been moved ages before. It was an inconvenience but she'd just have to wait things out.

She reached for her purse on the opposite seat and dug out her phone, thinking it best to let her assistant Monica know about the delay. She'd ask Monica to adjust her appointments as necessary. Before bringing up the contacts list she noted the text message icon on her phone was starred, and opening it she found it was from Tess Grey. Had Sower being lying about Tess arriving late to find Crawford Wynne, or was that too much to hope for? There was no hint in the message: Tess was only requesting assistance in tracing a vehicle-licence tag. Replying could wait, she'd check with Monica about any news coming out of Louisiana first. She closed the message without responding, and switched to her contact list and scrolled through for Monica's number.

A knock at her window brought up her head.

A man was standing close to the door, so that she got a view of the front of his jacket, and the zipper on his jeans. Emma reared back a little. The figure stepped away, and his hand came into view, rolling at the wrist, indicating she should open her window. Emma glanced in her mirrors. Behind her the second vehicle had drawn close to her car's trunk, but she could tell it was some kind of refrigerated van. The driver had alighted from the vehicle, possibly hoping to discover the nature of the delay from her. Little use her knowledge would serve, but she hit the button to lower her window. She craned for a closer look at the driver. 'Hi,' she said. 'I'm afraid I'm as much in the dark as you are—'

The man lunged for her, his arms darting in the opening window, and his fingers were in her hair before she could avoid them. His other hand fastened on her shoulder. Emma hollered, tried to wrench out of his grip, and was thankful she'd clipped her lap belt on otherwise he'd have yanked her bodily through the window.

But that wasn't his intention.

He was only restraining her while a second man came round the other side and opened the passenger door. The man leaned down, and pushed back his hood so she got a look at his face. It was the truck driver, but one glance told her that it wasn't his normal job. She recognized the face from the file of known associates of Albert Sower, though she was too shocked to dredge a name from her memory. The man snatched her phone out of her hand. Then he checked her purse for a firearm. She wasn't carrying.

'What are you doing?' Emma shrieked. She clawed at the hand in her hair. The second man shook her savagely.

'You're coming with us, Clancy,' the bogus truck driver announced. 'And it'll be easier on you if you don't give us any trouble.'

'You can't do this. I'm—'

'*We* don't give a shit *who* the fuck you are,' growled the man holding her. 'Now open the door or I'll drag you out by your goddamn hair.'

'I'd do as he says,' the truck driver urged. He slipped inside the car, and leaned past her to unclip her belt. Emma squirmed back from the closeness of his body. The man snorted in humour, then leaned to open the door. Emma grabbed at his head, sinking her nails into his scalp.

'Fucking bitch!' snapped the driver, and in the same instant her controller released the grip on her shoulder and jabbed his knuckles into the side of her head. The blow wasn't forceful, but it was still a shock to her system. Scarlet and grey flashes danced in her vision and a sharp pain shot down her jaw into her neck. On the verge of fainting, her fingers unlatched from the truck driver's head, and she was borne weightless out of the open door. She went down on her backside on the road. Her trousers were soaked instantly. 'Get up, or I'll make you,' her captor warned.

'Where are you taking me?' Emma croaked.

'We're going for a ride,' said the man. He wrenched her up, shaking her into compliance. He fed his free arm around her elbow, hooking her arm up her back. The truck driver slid into the seat she'd just vacated. No, he couldn't be the actual truck driver, because someone else had started up the semi and was pulling the tractor and freight trailer to one side of the road. Yet another man waited alongside it, and once it was lined up, he uncoupled two metal ramps and settled them on the road. Sower's people had planned in advance, and were ensuring that she, and any sign of her, disappeared completely. From his defence team – or someone much closer to her – they'd learned of her planned visit with Sower, waited until she returned to Portland, then carried out her abduction with little fuss. Jesus, she should've expected something like this! Sower had even warned her what was coming, the smug son of a bitch. Back in his cell, he'd be enjoying the moment, she bet.

'You won't get away with this,' she told her captor. 'I'm expected back at my office. When I don't show the police will be alerted and they'll be coming for me. They know who you all are, and where to find you.'

'They don't know jack shit,' growled the man. 'Nobody will be looking for you bitch, you don't think we know how to take care of that?'

'Where're you taking me?'

'I told you. We're going for a ride. Now get moving or I'll break your arm.'

Emma's car was driven up the ramps and into the freight trailer. That was all she witnessed of her vehicle's fate, because she was forced around the back of the refrigerated van. The doors stood open, and yet another of Sower's gang waited inside. He had a round face and thick body, and his Mediterranean complexion had paled to a sickly pallor, but not through the cold. The fridge's motor was off, and the interior of the van a dull grey echoing space. It wouldn't be soundproof. The man waiting for her held a roll of duct tape, and she knew exactly what for.

NINETEEN

Having showered and dried her hair, Tess felt more comfortable, if not recharged. She needed to sleep, but sleep still eluded her. Sitting in a tub chair at the hotel-room desk, she ran her fingers over the papers spread before her. Some were taken from the file supplied by Clancy's office, and she also had the electronic file up on her iPad now that she had Wi-Fi coverage. Other papers she'd printed off earlier on the hotel's laser printer downstairs, stuff she'd found while researching Albert Sower and his known accomplices. She could have done with a pin board on which she could arrange the mugshots she'd sourced from various agencies into a flow chart she could follow. Spreading them on the desk was inconvenient and she was certain she was missing something.

Po had looked in on her earlier, but finding her dressed in a hotel dressing gown, her bare legs poking out the bottom, he'd coughed his apologies and left her to it. She'd heard him banging around in his own room; slapping and grunting followed the commotion and she wondered what the hell he was up to. Lurid images went through her mind of the ex-con self-flagellating with his leather belt, until she recognized the rhythm of the noises as a rigorous workout. In the small hotel room he probably felt confined, and resorted to what he had done when locked up in a cell at Angola. He spent the time keeping fit and healthy, in mind as much as body. Afterwards, his door opened and clicked shut behind him and he padded away. After all his cardio work he'd gone outside to put a dent in it with a few well-earned cigarettes.

Of course, there was more to Po leaving his room than assuaging his nicotine craving. They'd made themselves targets of Sower's people, and Po was taking his role as Tess's guard seriously. She assumed he'd gone out to check she was safe from immediate harm while she worked.

She couldn't sleep, but neither could she think straight. She got up and went to the window, teased a gap between the vertical blinds, and peered out. It was early evening, but down here in the sub-tropics the sun had set, and it had done so much faster than the familiar slow roll to the horizon it made up north. Daylight to darkness in less than the half-hour since last she'd peeked outside. Street lamps made the street visible, but cast a yellowish nimbus around everything. Pedestrians on the opposite sidewalk were unaware of her scrutiny. Cars whistled by without pause. There was no hint of Po, he was probably around the other side of the building adjacent to the parking lot where he could watch both their car and the entrance to the hotel.

She'd sent down for coffee earlier, and room service had delivered a pot, but it was now tepid at best. She should send for a fresh one, but the caffeine wouldn't help her sleep. Did she really expect to sleep? Not with the kind of images that had been flooding her mind since they'd bugged out of Morgan City. She believed any sleep she might get would be fraught, disturbed by violently tortured faces, and two of them hers and Po's. Hell, were they actually setting themselves out as bait? Inviting Sower's pet killer to come after them? Should she be downstairs with Po, on high alert, not sitting in her room in a fluffy dressing gown?

But she didn't believe they were in imminent danger. His abductors would have had their hands full dealing with Crawford Wynne, and she didn't expect their day would end with another abduction attempt. But how could she be certain? She still had no idea who they were up against, but judging from how Mitch Delaney died, they were uncompromising in their violence. And they were good enough at their jobs that they'd outwitted Tess and Po, beating them to Wynne. So who knew how and when – never mind if – they'd come for them?

She checked her cell phone. Still no response from Clancy. What was keeping her? Then again, Tess hadn't exactly been reliable in getting in touch with her employer.

Tess hit the number for Clancy's cell.

It rang out and went to voicemail.

Hmmm. OK, it was out of office hours, but wasn't that why

Clancy had given Tess her personal number in the first place? So that she could make contact whenever she needed to?

She hit the end button. Waited a few seconds and then redialled. The phone went to voicemail again. 'Uh. Hello, Emma. It's me, Teresa Grey. I was just calling with a quick update and to ask if you'd gotten anywhere with that licence-plate number I sent you. Anyway, I appreciate that you might be busy, so, as and when you get this message, if it's convenient to do so, could you please call me back? I, uh, I'd really appreciate it . . .'

Tess hung up and immediately felt sick at the fawning tone she'd used. Hell, she sounded like a nervous wreck. What impression would that give Clancy? She'd best get her act together or Clancy might recall them without need of the police kicking them out of Louisiana. She tightened the belt on her gown, walked back across the room to where her notes were strewn on the desk. She flicked through various pages, then placed one on top. The page contained a photograph of a man in his late twenties, with longish dark brown hair, and a moustache and goatee. From the look of the photo it was a number of years out of date. It wasn't a professional shot, or posed, but one gleaned from a news agency website, where John Torrance had appeared in a story tying him to Albert Sower. Torrance had been arrested, but acquitted through 'lack of evidence' in an assault case. Tess studied the face in the picture, mentally removing the long locks, the facial hair. Was Torrance the second man she'd seen driving the car before it rammed theirs this morning? She couldn't be certain, because her view of him had been in the mirror, and fleetingly before she recognized the other as the man who'd planted the tracking device, and who she'd almost walked into at the airport.

She picked up her phone again and hit Clancy's number. When it again went to voicemail she hung up, scrolling through her contacts list for her brother.

Alex answered after only two rings. 'Hey, little sis, how you doing?'

'Hey, Alex. I'm good. Fine.' She exhaled noisily.

'How's Louisiana working out for you?'

'Hot. Sticky.' She grunted. 'It's a mess, Alex.'

More than fifteen hundred miles away her brother pondered for a second or two. 'Didn't that Po dude work out for you?'

'It isn't Po,' Tess reassured him. She thought about telling Alex everything that had happened since their arrival in the South, but it would only worry him. He'd be directly on the phone to their mom and Tess knew she'd then have to fend off calls from her supposedly well-meaning mother questioning her abilities and demanding that she return home immediately. She could do without it. 'It's only the situation I've gotten caught up in here. It's not as straightforward as I hoped.'

'Po'd best be treating you like a gentleman or I'll have something to say to him when you get back.'

Because of Po's volatile nature, Tess felt she should warn Alex about brushing his bristles the wrong way, but that would make him suspect there had been an issue with Po in the first place. 'Po's not the problem. In fact, he's been a great help, and you can relax. He hasn't tried it on with me or anything creepy like that.'

'Not that you'd tell me if he had, right?'

'That'd be too weird,' she said, and they both laughed in unison.

'Y'know, Tess, I'm not against you getting together with a guy. Hell, it's about time you did, but you could do a whole lot better than an ex-con.'

Yes, Tess wanted to say, you'd be happy to see me back with a clean-cut guy like Jim Neely. Well, given the choice, she'd take Po over that grade 'A' asshole any day! However, she clamped down on the response. Why the hell had she grown so defensive over Po anyway?

'For now I prefer my young, free, and single status, thanks,' she said.

'Well, two out of three aren't bad, sis. There's none of us getting any younger. You don't want to end up an old maid.'

'Speak for yourself, Alex. You're what now? Thirty-three? Isn't it time you had your own place, your own wife and kids? You can't stay tied to Mom's apron strings forever.'

'I'm working on it. But to be honest, I haven't found anyone who launders my clothes or cooks as well as Mom yet. I do

love my home cooking.' He was playing it up. It wasn't the
first time they'd had a similar conversation. When her relationship with Jim Neely had collapsed, Alex was the one to offer
a shoulder to cry on. He'd had his fair share of experience in
floundering relationships, and had been in a good position to
offer advice. In the last few weeks he'd been seeing a woman
he'd met through work, but he hadn't shared any details about
her, despite Tess's urging. Alex claimed he preferred to see
how things progressed before introducing his new girlfriend
to the family. Tess doubted it would last much longer than
Alex's other relationships. Not because her brother was
difficult, or wasn't a good catch, but because theirs was a
relationship Alex hinted might be deemed inappropriate, and
she thought he meant by Portland PD. He was equally as duty
driven as Tess, so would he jeopardize his career because of
this woman? She thought his reluctance to come clean about
her before their relationship grew serious was to protect his
position, and quite possibly his lover's too.

'How is the mystery woman?' she teased. 'I take it she isn't
a ready-made wife, then? Or is that the problem: she's already
somebody else's wife?'

'Hey, let's not go there, OK?'

'Suits me, bro. But that goes both ways.'

'OK. Deal. So what's up?'

'Are you on duty tonight?'

'Graveyard shift,' he said, and she pictured him glancing at
the clock, checking how soon he must leave for work. 'So,
I'm guessing this isn't a social call. What is it you want, Tess?'

'Who says I'm not homesick and want to hear a familiar
voice?'

'You've only been gone a couple of days. You haven't had
time to get homesick. What is it you're after?' He said the
last in a world-weary tone, as if she asked lots from him.
She didn't.

'I was wondering if you could run a licence-plate number
for me.' Tess waited. Police officers could be seriously disci-
plined if they used law-enforcement resources for personal
reasons. But, having been there and done it, she knew there
were ways and means of getting around the system. She'd

taken a sneaky glance at Jim Neely's record – actually his
lack of one – when first they'd begun dating, to ensure there
was nothing in his past that would come back to hurt her. She
also knew of cops who ran the sheets on boyfriends and girl-
friends of their children on the sly. Alex also knew the deal
and couldn't worm his way out of helping by quoting protocol.

'Give it me,' he said.

She told him the licence number and heard him scribbling
it down. 'I could do with the owner details ASAP. Can you
ring me back as soon as you have them?'

'I'll see what I can do.'

'There's something else, Alex.' She told him John Torrance's
name, and his age, the only details available on the printout
she had. 'Could you maybe get a glimpse at his rap sheet? I
could do with knowing as much about him as possible.'

'John Torrance? That'd be John "Jacky Boy" Torrance,
right? From here in Portland?' Alex grew serious. 'I know
that a-hole. He's a punk. What's he got to do with what you're
mixed up in?'

'Maybe nothing,' Tess admitted. 'His name just came up in
my enquiries. He might have nothing to do with anything. But
just in case he has, well, an idea what he's like, and what he's
capable of, would be a great help.'

'He's a low-level thug. But that means nothing. Watch out,
Tess, and I mean watch out. Sometimes it's the inconsequential
ones who turn out the worst to deal with.'

'Amen to that,' she said, thinking of the strung-out addicts
who'd ended her career, and who'd murdered their grandfather.
'I'll be careful, Alex.'

'See that you do,' he said, and sounded exactly like their
mom.

TWENTY

S leep must have crept up on her unaware.

Tess had reclined on the bed, checking through her notes, unable to piece together anything of use from the various strands to Albert Sower she'd gathered. She'd set down her cell beside her, bracing her iPad on her bent knees. The lights in her mind must have switched off abruptly.

Her phone rang and she kicked in surprise, and her iPad went flying. She struggled up, grabbing for the tablet and the cell phone at the same time. The cell slid away from her groping fingers and bumped to the floor. She rolled over, groping for the phone.

Flustered, she hit the button. 'Uh, hello!'

'Sis? It's me Alex. You OK?'

'Uh, yeah . . . uh, I must've dropped off for a minute or two.' Perhaps she'd napped for longer. She blearily looked around, searching for a clock. There wasn't one. She looked at her phone for a clue, but her vision was fuzzy from sleep. She smacked her lips. God, she could use some fresh coffee now.

'You composed now?' Alex laughed to himself.

'I'm fine. What've you got for me? Go ahead, I've got my ears on.'

'Ha, you're still using cop speak.'

'Old habits die hard,' she said.

'Then pin back those ears and get this. That number I ran for you?' She heard scratching as Alex leafed through some notes. 'It comes back to a Toyota Avalon, twenty-thirteen model in metallic bronze.'

Tess pictured the car and thought that the details matched.

Alex went on. 'Louisiana licence plate as you already know, registered to a private company in New Orleans.' He read out an address and Tess told him to wait up. She scrambled off the bed to the desk and scribbled the details on one of the printed sheets of paper.

'Gimme that company name again, will you?'

'Rutterman Logistics,' Alex said. 'Mean anything?'

'Not a thing,' she admitted, but she planned on researching the company and trying to find a connection with Albert Sower. 'No reports about the car being stolen or anything?'

'None.' Alex thought for a moment. 'It's one of a fleet of vehicles registered to Rutterman's, so it might not have been missed yet. What's the deal with it? Is it connected to Jacky Torrance?'

'I might have spotted him driving it,' she said, her voice guarded. 'I just thought it strange that he should be in Louisiana.'

Alex was no fool. He knew there was more she wasn't saying. 'I checked him out. His record's as long as my arm, but just minor stuff. His sheet's been clean for the past five years or so. But then again, it has been rumoured that he's been working for local organized crime the same number of years. Either he's being a good boy – which I doubt – or someone's keeping an eye on him and making sure he does nothing to attract our attention.' By 'our' Alex was referring to law enforcement. It felt good that he'd included her in that description. 'Hey, you're down there looking for witnesses in the Sower case, right? There have been rumours that Jacky Boy is on Sower's payroll. I take it that spotting him in Louisiana isn't as coincidental as you say. I should mention his name to the homicide detectives on Mitchel Delaney's case.'

'I never said it was a coincidence. I just wasn't sure it was him.'

'But you are now?'

'Couldn't really say, so it's too early to drop his name into the mix. I need a positive ID on him first; the only picture I have of him is years old. He's still doing the entire Bohemian look in it. Anything more up to date on the system?'

'The last time he was brought in on charges was over five years ago, but the photo on file might be more recent than the one you've got. Want me to send a copy?'

'Please. But, Alex, do be careful. I don't want you getting in trouble over this.'

'I know how to cover my tracks. Relax, sis.' He promised

to email her the most recent mugshot of John Torrance. Behind him there was a commotion. 'Uh, we just got an emergency call. Sorry, Tess, I have to go. I'll email you as soon as I'm back in the office, 'kay?'

'Thanks. Stay safe, Alex.'

'Should say the same to you.'

'I'm serious, Alex.' She wondered if she should tell him to check out the murder file on Mitch Delaney: if Sower's people discovered Alex was helping her they might turn their attention on him, and being a cop wouldn't protect him. It was one thing placing herself in their sights, but not her brother. If something bad were to happen to him, it would completely destroy her. 'Seriously serious.'

'So am I,' he said, and she gained the impression Alex knew more about this case than he was letting on. Before she could ask, he made a smacking noise with his lips, a kiss sent over the digital airwaves. Then he was gone.

After hanging up, Tess checked the time on her cell. It was 22:11. Whoa, she'd slept longer than she realized. She wondered if Po was back in his room or still standing guard outside. She looked for her clothes. After showering she'd bagged her dirty laundry in her suitcase, so went to the closet where she'd hung her clean stuff. She selected a pair of jeans and stepped into them. She put on a T-shirt, and over the top of it a thin cardigan in case the night turned chilly. She wormed her feet into the pumps she'd worn previously. Dressed, she glanced once at her iPad, wondering if she should research Rutterman Logistics before telling Po what she'd learned. It could keep. She left her room and stepped to the next door along. She knocked softly.

No reply.

Was Po sleeping? She doubted it. Someone who'd spent all those years in prison would have trained himself to wake at the slightest hint of noise. Nevertheless she knocked harder, but still got no reply.

She went downstairs. Po wasn't in the foyer, but that wasn't surprising. He'd be outside smoking. There was a night manager at the check-in desk. He nodded and smiled a greeting. He was a young man with cafe au lait skin and a beak of a

nose. Tess offered a smile in return, but once it was apparent
she wasn't in need of his service, he bent back to his computer
screen. Tess headed outside, and immediately felt a damp veil
of humidity slap down on her. If ever she returned to Louisiana
she'd ensure it was in the cooler months. She thought she
smelled cigarette smoke, but then the air was redolent with
other unfamiliar scents. Instead of trying to sniff Po out like
a bloodhound she moved out from under the exit awning, and
spied across the parking lot. There was no sign of Po, or
anyone else for that matter. Where was he? Their rental car
was parked where they'd left it, and she was conscious of the
transponder in the glove compartment still beaming out its
signal. To expect Po to be standing in the open was stupid;
he'd have positioned himself where he could watch the car
and the hotel, where he wasn't likely to be spotted. She looked
around but couldn't see him. Best plan? Stand there and he'd
spot her.

'Tess. Over here.'

Her hand went to her throat, and she stumbled back at the
voice. It was familiar, but not Po's. From the interior of a van
parked on the far side of the lot large eyes appraised her, the
whites glowing in the ambient light. The speaker's features
were lost in the darkness. She didn't need to see his face to
know who it was.

'Pinky! What are you doing here?'

The van wobbled on its chassis as Pinky adjusted his weight.
He flopped one of his unusually thin arms out of the window
and beckoned Tess closer. 'Hush now, pretty Tess. I'm under
cover, me.'

Tess moved towards the van, no hint of trepidation about
approaching the ex-con and current gunrunner. 'You're
watching for me?'

'Looking out for you,' he corrected. 'Nicolas asked me to
stand guard while he attended to an important errand.'

Tess glanced around, as if she'd spot her wayward employee.
'Po left?'

'Po? I can't get used to that name, me. You mean Nicolas,
right?' Pinky drummed his fingers on the van door. 'Come sit
with me. We can wait for Nicolas together, us.'

'Where has he gone?'

'He didn't say,' said Pinky, though he would never pass a lie detector. 'He only asked that I sit here until he returns.' He checked his watch. 'He swore he'd be back before midnight. He'd better uphold his promise, otherwise I'll turn into a pumpkin, I warned him.'

If she'd to be honest, Tess was pissed that Po had deserted his post. But she was also disarmed by Pinky's jovial manner. Something about the guy made her smile. 'Please tell me he hasn't gone off on a personal vendetta.'

Pinky laughed, and now there was an edge to his humour that she wasn't certain of. 'I couldn't possibly say. Not where an eavesdropper might overhear. Come, pretty Tess, sit up here beside me and we can keep each other company.'

Should she trust Pinky? He was Po's friend, and Po trusted him. That should have been enough for her, but now that he'd deserted his post, gone off on some 'private errand' without giving her as much as a heads up, how trustworthy was he? She moved towards the van, but halted and cast a look at the hotel entrance. She'd left her purse in her room. She'd left her gun in that purse. Was it wise to climb into a van with a man she barely knew, and whose word she had to take regarding her missing companion? For all she knew Pinky wasn't as beholden to Po as he made out and he'd claimed the bounty on Po's head himself. Maybe he was here with nefarious reasons in mind: maybe he was here to make sure there were no witnesses to Po's disappearance.

Jesus, talk about paranoia!

She moved around the front of the van and slipped in alongside Pinky. He looked uncomfortable on a seat designed for someone without his bulk. His stick arms looked odd as he drummed his fingers on the steering wheel. He offered a smile, and she squeezed one in reply. 'Nicolas told me you probably wouldn't leave your room before he got back.'

'Call me a rebel,' she said.

Pinky laughed. 'I'm glad you came down; this undercover stuff isn't as exciting as I thought. I was about to fall asleep, things are so quiet.'

'Did Po – I mean Nicolas – tell you what's going on?'

'He told me that some dudes might show some interest in your Honey Wagon over there.'

'Honey Wagon?'

'His words, not mine, pretty Tess.'

'Hmmm. Sounds like him, I admit.'

Pinky laughed again, his voice throaty. In the next instant his face grew serious. 'Nicolas warned that they might be interested in more than the car. I would not let them harm you, Tess.'

She smiled her thanks, but couldn't hide her doubt.

'I'm not as slow as I look.' Pinky prodded his stomach, his fingers sinking deep. 'This looks bad, but underneath I'm not as soft, me.'

Tess didn't know what to say, anything might be construed as insulting. Pinky grinned at her discomfort. 'I'm gay, I'm black, I'm ugly, and I'm shaped kind of weird. There's no insult I haven't heard before, pretty Tess, nothing I haven't shrugged off a thousand times and more.' His hand dipped down the side of the chair and it came up gripping an automatic handgun. 'Usually this shuts up the name-calling.'

'You're not ugly, Pinky,' Tess reassured him – then thought how bad that sounded when she hadn't fended off his other self-recriminations.

Pinky laughed in that throaty manner again, and she was happy when he put away his gun. 'Nicolas said you were a funny girl. He was right, him. I like you, pretty Tess.'

'I like you too, Pinky. Not too keen on Nicolas just now. Please tell me he hasn't gone after the Chatards?'

'He's no crazy man. There's a time and place to end that vendetta. This is not it.'

'Then where the hell is he?'

Pinky sighed. 'He's gone to pay his respects, Tess. Gone to say a few words over his daddy's grave. You wouldn't hold that against him, no?'

Shame burned her. She hadn't considered that Po's absence could have something to do with anything other than his unresolved feud with the Chatard family. She rubbed her fingers over her face, noting how rubbery with sleep it was. She wasn't thinking straight, that was it, her brain was still swaddled in cotton wool. Giving it some thought, an opportunity to visit his father's grave was probably a clincher on his decision to accompany her here. Before setting off she'd visited and laid flowers on both her grandfather's and her dad's graves, so why shouldn't Po want to do the same? As awful as it was, she hadn't considered that his father meant as much to him as hers did to Tess. He was a convicted criminal: did ex-cons even have feelings? Idiot!

'Ah, you probably have more on your mind.' Pinky reached across and patted her wrist. It was a gesture of compassion, but Tess discreetly drew her hand away and folded it in her lap. It was her left hand, not her injured one, but she still felt self-conscious about her scarring and occasionally forgot which hand she protected. If she weren't careful her damaged hand would become more a psychological encumbrance than the nerve and ligament damage.

Headlights flooded the parking lot.

In reaction they both hunched in their seats, but they weren't in danger of being spotted. The lights swept the cars on the opposite side as the vehicle angled in to park near the hotel entrance. A man fumbled his way out of the car, followed a moment later by the driver, who appeared to be his enraged wife. She gestured angrily, and her voice cracked across the parking lot and made the man flinch. He staggered for the entrance, and the woman followed, shaking her head at his drunkenness.

'I hope they don't have the adjoining room to yours,' Pinky laughed. 'I predict some shouting tonight.'

Po's room was on one side, she had no idea who had the other room. She sure hoped it wasn't an angry wife and her worse for wear husband. Then again, judging by his wobbling gait, she predicted that the drunkard would be face down, sound asleep within minutes.

They made small talk, Pinky asking how Tess liked Louisiana. Although she'd had a tour of the central areas she hadn't had much opportunity to enjoy its beauty. All she'd concentrated on to date was the locations they'd visited, and Gardere Lane, the Cottonmouths' clubhouse, and especially Crawford Wynne's home were nothing to write home about.

'It has a feel to it that I can't quite put my finger on,' she admitted. 'Something gothic, alien, or otherworldly.'

'Then I'm probably right at home, me. I too am slightly odd, right?'

Tess laughed. 'I wouldn't put it that way. If anything I'm the alien visitor here; you must find me rather strange at times.'

Pinky didn't reply. He simply sat back, smiling to himself.

They talked about the mundane. Favourite food. Drink. Movies. Books.

'I've never read an entire book,' Pinky admitted. 'I don't have the attention span. It's probably why I found sitting here so boring . . . before you joined me, I must add. Right now I'm thoroughly enjoying myself.'

Tess's smile was slow to grow. She wasn't certain if Pinky was being sarcastic or not. 'So you prefer movies to books?'

'Certain movies. It's such a shame isn't it, learned people quote Shakespeare while I can only quote Stallone!' He giggled at his own joke.

'Yo! Adrienne!' Tess said, and they laughed together now. 'It sounds as if we enjoy the same type of movies.'

'People look at me and jump to the wrong conclusion. They expect me to be a fan of *The Sound of Music*, or *The Wizard of Oz*, or something equally as camp. Huh! Give me a beefcake lead in a dirty tank top any time,' he said. Suddenly he turned to her, aiming a conspiratorial nudge with his elbow. 'Didn't you wonder why I fell for Nicolas Villere? Isn't he a ringer for that hunk Hugh Jackman?'

Not for the first time, Tess thought of Po as a Clint Eastwood lookalike, but now that she thought about it, Jackman too was a double for the young Clint. 'Oh, you knew him when he was younger,' she said. 'So you fell for him then?'

'Who wouldn't?' He watched her and his eyes had grown wide again. Tess looked quickly at her hands in her lap. 'Mind you, now that he looks more like grizzled old Sam Elliott, I'm more inclined to look elsewhere for my eye candy.'

'I, uh, think Sam Elliott's still an attractive man,' Tess said.

Pinky grinned at her. Then he wagged a finger, and an arched eyebrow. 'That Nicolas! He does still have a certain charm. But what about me, pretty Tess? Don't you think I have a look of Denzel Washington?' He laughed brightly at his own joke, waving off her politically correct response. 'I'm more like Eddie Murphy in *The Nutty Professor*. Sherman Klump, me.'

'You're doing yourself a disservice there, Pinky.'

'No. No. I know what I look like. My face won't win any prizes, even if my waist size does. But what about you, Tess? Who do you remind me of? Let me see.' He turned as far as his seat allowed, the upholstery squeaking in protest. 'Hmm, there's a definite hint of Charlize Theron there.'

'I wish,' Tess said.

Pinky flapped a hand at her. 'You did see her in that movie *Monster*, right?'

Tess opened her mouth in mock horror, and Pinky laughed uproariously. Charlize Theron played the serial killer Aileen Wuornos in that one, and had looked anything but beautiful in make-up. Pinky wiped his mouth, an effort to stifle the laughter. 'Silly of me. I meant "monster movie". Y'know the one about the big ape?'

'You're thinking of Naomi Watts in *King Kong*.'

'Hmmm. Excuse me, but I do know a big ape when I see one. I'm talking about *Mighty Joe Young*, and it was definitely Miss Theron in that one.' Pinky suddenly grew serious. 'And speaking of big apes, check him out.'

Tess followed his gesture, expecting to witness Po's return to the fold. Instead she spotted a figure shambling through the parking lot. It was a large man, heavy as Pinky, but fat all over. In contrast to his girth, his face appeared gaunt and pale, as if he hungered badly. His clothing was a mixture of styles, and even in this damp heat was wearing a threadbare trench coat over stained khaki chinos, and shoes held together with string. He was carrying a rolled sleeping bag, from which dangled other items in plastic bags fit for bursting. Tess almost disregarded him as a harmless street person until he paused at the rear of the Honda and studied the licence number.

'What's he up to?'

'No good.' Pinky drew his sidearm from down by his side.

'No. Wait on.' Tess leaned to get a cleaner look at the homeless man. He was standing, bent at the waist, head cocked as he rechecked the number. He straightened, nodding, and even from across the parking lot Tess could hear mumbled confirmation. He dipped a hand inside his coat pocket and pulled something out. He moved around the Honda and leaned across the hood.

'What's he doing now?' Tess's question was rhetoric; because it was obvious he was slipping something under the windshield wiper.

'Probably putting out flyers for pizza or hot chicks,' Pinky suggested. 'Sometimes the bums are given a bunch of flyers and told to put them out in return for alcohol or cigarettes.'

Pinky's explanation was feasible, except the man had bypassed all the other vehicles in the lot, going directly to the Honda. Now he'd completed his task, he shambled away, shaking his head and muttering at the sky, while ignoring the other parked cars.

Tess got out the van, while Pinky started the engine. Instructions were unnecessary, as they each knew what the other intended. While Pinky went off to corral the street guy, Tess jogged over to the Honda. She glanced around, checking she was unobserved as she approached the front. She reached for the small envelope wedged under the wiper. It was no advertisement, and a quick squint showed her name 'Teresa Grey' on a printed label on the front.

Her fingers shaking, she opened the envelope and slipped out a small card. It was bulk standard card, bleached white, and only printed on one side. Two numbers. She immediately recognized them as coordinates. There was no clue who the card had come from or where the coordinates led. Looking for Pinky, she spotted him out of the van, and talking with the street person next to the exit to the street. The man was shaking his head and flapping an arm at Pinky. Tess headed for them. As she approached she heard curses directed both ways, and was thankful that Pinky had left the gun in the van after all.

'Hey! Hey!' she said, making calming pats of her hands at the air. The street guy turned and looked at her, his gaze bleary. 'Let's calm things down, shall we?'

To Pinky, he said, 'Who's this, yo sister?'

'That's enough of your wise mouth, you,' Pinky snapped at

him, and jabbed one of his long fingers into the man's chest. The guy brushed at the spot as if Pinky's touch had smeared his coat. If anything, Pinky had left a clean spot.

'Don't you touch me, nigga!' The man turned to flounder away, but Pinky caught him by his shoulder. Pinky claimed he was stronger than he looked, and proved it when he brought the man to a jerking halt. The man took a swipe backwards with his elbow, but Pinky was in no danger. He looked at Tess for direction. 'You want me to slap this punk?'

'No. Let me handle it, OK?' She moved so that she was in front of the guy. He swore at her but she stood her ground. She wagged the envelope under his nose. 'You put this on my car.'

'You going to get me arrested for littering, huh?' Perhaps he wasn't as inebriated as he first looked. But that was a good thing.

'I'm only going to ask you a question or two,' Tess reassured him. She made eyes at Pinky to back off a little. Pinky rolled his, but took a step away.

'Are you a cop or something?' The man's accent wasn't typical of Louisiana. He was another out-of-stater just like Tess.

'No, I'm not a cop.'

'Then I don't have to answer yo' questions.' The man went to walk by her, but Tess sidestepped and halted him in his tracks. Pinky tensed, readying for action if the guy tried to bolt.

Tess shoved the envelope under his nose again. 'I only want to know who gave you this.'

The guy shrugged. 'Beats me. Some dude. Gave me ten bucks to push it under yo' wiper. I'm beginning to think that ten bucks wasn't worth the trouble.'

Tess suspected who was behind the message: John Torrance or his pal. But she had to be clear on it. She dipped in her pocket, searching for cash. She'd left her money in the hotel room with everything else. 'Pinky, can you loan me twenty dollars?'

'For this flimflammer? You want *me* to give him money when what he needs is some civility knocked into him?'

'I'll pay you back,' Tess promised.

Pinky snorted, but delved in his pants pocket and came out with a roll of cash. He peeled off a single twenty, extended it between two fingers. Tess reached for it, but the drunk got there first. He inspected it as if the note was counterfeit.

'There.' Tess raised her eyebrows at him. 'Is it worth the trouble now? All I want is a description of the man who gave you the envelope.'

The twenty went inside the man's grungy coat. 'Can't say much. They wus in a car, I didn't get a good look at them.'

'So there was more than one guy?'

'Uh-huh.'

'White guys?'

'Uh-huh. Two of them were white. Some other guy was in back. The driver gave me the cash and the envelope.' He pointed back the way from which he'd entered the parking lot. 'They were parked just over there, near the laundromat next to the intersection. Big black car. Don't ask me the type, 'cause I haven't a clue. I walk; I don't have anything to do with cars and such. Rich man's car, though, I can tell yo' that. One of them with the silver Olympic rings on the front.'

He was describing an Audi, Tess assumed. 'What did they say to you?'

'Asked me if I wanted to make some beer money.' He snorted. 'Ten goddamn dollars doesn't amount to much beer these days. He pointed out where yo' car wus, told me the last three letters on the licence, and made me repeat them so I got it right, and told me to leave the envelope on yo' wind-shield. I did what they asked, earned the cash. That's all.'

Tess checked across the lot to where Pinky's van had been parked before they'd spotted the drunk on his errand. There was no view of the intersection from there. From where they stood now, she could see to the laundromat but there was no 'rich man's car' visible. If Tess described those she'd already identified as her watchers, the drunk would simply agree to the description. It was better that she elicited the details from him without prompting, but nothing much was forthcoming. She'd no doubt it was Sower's men, so why push for more, except that he'd mentioned a third man.

'What about the guy in back?'

'I didn't look at him,' he said, but his eyelids flickered and she suspected he was lying. 'No good would come from looking into that face.'

'What do you mean by that?' Tess pushed.

'Nothin'. I don't mean a goddamn thing 'cause I never seen him.'

'Did he say anything? *Anything.* It might be important.'

'Jeez. I told you what they said already.' The drunk pushed past, and Tess got a face full of his stench. Sour body odour, vinegary, vomit-laced, it wasn't pleasant. She stepped out of his way. She'd gotten all she would from him, so there was little to be gained from keeping him other than an upset stomach.

Pinky called after the retreating drunk. 'Word to the wise, bra. Use that cash for something you really need. Instead of beer, I'd be buying soap, me.'

The street guy swore viciously without checking for a response. Pinky grinned at Tess. 'Sorry, I had to get some kind of return for my investment.'

'I'll pay you back,' she said again.

Pinky shrugged. He nodded at the envelope Tess clutched in her hand. 'So what's that about?'

'Coordinates,' she said. 'They want me to find something.'

'Or go somewhere you really shouldn't,' Pinky cautioned.

TWENTY-ONE

P o returned to the hotel in the early hours of the morning. By then Tess had already deduced that there was no imminent threat from Sower's people. They hadn't left the map coordinates only to come for her while she slept. She'd excused Pinky from guard duty and returned to her room, intent on finding exactly where she was supposed to go. Google Maps pinpointed the coordinates to swampland on the shore of Hammock Bayou, due south of New Iberia, west of Morgan City. Since discovering the location, she'd waited for her companion to get back, and it had been frustrating. She felt as if fire ants had invaded her clothing, she was so jittery, anxious to get moving. When she heard Po bumping around in the adjoining room she practically leapt for her door and into the corridor. She rapped on Po's door.

'It's me. Tess,' she announced, imagining Po approaching the door with his gun in hand.

The door snicked open. 'I knew it was you, I heard the racket you made leaving your room.' Po held out a palm. 'C'mon in.'

But Tess halted, and it wasn't because he held a sidearm or anything else. He'd stripped to the waist, the top button of his jeans loosened. Unbidden, her gaze swept from the tight weave of muscles in his abdomen, up to the thatch of dark hair on his chest, and down again, and in the next instant she was reminded of Pinky with his arched eyebrow and wagging finger. *I'm more inclined to look elsewhere for my eye candy*, he'd said and she didn't believe a word of it. She quickly averted her attention to Po's face, but, damn it, by the twinkling of his turquoise eyes, he'd caught her staring. 'I was just about to shower,' he said, and put a hand to his bare chest, again drawing her gaze. 'Does this bother you?'

'Could you, uh, pull on a shirt or something?' Tess asked, bustling over to his bed, where she laid down her iPad and the envelope. She kept her back to him, but swore she could feel heat radiating off him, and it was difficult not to check his state of undress. 'While you've been out, I've been busy working,' she said, and her tone was as flustered as the manner she rearranged her iPad on the bed, while listening to the faint rustling of cloth. Finally she couldn't help looking.

Po had closed the door to the hall, stood with his back to it, hands on the handle, barring her escape. He'd pulled on his shirt but it hung loose, still displaying more than was comfortable in the confines of the small room. But he wasn't totally shameless; he dipped his head and frown lines creased his brow as he stepped away from the door. 'I spoke with Pinky. He told me about your visitors. I'm sorry I wasn't here, Tess, but I'd something to do that I couldn't put off.'

'I know. You're not the only one who talked to Pinky.' She wondered exactly what Pinky had told him, and if he'd mentioned the admission Pinky made about whom he found attractive, and the one he'd also teased from her. She was positive her face was burning. 'Anyway,' she said in a rush, 'it doesn't matter. Nothing bad happened.'

To get back on track, she explained how her brother had run the plates for her and how they'd come back to Rutterman Logistics, and how she'd connected John Torrance to Albert Sower. Then she told how the street guy had played messenger boy for Torrance and his buddies, and how she'd figured that Sower's people wanted her to follow the clue they'd offered her.

'Torrance and his buddies,' Po asked, 'there were more than the two we've already seen?'

'There was a third man in back,' she said. 'But the guy didn't say much about him, claimed he didn't see him, but I think he was lying.'

'Frightened?'

'Crapping his pants,' she said. 'All he'd say was something like "no good would come from looking into a face like that". He claimed he was just given some cash to deliver this to me.' She slipped the card from the envelope and held it out to him. Po walked over, took it, angled it so he could read it, and his mouth quirked down. The coordinates wouldn't mean a thing to him. 'Sit down. Let me show you where they are on a map.'

Tess sat on the bed, and Po joined her, his knee brushing hers. She pitched the iPad so he could see the screen, discreetly shifting away an inch or so to break the physical contact, but could still sense the ghost of his touch as a faint buzz of electricity up her thigh. In the corner of her eye she caught him studying her face in profile, and thought he too had been conscious of their closeness, and was checking if she was too. 'Look here,' she said, diverting his scrutiny, and tapped the map to zoom it in. 'Do you know this place?'

'I've been to Cypremort Point before; it has some great restaurants and it's also a popular spot for family picnics,' said Po, indicating a small waterside community a short distance to the west of where the coordinates were pinned on the map. He swept his fingers over the land adjacent to Hammock Bayou. 'But that's all untamed swamp. If you want to go there we'll need to get you some appropriate clothing. You won't last more than a few minutes in those pumps.'

'I've Clancy's credit card. We can buy what we need on the way.' Tess got up, eager to be off.

'What? You want to go now?' Po leaned back, bracing his weight on both hands. His shirt slipped a fraction, and despite her resolve, Tess's gaze was drawn to his tight body. She turned away, telling herself she'd misread the undertones of his question.

'Why not?' she said, and her tongue darted across her suddenly dry lips. 'We're both awake. The sooner we get going, the sooner we get to the bottom of this.'

Po shook his head. 'You do realize what we're going to find?'

Sadly she knew exactly, and understanding brought her focus back to her job.

'A couple more hours won't make any difference to a dead man,' he counselled. 'In fact, it's unwise going there. I know we agreed not to earlier, but you should call the cops and hand things over to them. You're going to have to if we find Wynne out there. Why put yourself through it when you don't have to?'

Po had changed his tune. Not surprisingly. He'd spent the evening at a murdered man's grave, and was likely to spend his morning at another. She could understand his reluctance, but they'd journeyed to Louisiana to find Crawford Wynne, and she had to be the one to do that. Again he showed that ability of reading what was on her mind; was she so transparent?

'I'll go with you,' he reassured her. 'I just want you to think about what we might find.'

She expected no less than what she'd witnessed in Mitch Delaney's autopsy report. 'My stomach can handle it.'

'I'm not talking about Wynne. What if it's a set up? What if Sower's people are waiting for us? Maybe Wynne won't be the only one left to rot in the mud.'

'We're armed.'

Po grunted. His gaze flickered to her damaged wrist. Tess scowled at him. 'I'm not a damn invalid,' she said.

'Didn't suggest you were. It's just that we might be walking into a trap. They'll have the advantage of knowing where we are; we'll be stumbling about as good as blind.'

'You grew up around there. Sower's people are from up north. This terrain is alien to them. I'd bet on you spotting them before they do us.'

'Huh.' Po smiled with little humour. 'Flattery will get you everywhere. But it's not me I'm worried about, Tess.'

'OK, I'm a northerner too. And, yeah, I'll struggle in the swamp, but going there's something I'm prepared to do.' She was about to add 'with or without you', but that wouldn't engender the hoped-for response. She had no desire to alienate Po and it was time to admit that. 'I'm counting on you keeping me safe while I see this through. I want you to come with me, Po.'

He held up his hands. 'I said I'll come. I just want you to understand that it isn't the best idea I ever agreed to.'

'Noted. It's on me if the crap hits the fan,' she said, crossing her chest. She offered a deal-making smile, and it warmed his face.

'OK, so do I get chance to visit the bathroom before we go?' said Po. 'I was about to shower, remember.'

She hadn't forgotten. How could she when the closeness of

his partially bared torso, and her less-than-surreptitious study of it, made certain of that?

'I'll go get my stuff,' she said, and hurried to escape her train of thought.

Back in her room she braced her shoulders to the door, her hands clasped round the handle, a similar pose to the one Po had struck minutes ago. She shook her head in disbelief, exhaling. Get a grip, Tess! You'd think you'd never been alone in a room with a half-naked man before, she admonished herself. But that only forced her to picture Po again, and also to admit that though she'd been uncomfortable and embarrassed by his semi-nudity, it wasn't entirely unenjoyable either.

To divert her attention off him and back on her job, she grabbed her purse and searched for her phone. Checking the screen by auto-response she saw she had a new email. It was from Alex and came with an attachment. She opened the mugshot he'd sent of John 'Jacky Boy' Torrance. The man driving the Toyota Avalon like a stock-car racer was one and the same. OK, he was older now, with shorter hair, but there was no denying she'd identified one of their enemies. If she'd the time to spare she thought she'd easily identify the fair-haired man who she'd eyeballed on more occasions, if not the third man so easily, but they could wait. She stuffed her phone in her bag, but left the paperwork scattered on her desk, except for one sheaf. She didn't believe she required the legal papers she was supposed to serve to Crawford Wynne, but she took them anyway: she could live in hope that they'd find him alive, though it was only the smallest grain.

By the time she locked her room, Po emerged from his, hair damp and finger-combed back off his forehead, and he'd donned a fresh shirt and jeans. They hustled downstairs and out the exit, again with a nod and smile for the night manager, who didn't bother returning the gesture this time. Tess strode for the Honda.

'Uh-nuh,' Po said, and jingled keys. 'We aren't taking that chicken shack. We leave it, and the damn transponder, right here. No sense in advertising that we're on our way.'

'So how do we get to the bayous?'

'Think I walked to my father's grave and back, do you?'

He nodded towards a sleek Mercedes-Benz GL450 SUV parked in the opposite row. 'Pinky loaned me his wheels. You didn't really believe a guy like him drove an old Dodge panel van?'

Honestly, she hadn't given Pinky's choice of vehicle much more thought than that the van was inconspicuous during a stakeout, but now that Po mentioned it . . .

'Even a Merc isn't extravagant enough for Pinky,' she pointed out.

'I had a choice of cars,' Po smirked. 'The others I turned down flat.'

'They were so flamboyant they challenged your masculinity?'

'Nope. Too flashy. This was the least expensive of the bunch.'

Her eyes widened. Hell, the Mercedes probably retailed upward of sixty thousand dollars, and it was the least expensive of Pinky's fleet?

'Anyway, if we're going into the bayous, I want something more reliable than the Chicken Shack, and something that can handle a little mud if needs be. Go on, jump in, why don't you?'

'OK, OK, you've sold me on it,' Tess said, and aimed for the SUV. Behind her she suspected Po was grinning in triumph, maybe even flipping the bird to the abandoned Honda minivan. So allow him his moment, there might be fewer happy moments in the coming hours.

TWENTY-TWO

Ochre was the colour of death.

It was the colour of the sky, and of the water lapping on the mud between the cattails and reed grass. Way across Vermilion Bay, above the strip of treetops, the unseen chimneystacks of petrochemical plants belched smoke into the sky. Burnt ochre in their case.

Tess didn't doubt that she was tinged the same colour, because standing beside her Po had the caste of burnished brass, adding an unnatural hue to his usual pallor. She'd always thought of him as a man out of his time, and standing there in his worn jeans and denim shirt, a battered baseball cap shading the rising sun from his eyes, he looked like a photograph of a turn-of-the-twentieth-century farmhand, immortalized in sepia. The downturned lines in his face looked severe, shadowed as they were. To Tess his craggy features spoke of something more, though they were a contradiction in terms: strength and world-weariness. She knew he was in turn a man of sharp intellect and of savage bestiality. Some people feared Po – and rightly so – but right there in the swamp there was nobody she would rather have at her side.

'You going to call this in?'

When Po spoke to her now his accent was again untainted by his Acadian heritage, and good job, because when they'd stopped at a fishing and hiking store to purchase appropriate clothing for the trip she'd heard him converse with the locals and had been lost within seconds. The Louisiana bayou dialect was a foreign language even in their common country.

'Yes. We should,' said Tess, but she didn't reach for her cell phone.

Po cleared his throat, spitting between his boots. He was ankle-deep in mud, and unlike Tess hadn't elected to wear the fisherman's waders she'd purchased on Clancy's card. His boots were military issue, waterproof, though he'd never seen service. Not in any conventional sense. He glanced again at the device he held in his hand, and grunted as if agreeing with the read-out on the screen.

They'd parked Pinky's SUV beside route 319 approaching Cypremort Point and trekked through the swamps following the coordinates on a handheld GPS unit – also an acquisition charged to Clancy – to the northern shore of Hammock Bayou. The hike through the swamp had been taxing, the early morning air already thick with moist heat, buzzing insects, and bugs. More than once they'd swerved off trail to avoid snakes, some of them coiled in the low branches. Sweat had poured from Tess, dripped from her hair, gathered in her clothing. By contrast Po was still untroubled by the stifling humidity, which she found frustrating considering he'd been absent from these lands for years. He had no right to be so cool, not when she was practically melting. Of course, she'd forgotten about the wet heat as they'd stepped out from between the moss-covered cypress trees and onto the snarl of roots alongside the bayou. Instantly, she grew cold.

She'd witnessed violent death before, but experience didn't prepare her for what they'd found.

Tall pilings had been driven into the mud, poles to which a fisherman could hitch his flat-bottomed pirogue or nets, but the bayou was absent of fishermen. On one of the pilings something else had been tethered, and bathed in the sharp light of the sun, there were too many shadows on the naked corpse to tell at first if it was man or woman. It was difficult to tell if the body was even the correct way up. Minus its head and the way the limbs had been contorted and secured by steel wire, the corpse was at first an amorphous jumble.

Po studied the corpse with that stillness that always disturbed Tess. She on the other hand sunk to a crouch and pushed her slick palms through her hair. She'd thought ahead, plaiting her pale locks and fixing them behind her ears, but still her hair had frizzed and she distractedly smoothed down stray curls as she looked in horror at the upended corpse.

The victim was a portly man, or at least he had been. He'd been gutted like a steer and his belly was now an open cavity, the loose folds of flesh hanging down over what would have been pendulous breasts if gravity hadn't been defied. His genitals were missing. But if his murderer had followed his *modus operandi* then Tess suspected where she'd find them. Deep incisions covered the flaccid body, front, back, and sides, and Tess assumed the cutting had been done while he was still alive as a form of sadistic torture, prior to his decapitation.

'You think it's him.' Po's words weren't as much a question as a statement of fact.

Tess rose from her crouch, and she placed her fists on her hips as she nodded once. 'It's him. But we have to be certain, right?'

'We need to find his head.'

Tess searched around. If the killer had stuck to his MO, the decapitated head shouldn't be far away, a requisite to the way in which Mitch Delaney had been displayed.

Po looked again at the screen of the GPS unit, then held it out to Tess. 'I don't think there's any doubt it's him.'

Tess read a location named on the screen, then followed Po's languid nod towards a nearby peninsula crowned by cypress jutting into the bay. 'Crawford's Point,' she repeated.

'Our boys are having fun while they work.' Po's lips quirked at the grim humour, as if he found the killers' joke worthy of acknowledgement.

'They're laughing at us, more like,' Tess said.

Po shrugged. It didn't matter to him the way it did others, or to Tess in particular.

A breeze blew in off the Gulf.

A sour coppery tang invaded Tess's senses. Mitch Delaney's corpse had been washed, cleansed of all forensic evidence, and this one probably had too. But this one had sat out here in the sun for what she guessed must have been the best part of yesterday, and begun to decompose. The insides of her cheeks watered, and she was forced to spit the way Po had, or else she'd vomit.

'Look at the mud flats,' Po said, with a flick of a wrist towards the base of the pilings. 'No tracks. No human tracks at least. Tide's been in and out a couple of times.'

Tiny footprints dotted the mud, but they were wading birds,

and crabs. Some of the swamp dwellers had been feeding on the body, no doubt, but none of the larger scavengers had got to it yet. Tess ignored the obvious tracks and looked for something else.

'They must have brought him in by boat,' she said.

Po grunted. It was a fair deduction, because they hadn't found signs of anyone approaching on foot from the swamp. Even if Sower's two henchmen had helped the killer, it would have been impossible to carry the victim through the cypress roots and place him here without leaving a trail a blind man could follow. Hell, she'd almost passed out dragging only her weight through the swamp, let alone someone as hefty as Crawford Wynne. She was in no doubt who the victim was, but as she'd told Po there was only one way to be certain. 'There,' she said.

'Hmm,' Po replied. He too had spotted the faint trail twenty yards away. The tide had smoothed out the footprints down by the water, but higher up towards the mesh of entwined roots there were still uneven grooves in the muck. At the tideline a broken branch lay discarded: a makeshift broom thrown aside when finished with. 'Looks as if our boys tried to brush away their tracks as they returned to the boat.'

Without waiting for Po, Tess slogged through the mud to where the trail disappeared between the cypress roots. He gave her room, waiting until she again crouched and ran her hands through her hair, before moving in behind her. This time her pose was more controlled, thoughtful. She crouched to study her find. Wedged among the snarl of roots was the missing head. Crabs had feasted on it, nipping away the flesh of the cheeks and forehead, stripping it down to the bone in places. But the face was still recognizable by the swastika tattoo that extended from above the right cheekbone and round almost to the nape of the skull. It had been a defining feature of Crawford Wynne back when he'd been an active white supremacist, a brand that had marked him for the asshole he was in earlier life, and up to the day of his violent demise. His killer hadn't cared that the mud crabs would tear apart his face, but had taken pains to ensure they'd have a harder time getting at what was stuffed inside his mouth. Wynne's lips had been stapled together, thick steel upholsterers' staples driven through the flesh and into the bones of his jaws.

They'd have to wait until the pathology report came back to be certain, but she already suspected what would be found when Wynne's mouth was opened. The pathologist would also state clearly that Wynne's genitals had been removed and stuffed in his mouth while he was still alive. That was the punishment prescribed to all with the temerity to stand witness against Albert Sower, she realized.

Tess glanced at Po. He stood with his back to her, but it had nothing to do with his aversion to death. He peered back down the trail, and from this angle could see way across the Gulf. If there were any boats out on Vermilion Bay they were hidden by the haze on the water, the light now blazing orange as the sun pushed up from the horizon.

'You think they're out there watching us?' Tess asked.

Po grunted, then spat between his boots. 'Can't see why they'd set this up if they weren't around to enjoy the result of all their hard work.'

'So we don't give them any hint we're on to them.' Tess stood and walked away, concealing herself from view by the grey trunks of cypress trees. Now was the right time to call the police, and Emma Clancy. She could see Po scanning the swamplands, and his hand drifted to his holstered gun. Instead of taking out her cell, she reached for her Glock and racked the slide. She was glad that her hands didn't shiver with fear or from the misfiring of damaged nerves.

'What's wrong, Po?'

'Thought I caught a flash of yellow through the trees.' He stared into the shadows between the cypress roots. 'I don't see it now.'

'Yellow?'

'Could've been a bird,' he said without conviction.

'Do you think it's them?' Tess's heartbeat was suddenly loud in her ears, and the grip on her gun tightened.

Po continued to scan, listening keenly from the way he cocked his ears. Finally he rolled his head on his shoulders, and his hand fell away from his gun. 'Probably nothing,' he said, but Tess wasn't buying it. 'I don't hear a thing.'

But that was a problem even Tess recognized. It was too quiet.

There were no animal calls, and even the sound of the surf was hushed. They were on the bank of an inlet, so the tide was barely noticeable, but Tess was positive that the lapping water had been noisier before. The quietude was unnatural though, a response of her body, adrenalin coursing through her, and before long she again grew aware of her pulse beating within her. She was holding her breath, and she released it in a slow exhalation as she checked the shadows between the trees for anyone skulking.

'I don't like this. It feels like a trap,' she said, her words pinched by anticipation.

'Let's back out of here,' Po suggested. 'We've found Wynne and can direct the police to him with the coordinates. We don't have to hang around.'

'Wait. There's something I need do first,' said Tess, and this time she did pull out her phone. Gun in one hand, phone the other, she snapped a sequence of photographs, first of the severed head, then of the corpse tied to the piling.

'What do you want those for?' Po asked, his eyebrows beetling beneath the peak of his cap. He waved her away, and began following her back through the swamp.

'Evidence. No, proof. I need to show Emma that we got within touching distance of Crawford Wynne.'

'When news of his murder comes out, you might regret that decision.'

'Nobody in their right mind would blame us for this.'

'Don't kid yourself. Some cops have suspicious minds. Others are lazy. They might decide that concentrating on us is easier than trying to find the actual murderers.'

'You have a low opinion of cops.'

'They have a low opinion of me,' he reminded her. 'And don't forget, there are witnesses who'll state that we were searching for Wynne, and it was obvious we didn't have his best interests in mind.'

'We're here on behalf of the Portland DA's office,' Tess argued. 'We can prove that as fact . . .'

Po shook his head. 'I'm concerned about this scenario. We

thought Sower's guys left you those coordinates so they could set a trap. I'm beginning to think that it's more of a set up. You think they got us out here, not to ambush us, but to place us at the murder scene?'

Tess understood how rash they'd been by coming here. For all she knew, Sower's men could be lying in watch from across the bayou, or even way out on Crawford Point. Sower's people had sourced cars; she doubted their ability to lay their hands on long-range rifles, but a camera with a zoom lens would have been no problem. Even now, those photographs of Tess and Po standing before Wynne's corpse could be anonymously winging their way to a police email account. 'No. Too complicated,' she decided.

'What is?'

As they slogged through the mud she mentioned her fanciful theory, but Po wasn't buying it. 'Like you say, it's too much. No.' He thought a moment longer. 'It's much simpler, right?'

'Yeah,' Tess agreed. 'It's a warning. They wanted us to get up close and personal, so that we'd know what would happen to us if we didn't back off. That's what the previous murders were about: designed to strike fear into the hearts of witnesses. It's the same now that we're involved.'

'We should be scared,' Po cautioned.

'Yeah.'

'But you aren't?'

'No.' She was terrified. But more than that she was resolute. 'This has just made me more determined to stop the sons of bitches.'

'OK. Then let's get the hell out of this swamp, and we'll call the cops.'

'Anonymously?'

Despite all his previous encouragement to the contrary, Po dipped his head in agreement. 'I guess it has to be that way for now.'

Hector crouched, watching the reaction of the young woman through a handheld optical fieldscope that magnified her to a point he imagined he could reach out and touch her. He was a hundred yards away, concealed between jagged cypress

stumps, though, so the temptation to grab her was wishful
thinking. There was nothing more he'd enjoy than to get his
hands on her, and to do with her what he'd recently subjected
Crawford Wynne to, but he must deny his base desire. He'd
gone to great effort to display Wynne's corpse so it rang loud
and clear as a warning, and now to simply murder the recipient
of said warning would prove a waste of everything he must
achieve.

His confederates had urged him to slay Wynne and have
done. By all means display him as the warning Alberto desired,
but why do so way out here in the bayous? They had no
concept of irony, Hector believed, and didn't appreciate the
correlation of the victim and location the way he believed
Teresa Grey or her *caballero* companion would. He'd made a
point of Crawford within spitting distance of Crawford Point
because he found the irony meaningful in a way his helpers
would never understand. They didn't find it humorous the way
he did, and had complained at what they deemed an unnecessary workload for what they hoped to achieve. But they hadn't
protested directly to him, preferring to grumble to each other
when they thought he wasn't paying attention. They knew
better than to question him outright, and it were best they heed
that advice if they hoped to continue working for him after
this.

Twice the trio had come to this bog, the first time to deposit
Wynne, and there was no avoiding that trip, because the coordinates were already delivered to Teresa Grey, and therefore
Wynne had to be here to be discovered. This second time
they'd arrived in anticipation of Grey's arrival, and Hector's
companions had muttered under their breath about having to
wade through the cloying muck a second time. In fairness
Hector also hated the mud with a passion, and was thankful
for the waterproofs he'd donned on both occasions, though he
wondered now if wearing garish yellow and orange was a
good idea. He was certain that Grey's companion had spotted
him moments before when he adjusted position. Not that he
feared the tall man, but this was neither the time nor place to
confront him. The man looked at home in this swamp, and
would be at an advantage, and Hector preferred that when the

time came to kill him it would be under circumstances and at a location more suitable.

Besides, luring the duo here was never about trapping them in order to kill them, but about manipulating them, making them dance on the end of the strings he jerked. Murdering the witnesses who'd dare speak against Alberto was designed to engender the greatest reaction from his enemies. Stringing up Wynne's corpse in this grotesque but fascinating fashion, in this equally evocative gothic setting, sang to Hector's dark soul, and he knew its impact would be more shocking as a result. When it came time to kill Grey and her companion he'd repeat the hunt and kill pattern he enjoyed, then display them for all to see, not simply have them gunned down and gutted out here as his helpers had suggested. He'd sent the two fools to wait at their boat, preferring to relish the moment Grey discovered Wynne on his own. Jacky Boy argued that she wasn't even coming and it was a waste of their time: he relied too much on that transponder they'd placed on the couple's car. Hector knew they were coming, and his surety was rewarded sooner than he'd thought. In their urgency, Grey and the *caballero* must have driven through the night in another vehicle. He was glad he'd waited.

Through his scope he studied Grey's reaction, noting the mixed emotions of revulsion, nausea, anger, confusion, and some form of resolution pass through her, and found the latter most satisfying. Grey was proving to be a worthy opponent, and admittedly if she hadn't led him to Wynne he couldn't share this moment with her now. It would be agreeable to snatch her, show her how appreciative he was, before taking her head as a trophy, but it wouldn't be as satisfactory as waiting for an opportunity when he could take his time with her.

He turned the scope on the man, whom he'd learned was called Nicolas Villere. He was positive that those deep blue-green eyes peered directly at him, and a tremor went through him. He recognized something in Villere's gaze that he occasionally saw staring back at him from mirrors. That was the look of a killer if ever he'd seen it, but Hector would never venture that they were alike. That would be like accepting that there was someone to be feared, and the very notion was anathema to him. Hector was the one to be feared, and he would allow no man to take that title from him. He lowered the scope, denying the trickle of unease that had gone through him as their gazes met, telling himself that what he felt was anticipation of their future meeting, and some disappointment that he couldn't take the time to slay Villere now. Hector's presence was demanded elsewhere, and he took some consolation in the fact. Word had reached his ears that Alberto had taken their campaign of terror up a level, and Hector's special skills were required up in Maine. Alberto's lackeys had snatched his latest prize and he couldn't wait to unwrap it, and his satisfaction would be two-fold.

When it was done and his latest victim displayed in a manner that would shock the nation he knew that Alberto's plan would implode. By following this path it guaranteed an end result Alberto had never anticipated: he'd planned on evading justice through the extermination of anyone who could bear testimony against him, but by doing so he'd only ensured his imprisonment. Once news broke of the mutilation of Emma Clancy the lid would be sealed on the box that Alberto was building himself, and Hector's actions would nail it shut.

Alberto had once saved his life, for which Hector swore fealty. But in doing so, the balance of power had shifted between them, with the leader now relegated to follower. Hector was a man of honour, and would uphold his pledge to serve Alberto unswervingly. Ironically, and Hector loved the concept of irony, by following Alberto's commands to the letter, that power shift would swing back in Hector's favour. Once Alberto was caged for life – and Hector didn't expect him to survive long after that – Hector would assume his vacated throne, one that should rightfully have been his all along.

TWENTY-THREE

P o aimed the Mercedes-Benz at New Orleans, picking up Route 90 as the most direct. It meant passing through Morgan City, but it didn't matter because they'd no intention of stopping there. They did however stop prior to reaching the city from which Crawford Wynne had been abducted, choosing a gas station in the small town of Baldwin. There, Po elected to make the call, claiming it would sound more authentic coming from him. Tess stood adjacent to him as he bent to a telephone on the gas station's outer wall and hit 911, listening as he affected the accent he'd used in his youth. He played at being a shocked fisherman who'd stumbled on a corpse out in the bayous, and gave the police dispatcher the exact GPS coordinates where Wynne could be found. He, of course, neglected to give his name, and hung up quickly. 'It's over to them now,' he told Tess, urging her to the SUV. The cops would have identified where the call originated and a car dispatched to their location. They had to be back on the road before the cops showed up.

They were passing Harry P. Williams Memorial Airport before the first responding cruiser zipped by in the opposite direction. Another two cruisers rocketed by as they skirted Bayou Vista, these with their lights flashing. Then they were through Berwick and on the bridge spanning the Atchafalaya River and Morgan City was dead ahead. Route 90 took them straight through town, then snaked above the wetlands bordering Lake Palourde. They passed within spitting distance of where Sower's people had brought violence to the Cottonmouths MCC clubhouse, and Tess tried to avoid thinking about Marnie or the others who'd been struck down but couldn't. She'd viewed a more recent report of the attack on her iPad and learned that Marnie Ross and a male called Henry Thibodaux had both been fatally shot. James le Boeuf, another of the Cottonmouths, was stabbed and in intensive care, but the last man – Tess assumed the one who'd been observing the seated checkers players – had managed to escape unharmed, but as yet was still avoiding the police. He was probably fearful of being targeted by his friends' killers if they discovered his name, and he was right to be. Tess hoped he stayed on the run, because once questioned he'd tell the cops about her and Po's visit only minutes before the shooting began.

It was mainly cross country beyond the outskirts of Morgan City, a landscape of grasses stirred by breezes off the Gulf, still water, and the occasional copse of dead cypress. But as they approached the winding Mississippi, industrial complexes and small conurbations replaced the wild terrain. Po stayed south of the river, avoiding the bridges that would take them into New Orleans, and began looking for somewhere to pull in. He chose a Best Western motel just off the expressway, but first visited an Exxon gas station and refuelled the SUV. He paid cash from his own billfold, and Tess understood he was covering their tracks. She waited in the SUV while he went inside and secured them a room in the motel – she guessed he also paid cash there, and perhaps offered ID that had no connection to him in the real world. Best she didn't ask.

'We need to get cleaned up, then get our heads together,' Po said on his return to the SUV. He'd grabbed some Diet Coke and pre-packed sandwiches from the attached convenience store. 'A little rest and recuperation wouldn't go amiss either.'

After floundering around in the mud, Tess had stripped out of the fisherman's waders and dumped them in the SUV's trunk, but still her clothing was dotted with muck, and her skin and hair was grimy. She'd picked more than one dead bug out of her ears on the drive over. Po had also knocked the clods from his boots, but he was muddy to the knees, and equally as dirty. Thankfully their room was situated in the courtyard and there was no need to trudge through the entrance foyer. It wasn't until Po inserted the key in the lock that she understood he'd only rented one room. It was standard, a small room with a smaller en-suite bathroom. A suspended counter ran along one wall, a small flat-screen TV and a coffee maker the extent of the conveniences on it. There was one small tub chair and one queen-sized bed.

'Are we going to sleep in shifts?' Tess asked, eyeing the bed warily.

'I'll take the floor,' Po said. 'But that also means I get first use of the shower.'

'We couldn't stretch to two rooms?'

'We won't be staying, Tess. It's for a few hours only. And like I said, we need to get our heads together, we can't do that through a separating wall.'

Tess paused another beat at the threshold. She hadn't even brought fresh underwear. She doubted her companion had either. Hell, all her clean stuff was in the room back in Baton Rouge, and she didn't have as much as a toothbrush with her. She wondered if she could find a few necessaries at a nearby store, but there was no way she was going to show her face in the unkempt state she was in. Sighing, she came inside and knocked the door to with her hip. 'Don't use up all the hot water,' she warned.

Po entered the bathroom and she heard the shower go on. She sat on the bed, broke the seal on the bottle of cola and took a deep slug directly from it. She peeled back the wrapper on one of the sandwiches. Po had selected chicken salad, with some kind of dressing masquerading as mayonnaise. It didn't look appetizing, but she needed the calories, so set to nibbling at the seeded roll. She'd little appetite, but after their recent discovery it was no wonder. There was she worrying about having no clean panties and a man had been viciously slaughtered. Crawford Wynne's record had never engendered any pity for him, but even a racist thug like him didn't deserve to die that way.

She managed half of her sandwich, but put the rest aside. She felt horrible. Her clothes chafed in all the wrong places, and where they didn't rub they were sticky. She leaned to peel off her pumps and was horrified to see how gummy with sweat her feet were; even with protective waders the swamp had got in – there was a tidemark of grit around her ankles. She hoped Po wouldn't be long in the bathroom. While she waited, she pulled out the plaits and shook her hair loose. Unidentifiable detritus fell around her. She determinedly avoided the mirror and reminded herself to keep her head lowered when Po finally showed himself.

When he opened the door Tess attempted to avert her gaze. She failed. Po stood with a towel tastefully wrapped about his hips, but that was all he wore. He clutched his discarded clothing in one hand, holding it away from his freshly scrubbed body.

'It's all yours,' he said.

Tess was a second too slow in tearing away her gaze. It had been tracing the muscled contours of his chest, the flat stomach, the first smattering of curly hair around his navel, lingering where it shouldn't. He didn't have the body of a man in his early forties but of someone younger, and more virile. Hell! What did he just say? In her stunned state she misconstrued his words, thinking he was offering himself and not the vacated shower stall. Her face blazed red, and she rushed past him. As she swept by, he pirouetted like a matador, whipping his dirty laundry out of her path, and she caught the fresh scent of soap off him. Inside the bathroom she grabbed at the door to hide her embarrassment, but their eyes met. Po's were amused; Tess's squeezed out an apology. Po only laughed and turned away. She slapped the lock in place.

Swearing under her breath, she pulled out of her clothing, using the rancour she felt at her sticking garments to divert her from her actual self-directed anger. She'd acted like a goddamn fool. What impression had she given Po, watching him like some libidinous slut? Then again, he might have warned her he was about to step practically naked into the room. Had he no shame?

Tess, she told herself harshly, shut up! You're acting like you've never seen a man before. But that was the problem . . . she'd never seen a man like Po before, one who evoked a thrill that was at once visceral and sexual.

She concentrated on showering, then shampooing her hair thoroughly. The soap came from a dispenser on the wall, and wasn't the most luxurious, but under the circumstances it was wonderful. She washed until she thought she had sluiced away the dank smell of swamp. When she looked for her clothing, she was horrified to find it stank of the bog, still damp and creased. But what else could she wear? There wasn't even a gratis bathrobe she could don, only a few towels stacked on a shelf. She dried herself on one, then used it to wrap around her damp hair. The other she wrapped tightly around her, fastening it at her breasts, but only after stepping back into her panties.

She knocked on the door. 'Uh, are you decent out there?'

'Come on out, Tess. I'm not going to bite you.'

She opened the door a crack and saw that Po was seated in the tub chair. Thankfully he'd pulled on his jeans and an undershirt. He'd washed the mud off his jeans and they were damp to the knees. He'd propped his boots and socks on the window ledge, to dry them in the breeze. She retrieved her clothes with a similar idea in mind. Then tentatively she moved out, ensuring the cinched towels stayed in place.

Po had eaten his sandwich, and some of the cola was gone. He nodded at her leftovers. 'Aren't you going to eat that?'

'It's yours if you want it.'

Po reached for the sandwich.

Tess sat on the bed. It should have felt odd, as vulnerable as she was, but it wasn't uncomfortable. She'd barely known Po for a few days and for most of them she'd been irritated by their constant jostle for power. When had things changed between them? As he chewed the remains of her sandwich, he watched her with interest, nothing lascivious in his gaze. His eyes played over her face, not the expanses of bare skin the towels failed to conceal.

They'd already discussed why they'd come direct from Crawford Wynne's corpse to New Orleans, and it had nothing to do with taking in the carnival ambience of Bourbon Street. 'When do you plan on hitting Rutterman Logistics?' Po ventured.

'Later,' she said, without specifics. 'Once we're rested and have clearer heads. I don't know about you, but it feels like someone jammed a stick in my ear and gave my brain a whisk.'

'It's lack of sleep,' he said.

At least Tess had grabbed a few hours last night, but Po had been on the go since early the previous morning. He had to be riding on fumes by now. 'You should get your head down for a few hours,' she suggested. 'I've some notes and stuff to do, and I need to speak with Emma Clancy. Why don't you take the bed, and I'll have the chair?'

Po rubbed his fingers over his face. She glanced at his hands; the ingrained oil hadn't shifted from his knuckles, despite the fresh glow of his scrubbed skin. The staining was a feature of his character, the way the scar on her wrist was of hers. He looked at the bed. 'I'll be OK on the floor, but I'll take one of those pillows.'

'I'm not using the bed. You take it for now.'

He shrugged, OK.

Tess swapped places and he lay down on top of the spread. He crossed his ankles, and placed his folded hands on his stomach. He went out in seconds, snoring faintly. Tess watched him sleep. The deeper lines in his features smoothed out, and he looked ten years younger. Smiling for a reason she couldn't define, Tess went to the window and opened it wider. She hung her clothes to dry, though the damp fecundity of the atmosphere might be a problem. She sat in the tub chair, and typed up a report. Chronological bullet points rather than an elaborately detailed chain of events. When it came to the legal process that was sure to follow, she wanted everything down on record, so that when she was questioned under oath she could answer truthfully but contritely. Questions would be raised concerning her decisions, no less her reluctance to inform the police at the first opportunity, and she wanted to show why she felt it necessary to continue her own investigation, based upon the meagre details she had at hand.

Her cell phone was lying on the shelf. She had received a few notifications from her Facebook and Twitter feeds, some junk emails, and an enquiry from an old girlfriend about her availability for drinks while she was in town – Portland, that was – but Tess ignored them all. There had been no reply from Emma Clancy. What was keeping the woman?

Po still slept soundly. Having no desire to wake him, she took her phone into the bathroom and closed the door. She hit Clancy's number and it rang out to voicemail. Had the woman given her the wrong number? She scrolled through her received calls and found the number for Clancy's office, the one she'd originally used when first contacting Tess with the employment offer. It'd be lunchtime in Portland, but she trusted someone would pick up in the office.

She wasn't disappointed, until she found the voice on the other end wasn't Clancy's. A young woman gave the company name and asked how she could help.

'Hello, this is Teresa Grey. I was hoping to speak with Emma Clancy; is she available, please?'

'Oh, hi, Miss Grey. This is Monica Perry, Emma's assistant. I know we haven't spoken in person, but I was the one who sent you those files.'

'Hi, Monica. Yes, I got those, thank you. Look, I've been trying to get hold of Emma for the past couple of days with no luck; can I check I've got her number right?'

There was a moment's silence that felt as solid as a brick wall to Tess.

When Monica came back on, Tess pictured the young woman bending over her phone, cupping it so that others wouldn't overhear. 'I can assure you it's the correct number, Miss Grey. The problem is that Emma hasn't been answering *any* personal calls. I've had to field dozens from people hoping to speak with her.'

'She must be very busy . . .'

'No. That's not it. She simply isn't replying. She doesn't pick up even when I call her.' Monica made it sound as if she'd been betrayed.

'Wait a minute. She isn't at work?'

'Not since she went out to a meeting yesterday morning. She emailed that she'd be incommunicado and that she'd make personal contact when necessary.'

'Is that normal?'

'No. Back when she was an active investigator she would sometimes work under cover and stay off the grid. But not since she crossed to a managerial position, not while I've worked under her.' Monica halted, steadying her breathing. 'I'm a little concerned. This is *soooo* unlike Emma.'

'What about others in the office? What are their thoughts?'

'They're not overly worried, or at least they're not showing any untoward concern. When I mentioned Emma's silence to Mr Jackson, it was pointed out to me that she'd emailed instructions not to be disturbed. I was more or less told to keep my nose out of her business.'

Perhaps Clancy's boss knew more than he was letting on, and what she was up to, and it wasn't in a personal assistant's remit to know. Having received the email message from Clancy, there was surely nothing to worry about, because it was apparent she was engaged in a task that demanded all her attention. She'd reappear in a day or so. In one way, Clancy's state of incommunicado was a small blessing for Tess. She fully expected that by calling her employer she would immediately be pulled off the job, so this gave her some wiggle space. 'I was going to send Emma a status report,' Tess said. 'But there were a couple of details I wanted to talk through with her first. I'll hold off on doing that for now. When she does get in touch, could you ask her to call me and I'll email the report then?'

'No problem, Miss Grey. Is there anything else I can assist you with?'

There was the text and the voicemail message she'd sent Emma, still unanswered, but they weren't an issue now she'd learned what she'd needed from her brother. 'No. That's all. I was just hoping to speak with Emma in person. When you see her, she might have caught the bad news coming out of Louisiana: I'd prefer to speak with her before she jumps to any snap decisions.'

Immediately Tess regretted her words. News of Crawford Wynne's murder might not feature in the news as far away as Maine, but now that she'd intimated that something bad had happened she fully expected Monica Perry to check it out. With Emma out of the office, someone else would still be on board with the case against Albert Sower. When they discovered their prime witness had been slaughtered it would cause massive repercussions, both for the case and for Tess. Before Monica's interest was further piqued, Tess said goodbye and hung up.

She stood looking at her phone. Clancy's silence was unusual, and worrying. Expecting Tess to call she might have at least left her a message or alternative instructions. Someone in the office had to be picking up Clancy's case threads, and a contact name for Tess would've been helpful. Hell, if she had managed to snag Wynne and drag him back to Maine, there should've been someone available to hand him over to. Should she call Richard Jackson directly?

She tapped the phone against her thigh. It was academic now. Wynne was dead, and the only place he'd be going was the morgue. The only way something good could be salvaged from the mess was if Tess could tie Wynne's death to those working for Sower. Find John Torrance and his pal, and from them discover the identity of the nefarious murderer on Sower's payroll. Do that and it would strengthen, and most likely break, the case against Albert Sower and his criminal organization. Yeah, that was all she need do. Some contingency.

She brought up Alex's cell number and hit the call button. Though she preferred that Alex's involvement remain minimal, there was perhaps some information compiled about Sower's associates he could field her way. Alex's phone rang out, and went to voicemail. Tess frowned at the phone, wondering why he hadn't picked up. A trickle of unease wormed through her: what if Sower's people had discovered that he'd helped her and targeted him? No. Don't even think like that, she told herself. Alex is fine, probably just out on a lunch date with his girlfriend and ignoring his phone. Anyway, you wanted to prove yourself, and calling Alex for help every two minutes isn't strengthening your case. It's down to you, girl, so get to it.

Good advice, except the magnitude of the task hit her, and it was as if her circuits frazzled. She slumped, fatigue washing over more thoroughly than the shower she'd recently stood under. Exiting the bathroom, she placed her cell gently on the shelf. Po's cheek twitched, but that was all. He lay as she'd last seen him, ankles and hands crossed. She couldn't wake him, not after such a short time. She looked at the floor, then at the empty side of the bed. There was no contest for her affections, she decided, and plenty room to hold on to her dignity. She stretched out alongside her reposed partner, ensuring her towels were modestly cinched.

She was asleep in seconds.

TWENTY-FOUR

R utterman Logistics enjoyed a prime location north of the Mississippi, adjacent to an area Po referred to as 'Gatorland'. At first Tess expected swamps, and actual alligators crawling about the streets, ready to snap up straying pets and unchaperoned children, but Po had laughed. 'It's where the moneyed N'Orleanians live,' he explained. 'Y'know, where they tie pastel-coloured sweaters round their necks and have little gators on the front of their shirts?' He was quoting an old joke that was somewhat wasted on her, his eyes twinkling. Under his scrutiny she'd looked away, feeling heat in her chest, but not at a lack of humour.

The logistics depot was one of dozens of freight storage and transport companies on the waterfront. They parked on a slip road opposite, with a view of Rutterman's fenced compound. It was approaching evening, but they'd still some time to wait until the workers left for the day. While they waited Po ticked off a few facts they'd confirmed.

'OK, so we know that John Torrance and his buddy, who have connections to Sower, followed us here from Maine. We know they were the assholes that planted the tracking device on the Chicken Shack, then made the mistake of getting too close and had to ram us like a pair of amateurs to escape. We know that the car they were driving is registered to Rutterman Logistics over there. But that's all we know as fact. Whether they were with the guy that snatched Wynne is still debatable, as well as if they'd anything to do with his murder. We've only a very basic description, from a drunken hobo, that they were the same guys that left the coordinates that led us to Wynne's body.'

'I'm positive it was them,' Tess said. 'Who else could it have been?'

Po didn't offer an alternative. 'They were driving an Audi when they left the card, but I doubt they returned here to

collect it and it was probably sourced up in Baton Rouge after
they dumped the wreck. I'm not certain they'd have any reason
to come here. In fact, now that Wynne's out of the picture, I
fully expect they've flown back to Maine, and the murderer
has gone with them.' He peered across at Rutterman Logistics,
contemplating. 'We could be wasting time here, but we still
have to take a look inside, right?'

'We're here now. We'd be fools not to.'

'The thing I hate most is being made to feel the fool,' Po
remarked. 'Thankfully it doesn't happen too often.'

Tess wished she could say the same.

When she'd wakened on the hotel bed, she'd been snuggled
up on her side, practically nose to nose with Po, his breath
mingling with hers. He was already awake, just lying there,
his turquoise eyes twinkling brightly as he watched her rouse.
Tess had launched off the bed with a squeak, as if she'd caught
him with his hands inside her towel, although he had them
discreetly folded on his stomach. If anything, her hand was
the one that had made an improper crawl across the bed to
drape itself over him while they snoozed, her fingers playing
across his chest in the very moment she'd started awake. God!
How long had he been awake before her? She'd stammered
an apology, while also staring daggers at him.

'You were so sound asleep I didn't like to disturb you,' he'd
said, and it wasn't the counter-apology she'd expected. 'Not
when you seemed so comfortable where you were: nice dream,
was it?' She'd fled to the bathroom, splashing water over her
face, more to be doing something other than light up like a
bonfire before him. Now whenever she looked at him the
twinkle was still there, and she was sure he was enjoying every
second of her lingering embarrassment. She had mixed feelings, because even though she'd been horrified to wake in
such an intimate embrace with Po, she was secretly thrilled
that he hadn't pushed her hand aside and climbed out of bed.
Jeez, there were worse things to wake up to than a good-
looking guy like Nicolas Villere.

No sooner had that thought crossed her mind than she took
an unbidden trip back in time to earlier that morning. Crawford
Wynne's decapitated head, lips stitched, face nibbled by crabs,

lurched out of her memory, and she squirmed in her seat to avoid it.

'You OK, Tess?'

'I'm fine. Don't worry. It's just been a strange day, that's all.'

'Let's hope it ends on a more positive note than earlier,' he said, and she couldn't decide what *exactly* he was referring to. When she looked at him for confirmation his eyes twinkled. Rakish bastard! 'You aren't having second thoughts about breaking in?'

'Second, third, and fourth,' Tess admitted, 'but I'm not going to back out. If we're careful no one will ever know it was us. If we're not careful, well, a breaking and entering charge might be the least of our worries.'

Surprisingly it was Tess's decision to sneak inside Rutterman Logistics. Tying events together might prove difficult when all they had to go on was that some men had crashed a car registered to Rutterman's into theirs. It didn't prove that those same men had planted the coordinates to the murdered man on their car, or that they had anything to do with the abduction and murder of Wynne. If there were any connections between Sower, his hired thugs, the murderer, and Rutterman Logistics then they had to find it. To do that meant employing unconventional means, and there was always the chance of being caught. How could she explain their illegal actions even if they were performed with good intentions? Hell, why worry? They could end up dead in there, so best put any lesser concerns aside until another time.

Finally the workers began to leave, the lights went off behind the barred windows, and a steel shutter was lowered over the entrance doors. An old guy in coveralls ambled out and secured the gates with a solid padlock and chain, before he drove away.

'Locked down as tight as a beaver's butt,' Po announced.

'Empty,' Tess said.

'No. Not empty.' Po adjusted in his seat so he could face her. He pointed at a van sitting in the compound. It had arrived earlier and disgorged two Latino women and a black man. 'There's a cleaning crew still inside. Probably a night watchman as well, who'll let them out when their work's done.'

'Do we wait until the cleaning crew leave?' Tess asked.

'That'd leave only the watchman.'

'Yeah. Easier to control if necessary.'

Po shook his head. 'It's best to enter while the workers are still there. It'll be noisier, and the watchman will be less vigilant while the others are still there.'

'It sounds as if you've done this kind of thing before?'

'I plead the Fifth,' Po said.

'Fair enough, I don't really want to know.'

By the time the sun had dropped below the horizon, and Po shifted wordlessly to get out the car, Tess was shivering with anticipation.

TWENTY-FIVE

K eeping it cupped in her palm, Tess aimed her pen light into the darkened space ahead. Subdued as it was, the beam barely caressed the walls, but there was enough of a gleam to tell the corridor was empty of obstructions. Po followed close on her heels, allowing her to take the lead as he scanned both front and back. Outside, while gaining entry to Rutterman Logistics, he'd taken charge, but was happy now to revert back to his guard role, and that eased her too. Under these circumstances there was no place for jostling for control as they'd done in the past.

They'd come over the perimeter fence, then angled towards the nearest structure, a single-storey addition to the larger main building, where Po boosted Tess up to the roofline. Po scrambled up by his own power, and together they crept along the sloping roof to a window on the upper floor. The window was barred, but they used it as a stepping-stone to get higher. Once on the roof of the building proper, they tiptoed to a skylight, and Po had it open in seconds. Tess didn't comment on the knife he slipped from his boot to lever the catch from the frame, but wondered how long it had been secreted there. There were things about Po she didn't know, and some things she'd best never ask about.

They dropped into an empty storeroom. Using her flashlight, Tess found the place deserted but for cobwebs and dust balls. Po opened the door and craned out. From a distance came the strains of music, thin and reedy, and an incessant whir that Tess identified as a floor-polishing machine. The cleaning crew was being industrious. Po led the way down a narrow stairwell lit by the faint glow of emergency lights. They gained the first floor unchallenged. Hopefully things would stay that way, though the odds were against them.

A cramped corridor allowed access from the stairwell alongside a set of four offices. Down it they moved with Tess cupping the flashlight so that the beam wouldn't carry inside the offices. In one of them the night watchman could be sitting, and an errant flash of light might be enough to alert him.

'Where now?' Po whispered.

'We might as well start here.'

Po remained in the corridor while Tess entered each office in turn. They were the usual cramped spaces found in most workplaces, packed with what you'd expect in a logistics hub. Given weeks, Tess might find something useful, but the workload was too much. Returning to the hall she shook her head in the negative at Po's raised eyebrow.

'Let's see what else there is through here.' He'd discovered an access door to the warehouse. It was a cavernous space, but they didn't have a great view of the floor plan because of the nearest row of shelves, stacked high with boxes. Identical rows of shelves formed serried ranks in the echoing warehouse. The music was louder now, emanating from somewhere on the other side of the building. The polishing machine fell silent. Voices batted back and forth, laden with humour, but distant.

They moved down the aisles, pausing to check boxes. Primarily the goods stored on the shelves were bathroom furniture, appliances, and accessories. They ignored them and moved on. On the next aisle they found household goods, on the next sports equipment. Arriving at aisle four, Tess held up a hand to halt Po in his tracks.

'Will you take a look at that?' she said, breathless.

Po craned past her. The shelves were stacked with boxes containing random electrical devices, from kettles to waffle makers to George Foreman Grills. But Tess had paused at one box on which the tape had been sliced open, and one flap was bent back.

Po shook his head in incredulity. 'I'll be damned. What are the chances of finding these? Remind me to buy a lottery ticket once we're out of here.'

Tess leaned over the open box, using her flashlight to flip aside some shredded packing paper, disclosing a gap where a smaller box had been removed from the larger one. She swept the beam over the others still inside, and a grin of triumph flared on her face. The consignment held the same type of tracking devices that had been fixed to their Honda by Sower's people. Tess would bet her hide that the missing device was the one still in their car up in Baton Rouge. Showing that it was the same device didn't prove who Crawford Wynne's murderer was, but it vindicated Tess's actions in coming here.

Fixed to the box was a semi-opaque document pouch, and when the tracker had been removed, the delivery manifest had been left inside. The manifest listed twelve 'GPS locator devices' and each came with a sequential serial number. She tucked the papers inside her pocket, then took out her phone. She pulled out two of the smaller boxes, arranged them atop the larger one and snapped a series of photographs, ensuring that the serial numbers on the sides of the boxes were clear. It showed that there was a break in the chronological sequence, and Tess was positive that once they returned and retrieved the one from their Honda it would sit numerically between the two.

'Ideally I'd prefer to take the entire box with us,' she whispered, 'but it's best left here.' She carefully repacked the box, pushing down the flap, then took a final photograph to show the box's position on the shelf. While she did so, Po moved away, and before she understood why, a flashlight beam blazed over her.

In her urgency to record the evidence she'd grown snap-happy with her phone. The camera's flash had drawn the attention of the night watchman. Her saving grace was that he had no idea who she was, or why she was standing in the aisle taking pictures. He might've assumed she was one of the cleaning crew: until he played the light over her.

'Hey! What you doing over there?'

Tess was caught red-handed and acted like it. She turned towards him, mouth open in shock, her phone held out to one side as if she was about to drop it and run.

'Don't move!' He'd made her as a stranger. 'What are you doing? You've no right to be here.'

'That's fine,' Tess told him, slipping the incriminating phone into a pocket. 'I'll happily leave.'

'You're going nowhere 'til you give me some answers.'

Behind the bright torch the guard was a silhouette. But Tess could tell he was muscular, tall, and from his voice, young enough that he'd catch her in a foot race. It made no difference; she spun and raced away along the aisle. A bark erupted from the guard, and the slap of his boots announced the chase was on. From elsewhere, voices lifted in query as the workers recognized something was amiss. All Tess needed was for them to join in the chase and she was done for. Where the hell was Po? Just when she needed him most, he'd freaking disappeared!

She hurtled out the end of aisle four, skidded right, and headed for the only exit she knew of. The guard charged round the corner, dogging her trail, one hand reaching for her collar. His fingers snagged the cloth, and only a yank of her shoulders freed her. She almost fell, her soles squeaking harshly on the floor as she fought for balance. The guard snapped a hand on her shoulder. Tess fought for her freedom, wrenching against his grip, lurching low to gain power. But the guard had her now, and he wrestled her to one side, her shoulder slamming the shelves. A tremor went through her, an echo of the one that set the shelves rattling. She half-turned, getting her hands between her and the guard, palms thrusting at his chest. He felt as solid as sun-baked clay. His face was set in triumph as he thrust his right arm up, knocking aside her arms and jamming his elbow under her jaw. He hadn't relinquished his flashlight, and the backwash of its beam flared in her peripheral vision, half-blinding her. Scarlet shapes swarmed, ghost images burned on to her retina.

At first she didn't notice the figure looming behind the guard: it was one of many swirling shapes. In the next instant the figure moved to one side, leaning in close to the man. Was it one of the cleaning crew coming to the guard's assistance?

No.

A sinewy forearm encircled the guard's neck, burying it deep in the crook of an elbow. Tess gagged as the pressure went from her throat, and there was a corresponding gasp from her would-be captor. He was hauled backwards, and as Tess rose up, she saw Po twist so that he was back to back with the guard, his hip jamming into the man's lower spine. Po hauled with his bent arm, pressing back and upwards with his hips, and the guard catapulted over the fulcrum, completing a full somersault and crashing head first to the floor. Such a throw was banned in judo and wrestling competitions, and for obvious reasons; there was no safe way of breaking the fall. Face, chest, knees, and ankles, all took the force, and the guard hollered in agony. His flashlight skidded under the shelves, its beam playing over his contorted features. Po stood over him, fists cocked, but the fight had left the guard: the man rolled into a foetal position, cradling his injuries, moaning in anguish. Po looked at Tess. She looked back.

She looked again at the injured man. He was hurt and needed help. She wondered why she was relieved, and understood that the alternative was it should have been her lying there.

'Let's move,' Po snapped.

Tess ran.

TWENTY-SIX

'You do your thing, Tess. I'll just be over there.' Po waited for Tess's nod before moving.

It was almost an hour since fleeing Rutterman Logistics. Po had parked Pinky's SUV out of sight of the nearby highway, beneath a graffiti-scarred underpass – the underside of a bridge that spanned a tributary of the Mississippi. Trash had accumulated in the angle between hard-packed dirt and concrete, a shopping cart piled high with cans and bottles marking it as a hideout for some homeless person. Broken glass littered the sloping bank, and the reeds poking up from the diseased earth were sickly and stunted. Even the lily pads on the river looked diseased, like purple scabs on the surface. There was a stink off the sluggish water that was acidic and agitated Tess's sinuses. She needed to sneeze, and her roiling stomach contents also demanded some kind of release, but more than anything she absolutely had to pee. While she'd been flooded with adrenalin the desire to empty her bladder hadn't troubled her, but now she was finally calming down it had become a necessity. Po did the gentlemanly thing, walking away to give her some privacy while she peed behind the SUV. After she was finished she walked to the front of the SUV, to get away from the incriminating puddle. She heard the crunch of Po's boots on the gritty earth.

'Done?'

'Much better, thanks. But can we talk about something else?'

'F'sure.' Po waited. 'Maybe we should just get moving again. We can talk while I'm driving.'

Po drove out from beneath the underpass, following a levee road that stood fifteen feet above the riverbank. He was driving by instinct, heading for Baton Rouge. 'So what would you rather talk about, Tess?'

She touched the folded delivery manifest in her pocket. 'We

have evidence that ties Rutterman Logistics to those who rammed our car, the same ones who undoubtedly fitted the tracking device to it. But does it really help? It doesn't prove that they were the same men who abducted Crawford Wynne, and certainly doesn't prove they had any part in his murder. It'd have been much better if we'd found something more damning in that warehouse. Illegal guns, drugs, a cell full of sex slaves. I don't know what I expected to find, but I was hoping for more. Maybe if we'd more time . . .'

'We didn't. So it's not worth getting pissed about again.'

'Again?'

'You're often pissed at me, and for the life of me I can't figure why.'

'I'm not pissed; I'm disappointed.'

'With me?' He frowned.

'No . . .' she said. 'With the lack of evidence.'

'It's good that we got away with what we did. The guard almost got the drop on both of us.'

'You heard him approaching. Why the hell didn't you warn me?'

'It worked out better in the end. If I'd warned you, he'd have probably come running and caught the two of us. I moved away to get round behind him. Luckily when you ran, you went the right way.'

'So I was bait?' Tess shook her head. 'Nice.'

'You were never in any real danger.'

'I wasn't? Having his elbow jammed in my throat wasn't exactly comfortable.'

'He saw you as easy meat and underestimated you. It meant he didn't bother drawing his sidearm. If he had, things might've ended much worse.' Po twiddled with the air-con buttons. 'Anyway, you were just gathering yourself: I trust you'd have handled him even if I hadn't intervened.'

'I ran.' Tess felt a prick of shame. 'In all my years as a deputy I never feared anyone; hell, back then I was the one doing the chasing.'

'It's psychology at work, Tess. You felt you were up to no good, and the natural instinct was to run away when cornered. Under the circumstances anybody would do the same: it's only once you began thinking straight, forced down the natural instincts that your training would've kicked in. I had the benefit of forewarning, and was able to take the initiative sooner.'

'I have to admit that was a crazy move you used. What was it, some kind of jiu-jitsu throw?'

Po frowned in consideration. 'I guess. But I never took martial arts classes, not in the usual sense. You ever heard of Jailhouse Rock?'

'Elvis, right?' She curled up the corner of one lip, mimed a couple of hokey karate chops. 'Uh-hu-hu.'

His mouth pinched in humour and she felt immediately foolish at her antics. 'I guess that's where the name derived, if not the moves,' said Po. 'No, I'm talking about the fighting style formulated by inmates. It's down and dirty, and not pretty to look at. Designed for fighting in close quarters, and it's about life or death. In prison, someone comes at you, well, they're going to stick you with a shank or worse. There's no place for fancy techniques: it's you or it's them, no mercy. Job done.'

'Nasty.'

'Necessary,' he countered, and she was reminded of the scars on his forearms and conceded his point.

'Still, you showed that guard mercy. You could've done him real harm but didn't.'

'It's been a while,' he said, 'I guess I've grown rusty. You'd prefer if I'd hit him with a finishing blow?'

Actually, she believed there was more to his reluctance to permanently maim the guard. For all they knew he was an innocent party, simply performing his duty, and Po had tempered his response with that in mind. He wasn't a hard ass all the time, just some of it.

'A soon as he recovered he'd have reported the incident to his bosses. And once they realize what I was photographing they'll put two and two together. They'll guess it was us, and probably let Sower's people know.'

Po pulled the Mercedes-Benz over at the side of the track. He pulled his phone and hit buttons. 'Yo, Pinky!'

Pinky's reply was a thin whistle to Tess, but Po kept his phone pressed to the side of his head.

'Need you to do something as a matter of urgency, my friend,' said Po. The high-pitched voice raised a decibel or two. 'It won't take you more than an hour. Yeah, sure, I know you already gave up last night for me, but this is urgent. Uh-huh. I need you to go retrieve the tracking device off the Chicken Shack. It's served its purpose, and I'm concerned someone is going to come and take it away before we get back. Trust me, buddy, we need that thing in our hands. I don't want you getting hurt, but if anyone's there when you arrive and they try to take it, you don't let them. You get me?' Po laughed at Pinky's response. 'Just do what you have to do, OK?'

'That was good thinking, Po,' Tess said when he'd cancelled the call. 'The evidence we got at Rutterman's is worthless without the tracking device. Of course, they could always claim we stole the tracker from the box when we broke into their warehouse. Their word against ours. Considering we were conducting an illegal search I guess I know whose side a jury would take.'

'We've no reason to set them up, but, yeah, you're probably right.' Po got the SUV moving again. 'But let's go get that tracker from Pinky. Who knows, maybe those guys weren't too careful when they placed it. I don't recall Blondie wearing gloves when we caught him in the act; we might get a finger-print or DNA or something.' He looked hopefully at her, Tess being the expert. 'You've contacts for that kind of stuff, haven't you?'

'Once we're back in Maine, I'll get Emma Clancy's office on the case.' Supposing that Clancy had come out of hiding, of course. There was something troubling about Clancy's disap-pearing act, and this wasn't the first time she'd wondered about the unusual circumstances behind it: Tess was starting to believe something was wrong with the entire scenario.

'I promised I was driving back, but I guess there's a matter of urgency to all this now.' Po exhaled deeply.

'Not looking forward to the flight, huh?'

'Nope,' he said. 'But I'll persevere.'

His decision brought a smile to her. He was still in body-guard role, not about to give in to his stubborn fear of flying. She was glad, because after everything she'd said to the contrary she wouldn't feel whole without him by her side if taking the trip home alone. Hell, she needed him. And not just for the calm-under-fire-attitude he'd shown when escaping Rutterman Logistics – when she'd have run up two flights of stairs seeking the skylight exit, he'd grabbed her by an elbow, guided her to a fire exit and booted the door open, ushered her to the front gate, and boosted her over. No, there was more to it than that. He'd followed her to Louisiana as an employee, but the dynamic of their relationship had shifted. Each had a stake in this case; each had a desire to see it through to a satisfying conclusion. They actually were partners now, she realized. She sneaked a glance his way; he was watching the road ahead with intensity. He must have sensed her observation because he snapped his head towards her, his eyes reflecting the dashboard lights. His mouth bowed in humour, or was it affection? She was immediately reminded of waking to that same scrutiny earlier, and felt a tremor go through her. This time it was an enjoyable sensation.

TWENTY-SEVEN

Tess went through her Baton Rouge hotel room as wild as a dervish, snatching up her things, packing away her laundry, throwing the paperwork off the desk into a carry bag. There was no rhyme or reason to her method, and she simply dumped everything in, haphazard and messy, keen to be off. Some of the papers spilled across the floor in a mini-landslide, and she crouched, puffing and huffing to draw them back to hand. More speed less haste, she told herself. Why hadn't she travelled as light as Po had? What he owned, he had with him in his knapsack, so there was no need for him to visit his room. He was downstairs, in the lot, prepping their car while waiting for Pinky. His friend had been and gone earlier, and had successfully retrieved the tracking device off the Honda, promising to return and hand it over once they got back.

Ready to go, Tess took one last lingering look around the room. She could guarantee she'd missed something. Her toiletry kit! She headed into the small bathroom, snatching up her toothbrush, wash kit, and other feminine necessities, and pushing them into a drawstring bag. OK, now it really was time to go. They'd booked a 06:20 United Airlines flight out of Louis Armstrong International to Newark, with a connecting flight to Portland, Maine. They'd plenty of time to make departure, yet Tess still felt rushed by ill-restrained urgency. Not only did she wish to get home, but also since their escape from Rutterman Logistics she'd felt like an outlaw, concerned that they'd been identified as violent burglars and were now being hunted by the police. Hell, it felt odd being on the wrong side of the law. It had only been a few hours and the paranoia was eating at her.

She headed downstairs. The same night manager as last night was on duty. As she approached, he lifted his hawkish nose in greeting, his teeth flashing white against his dusky skin.

'Good evening,' said Tess, humping her case close to the counter.

'Evening, ma'am.'

She set hers and Po's door keys down. 'I'd like to check out. Two rooms; numbers twenty-eight and thirty, please.'

'I hope everything was to your satisfaction, uh, Miss Grey?' he said, after a quick glance at his computer screen to check her name.

'Everything was lovely,' she said. They were checking out early, and at an unusual hour, and the manager was wondering why. Let him wonder.

He tapped and rattled at his keyboard, made polite noises about how – unfortunately – she'd be charged for the remainder of the night on both rooms, to which Tess agreed it was fine. She'd already registered Clancy's credit-card details, and the bill was cleared with no fuss. Despite the extra constraints on her time she turned down the offer to have her receipt emailed to her, and asked instead for a printed copy. The man obliged, and she headed for the exit, tugging along her unbalanced suitcase. It snagged in the doorway, and she had to tug it loose, and practically spilled out from under the entrance canopy onto the parking lot.

Three faces turned towards her, and only one of them she recognized.

A large pickup truck stood with its engine idling a few yards from the trio, its doors wide, signifying the speed at which the two strangers had jumped out to confront Po.

Instinctively Tess pranced away, heading not for the Honda alongside which Po and his two admirers stood, but for Pinky's SUV parked on the other side of the lot. She averted her face, hauling on the case as if she were simply another harried traveller on her way to parts unknown. The two men standing too close to Po for comfort watched her out the corners of their eyes, aware of a potential witness, but more wary of losing sight of their captive. Tess played the part of rushed and frustrated with almost natural results; equally she hid her fear. She rattled the suitcase along, then deliberately allowed the handle to snatch out of her hands, and she uttered a howl of irritation. The suitcase toppled, and the men again glanced at her, annoyed at her unwelcome intrusion. Sadly neither of them lowered the weapons they aimed at Po's belly.

It didn't matter, because as Tess leaned down, pretending to right her case, she dipped her hand into her purse and stood again. Her Glock was hidden alongside her thigh as she turned, but only until she snatched it up. 'Police!' she hollered, the gun in a two-handed grip, her knees flexing and her feet set. 'Lower your weapons. Now!'

She didn't expect them to comply, and her ruse would backfire if it turned out *they* were police, but she didn't think that was the case. She moved forward quickly, so that she'd more chance of getting off a shot that would actually hit something. The two men gawped at her, but held on to their guns. Thankfully they were now aimed low, towards the floor, and Po wasn't in immediate danger of being gut shot.

'Drop your weapons!' Tess yelled again, and by now she'd crossed half the lot.

Instead, the two men raised their firearms, coming up to meet hers. Outnumbered, outgunned, Tess knew it was now or never. Po threw himself into the nearest man, ramming him off his feet and into his pal. Both men staggered, and one of them discharged his gun. Tess felt the snap of the round pass close by, and she flinched in response. Remarkably there was no corresponding bang; the gun was suppressed. Cops didn't use silenced weapons: assassins did. She almost returned fire.

However, Po hooked a heel around the nearest man's knee, continued forcing him backwards, and all three went down in a heap on the asphalt. Po's fists were a blur as he pounded each man in turn, but he was one against two and they were still armed. Any second and the situation could turn deadly. Tess rushed in just as one of the men pulled away and got a knee under him. His gun was swinging towards Po's head when Tess's foot clattered against his wrist. The bullet went skyward, the gun spinning away. Tess backhanded her Glock, and felt the solid thunk of metal against bone. Only when the man went over on his butt, hands cradling his face, did she know where she'd struck. She didn't stop to admire her handiwork; she threaded her fingers through the man's hair, and rolled her fingers into a fist, yanking him over backwards. She jammed the muzzle of her gun in his throat, snarling at him to hold it.

She searched the tangle of limbs opposite them, saw Po heave up and roll on top of his opponent, straddling his chest. His left hand grasped the man's gun hand, forcing it against the ground. His right hand went to his boot, and a flash of silver arced towards the man's throat. Tess squinted, anticipating a horrifying jet of blood.

'You son of a bitch,' Po snarled, as he repeatedly slammed the man's gun arm on the ground. 'Let it go.'

When Tess next checked, the gun was out of the man's hand, four or five feet distant, and the man craned to avoid the needle tip of Po's knife, which was in the hollow under his left ear. Thankfully his throat wasn't an open geyser.

'One more move and you'll be brain dead,' Po promised. He snapped a glance at Tess, and saw that she had her captive under control, fully submissive. The man she kneeled on bled profusely from a gash in his cheek. Po nodded. 'Can you get that asshole to his feet?' he asked. 'If he tries anything, shoot the fucker in the face.'

'Oh, don't you worry. I've got him.' Tess switched her attention to the injured man and snarled through her clenched teeth, 'Are you going to give me any trouble?'

'Jesus, bitch, you broke my face already.'

'Trust me, things could get much worse. Just try calling me *bitch* again and I'll show you how much. Now sit up.' Tess jammed her gun against the side of the man's neck, hauling him to a seated position by his hair. She switched round behind him, transferred the gun to the nape of his neck, and the man struggled to standing. He was unsteady on his feet. Tess pushed him up against the parked truck, kicked his feet apart.

Po also had his man standing. His knife had disappeared, and in its place Po had drawn his gun. He prodded the guy over, and he too ended up with his chest forced against the truck, his feet splayed wide. Po checked him for other weapons but came up empty.

Sower's people? Tess mouthed the question to Po, but he

shook his head. He didn't offer an explanation, but it was unnecessary. There was a more obvious answer.

'So you thought you could claim the bounty on me, eh?' Po said, his voice amiable now. He directed it at his captive, because Tess's guy was busy moaning about his bleeding face.

These guys weren't members of the Chatard family as Tess assumed, just guys hoping to claim the reward on Po's head.

'We were told you were in town; we were told to make sure you left.' The man dipped his head; he'd obviously failed his instructions. 'We aren't in the business of killing.'

'Silencers on your handguns tell a different story,' Po said.

'If we were going to shoot you, we would've done it from the truck. We didn't have to speak to you first.'

The man had a point, and was possibly telling the truth. Perhaps the suppressors on their guns were props to add menace to their warning. By the look of things, Po had come to the same conclusion as Tess. She was about to mention that they were leaving anyway, that they'd wasted their time and taken a beating for nothing. She kept her mouth shut. This was Po's business.

'The Chatards thought a couple of bums waving guns would make me run away?' Po snapped out a laugh of derision. 'How did you think this was going to end: with me making polite goodbyes?'

'We hoped you'd see sense,' said the man glumly.

'Sense never comes at the end of a gun,' Po told him. 'Or does it?' He pushed his weapon under the man's ribs, digging into a kidney. The would-be tough guy squirmed in fear.

Tess held her breath.

But Po lowered the gun. He stepped away. 'Turn around.'

The man complied, but raised his empty hands to his shoulders. He had a thick monobrow, beetled in a frown.

'Put those down, will you?' Po grunted, meaning the hands. He looked at Tess, and she took the hint. She unwrapped her fingers from her prisoner's hair, taking a few steps back. Her guy was slower to turn and he did so cupping his face. His hair stood wildly where she'd tangled her fingers, and his eyes were red-rimmed, almost bulging out their sockets. She'd bet that all he was interested in was chugging down a handful of painkillers at his first opportunity.

Po looked at the ground, shook his head wearily. 'Here's what's going to happen. We're leaving, but so are you. You go back and tell the Chatards whatever you want about what went down here. Save face: tell them you chased me off, claim your reward, I don't care.' His face grew serious. 'But tell them this. I didn't come here for them. Not this time. But I will come again.'

His delivery was calm, controlled, spoken without rancour. Yet Tess felt a wedge of ice push through her chest at the weight of his promise. The faces of the two thugs told her they'd received the message loud and clear.

Po wagged the gun towards the truck. 'Git. And don't come against me again. I'm not usually the forgiving type.'

The bleeding man looked to his friend for instruction.

'Get in the truck,' said the man, and the bleeder shambled off. He glanced for where their guns lay.

'Leave them,' Po ordered.

An engine rumbled.

'Somebody's coming,' Tess warned Po.

He was unconcerned.

He thumbed towards the truck. 'Git.'

The guy nodded sullenly, but moved for the driver's door. His bleeding pal had already clambered inside and was resting his head in his hands. Tess went and kicked the dropped weapons towards Po, while shoving her Glock in her purse. He didn't retrieve them, just stood and waited while a Dodge panel van pulled into the lot. Tess recognized Pinky in the passenger seat, a younger, slimmer black guy driving. They both eyed the truck, faces grimly set. There was no eye contact from the two in the truck. It pulled away, the thick rubber tyres whistling on the asphalt as it made a wide turn towards the exit ramp.

'What was with Bert and Ernie?' Pinky enquired after he'd got out of the van. Tess smiled at the description, fondly recalling the Muppet characters from *Sesame Street*.

'Messenger boys,' Po explained. 'No sweat.'

'Damn, it looks like I missed all the fun, me.'

'You didn't miss much. I had everything under control.' Po flicked a veiled smile at Tess. Hell, if she hadn't intervened, God knew how things would have turned out. She didn't comment; let him enjoy his macho moment. Pinky beamed a smile. He was impressed, Po still his object of worship.

'The Chatards send them?' Pinky asked.

Po only rocked his head.

'Something needs to be done about them,' Pinky said. 'You want me to send my boys down to New Iberia?'

Po shook his head. 'Their beef is with me, old friend. I'll deal with the Chatards when the time is right.'

Pinky shrugged his rounded shoulders. 'You know you just have to say the word and the Chatards are out of your hair, Nicolas.'

Po rested his hand on Pinky's arm. No words necessary.

'I'm glad I got to see you before you left,' Pinky said, and his eyes were glassy. He leaned in and hugged Po. Po returned the embrace, unashamed at the big guy sniffing alongside his ear. Po slapped Pinky's back and they parted. 'Promise not to leave it as long in future, you,' Pinky scolded.

'I promise.'

'Good.' Pinky turned to Tess, opening his arms. 'And you, my pretty Tess, you are always welcome in Baton Rouge. Come here, girl.'

Tess was engulfed by his warm weight, and Pinky even lifted her off her feet a few inches. His stick arms *were* stronger than they looked. He laid a smacker of a kiss on her cheek before setting her down. 'Maybe next time you can come visit alone,' Pinky offered with a wink and nod for Po. 'I told you, for a woman like you, pretty Tess, I'd change my ways for good.'

'I'll miss you, Pinky,' Tess said, and she meant it.

Po approached; he'd collected the discarded guns. 'Going away present for you, Pinky. You can use these, yeah?'

Pinky waved at the van driver. 'DeAndre, fetch me that bag, you.'

The driver got out the van, toting a thick orange sack. Tess recognized it as an anti-ballistic 'safe bag' from her law-enforcement days. By the clean cut of him, she wondered if

DeAndre was a cop moonlighting as Pinky's driver. She didn't ask and he didn't say: probably best that way. He held the bag open and Po dropped the liberated guns inside. Po then unfastened his shoulder rig and dropped it in too. He dipped his boot, came out with his hidden blade. He turned it over in his palm, shrugged and dropped it inside. 'Call that a bonus.'

Shoving it in the bag, Tess was relieved to be rid of her Glock, but had to admit that the weight in her purse had grown familiar. Although she had loathed carrying the illegal weapon it had tipped the scales in their favour minutes earlier. Now it was gone, she didn't hate it as much.

Pinky took the liberated transponder from his pocket. He'd wrapped it in a plastic bag. He passed it to Tess. 'You'll want this.'

'You'll want these too.' Po handed over the keys of the Mercedes-Benz. 'So it's back to the Chicken Shack,' he said ruefully. The Honda was bashed up. 'I guess we're going to lose your deposit,' he aimed at Tess.

'It's on Emma Clancy's ticket.' Tess had no idea how damning her next flippant statement was. 'I'm sure she's got more to worry about than paying the excess on an insurance policy.'

TWENTY-EIGHT

Their flight to Newark, New Jersey, went without a hitch. Po took the journey in his stride, not so uptight this time, but silently relieved that the airplane hadn't plummeted to earth when they finally touched down. There was an hour or more to kill before their connecting flight, but they had to change terminals so it wasn't all time they could spend lounging around. Once they'd caught the sky train to their connecting terminal, Po made his excuses and went outside to top up his nicotine levels.

'You'll have to pass back through security again,' Tess warned him. 'Try not to miss the flight.'

'If I miss it, I won't be crying, Tess. I can drive from here in a few hours. I'm seriously tempted to do just that, I'm just put off by the fact the rental companies will only have goddamn granny cars available again. If I had to choose between a short hop on a plane or drive all that way in another minivan, the plane wins out.' He winked at her. 'Don't worry, I won't be late.'

Tess headed off to find food, got coffee and donuts, but took them with her to the boarding gate. According to the flight information, their plane was on time. She sat on a seat against the wall, surrounded by weary travellers whose heads were buried in a variety of electronic gadgets, only periodically glancing up to check the boarding info. Tess had kept her nose equally buried in her iPad on the way over, checking over her typed notes, and wondering how much she should add to them concerning what had recently occurred. No mention would be made of what happened with the two guys last night, or their goodbyes and exchange of gifts with Pinky Leclerc. She had been tempted to leave out their breaking and entering of Rutterman Logistics, but if they were going to use the tracking device and the accompanying proof that it originated from a box on a shelf at Rutterman's there was nothing

for it. Of course, little would be alluded to concerning Po's
Jailhouse Rock moment with the guard: the assault had obviously gone unreported, because their identities hadn't raised
as much as an eyebrow while checking in for their flight out
of New Orleans. That surprised her; she had expected to answer
difficult questions from the local PD before they were allowed
to leave Louisiana, but the crime going unreported made sense
when she thought about it. Rutterman Logistics had much to
hide, more than it was worth mentioning a breaking and entry
to the local authorities for. She would bet that the box of
trackers and the corresponding paperwork had been spirited
away from the premises by now, and was glad she'd taken
photographs for her records. She didn't doubt that word of
their escape had reached the ears of Sower's group by now,
and they could expect some sort of retaliation from that, but
that was OK, because Sower's killer must have known all
along that they'd ignore the warning he'd made of Crawford
Wynne. Hell, Tess was beginning to suspect that it wasn't so
much a warning as a prompt that would lead to a full-blown
confrontation. Wynne's death had served more than initially
believed: Sower's killer wasn't only hoping to strike fear into
his opponents; he was stepping up the conflict between them
and Sower's gang, his way of declaring war. It was an insane
agenda the killer had set, and she had to wonder at its end
game.

The gate opened and arriving passengers trickled through.
Their plane had landed. She began watching for Po, but he
was a no show. 'C'mon, Po. Don't you dare make me miss
this flight.'

She'd already resolved herself to the idea: it was imperative
that she returned to Maine, but if Po was late to the gate, she
wasn't boarding the plane. They could wait for the next, or
she'd join him in the long drive home, whatever, but she wasn't
completing the next leg alone. Although this had originated
as her task, Po an employee drafted in to help, their dynamic
was now definitely a partnership: she couldn't imagine arriving
home in Maine without Po alongside her. His presence at her
side when finally she delivered her report to Emma Clancy
would definitely help. Clancy would go ballistic on hearing

of their decision to complete their own investigation, and to keep pertinent information back from the Louisiana law-enforcement agencies in order to do that. Perhaps the two of them could convince her it was the right thing to do. Clancy had engaged her services because she wasn't confident that a private investigator local to Louisiana was giving value for money, well Tess could argue that Clancy was getting two for the price of one, and she couldn't deny they had gone beyond what was expected of them.

She took out her cell, recalling she'd turned it off for the duration of the flight. Hopefully Clancy had made contact.

Nope. Her messages were nil. It wasn't right.

She rang Clancy's personal number, but it went directly to voicemail. 'Hi, Emma, Tess Grey checking in. Just to let you know I'm at Newark, on the way back to Maine. Should be on the ground in a couple hours and I'll try you again.' She considered adding that Clancy's silence was worrying, and please, if she could, at least let her know everything was OK, but was reluctant.

She ended the call, and rang the office number instead. When that call went to voicemail too she frowned at her phone. She rejected the instruction to leave a message, and redialled, waited, but got the same automated voice again. She checked the time. It was within office hours, so why wasn't anybody answering the phone? She hit Alex's number, but her brother's phone rang out as well. What was going on up there? First Clancy and now Alex had gone silent on her, and considering they were her direct contacts in Maine, she didn't like what that suggested.

Frustrated, and now worried, she hung up, deciding to Google an alternative number for Clancy's office, but around her there was a stir of motion and she saw her fellow travellers readying for action. Boarding was about to begin. She put away her cell, staring intently towards the walkway down which she hoped Po would hurry, now more eager than anything to get home.

She was surprised when he stepped out of a nearby gents' washroom, nodding at her. She'd missed his arrival at the gate while concentrating on her cell. He moved towards her, his bag slung from his shoulder, while he dry-washed his hands. Despite washing, she still caught a waft of smoke from him, though the sweeter aroma of soap leavened it. It didn't bother her; in fact, his scent had grown familiar these past few days, and was welcome. 'Thought I'd best freshen up after having a cigarette,' he said by way of explanation. 'This us; ready to go?'

She'd held on to their boarding passes. She handed over his, waved hers towards the doors by way of instruction. 'We'll be up and away in no time.'

'I guess the sooner we're up the sooner we touch down again. Let's do this, then.' He led the way, joining the queue filtering past the flight crew. Standing behind him, Tess spotted the cold sweat on the back of his neck. Flying wasn't easy for Po, and the idea that he was doing this for her wasn't lost on Tess. She wanted to hug him, but now wasn't the time or place. They filed aboard, this time on to a twin-prop, and found their seats. They sat side by side, the smaller craft coming with fewer seats, rows of two on one side, a single corresponding seat across the gangway. Taxiing out to the runway, the plane joined the queue of aircraft wending their way up and down the tarmac, awaiting their take-off window, and in no time they sailed up into the blue. As Po gripped the arms of his chair, fingers digging into the plastic, Tess placed her hand on his, offering a gentle squeeze of support. Before they levelled out, her hand was in his and their fingers were entwined. Later when Tess became conscious of their intimacy, she stole a glance over at him, expecting the amused twinkling of his eyes. But Po was sitting with his head back, eyes closed, and this time he wasn't enduring: a smile smoothed the lines in his face.

TWENTY-NINE

Tess lived on Cumberland Avenue, within a stone's throw of the Portland Public Library, assuming of course her throwing hand wasn't damaged and the stone small enough to skip along the pavement the last hundred yards or so. Her apartment was on the upper floor of two storeys, over a curio shop that closed by six every evening. Private access to her rooms was gained by a flight of wooden steps alongside the building. She'd lived there since her acrimonious split with Jim Neely, requiring less space. If she desired more room, Deering Oaks Park was only a short stroll away, and she often jogged along the shore of the pond when feeling energetic. There'd be no jogging today, she was worn out, and the desire to collapse on her own bed was almost overpowering. She'd moved to Cumberland Avenue for a couple of reasons – the first being the small apartment was affordable on her reduced income, but primarily because the library was where she conducted much of her research, her office away from home. There were plenty of local amenities, and nearby a plethora of high-end boutiques, restaurants, and coffee shops could be had on Congress Street, and adjoining roads. Close by was the neurological-rehab centre in which she'd spent many hours while recovering from her debilitating injury: recently she'd halved the frequency of visits, but had an appointment early next week.

She'd only been away a few days, but the atmosphere in her apartment felt flat, abandoned, deserted. It smelled different. The air was still and chilly to a point that she shivered. Standing in her living room, her bags and suitcase at her sides, she made a slow perusal of her home, her gaze skirting over all her familiar belongings, and felt an odd sense of dislocation, as if she didn't belong. Wasn't she relieved to be home? Yes. In a way she was. But there was also a discomfort about being back she couldn't quite put her finger on. It took a moment before she realized the tangible weight pressing against her heart was loneliness. When she first split with Jim, the new freedom had been welcome, and surrounding herself with all her favourite items had been a pleasure. But now it was as if she was missing out on something, by not having a companion at her side to enjoy them with her.

Hell! It was less than half an hour since she'd parted ways with Po, and already she was missing the irascible lout.

'Get a grip, Tess,' she said aloud. 'You're meeting him again in a few hours.'

Her words sounded invasive in the small space, and she would swear that they reverberated back at her from the walls, set the light bulb swaying in the ceiling rose. Nonsense, but she felt the room had been sealed as tight as a mausoleum these past few days and her breathy exclamation had stirred the atmosphere to a frustrated buzz. She ran her fingers through her hair. It felt gritty and in dire need of a wash. It coalesced her thoughts. It's why she'd returned home, because she was desperate to bathe, and to get into some fresh clothes. She was positive she still stank like a swamp.

Memories of slogging through the ochre-tinged mud flooded her, and unbidden Crawford Wynne's mutilated corpse. *That is what Sower does to witnesses*, she reminded herself.

She swore under her breath, banishing any insecurities from mind. For too long she'd allowed doubt to control her. That snow-filled night when the innocent store clerk died had been a personal shortcoming that she'd carried since, and it was more debilitating than her physical injury. When the robber's blade cut at her wrist, and her gun had gone off, plunging a bullet through the counter and into the clerk, part of her had perished along with him. As much as her wound hurt, it was nothing to the pain searing her heart when she discovered she was the slayer of an innocent man. She'd told herself it was an unfortunate accident, not her fault but that of the thug trying to cut an escape route through her, but she couldn't expunge the guilt. She'd fought to keep her job, but inside she knew that it was a battle she couldn't win, one perhaps she didn't really want to. How could she ever perform her duty again, knowing that the fear of consequences would ever stay her hand? Despite railing against the notion, she'd been secretly relieved when forced out of her job. Yet now, in hindsight, those feelings were displaced. When she'd walked out of the hotel last night and found Po terrorized by armed men she hadn't paused in going to his assistance. She'd selflessly put her safety before his, and though she hadn't known it at the time, something inside her had changed – for the better.

Albert Sower was to be feared; being no less dangerous while directing murder from his prison cell than if he was out on the streets. His faceless killer was to be feared also. Yet her internal warning fell on deaf ears. In fact, after everything she'd learned of Sower and seen done on his behalf, it made her more determined to see the bastard imprisoned for a very long time, preferably until he expelled his final breath. For his malicious henchman, she hoped his punishment was instant and more agonizing than languishing for decades in a cell. A cold shiver assailed her again, but this one more of anticipation of the inevitable.

But despite the certainty of the future, she locked the door. Clearly she'd been spied on from Maine to Louisiana, and possibly back again. If Sower's people didn't know beforehand, they would've learned her home address by now, and sooner or later they'd come looking for her.

Tess moved through her apartment, switching on lights, adjusting the dial on her heating, turning the temperature up a few notches. She'd only been in the balmy south a few days, and despite bemoaning the sticky heat some acclimatization must have occurred. Next she hit the bathroom, and turned on the shower, but had second thoughts. She began to fill the tub instead: a luxury she was owed.

Bathed, pampered, and perfumed, she left her bags where they rested, planning on leaving her apartment, and getting back inside her Prius for the short drive across town to Charley's auto shop. As she approached the door, knuckles rapping on the frame halted her. Her first thought: Sower's people had come for her sooner than expected. She crouched instinctively, and began looking for a weapon.

'Tess? Tess? You home?' The rapid knocking came again.

She recognized Alex's voice, and relief flooded her. But

why the urgency? After landing, she'd sent a text to let him know she was on her way home, and demanding that he let her know he was OK, but hadn't expected an immediate visit.

Opening the door she found Alex leaning with one shoulder against the frame, as if he lacked the strength to stand. His Portland Police Department uniform was rumpled, and his features hollowed out with concern. Like hers his hair was fair, but sweat darkened it. His forehead was dotted with perspiration. Beneath the glow of the porch lights pale streamers of steam rose off him. He smiled when he saw her, but it was one of desperate thanks. He said, 'Oh, thank God.'

Tess pulled him inside, and he hugged her.

'I've tried calling you,' she said tersely as they broke their embrace. 'You had me worried when you didn't reply. I thought . . .' Should she admit to fearing that Sower's people had got to him?

'I've been, uh, busy,' he said, also reticent about admitting something. He put a hand over his face and shuddered out a moan.

'What's wrong? What has happened?' Panic gripped her, and her first concern was for family. 'It isn't Mom?'

'No. No. Mom's fine.' He sagged noticeably. 'It's someone else.'

'Who? What are you talking about, Alex?'

'Emma,' he said, and the familiarity in which he mentioned the name surprised her.

'Emma Clancy? You know Emma?' She experienced a shifting sensation inside her chest. 'Oh, don't tell me . . .'

It all made sense now. She remembered that first opening statement of Emma's, how Tess had 'come highly recommended', but how she wouldn't divulge who had made the recommendation. At the time Tess thought Clancy was being coy about her source, and now she understood why.

'You've been seeing Emma Clancy?' she asked, to make certain that she hadn't misread anything. 'The DA's investigator who I just happen to work for? Jesus Christ, Alex! Emma has a husband! Are you trying to wreck her marriage?'

'She's already getting divorced,' he said lamely. 'It's why

we had to keep our relationship secret: their divorce is based on her husband's adultery; it wouldn't look good if it came out she was also having an affair. Anyway, divorce proceedings were underway before we met . . .'

'Yeah? So how long has this been going on? Oh, I see now . . . it was you that recommended me to—' The words caught in her throat, as she didn't know how to react. She had mixed feelings – insulted that she'd only got the job because Mrs Clancy's illicit beau had whispered Tess's name into her ear, but also thankful to Alex that he'd given her the desperately needed jumpstart to her career. She was angered by the first, but a wash of endearment went through her for the second. She shook her head at him.

'Tess, you don't know what you've got yourself tangled up in,' he said, and she watched his face tremble with regret, 'what *I've* got you tangled up in. Shit.' Alex stepped away, shoving back his mussed hair. When he wiped his palms on his thighs his trousers held moist streaks. He glanced at her TV, but it was inert. 'You haven't caught the news since you got back?'

Pointlessly, Tess also glanced at the dead TV screen. 'No. I haven't had the chance. What's going on, Alex?'

'Emma's missing. It's why I've been unable to answer your calls; I've been too busy looking for her. I was hoping you might know—'

Tess stopped him in his tracks. 'I haven't once been in contact with her. Damn it, I knew something was wrong!' She thought about the brief telephone conversation when Monica Perry had expressed her own concern over Emma's silence. 'Surely Emma's boss suspected she was in danger; why didn't he do something sooner?'

'That's a question being asked by Portland PD, but we might not get a straight answer soon.'

'Why not?'

He stared at the floor. 'You should come with me now.'

'Where to?'

'Just come on, we've wasted enough time. Grab your jacket. It's best you see for yourself.' Alex was already rushing to the door.

'I was about to go and meet Po,' she said.

'Call him. Tell him to meet us.'

'Where?'

'Baxter Boulevard,' he said. 'Tell him to come to the attorney's office near Belmeade Park.'

THIRTY

The breeze gusting inland from Black Cove pushed the smoke over Portland, but where she stood alongside Alex's PPD cruiser it didn't do much to shift the acrid bonfire stench impregnating the air. The fire crews had dampened down the fire, but had been too late to save the building itself. The entire structure containing the District Attorney's Office and the adjoining law firm premises where Emma Clancy worked was a blackened, crumbling husk, the windows blown out, the roof caved in. Singed timbers jutted skyward, and fallen masonry littered the ground. Blackened furniture lay in piles where the firefighters had dragged it outside so it didn't feed the conflagration. Runnels of filthy water ran into the kerb, carrying the detritus of ash and cinder. The stink of molten plastic, and something worse, was almost poisonous. The evening was filled with strobing lights, competing flashes from the emergency vehicles and the cameras of journalists who'd descended on the scene en masse. Emergency workers moved back and forward, and a line of police officers and some of Tess's old work colleagues from the Sheriff's Department assisted in keeping back the crowd of onlookers. Having driven her to the fire, Alex had gone to assist, though Tess fully expected he'd rather continue searching for Emma.

From what her brother told her, the fire had started hours ago, following a small explosion on the first floor. It was suspected that accelerants must have been present, because the fire spread at an exponential rate, engulfing the building in no time. Two people had perished in the initial explosion, another three receiving severe burns, but most of the other staff and civilian visitors made it outside before the building began collapsing in on them. Nobody was certain how many others might still be inside, and now that the fire had been put out, the firefighters were concentrating their search for victims. Tess watched the crew work their way inside, in full breathing apparatus, and armed with tools and even a thermal camera. From their body language, none among them expected to find any survivors, and Tess wasn't hopeful either. Only one EMT vehicle sat on standby, but if anyone was carried from that hellish place, she thought it'd be beyond the paramedics' abilities to bring them back to life.

Counting back the hours, it was now apparent why Tess received no answer when she'd called Clancy's office while waiting her departure from Newark. She'd been calling while the fire was consuming the structure, so little wonder nobody had picked up. She hoped that Monica Perry had made it out unscathed, then immediately felt guilty that she hadn't extended the same wish to the as yet unnamed victims. That Emma Clancy was AWOL at the time of the explosion came with mixed emotions. Partly, she was relieved Emma had escaped injury, but it made Tess more concerned for her employer. Even off on some undercover venture, she expected that Emma would have broken silence after this tragedy. Unless she'd no intention of doing so.

Wasn't it too convenient that Emma's office had been reduced to ash? Tess had to consider the possibility that there was more to Emma's disappearance than she first thought. Albert Sower was a powerful man, and his influence ranged far beyond the confines of his cell. What if he had got to Emma somehow, either through threat or reward, and she'd been assisting him in derailing the case against him? It was an absurd notion, but Tess couldn't deny the fact that Sower's people had been on to her almost from the moment she first stepped inside Emma's office. For all she knew, Emma had engaged her while secretly instructed by Sower to hire someone unconnected with his people to trace Crawford Wynne, so that his murderer's part could remain anonymous during the search. Someone in that office had given the details of her travel plans away, and Emma was the prime suspect.

That's ridiculous, she warned. That would mean Emma was not only playing her, but that she'd also played Alex, and it was just too far-fetched. Why would she use her boyfriend's sister when she could hire someone with no connection back to her? No. Emma couldn't be behind this, it had to be another person in that office, and when she thought about it, she had a suspicion.

Cold shivers racked her. She pulled her jacket closer, holding it tightly with crossed arms. She watched as Alex broke ranks, heading towards her. He'd the same haunted look he'd worn since arriving on her threshold.

'It's terrible. Just terrible,' Tess intoned as he approached her.

Alex raised his brows. 'Two deceased. Three others with serious burns. It could have been worse.' He wasn't being flippant. 'But, yeah, terrible enough.'

The bitter stench of smoke wafted off Alex as he stepped alongside her. 'How are you holding up, sis?'

Tess looked at him.

'You do know why this happened?' Alex prompted.

He'd told her on the way over from her apartment. While she was in Louisiana, Albert Sower had publicly proclaimed a personal war against his persecutors. Through a hand-written and signed release presented under duress by his defence attorney, who'd since been placed in protective custody, he'd warned what would happen to those who chose to treat him as an enemy. He bragged on how his reach was long, his will strong, and that the fingers of retribution would claw the hearts out of the people of Maine. He sounded insane, but that didn't mean his promise was less terrifying. However, in some corners, his ranting had been met with derision: how exactly was he a threat while incarcerated awaiting trial? Sower had been quick to respond to those brushing off his threats, and this was the first act of terrorism in the wake of his boast. His reach was extended by proxy. But Tess had already known that. She'd borne witness to what Sower's people were capable of, and she didn't believe things would end with the burning of the DA's office.

'There's no doubt Sower was behind this?' she asked.

'There's no proof yet, but he more or less warned us what was coming. I just bet that he'll take responsibility for the fire. Considering he has nothing to lose now, he'd be a fool not to.' Alex shrugged. 'I hear the son of a bitch is delighted by his new status of most hated man in New England.'

'Surely there'll be some sort of concerted response now? Sower's known accomplices will start being rounded up?'

'Yeah. There's an FBI task force on it that've been desperate to bring them in since Officer Delaney's murder. But you know the score, Tess. They can only do so much, and can only bring in so many. We've identified the key players, Sower's lieutenants, but they've dropped off the radar these last few days and we've no idea where they're hiding. There are the others, the faceless minions we don't know about. I'm betting they have their instructions to continue the fight. There's no doubt that some kind of agenda was put into motion the instant Sower was arrested.'

'Like the murder of anyone prepared to stand witness against him,' she said. 'That would now include *me*.'

'I'll speak with my captain, arrange protection for you.'

Tess shook her head. 'I'm not afraid.'

'I'm not challenging your bravery, sis, just your good sense. You should keep your head down until we have everything under control.'

'You're beginning to sound like Mom again, Alex.'

'Occasionally she's right.'

'In this case she isn't.'

Alex faced her, placing his hands on her shoulders. 'I'm your big brother, Tess, and I'm concerned for your safety because I love you. But I'm also a cop, and I'm more concerned for your safety because there's a possibility you'll be hurt, the way I think Emma's been hurt. I'm terrified for the two of you, but I'm going with my head over my heart here. Work with me on this, or I might be forced to take you into protective custody.'

Tess couldn't help the smiling. 'You're kidding, right?'

'If I've to place you in handcuffs and force you into that car at gun point, I will.'

'You'd best get your cuffs ready then,' she warned.

'Aw, come on, Tess. Don't make this difficult for me.'

'You've enough on your plate with Emma's disappearance without worrying about me.' She peered over at the smouldering ruin again. 'I can help rather than being a hindrance. Some of those faceless minions you mentioned, well I think I can identify some of them.'

'Jacky Torrance? You already identified him. But he's out

of the picture. You said it yourself, he's down in the bayous and his involvement can't be tied to this. Hell, if anything you've given him a goddamn alibi.'

He was correct, but the alibi also tied Torrance to the abduction and murder of Crawford Wynne, and nobody could reasonably deny that they were by order of Albert Sower.

'There's nothing to say he's still in Louisiana. In fact, I want to do some checking, see exactly where the asshole is right now.'

Alex held up his hands. 'No way. Stay out of this, Tess. Stay safe, for God's sake.'

'I intend to. But if I can help keep someone else safe then I also intend doing that, starting with Emma.'

'I hear you, Tess, but it's not your responsibility. You're not a cop now, remember?'

Tess recalled sitting in the coffee shop opposite Charley's Auto Shop, that first time she'd met Po. *Funny, isn't it?* Po had ventured when claiming she'd left her law-enforcement career behind. *I was a con. Now I'm an ex-con, and will be for the rest of my days. Is it the same for cops? You're never anything but?*

There's probably something in it, Tess had admitted then, and she wanted to say the same to Alex now. But claiming as much would evoke the wrong reaction from him. He'd start warning her against taking the law into her own hands, and probably demand that a marked unit be parked outside her home, not to protect her but to ensure she didn't run off on some crazy vigilante quest.

'I'm not standing down.' She touched her brother on the cheek, using her thumb to smudge away a flake of ash. It was an innocuous touch of fondness, because ashes formed a blizzard around them, swept from the ruins by the rising wind. 'I know you're thinking of what's best for me, but you needn't, Alex. I'm not a helpless girl in need of your protection.' He stiffened, about to argue, but she patted his cheek. 'And besides, I have a friend watching my back.'

'You're talking about Po? Nicolas "Po'boy" Villere?'

'I am. Po watched my back while we were in Louisiana, I trust him to watch it now.'

Alex snorted. 'Don't you get it, Tess? Po is also a potential victim; he's as much a target as you are.'

'Then I'll watch his back.' She smiled.

'Freaking Po'boy Villere! He's an ex-con, Tess. It wouldn't surprise me if he's on Sower's goddamn payroll.'

A twinge of doubt nipped at her. Could Alex be on to something, and the very person she'd laid all her trust in had taken her for a fool? There were instances where Po had given reason to distrust him – that time he was supposed to be at his father's grave could've been a lie: had he secretly kept out of the way until Sower's people delivered the coordinates to Wynne's corpse? – and other occasions where he'd steered her down a different track than she might have followed. When she thought about his crazy antics when spotting their tail, had his overreaction been a ploy to keep any association he might have with Sower's people far from her mind? Did it explain why there was never a direct attack on them – even following their discovery at Rutterman Logistics – and how they'd avoided injury at the hands of Sower's men because Po was actually one of them?

As brief as they were, her doubts about Po shamed her, and she turned her anger on Alex. 'He isn't. And don't dare say anything like that again. If you knew him the way I do, you'd understand how stupid that accusation sounds.'

Alex kneaded his forehead. 'It's a possibility . . .'

'Only if you are on Sower's payroll too.' Tess pushed a finger in her brother's chest. 'You were the one that sent me to Po, remember? Oh, I know that accusation sounds ridiculous, but so does yours. You trusted Po was a decent man then, so what has changed? Don't tell me it's because I like him? That's the kind of protection I don't need, from anyone. And I certainly don't need relationship advice from my big brother.' She gave him her sternest look. 'When exactly were you planning on telling me you were sleeping with my boss?'

Alex glanced around wildly, but Tess had already checked. Nobody was in earshot. She touched a finger to the side of her nose. 'Your secret's safe,' she said, softening now they'd cleared up their disagreement, 'so you can keep your personal business to yourself. I'll do the same with mine.'

Alex laughed in defeat. 'And you accused me of sounding like Mom. That's why you two don't get along. You're too alike. Stubbornness must be a family trait on the female side.'

'Don't forget we also got the good-looking genes, unlike you, Monkey Boy,' Tess mugged at him. When he grinned she leaned in and hugged him again. 'But I still love you.'

'Love you too, sis.'

There was a distant roar. From the burnt-out building a cloud of oily smoke plumed skyward. The blizzard of ash intensified. The crowd stirred in response, pushing and shoving for a closer look. There was a larger drama going on than their little family ones. 'You should get over there and help out,' Tess suggested. 'It looks like they need all the hands they can get.'

Alex watched his colleagues forcing back the ghoulish onlookers. 'They've got it under control. I should take you home again.'

'I called Po like you said. He's coming here. He'll give me a ride back.'

As if summoned by the mention of his name, Po arrived. His choice of chariot was the 1968 Ford Mustang Tess had seen Charley working on that first day at the auto shop. It didn't surprise her that the muscle car belonged to Po; it suited him and explained his derision at driving something as mundane and utilitarian as a minivan.

'Man, who's he trying to impress?' Alex grunted. 'Does he think he's goddamn Bullitt?'

'I don't think he's trying to impress anyone, just making a point.' Tess waved at him as Po brought the souped-up car to a halt with a throaty rumble of the engine. Po flicked a salute for them both.

'Sheesh, give me a break,' Alex muttered. But he began backpedalling. He raised forked fingers to his eyes, then pointed them at Tess. 'I'll be watching.'

Tess offered a single finger. 'Watch this.'

They both chuckled in good humour.

'That's your brother, right?' Po said as she approached the car.

'Yes. That's Alex.'

'I recognize him now. He came around the shop looking for stolen cars one time.'

'Did he find any?'

Po only smirked. Adroitly he changed the subject. 'You guys look alike.'

There was no denying the family resemblance. If Tess was six inches taller, stockier built, and had a wider chin, she'd pass as Alex's identical twin. Their obvious difference – discounting their genders – was the colour of their eyes. Tess would love Alex's startling pale blue eyes, inherited from their dad, instead of the brown ones she'd gotten stuck with from their mom.

When Tess didn't comment, Po switched his attention to the activity around the law offices. 'I was worried about Charley getting drunk and burning down the shop while we were away, seems my concern was misdirected. This is Sower's doing, right?'

'That's the general consensus.'

'Charley told me about Sower's violent rant. He thinks he can terrorize his way out of a life term? Guy's a fucking psychopath. Uh, excuse my language.'

'You're right. He is a *fucking* psychopath.'

Tess got in the Mustang, taking a moment to admire the plush leather interior, the bucket seats. But she concentrated on the cardboard air freshener hanging from the rear-view mirror; it was shaped like a naked woman. 'Nice touch,' she said.

'That's Charley's doing. He hung it to take away the smell of smoke.'

The charred smell coming off the burnt building was over-powering. It clung to Tess's hair and clothing. 'Maybe I should rub it on me,' she said.

'I'll leave the windows open once we get going. You still want to do this?'

They'd discussed their plan of action on the way back from the airport. Now that Tess had learned that Sower had upped his game, it was time to up theirs. To do that was to follow the only route they had. 'Let's go get Jacky Boy,' she said, convinced that to help Sower's campaign of terror John

Torrance had been summoned back to Maine with his blond friend, and most assuredly with Sower's pet killer. 'Hopefully he'll lead us to Emma in time to save her.'

'We can only hope,' Po intoned. A faint smile plucked at his lips, but on noticing her perusal his expression grew unreadable. There had been finality to his words as if he knew something of Emma's fate that she didn't. Please let me be wrong, she prayed.

THIRTY-ONE

They didn't set off on a wild-goose chase, despite their urgency. They were better served using Tess's locating skills than randomly driving around in the hope of spotting a familiar face. Po took her to his auto shop, and gave her access to his computer. 'May as well get some use out of it, I rarely turn the damn thing on,' he announced.

'Only when you want to see some nice pictures of cute puppies and kittens, eh?'

He grunted in mirth. Left the cramped office to her.

Following the same investigative trails she did to collate family trees, Tess was able to identify the known haunts and accomplices of John Torrance. Her task would've been simpler if she'd had access to law-enforcement databases, but instead she had to rely on media websites and social networks. It might surprise some people to learn how much could be gleaned by tracing social network updates back to their sources, if not to the extent that people wore their hearts on their sleeves when it came to those very public forums. Rapidly she found an ex-girlfriend, who'd publicly shamed Torrance's sexual prowess after she caught him with another 'ho'. It was then a simple task to follow the torrid stream backwards along the timeline to a point where they were both still loved-up and sharing selfies of them enjoying themselves at various locations. Hell, the girl had unwittingly made things easier by turning on the 'tag location' function on her status updates and Tess found a handy map attached showing exactly where Torrance called home. It didn't give an exact house number, but the street was good enough. Other snaps taken by the girl showed the garden and exterior of the Torrance household, and by driving the street, Tess was confident she'd be able to identify the property.

Before setting off to front Torrance, Tess had also identified his blond partner in crime. He was in a number of the photos, handily tagged back to his own Facebook account. He had an everyday name, nothing that would ordinarily stand out, but Kenneth Jones was better known to his Facebook compadres as 'Welshy'. Tess had also identified his address easily enough, but this time via a news media channel reporting a drunken brawl the man had been involved in mere months ago.

She searched their 'trees' for any hint of who the faceless killer might be, but there was nothing of value. He could be any one of dozens of friends appearing in photographs on the social network sites, or any one of dozens more commenting on statuses, or he could be none of the above. Tess even looked for a page dedicated to Albert Sower, and one for his *nom de plume* Alberto Suarez, but it seemed Sower came of a generation with neither the time nor the inclination for social networking. Or he was too subtle a criminal to make his every move so obvious.

And thinking about the subtleties of criminals . . .

When he wasn't looking, Tess quickly keyed in Po's name, in its various combinations, but also drew a blank, for which she was relieved. When he'd originally been tried for his revenge killing of his father's murderer, the Internet was in its infancy and perhaps the *Times Picayune* hadn't yet got round to digitizing all its back copy yet. The name Nicolas Villere did crop up in search engine results, but not in a way she could be sure had anything to do with Po, and certainly not in connection to Sower or his associates. She clicked off again, feeling like a sneak thief digging through his personal things. Anything she wished to know about him she should ask. If he didn't want to reply, then so be it.

'You're making that funny woodchuck sound again.'

Tess glanced up from the monitor, immediately halting the unconscious clucking of her tongue. Po stood in the doorway, his left arm extending up the frame. He was dressed in a tight black T-shirt tucked into black jeans. He was wearing the same military issue boots she'd always seen him in. He clutched a thin black jacket in his right fist.

'What's this, your ninja costume?' she asked, while discreetly deleting her recent searches from the computer's history.

'It takes a ninja to catch a ninja,' he said, one eyebrow

lifted, and it sounded like a quote from some cheesy movie she'd watched years ago. 'Found us a starting point yet?'

'I have,' she said, and told him Torrance's street address.

'You expect him to be there?'

'No. But we won't know unless we check.'

Po nodded, and she closed down the computer. She followed him into the workshop. He paused at a large toolbox. 'Maybe you'd like to grab something,' he offered.

'What, there's no equivalent to Pinky Leclerc in Portland?' she asked.

'Despite what you might've heard, I've suppressed my criminal tendencies while living in Portland. So no, I don't have a handy gunrunner on call to get us what we need.' He shrugged his tall frame. 'I never was comfortable with guns anyway.'

'So what have you in your box of tricks? Throwing stars and nunchucks?'

'Best I can do is knives, or a hammer if you prefer.'

Tess puffed out her cheeks. Since her accidental slaying of the clerk she hadn't felt comfortable around guns either, but given a choice she'd rather have Pinky's Glock than resort to sticking someone with a blade, or bashing in their skulls with a blunt object. 'I'll pass,' she said.

She waited for Po to choose a weapon, but he simply stood. It was likely he'd already secreted his weapon of choice in his high-top boots.

'If we can go by my place there's something there I'd like to collect,' she said. Po's mouth turned down briefly, but it was a sign of agreement.

Back in the Ford Mustang, they were at her apartment in no time. Po waited with the car while Tess jogged up the steps. Caution slowed her as she approached the door. She checked for signs of forced entry; Sower's people might have arrived while she was out and were now lying in wait. The lock was untouched. She keyed it open and stepped inside, forced to turn on lights to see where she was going. Her apartment didn't feel as empty this time, more familiar and comfortable. She went through to her bedroom, opened her walk-in closet, and crouched to pull out a heavy steel box. It had a digital keypad, and she tapped in her grandfather's birthdate, and lifted the lid. Inside was his old NYPD revolver, a Ruger .38 Service Six, handed down from father to son and then bequeathed to Tess following her dad's untimely death. Tess had never used the gun during her service, but had maintained it, and occasionally test-fired it at the range. It was ready to go, and she'd two speed-loaders of ammunition. She fed rounds into the cylinder, then put the spare loader in her jacket pocket and slipped the gun in her belt. The revolver was licensed for home defence, and carrying it on her person was illegal, but to hell with that! Under the circumstances she'd take the rap to her knuckles, rather than face off against Sower's killer empty-handed.

Next, as another tool of choice, she collected her iPad, which she'd left charging while she was out.

Returning to the Mustang, she found Po out on the kerb, smoking a cigarette. That was how it appeared at first glance, but really he was patrolling. He too had thought that the bad guys might target her apartment. If he were in cahoots with them, would he stand guard against them? Time to put those doubts aside. She got in the Mustang and asked Po to drive; best to divert attention away from her home. As they drove away she glanced back, picturing the devastation a firebomb would wreak on the wooden structure.

John Torrance's address was tagged to a cul-de-sac off Brighton Avenue, nestled adjacent to a dirt track giving access to the Capisic Brook Trail alongside the Fore River where it spilled into a large pond. It would be a pleasant place to live in daylight, but in the dark it took on sinister tones. Tess wouldn't willingly walk down that trail without her gun in hand, for fear of being set upon by muggers or rapists, even if the fear were all in her mind. Po elected to take the back way in, for which she was grateful, while she waited by the Mustang to allow him time to get in place. He disappeared the second he ducked into the trail, beneath the overhanging boughs of trees and shrubs. Tess silently counted to one hundred, then went forward and knocked on the front door. She didn't expect Torrance to answer, because there were no lights on inside. When the door crept open, Po glanced out.

'Found an unlatched window back there,' he explained.

Tess checked behind. There was no challenge from any of the neighbouring abodes. 'OK, in and out as quickly as possible.'

Torrance had been a thug in his earlier years, and Tess almost expected a similar hovel to the one they'd searched for Crawford Wynne in Morgan City. But Torrance had aged since his wild drunken days, and his tastes had obviously matured too. His house was nice, without being overdone. Not too cluttered, which actually helped them make their search. Tess found his travel case on his bed. He'd only gotten as far as opening the suitcase, without taking the laundry to the wash basket yet. But it was enough to tell them that he had arrived back from Louisiana not long before them. Going downstairs she joined Po in the kitchen, he was playing a small flashlight around the room. As she walked in, he settled it on an opened can of chilli-con-carne sitting on the breakfast bar. A spoon jutted out of it. 'Looks as if Jacky Boy left in a hurry,' he said.

Tess leaned and sniffed. It smelled like dog food, but fresh enough. The sauce hadn't begun drying yet, which suggested the tin hadn't been open long.

'Think he got a taste for spicy food down south?' Po asked.

Tess said nothing.

She frowned, then went to a notepad on the breakfast bar, hoping to find some handy clue scrawled on it. There was nothing, Torrance not being much of a note taker. She opened a drawer and found it full of the usual stuff packed out of sight in drawers everywhere, but again nothing of importance. She closed it. Po had walked away into the hall.

'Here,' he whispered.

She joined him and frowned down at the old-fashioned landline phone on a small wooden stool. 'What?'

Even as she posed the question, a red light blinked on the phone.

'Voicemail message,' Po said. 'Should we listen to it?'

'Hell, yes,' said Tess and lifted the receiver. She hit a chunky button on the keypad, and put it on speaker.

'*Hey, Jacky, it's me, Welshy.*'

Tess lifted her eyebrows at Po, but continued listening keenly.

'*D'you believe the shit that's going on? These times they are a-changing. If you want to be part of the new regime you'd better get over here, man. The greaseball's called the troops together and isn't taking no for an answer.*'

The message was cryptic enough without giving much away, but Tess got lucky.

'*Get your ass to pier-side ASAP. The Greek's boat, right? And, Jacky, if you've fallen asleep, well, I pity you, man. The greaseball's looking to cut something and it might just be* your *balls.*'

THIRTY-TWO

Tess built the series of events from the bottom up, and thought she might not be far off the mark. Fatigued and hungry from a hectic few days, John Torrance must've returned home alone. After dumping his case, deciding it was too much trouble to unpack, he had then gone to the kitchen to prepare some food. Again, cooking must've been too much effort, and instead he'd opened the canned chilli and spooned it cold into his mouth. Tess could imagine him sitting at the breakfast counter, greasy chilli sauce on his teeth, groaning in frustration when the phone rang. Perhaps he chose to let it go to voicemail, but the alarm bells were ringing inside him and he'd downed his meal and listened to Kenneth Jones' message. His absence spoke volumes: he'd taken the warning seriously, and had responded to the summons with more alacrity. It was a lucky break that in his haste he'd forgotten to delete the message, otherwise Tess and Po would have no direction to follow. As it was, Welshy's instructions were vague but expecting him to be helpful by adding pertinent detail was asking too much. When she checked when the call was recorded, they were nearly two hours behind Torrance. She wasn't about to give up yet, though, even if the odds of catching up with him were difficult.

Portland was a city of piers. There were dozens of them, spread along the rugged coastline from Falmouth to the north down to South Portland across Portland Harbour. The main proliferation of piers and wharves was on the northern bank of the Fore River where it spilled into the bay, adjacent to Commercial Street. Along that front there were scores of fishing and pleasure boats, and the various ferries to nearby Cushing, Peaks, and the Diamond Islands. But it was a fair guess that a criminal organization would choose somewhere less public to ply their trade.

'The Greek's boat.' Po had repeated the phrase a number of times as he drove.

It was the best lead they had, but was so vague it could go nowhere useful.

Tess began clucking her tongue against the roof of her mouth. She caught a glance from Po.

'What's on your mind?' he asked.

'Pull over.'

They'd been driving with no clear destination in mind, heading instinctively for Commercial Street. Earlier, Tess had employed her iPad as a guide to Torrance's house, but had left it on the back seat while they were inside. Po brought the Mustang to a halt on Deering Avenue, on a bus stop servicing Tess's old middle school. She didn't give the school as much as a nostalgic glance; she went head down to the iPad as she brought up her records. She couldn't find what she was looking for. Recalling her hotel room in Baton Rouge, she rearranged her memories, and again saw herself laying out her files and paperwork so that she could view and order them into some kind of tree, showing connections back and forth to Albert Sower.

'The Greek's boat.' Now it was Tess who repeated the phrase. She looked over at Po. 'It might be nothing, but I recall there was a name connected to Sower, a known associate. It sounded Greek.'

'But you can't remember who it was?'

'I could find the name among my papers, but I just dumped them all in my case and it's back at my apartment. Damn it.' She waited for Po to suggest taking her back to Cumberland Avenue, which wasn't far away, but he didn't start the engine. Returning to her house might place them in the firing line. It forced Tess to think harder. She might be able to find the name if she went through the process of following Internet searches once more, but that was time they couldn't spare. She took out her cell and rang Alex.

'Are you still at the fire?' she asked.

'No. I'm back on . . . patrol.' Really, he meant he was on the lookout for Emma. 'What's up, Tess?'

'I need your help.'

'Uh? To do what?'

'I need a name, and hopefully an address.'

'Why?'

'You know why, Alex.'

'I told you already; you have to stay out of this, Tess. Keep your head down and stay safe.'

'When did I ever do anything that was expected of me?' Tess grinned at his coarse response, even though her brother had no way of knowing.

'Where are you?'

'I'm with Po.'

'Not sure how I feel about that, but I guess he's better than nothing.'

'He can hear what you're saying.' Though she was kidding, she suspected that Po could indeed hear their conversation judging by the ghost of a smile he wore.

'Be more specific this time, sis. Where *exactly* are you?'

'So you can come and put me in cuffs?'

'No. So I can help. Do you want my fucking help or not?'

'OK, chill out, bro. We're opposite King Middle School on Deering Avenue.'

'Wait there. I'll be with you in a couple of minutes.'

'You don't need to come here, I just need a name and address from you,' Tess said.

'Let him come,' Po said.

Alex was saying something but Tess's attention was on Po. 'He's only going to try to talk me out of doing this.'

'If Emma has been taken, he has a right to try and help her as much as we do. Plus, we might need him,' Po counselled. 'We don't know what we'll find at the Greek's boat. Having a cop along might prove useful.'

'Po's right,' Alex said, obviously having listened in. 'What was that about a boat?'

Tess exhaled.

'Alex, this might be a wild-goose chase. But it's something I have to check.' She wondered how much she should share with him: he was her brother but he was still a cop and duty could win out, forcing her off the hunt. But then, he was also Emma's boyfriend. 'I think Sower's people are holding Emma on a boat. The problem is I don't know where it is or even its name.'

'Why the hell didn't you mention this when you were with me earlier?' Alex's voice was strident, but it was pretty much what she'd expected. 'I could have—'

'I didn't know then, it's something I've just learned myself,' Tess explained. 'It's why I called you *now*. We have to find that boat, Alex.'

'I knew something was wrong,' Alex said, his voice barely a whisper. 'She's been missing for two days now, but nobody has seemed too concerned.' Apart from him of course, but how could he push to find Emma without coming clean that he had a personal stake in her welfare? 'I did try to get someone at her office to contact her on the pretence I was following up on a case she'd handled, but I was given the bum's rush, told that she was unavailable. I didn't buy it, sis, but what could I do?'

'I got a similar response from her office. Her assistant said they'd received an email from Emma stating she was incommunicado, but the message could've been sent by anybody. If Sower's people snatched her, they could have access to her phone or laptop. Hell, they could've forced her to send the message herself to allow them more time with her. But – as bad as it sounds – I'm hoping that's the case. The alternative is that we would've found her earlier, displayed like the other victims.'

'I hope to God you're right,' he said.

'Alex, when I spoke to her assistant, Monica, the girl was concerned. She knew it was out of character for Emma to disappear like this, but when she raised the subject with their boss he stonewalled her. I've suspected for a while that someone in her office was passing intel to Sower's people and have a good idea who. The victims from the fire, one of them was Emma's boss, Richard Jackson, right?'

'Jesus . . .'

'The fire wasn't simply a terror attack on his enemies, Sower was cleaning up witnesses again,' she said. 'I bet when we dig deeper into this, we'll find Jackson was either in Sower's pocket or he was being forced to work for him. Arson's a different MO, but it stands to reason because Sower's mutilator was still out of town and one of his other lackeys got the job of doing away with Jackson. But we haven't time to worry about any of that now.' Tess had grown breathless, and forced herself to slow down. 'I guess that following Sower's boast about destroying his enemies, he's more or less given the DA the rope to hang him with, but he isn't beyond making more examples. We all know that Sower pointed the finger at those other victims. They were punishment killings. Well, doesn't it stand to reason he might want to punish the woman determined to ruin him?'

'This Greek you asked me about; you think *he* has Emma at his boat?'

'If not him, then some others visiting with him right now.'

'I'm on Park Avenue, just passing the Expo building. I'll be with you in seconds. Sit tight, sis.' Alex breathed out in decision. 'If there's anything I can do to help, I'm with you.'

THIRTY-THREE

A dripping noise roused Emma Clancy, and of all the abuse she'd suffered, this latest debasement hurt most. She screamed in torment, throwing herself against the bonds holding her upright, caring less that the Velcro straps rubbed raw spots on her wrists.

'Keep it down, why don't you?'

The voice came from the swarthy fat man who'd originally gagged and tied her up during her abduction; also her unhappy jailer who'd kept watch over her for the past few hours. He was only one of at least half a dozen men who'd taken a turn at guard since she'd been brought here. Strung up trophy-like, stripped to her briefs, the men had enjoyed private moments with her, pawing at her breasts and backside, then laughing as she kicked and spat at them. Pigs! They were disgusting scum, taking enjoyment in her torment. The fat man was different, but her ordeal had nothing to do with her latest jailer's displeasure.

'I've wet myself!' Emma sobbed. 'I warned you I needed to pee and you wouldn't let me!'

'And I told you that you were going nowhere. So you've pissed yourself. Get over it.' The fat man rubbed a palm over his balding crown, and grunting, he pushed up from his seat. 'Believe me, you think you've got problems now, you've no idea.'

'You can't treat me like this,' Emma cried.

'It's not my decision. But unless I'm ready to trade positions with you, I have to do as I've been told. Trust me: this isn't fun for me either.'

'Fun? You talk of fun while a woman is tortured in your place? You're as insane as all the rest of them.' Emma aimed a kick at the man.

Her foot fell short by a full yard, yet he still flinched.

'Stop that,' he warned. 'So I'm unhappy that you've been

brought here. But it is what it is, and there's nothing I can do to change that. So try hurting me, and I will bust your face.'

'You won't touch me!'

'Try me, we'll see.'

'No. You're not like the others. I can tell you don't want any part of this. It's Albert Sower. He's making you do this. Listen to me . . . if you let me go now, if you help me get away, I promise I'll speak in your defence. I'll explain how you were being coerced under threat . . .' Her words fell silent as he sharply raised a palm.

'You seen what happened to Mitch Delaney, right? That's what came of working with you.' The fat man moved towards her, looking her up and down. There was nothing lascivious in his gaze as it swept over her bare breasts, or down her flat stomach to her wet panties. 'This! This is what happens to *anyone* who goes against Sower. Don't you get it?'

'Sower's caged in the special management unit, on twenty-three-hour lockdown. He can't touch you. He—'

The fat man rushed at her, and his hands went round her throat, choking off her words. He squeezed, his face pressing close to hers. His spittle was hot on her face, but he released his grip. 'It's not fucking *Albert* who terrifies me, you stupid bitch! His hand is in this, yes, but he only thinks he's guiding the knife. He's not the one who's fucking holding it, and he won't be the one still holding it after all this is over with.' His hands fell from her neck, and he stepped back, his eyes dazed as he shook his head. 'Don't you get it?'

Emma thought she did. Albert had sealed his fate, though he'd had assistance in doing so. He would never be released from prison now, and the latest killings, and even her abduction, had been designed to ensure that. When she'd visited him at the prison he'd boasted that the personification of his will was strong and directed, but he was only partly correct. This was more about free will and misdirection. A power play was afoot, a coup where Albert's prime position at the head of this criminal empire was about to be usurped. Emma understood that her murder was the event that would crown the new king.

'You have to let me go,' Emma wheezed. 'How does anyone expect to get away with this? You're lucky there's no death penalty in Maine, but trust me, you will all go to prison for a very long time. That includes you!'

'Only if anyone discovers you were held here. If I have my way you won't be found anywhere near.' He walked away, approaching a galvanized steel sink. 'We know that Albert isn't getting out, and probably never will, but that's the way it's supposed to be. He won't be seen to go down easily. That's why it's been made to look as if he's taking out everyone he has a beef with. That includes you, Mrs Clancy, and anyone else working for the DA on his case. There'll be nobody left who can tie me to what's been going on here.'

'The investigation won't end with Albert. Every last person involved in this madness will be hunted down and arrested!'

'That's the thing; the cops will be chasing bigger prizes than the likes of me. All I have to do is keep quiet, do as I'm told, and once it's over and done with, I'll go back to doing what I do best. Selling fucking lobster and crab cakes to tourists.'

'No. You won't get away with this. You'll go to prison with all the rest.' Emma was almost breathless. 'They'll find this place, and when they do . . .'

The man turned on a faucet.

'They'll find nothing evidential,' he said, and aimed the nozzle of a sluicing hose at her. The water was icy as it spattered her body, and she recoiled from it. The man followed her jerking movements, washing away the urine that had dripped down her legs. When he was happy she was clean, he directed the stream of water at the puddle, forcing it into the gutter between her feet. Emma still danced to avoid the blast, and the man shook his head at her ingratitude. He directed the spray at her again, making her shriek.

'Had your fun yet, Vas?'

The new voice brought them both to a halt.

A stranger had entered the room, a fair-haired man with a cruel twist to his mouth. Emma forced herself around in her bonds, eyeing him as a possible saviour. He wasn't, not if Vasilis Katsaros' reaction was anything to go by. The fat man visibly deflated, but it was in relief.

'You're back, Welshy! Thank God. If I'd to stay here much

longer I'm sure this bitch would send me nuts. The sooner this is over with the fucking better. Does that crazy man realize how much business I've lost shutting up shop like this?'

Welshy held up a warning finger. 'Don't let Hector hear you calling him that, and do you really think he gives a goddamn *fuck* about your business?'

'All he cares about is getting his own sick rocks off,' Vasilis muttered.

Shaking his head, Welshy glanced at Emma, and for her benefit said, 'He cares more about avenging Albert.'

'We all know that's bullshit,' Vasilis snorted. 'And so does she.'

'You fucking told her?' Welshy stepped forward, his right hand curling into a fist.

'Why not?' Vasilis challenged him. 'It's not as if she's going to be able to tell anyone, is it?'

Welshy considered the truth. 'OK,' he conceded, 'maybe Hector does have his own plans, but they're not at the expense of avenging Albert.'

Vasilis sneered. 'So he says, but even if he wasn't on some revenge trip he'd still be hacking people to pieces.'

'Just be thankful it isn't you, Vas.'

'Where is the mad bastard anyway?' He glanced at Emma. 'Sharpening his knives?'

'He's getting kitted out. You know how Hector enjoys dressing for the occasion, right?' Welshy stage-whispered at Emma. 'He wants to look his best for you, m'dear.'

'Who . . . who is Hector?' When Albert Sower had spoken of his killer it had been through metaphor, and Emma had conjured in her mind some kind of shadowy bogey man: giving him a name made him more terrifying than the faceless figure lurking at the edge of her imagination.

'You don't know? Even after all the extensive files you must've compiled on Albert Sower, you don't know about Hector Suarez?' Welshy laughed at her ineptitude. He had also come to the same conclusion as Vasilis, telling her the truth would make no difference considering she would very soon be dead. 'Surely you looked at Albert's family connections from back in Bolivia, from before he arrived here?'

'You're talking about his brother? But . . . Hector Suarez died,' she croaked, realizing that her information was woefully misinformed. 'When he was killed, didn't Albert replace him as head of the family . . .'

'Yeah, Albert took the reins. But he also saved Hector's life, and Hector has worked to repay him as *honour dictates*.' He delivered those final words in a poor attempt at a Spanish accent. 'Don't ask me, Clancy: those greaseballs have some fucked-up ideas about honour traditions. All I know is Hector feels he owes Albert one last act of servitude, then his debt is paid and he'll be his own man again.'

He grinned maliciously.

'Vas has a point: even if Hector weren't on this supposed revenge kick, he'd still be doing what he does best. He's kind of fucked up in here.' Welshy tapped the side of his head. 'Mrs Clancy, you won't believe what Hector's got planned for you. But don't worry, you'll find out soon enough.'

Emma lost the power of speech. Shivers assailed her, and her shaking jingled the overhead pulley. Welshy coughed out a laugh, then turned his back on her. Vasilis still stood with the sluicing hose, though he'd turned off the faucet.

'Jacky Boy's back too. We had quite the little adventure down in the boonies with Hector and our old buddy Crawford Wynne. I'm sure Jacky'll be happy to tell you the story. Go find him, Vasilis, have yourselves a smoke.' He aimed a thumb over his shoulder. 'I'm not sure you've the stomach for what Hector's got in mind for Mrs Clancy.'

Jamming the hose in the sink, Vasilis wasn't about to argue. He rubbed his hands over his head, moving past Emma for the door. Emma twisted in her bonds. 'Please,' she said. 'Remember what I told you.'

'Shut up,' Vasilis snapped, his gaze darting for Welshy. The fair-haired man was watching. 'Huh! She promised if I helped her escape she'd have the law go easy on me. Idiot!'

'I'm happy you weren't tempted by her lies,' said a new figure that filled the doorway with his stocky frame.

Emma craned to see, and her mouth fell open.

Vasilis had come to a skidding halt. He had to be worried

that the large man had overheard more than his final statement.

The man entered the room, and he was carrying a roll of duct tape in one gloved hand. 'I wish to enjoy my time with our guest, and don't want to miss a second while wondering how I'd deal with you, Greek.'

The man in the yellow fisherman's slicker and orange waterproof trousers had to be Hector Suarez. Emma knew simply by Vasilis' reaction to his unannounced arrival, and didn't need the added detail.

'I . . . I promise you, Hector, I didn't believe a word she said,' Vasilis bleated.

'Then go have your cigarette with Jacky Boy.' Hector's smile was sadistic as he nodded at the door. He had been listening, and Emma wondered if the fat man would be punished for his insolence: somehow she felt no pity for him. Right then she was more concerned for her own hide.

Hector leaned down, wrapping the loose end of the duct tape around the cuff of his pants, sealing it to the gumboots on his feet. He'd already taped the cuffs of his coat to his gloves. His preparations were fastidious and all the more terrifying for it. There was only one reason he was proofing his clothing, and it wasn't through a fear of being soaked by water.

'Uh, you want me to stay?' Welshy asked.

'I need you and one other. The Greek is a weakling. Fetch another man, and have him bring a – how do you call it? – *mop* and bucket.' He stood directly before Emma as he made his next announcement. 'When I open your stomach, Emma Clancy, I think there will be much mess to contend with, no?'

'You . . . you can't do this to me,' Emma croaked.

Hector snorted, then ran his tongue over his teeth. 'I can, and I will. You have borne witness to my handiwork before, why would I change my ways now?'

'I work on behalf of the Cumberland County District Attorney's Office. Don't you realize what they'll do to you if you harm me in any way?' Even as she said it, Emma knew she'd made a fatal mistake. Her words only bolstered his desire to hurt her. Albert Sower had declared war on the DA and all who worked for him, and this monster was the weapon by which he'd wage his war: the personification of his will. No, she remembered, as she stared back into the man's lumpy, scarred visage and the bottomless pits of his eyes, this man didn't work on Albert's behalf. He was wilful in his own right, and this was about sating his warped desires. He delighted in pain and savagery, and there was no pity in his shrivelled heart. She shrieked in abstract terror, and even that was a mistake, because it brought him to her immediately.

THIRTY-FOUR

Of all the places on the Maine coastline Sower's group couldn't have picked a location more fittingly named to their base of operations than Smuggler's Cove. The criminal organization was suspected of numerous crimes, but mostly trafficking narcotics, workers headed for the sex trade, and illegal weapons. Some of their routes were over the Canadian border, but most of their activities were conducted by sea. With the best will in the world, not to mention unlimited funds and manpower, the Coast Guard couldn't possibly control the rugged Atlantic seaboard, where there were dozens – if not hundreds – of places where a boat could sneak to port unchallenged. Smuggler's Cove was of course named for a historical landfall of eighteenth-century ne'er-do-wells, and had nothing to do with Sower's modern accomplishments. These days it was better known as a vacation and pleasure destination, because of its ruggedly captivating coastline, vistas of open water, and towering lighthouses, where people came to fish, kayak, pleasure cruise, and sail, or to avail themselves of the local amenities. Throughout the region there was a proliferation of hotels, resorts, cabins, and camping facilities, and in line with demand equal numbers of restaurants, diners, and teashops. Tess had visited the area many times over the years.

It was easy to assume that the Greek's boat was one of hundreds of pleasure craft or trawlers dotted along the coast, but it was a misnomer. It wasn't a boat or ship, but a structure on a promontory overlooking the cove, designed and erected in the fashion of a rising prow, in keeping with the nautical theme of buildings nearby. In a coastal area where people usually gorged on Maine lobster, Vasilis Katsaros cornered the market on eastern Mediterranean and Aegean cuisine, serving food from his aptly named restaurant, Macedon. Neither was Katsaros a true Greek, he originally hailed from Cyprus, but that was nit-picking.

When Alex had joined them on Deering Avenue, he'd phoned a colleague in the office who owed him a favour, and asked for a list of Sower's suspected associates. The list was long but only one had a name of Greek extraction, and as soon as he'd shown it to Tess she recognized it. Rather than risk Alex's career any further, she interrogated the Internet for the further information she required. At first following a false trail, looking for a boat registered to that name, she'd stumbled across the Macedon instead, and everything had fallen in place once she'd brought up an image of it and spotted the nautical theme of the restaurant. Hell, she even remembered eating there four or five years ago while on a date. As she'd dined, she'd no idea of the owner's involvement in a crime ring, and good job, because it would've probably soured her stomach and spoiled her meal of vine leaves stuffed with lamb, garlic, and sautéed onions. Oddly the delicious meal had stuck in her memory in a way her boring date hadn't, and now she couldn't say if he was called Will, Bill, or Phil.

'Smuggler's Cove is well off my patch,' Alex had pointed out, 'but I'm still coming with you.'

'You could lose your job,' Tess argued.

'You could lose your liberty,' he countered.

'We could all lose our heads,' Po added, and it sobered them. But it also clarified what exactly they hoped to achieve, and that was to save the head of another person. Alex advised his dispatcher that he was following up on enquiries, but didn't specify. With everything else that the Portland PD were dealing with that night, his status update was acknowledged but unchallenged, and he was relying on being lost in the shuffle, and could hopefully go unmissed for an hour or two. If not, well, he could argue that he really was following up on enquiries, just not on a case he was actively engaged in. If everything went to order, he might get away with a stiff reprimand, but if the opposite was true then it didn't really matter.

To get them quickly to their destination, he took a liberty with his emergency lights, leading the charge over the harbour bridge and through South Portland with Po's Mustang tight to his tail. Alex was an expert driver, and negotiated the roads at speed, but with care, but Tess could tell that her companion was itching to overtake and show how it should really be done. She caught Po tutting in frustration a few times. 'Who's the freaking woodchuck now?' she demanded, unable to hold in a chuckle.

They followed the aptly named Shore Road, passing Portland Head Light, Chimney Rock, Pond Cove, and other places of local interest until they found a turn off for Smuggler's Cove. Here wealthy residents kept houses, or summer homes, and it was highly likely that a Portland PD cruiser and souped-up muscle car would draw untoward notice. Alex set his blinkers flashing and pulled off-road, following a dirt track down a slope towards a deserted jetty, alongside which a small pleasure boat was moored. Tess guessed what he was up to, because from the shoreline the Macedon's glass-fronted prow was visible, rising above the promontory across the bay.

'A frontal approach probably isn't wise,' Alex said as they gathered on the pebble shore.

'Best we keep a low profile, until we know what we're up against,' Po agreed. 'We should go in on foot, take the beach, and approach from the water. They won't be watching that way.'

'Agreed,' said Alex.

Tess glanced between them, typical men doing all the planning without asking her opinion.

Alex held up a cautioning hand. 'We scout the place only. We don't get too close; we just take a look. If we get any hint that Emma's inside, held against her will, we back off and I call in tactical support. I can get the ESU team here quick-time if need be.'

'Makes sense,' Po said, but he gave Tess a subtle wink that anyone who didn't know him would barely register.

'We should put our cell phones on silent,' Tess proposed, 'but use them to communicate if necessary. I don't suggest we go in together like this, we should split up.'

'Po,' said Alex, 'can go in alone. But you're sticking with me, sis.'

'Who made you the leader?' she demanded.

He tapped his shiny PD badge. 'This does. And if that doesn't work for you, then I'm pulling sibling rank. I'm your big brother, don't forget.'

Tess opened her mouth, but Po forestalled her. 'He's right, Tess. You should stick with him. You can pinpoint Clancy and he can call in the cavalry.' Po also took a pointed glance at the gun holstered on Alex's belt. 'He can also protect you better than I can.'

'He's not the only one who can shoot,' Tess said.

'I'm the only one with a firearm,' Alex replied. Then his eyes creased. 'Oh, don't tell me . . .'

Tess withdrew her grandfather's service revolver.

'Jesus, what are you doing with that thing?' Alex cast a disapproving glance at Po, as if the ex-con's bad influence was already rubbing off on her.

'Nothing to do with me,' Po said.

Alex glared at the revolver. But in the end he shook his head. 'OK. You know how to use that thing; I'll give you that. But it's for show only. You do not fire it. Understood?'

'I hope I won't need to,' Tess admitted, but remained noncommittal on his instructions. Her vague promise would have to do because she wasn't going to stand by and watch while anybody important to her got hurt.

'OK. Put it away for now. Damn thing's that old it might blow up in your hand,' Alex muttered, but he was about done with the subject. He pointed along the shoreline. 'We'll head along there; once we're past those pilings we'll head up the slope. Po, you OK going further along and up the promontory on the far side of the restaurant?'

'I'm good with that.'

'If you spot anyone, or if you're spotted, get out of there, and try to warn us. Use your phone like Tess suggested: we'll have ours on vibrate so we know there's an incoming call.'

Po said nothing.

Taking his silence as agreement, Alex turned to Tess. 'Same for us, Tess. We see Emma, I'll call it in. But if we're spotted you get the hell out of here.'

'While you do what?'

'What do you mean?'

'You said I've to get the hell out, but what about you?'

'I show my badge, take things from there.'

'And you seriously expect them to give up quietly?'

Now Alex said nothing.

But neither did Tess. They all had their instructions, but none of them would abide by the rules. Rules were made to be broken, in this case before they'd even initiated their plan.

It was dark, but an ambient glow was cast from the phosphorous wash of tide, so they kept to the head of the beach to remain invisible. Tess could barely see her companions, so it was unlikely any of them would be spotted. It'd be different once they approached the Macedon, because light spilled from its huge glass walls and on to the promontory it stood abreast. Po must negotiate those pools of light to gain his approach route up the far side of the rocks, and Tess suspected that was why Alex had sent him that way. Nevertheless, she doubted Po would be sighted. She'd jokingly called his garb a ninja costume, but there was value in wearing black on black.

'Be careful,' she whispered to him, and touched him gently on the back of his left hand.

'Don't worry about me.' Po loped off, and he was lost among the shadows in seconds. All that pinpointed him was the soft scuff of his boots through loose pebbles, but the sound could be mistaken for the lapping tide. Tess listened a moment longer, and then even that hint of his location vanished.

'We'll give him a minute to get in position,' Alex said close to her ear.

Standing alongside her brother, Tess looked up at the sharp prow of the building rising above them. From their position there was no sign of movement inside, but it was unlikely that Sower's henchmen would be gathered in the restaurant's seating area, with Emma Clancy displayed on a platter between them like the 'special of the day'. If she were there at all – if indeed she were still alive – she would be held out of sight while Sower's killer completed his work. Did the others have the stomach to watch, or was the mutilation too much even for them? She hoped Jacky Torrance or Welshy would show their faces, because theirs were the only ones she could confidently identify. She now knew of Vasilis Katsaros, and had a vague recollection of his looks from the photo in her file, but there was no proof he was involved, the link to his restaurant being only tenuous until proven otherwise. Concern washed through her; what if she'd brought them to the wrong place? She exhaled, shivering, afraid for Emma if she was wrong. Then again, she was equally afraid for Emma if she was right. But there still remained a trickle of caution running through her. She barely knew the woman, and for all she knew Emma could be as complicit with Sower in the way her boss, Jackson, could prove to be, pulling the strings Sower required to find and eliminate Crawford Wynne. What if Emma had used her, and her brother alike, to get what Sower demanded? If Tess was right and extreme precautions had been taken to cover up Richard Jackson's collusion with the gang boss, what if Emma's disappearance was to ensure the same end? But what if, instead of being snatched, Emma had been assisted to disappear? Did Emma need rescuing at all?

'Are we doing the right thing here?' she whispered to herself.

Until then Alex had remained silent. Perhaps counting down the minute he'd given Po. But he must've heard her doubt, because he patted her on her lower back. 'C'mon, Tess, we'll only find out if we go take a look.'

'How well do you know Emma?' she asked. '*Really* know her, I mean.'

'Enough to know it'll destroy me if anything bad has happened to her.'

That was enough for Tess. 'Let's go get her, then.'

Accompanied by a uniformed presence, Tess felt different than when she'd followed Po inside Rutterman Logistics. It was a throwback to the old days, like being a cop again, and as doubt diminished confidence swelled. She trotted alongside Alex, making their way up a sloping footpath used by diners who enjoyed after-dinner strolls on the beach. As they crested the rise and onto the parking lot adjacent to the Macedon they crouched and surveyed the land. A driveway followed the back slope of the promontory, down to a service track that led to Shore Road. There was a number of assorted vehicles parked at the front of the building. The restaurant was closed to the public, so the presence of so many cars spoke volumes. One of the vehicles was a large refrigerated van. Tess and Alex shared a glance. 'Ideal for transporting a subdued woman in?' Tess whispered.

'Or maybe it delivers chilled food to the restaurant,' Alex cautioned. The presence of a suspicious van wasn't enough to go on, it didn't give him probable cause to enter and search the premises.

'We have to get closer. We have to get a look inside.' Tess made to rise, but Alex's hand on her shoulder stalled her.

'Wait up, sis. We have to think this through. We can't just sneak inside and hope for the best.'

'We've no option.'

'I should call in backup. Hell, we need a team here to conduct a full search. We could always claim we received an anonymous tip-off that a woman is being held against her will. But what if we're wrong and Emma isn't here? What then?'

'Listen,' Tess said to waylay his growing doubt, 'wasn't that just a scream?'

There was no scream.

'Good try, but we need something more.'

'I'm just trying to cover your ass, Alex. I don't care about the legality, I just want to get in there.'

Alex remained crouched. His breath whistled in his throat. 'OK, we get closer. But you don't go inside unless I allow it.'

Tess shrugged, and before he changed his mind she rushed across the lot and bent low, hiding between two parked cars. A series of scuffs confirmed that Alex had followed, and was close. She checked over her shoulder and found him a few feet away, his face set. 'You're supposed to be sticking close to me,' he whispered, 'not the other way around.'

She held up a finger. There was a soft buzz against her side. Tess dipped her hand in her purse and brought out her cell, cupping her other hand over the screen to douse the soft glow. It was Po calling.

'I've got eyes on a couple of guys around this side. One of them's an old pal of ours. Blondie, the guy who put the transponder on the Chicken Shack.'

He meant Kenneth Jones – Welshy – and Tess felt instant vindication for bringing them here.

'What about Torrance?'

'No sign of him. No sign of Emma Clancy either, but that's not to say she isn't here. Blondie and this other dude have stepped outside for a smoke, but when they came out I heard other voices from inside.' Po waited. 'I can get by them. Better still, I can have a quiet word in Blondie's ear.'

'Wait, I'd best check with Alex first.'

'He's not the boss of me,' Po said, and she caught the subtle hint in his announcement. On occasion she'd questioned Po's loyalty, even to a point of fearing he might be working for the opposition, playing her for a fool, but that had never been it. She understood the simple truth from his statement: he was his own man and did things his own way, and conforming to her way of working must have been frustrating for him. He'd trusted her safety to Alex so he could do his thing again – without the hindrance of having to worry about her. Before she could caution him about doing anything rash, Po hung up.

Tess looked at Alex, and he read her expression.

'Damn it,' he wheezed. 'That's what comes of working with an asshole. You could stick a bunch of flowers in their butt but it doesn't make them a Ming vase.'

Under any other circumstance Tess would've laughed. Not now though. She wondered what the hell Po was about to do, and more than anything she wanted to join him on the far side of the building. She swapped her phone for her grandfather's revolver.

THIRTY-FIVE

B lood leaked from Emma Clancy's hairline, invading her eyes, making it difficult to see. For that contradictory blessing, a tiny part of her was grateful. She couldn't bear to meet the gaze of her torturer any longer and she screwed her lids tight. It was akin to proverbially burying your head in the sand; it didn't defy the horrifying reality. Hector still delighted in tormenting her, making the smallest of painful cuts long before he was prepared to deliver the coup de grâce. In fact, there was no hope of a stroke of mercy, because delivering a decisive cut to end her suffering was an alien concept to him. He wanted her to experience agony, and for it to linger. As far as the cutting went, it was only part of his devilish plan, and her torture was as much mental as physical. He'd sliced along her hairline while explaining how he was going to peel her face from her skull like a mask. With a male victim, he targeted the genitals, taking away his masculinity; with a woman he was more interested in destroying her through vanity. He'd nipped and stabbed at her breasts, the cuts and bruises superficial, but incredibly painful and soul destroying. Twice already he'd promised to slice off her nipples, but twice he'd held off, but the attack on her femininity and possibility of future motherhood was still on the cards.

As a career-driven woman, with her eye on continual advancement, becoming a mother had never rated highly on her 'to do' list before, and she blamed that on the breakdown of her marriage, but since entering a relationship with Alex Grey, her maternal instincts had stirred, blossomed, and she had begun to yearn for a baby. Until her divorce was finalized, Alex had agreed to keep their relationship a secret, despite how much he wanted to shout about their love. She loved Alex with equal passion, and for the first time in her life hopes of a future family were as important as succeeding in this man's world. Would Alex still love her if she were grotesque and violated, unable to bear his children? It was as if the monster knew her deepest desires and was determined to wrench them from her. More than once he'd inserted his hands in her panties, threatening to *spoil* her, and the presence of the thick rubber gloves denying his flesh from hers were no less invasive. She'd travelled beyond screaming, both in anger and terror, and now barely mewled as he continued his assault. She couldn't see the knife he wielded, but she could feel its icy presence alongside her skin. A pinprick in the flesh told her he was testing it against her lower abdomen.

'I'm going to cut you long, deep, and wide,' he whispered into her ear. 'I'm going to pull out your womb and make you eat it while I watch you swallow every mouthful.'

She believed he would too.

But his attention had fastened on her breasts again.

'I'm going to take off your *tatas*: one of them I will make into a pouch for my cell phone, the other I'll stretch over your skinned head.' He giggled at the loathsome image, and directed his next words at the other person in the room. 'She would look cute in a *tata* hat, no?' Welshy had left the torture room on some personal errand, but another man attended to Hector's whims and his disgusting humour, labouring to keep the area clean with a mop and bucket while he forced out a strangled laugh. Hector had proven to be fastidious about cleanliness, a total abstraction considering the amount of blood and viscera he intended spilling. The cleaner was an unwilling participant in Emma's treatment, but he was wise enough to keep his opinion to himself, and to laugh on cue. Emma hated the stranger for his cowardice almost as much as she despised Hector Suarez.

The flat of Hector's palm smacked off Emma's backside.

'Pay attention,' he told her.

'G-get away from me you . . . you . . . animal.'

'Ha! So there is some spirit left in you? That is good. *Eso es bueno, la señora Clancy.*'

There was a noise from beyond the room.

An angry shout followed.

Then the distinctive crack of a gun.

Hector's prattling fell silent, and the atmosphere grew sharp with expectation.

There came a series of thuds and clatters, the pained yelp of a man, and Emma's eyes snapped open.

'*Qué fue eso?*' Hector breathed. When got no reply, he switched to English, directing his question at the cleaner. 'You. What was that?'

'Beats me, man. But you heard the gunshot, right?'

'I'm not fucking deaf,' Hector snapped. 'Go find out what is happening.'

'You want me to go out there? Isn't it obvious what's happening?' The cleaner aimed an accusatory nod at Emma. 'My guess is they've come for her.'

Hector swore under his breath. He slipped his knife into his slicker coat pocket, reached for the pulley holding her upright. To Emma he promised, 'You're mine.' He began unlatching her bonds, zipping apart the Velcro from one of her wrists. Emma sagged to her knees. Hector glared at the cleaner.

'You. I told you to find out what is happening.'

'I'm unarmed, man. I'm not going out there to get shot.'

'Coward! Dog! Do something useful. Do not let anyone in that door before I am finished with this *puta*.' He tore the last strap from Emma's wrist, and now she almost went down on her face. He fisted a hand in her hair, hauling her up. Emma grasped at his fingers, but his grip was remorseless. He dragged her across the tiles, her toes scrabbling for purchase as he headed for a door in the far corner.

As they reached the door, Emma tried to dig in, pressing her elbows against the jamb. Hector yanked her head savagely, and a clump of hair ripped loose. She collapsed on one hip, spinning on to her backside.

Against the pearlescent tiles and stark strip lights, the figure that swept into the room was a living shadow. He was tall, broad-shouldered, dressed in black, and he wielded a knife. His face held some colour, but it was a sickly pale green under the unnatural lights. His eyes were shards of turquoise when they swept the room, registered the man stabbing towards him with the broom handle, the monster in the yellow coat, and then settled for a fraction of a beat on Emma.

'Help me!' she screeched.

Then she was being dragged away, and was lost to her would-be saviour.

Hector grunted and cursed as he hauled her along, and the noise of his exertions almost covered the scuffle back in the torture room. Emma listened keenly, hoping to hear the slap of boots in pursuit. But the sounds of combat were indefinable. Bumps, bangs, the ringing clang of something metallic. A solid thud as someone went down, and in that moment she was lost.

All faith in an eleventh-hour rescue fled her, and she truly collapsed now. Her mind closed down to a point, a single lucid spark that danced in her vision, like a candle flame at the far end of a tunnel. The light receded, dimming, and she knew that it was a symbol of hope she must grasp at. But she didn't have the strength to lift her hands, or even the will to struggle against the inevitable. Hector doubled his efforts, dragging her dead weight without care that she banged forcefully against each riser as he manhandled her up a flight of stairs. She couldn't feel the bruising impacts; she'd sunk into oblivion.

THIRTY-SIX

'Alex, we can't just sit here all night,' Tess had whispered only moments ago. She watched her brother chew his lips in indecision, and decided enough was enough. She exhaled, and shifted so she could move easier.

'Wait!'

Alex's hand jerked up. Tess followed his nod, and saw a figure emerge from the front door of the Macedon. He was short, stocky, dressed in jeans and a football jersey hanging outside his pants. Even partially silhouetted by the internal lights, the man's face was pale. He bent at the waist, hands on his thighs, and Tess waited for him to vomit. He didn't throw up, but he was on the verge of losing his last meal. What had he witnessed to induce such nausea? She dreaded to think. She was tempted to rush over, stick her gun in his face, and demand answers. But Alex fisted his hand around the tail of her jacket.

The man wiped his hands over his face, pushed them through his hair, and stood. He rocked back on his heels, face to the sky. His exhalation was vocalized loud enough to carry to them. *Woo!*

The man scratched through his pockets and came out with a pack of cigarettes. He lit up, stood there drawing on the cigarette as if it were a lifeline. With each inhalation the glow lit his face, adding a demonic caste to Vasilis Katsaros. Actually, he didn't so much look like a demon as someone who'd peered into hell and seen it staring back.

Finally, the restaurant owner flicked away his stub, turning back for the door reluctantly. Tess raised a few inches on the balls of her feet, but Alex still controlled her. Good job. In the next instant Katsaros stepped aside, giving clearance for the door to swing open. Jacky Torrance almost staggered out on to the front step. Tess heard Alex's breath catch in recognition. Torrance snapped his hand at Katsaros, demanding a smoke. His face was as pale and sweaty as the Greek's. There was also a dark smudge on his shirt and it didn't take much imagination to colour it red.

Thinking back to the transponder she'd left packed in plastic in her suitcase, Tess pointed to Torrance. 'Alex. I've evidence pointing to John Torrance's involvement in the murder of Crawford Wynne. That man is a murder suspect, is that the probable cause you need?'

'That will do for me, sis.' Alex thumbed his radio mike, and gave a breathless announcement to the PPD control room. Before he could key down the volume, he received a responding squawk. He flinched at its harshness, but it was too late. Both Torrance and Katsaros gawped towards the parked cars.

'Now or never,' Tess decided, and she stood up, her revolver extended.

The two men responded by instinct. But it wasn't to her appearance. They'd heard the screech of Alex's radio and recognized what it was. But more so they'd heard the yell and the crack of a pistol from the other side of the building. Both men rushed for the door, momentarily fighting each other to get inside. Then Torrance disengaged, pulled aside his coat, and hauled out a gun. He blinked in surprise, spotting Tess.

'It's you!' His gun swung on her.

'Police department! Drop your weapon!' Alex's challenge was instinctive, but pointless.

Torrance fired, the night lighting up with muzzle flashes.

By then Tess had already dropped, but she heard the rounds carom off the roof of the parked car, sparks showering over her.

'Drop your weapon now!' Alex hollered.

Torrance was either deafened by his gunshots or desperate. Whatever, he came forward, holding his gun out as if it were too heavy to control, straining with it in his grip. He fired again, and the round zinged overhead.

Alex returned fire.

Torrance lurched aside, putting his shoulder to the door-frame. His gun rattled on automatic, and Alex went to his knees beside Tess.

'Alex?' her voice was a croak, fearing the worst.

'I'm OK. What about you? Are you hurt?'

'I'm OK.' Tess crawled forward, her revolver elevated, making it to the front of the parked car. She poked her head out as Alex stridently summoned assistance from his colleagues.

'Fucking bitch!' Torrance screamed. His gun rattled again. A spray of asphalt spattered Tess, one piece of tarry shrapnel striking her neck. She hissed in pain and ducked behind cover.

Behind her, towards the rear of the car Alex popped up, and braced his arms over the trunk. His aim steady, he fired: two rapid pops of his sidearm. The first round splintered glass in the front door, the second won him a throaty grunt from Torrance. From within the restaurant there was a corresponding rumble, and it had to be Sower's men rushing to take cover or to support their injured comrade.

Torrance fired again, but the bullet didn't come close. It was a pot shot, to cover his ass as he clawed to get through the door. Alex swore under his breath, aimed, and fired. Torrance grunted again, and this time, as he pushed inside, he fell to his knees, scrambling to get away.

Tess also scrambled, hauling herself up with a handhold on the parked car. She took a step.

'Tess! For God's sake, stay down!'

Alex came after her, but her mind was already made up. There was only one explanation for that first gunshot they'd heard. Po had been spotted and shot at: he could be injured, or, God forbid, dead. She raced for the building, and Alex had no option but plunge along in her wake.

The door opened.

A gun barked twice.

Tess felt the tug of a bullet through her jacket lining. When she didn't fall, she knew she'd been spared a round in her side. She ran on, but angled to one side, out of the line of fire. If it was Torrance beyond the door she couldn't tell. Behind her, Alex skidded to a halt. He braced his bent knees, gun extended in a two-handed grip. His gun flashed and whoever was inside the doorway instantly gave up the fight. Still, there was no point in assaulting the front entrance. Torrance, Katsaros, and at least one other could be just inside and they'd be running into a shooting gallery.

Tess had no intention of going that way; she wanted to see where Po was. If he needed help . . .

Alex tackled her.

They went down in a jumble on the sidewalk perimeter of the lot. His intention wasn't to stop her, but save her being ripped apart. Another of Sower's people had materialized around the corner she was racing towards, and he was holding some kind of compact machine gun. The gun chattered, but thankfully the rounds went over them, metallic pings and tinny shrieks announcing where they hit among the parked vehicles. Alex disengaged, rolling to get his elbows propped.

The machine-gunner needed only lower his aim.

Tess fired before any of them.

There was more chance of the building falling on the gunner's head than her bullet hitting him. But it didn't matter. He flinched, expecting to be struck, and his gun again spat rounds into the open air. Alex clipped him once in the gut, then once again, this time marginally higher up, and the man sank sideways, the gun rattling free of his outstretched arm on the sidewalk. Alex scrambled to his feet, never relinquishing his aim as he approached the man. Tess was close to his shoulder. The gunner was finished; Alex's final shot was dead centre to the chest. Alex kicked aside the gun that Tess now distractedly identified as an Uzi. Serious firepower, but considering the war that Sower had fanned it was unsurprising.

'Get back behind cover,' Alex said, pushing her to get her moving.

Tess elbowed past him. 'I have to help Po.'

'He's dead or he isn't,' Alex said, grasping her jacket. 'Run around that corner and it might be directly into the sights of another goddamn machine gun.'

'It's a chance I'm willing to take,' said Tess, wrenching to get free.

'I'm not.' Alex grappled her, picking her bodily off her feet, and lurched towards a low cinder-block wall. He slung her over the wall and dropped down beside her. 'Backup is coming,' he snapped. 'But it'll take a while to get here. We can't fight all those bastards inside. We just need to keep them there until the ESU team arrives.'

'We don't know how many there are,' Tess argued. But she knew he was right, because even if each vehicle on the lot had arrived with only a driver, it still amounted to a dozen people inside. Each car could have brought more.

'They don't know how many of us there are either. For all they know they're already surrounded. We keep them pinned down, Tess, wait for support. Then we go in.'

'By then it could be too late. If Emma's in there, if she's still alive, do you think they'll let her live?'

'She'll live if they decide to use her as a hostage,' Alex said hopefully. Tess knew he was struggling to contain himself – he wanted to rush to Emma's rescue as strongly as she did to help Po – but he was also fearful of anything happening to his sister, and was fighting the urge, thinking like a cop instead of someone protecting his loved ones.

She thought of the voicemail message left for John Torrance. *'The greaseball's looking to cut something,'* Welshy had warned, and he could only have been referring to Sower's pet mutilator. Thinking back to the sick pallor on Vasilis Katsaros' face when he'd stumbled outside for a smoke, the killer had already begun his work. Judging by how sickened the Greek was, Emma would be in no fit state as a hostage, more like another demonstration of Sower's power. It was probably too late to save her, but if Tess voiced her concern it might send Alex over the edge. Perhaps it was best that one of them kept a clear head, and she preferred that it was Alex.

The radio traffic over Alex's mike was almost indiscernible. The voices of dispatchers and responding officers babbled, but it was comforting. It meant that the troops were responding in numbers. But it was as Alex pointed out, it'd take time for them to arrive at the Macedon. Keeping Sower's gang pinned inside possibly was best practice, but that was under different circumstances than Tess and Alex were up against. From somewhere inside the restaurant a firearm crackled, and there could be only one good reason. Even if Emma was dead, Po was inside, and he faced overwhelming numbers, and was woefully outgunned.

'No. We can't just sit and wait,' Tess croaked. 'Po's inside. He needs *me*, Alex.'

A voice hollered a challenge: curses that blew overhead. Whoever was shouting, he had no idea where Tess or Alex was. Alex popped up from hiding, fired, and his round clacked against a wall. The shouter shut up as he took cover. Alex dropped down again, shaking his head in regret.

'Idiot!' he snapped in self-derision. 'That bastard was drawing fire, gauging our numbers. They'll know they're up against a single armed officer. They might try to force a way out past me. Better get ready, Tess. If the worst comes to the worst, you haul ass. Got it?'

'We've two guns,' she reminded him. 'I'm not leaving.'

'Fuck!'

'Alex, don't forget I was a cop too. I'm not a helpless little girl.' She crawled away from him. 'Let's give them something to think about, shall we?'

When she was a dozen yards away, she went to her knees. Nodded at him and was relieved to catch his return nod. Simultaneously they rose above the low wall, firing, placing their rounds in the glass doors and windows where they'd do most damage. Anyone inside would assume they were under fire from a squadron.

With only one bullet left in the revolver, Tess dropped low again, then made the crawl back to her brother. He'd already snapped a spare magazine in his semi-automatic, and now covered her while she braced her shoulders to the wall. She opened the revolver, knocked out the last round, and fed the spare speed-loader into the chambers. Six bullets back in her gun, and one she slipped into her jeans pocket. Seven rounds wouldn't last if Sower's gang attempted a concerted escape, but she must make do. There'd be no spending rounds through windows again.

There was no way to accurately predict any outcome, but their only chance of success was in taking the initiative. There were other exit and entry doors to the Macedon, and with only Tess and Alex outside, crouched behind the same wall, they'd no hope of controlling all routes. If Sower's people wished to flee, they could escape via the public restaurant, clamber down the promontory and on to the beach. But that would put them on foot and within the noose of approaching police. If those inside intended to evade capture they'd have to make a try for the cars and use speed to outmanoeuvre the responding cops. From their position Tess was confident they could stop any attempt at the vehicles, unless the group charged out en masse, all shooting. The cinder-block wall was poor defence against a blistering volley of gunfire and would be chewed to pieces in seconds. They must gain ground, enter the building, and force Sower's people back. She'd promised Po she'd have his back as he did hers, and that was impossible while hiding outside.

She craned for a look. The glass doors were shattered, splinters of glass littering the ground at the entrance. There was no hint of movement inside, though she could hear rapid footsteps pounding through the building. Faint shouts and instructions were bandied back and forth.

Nobody was shooting, but that wouldn't last.

'Come on, Alex. We have to do *something*.'

'We wait.'

'Waiting's going to get Po killed.'

'Not waiting will get us *all* killed.'

She shook her head. 'I'm going in. I'd prefer it if you were with me.'

'No, Tess. You're staying put.' His hand reached for her. 'If anyone goes in it should be me.'

But she'd made her decision. 'Cover me.'

His fingers fell short as she crawled away.

'Tess . . .'

She continued crawling.

'Son of a bitch! Get back here!'

She ignored Alex's irritation, it was born of his concern for her welfare, and she loved him for it, but it wasn't going to deter her from what was admittedly a stupid idea. She gripped her revolver, faintly aware of the ache in her damaged wrist, legacy of controlling the recoil while shooting out the windows. But surprisingly there was no weakness in her fingers. Resolve, determination, call it what you will, steadied her hand. She looked back at Alex, and saw that he'd planted his heels, ready to bob up and cover her. She mouthed a silent thank-you at him, but he just formed a bitter line of his mouth, concentrated on target acquisition instead. Tess hopped up, and sprinted for the corner where the machine-gunner lay dead. She made it to cover, paused with her back to the wall. The Uzi was at her feet. She'd fired automatic weapons before, but wasn't confident she'd be able to handle the machine gun, but she knew someone who probably could. She snatched it up and slung it by its strap around her neck. She moved on.

Being out of public view, this side of the Macedon was in darkness, but for one dim glow ahead, marking entry to a side door. There was enough ambient light to tell nobody lurked in ambush on the narrow tarmac path, but it wasn't totally deserted. A recumbent form presented their heels as she approached. Tess covered the man with her revolver, padding to his side. She was thankful it wasn't Po, but also realized that the man had fallen victim to her partner. Blood poured from both nostrils, but that wasn't the worst of his injuries. His head was canted unnaturally to one side, and more blood dripped from his right ear. If he lived, it would be in a wheelchair for the rest of his miserable days. Perhaps it would be best if his broken neck had instantly sheared the nerve functions of his heart and lungs.

Po had reported sighting Kenneth Jones and one other man, taking a smoking break away from the nastiness going on inside. The victim wasn't Welshy, but some other man, a stranger who'd chosen the wrong path when following Albert Sower. She felt no pity for him. But she wondered what had become of Welshy, and if that was who had shot at Po earlier. A quick check of the broken man found no weapons, and there were none she could find alongside the path. She went to the fire door. Light from within etched its frame, and also a two-inch gap down the centre. Luckily the door hadn't fully closed after Po or Welshy had gone inside, and the locking bar hadn't engaged. She fed her left hand into the gap, manipulated the bar, edged the doors open, and snapped a quick look inside. She saw a corridor that ended at an intersection about twenty feet away. Doors on either side were utilitarian, and the rooms probably housed stock or equipment. Nobody waited to shoot her dead. She inhaled, prepared to enter.

Shots rang out, the muzzle flashes cracking the darkness over her right shoulder. She couldn't see Alex but there was plenty of thunder and lightning to indicate he was busy.

Alex shouted an officious command. Briefly the shooting abated and she hoped it meant the situation was under control. It wouldn't last. She was torn: she should go back and support her brother, but she must also help Po. A few days ago there'd have been no debate about whom she'd have gone to. But that was then. She pulled the doors wide and entered the corridor.

She went cautiously, passing the utility rooms, checking handles as she progressed and finding them locked. Underfoot the linoleum crackled. She saw dots of fresh blood on the floor. Whose blood? With no idea she put it out of her mind, and hurried to the intersection. She checked both ways, then, following logic, she chose left, forging deeper inside the building. From somewhere ahead there was a rumble, a clatter. Something metallic but unsubstantial spilled across the ground, clinking and tinkling. The air smelled of heat and cooking, heady mixed scents and aromas forming a panoply where she couldn't define one smell from another. It was nauseating.

Ahead was a set of swinging doors with porthole windows. The doors were brushed steel, scuffed and gouged at ankle height. A bloody hand had slapped a way through them. Tess cringed back from the crimson smear as if it were diseased. Instinctively she knew it wasn't Po's blood. Avoiding the blood, she leaned to get a look through the porthole to the left. She'd expected to discover a kitchen, but the room was for storage, with long steel trestle tables, tall fridges, and freezers. The floor was tiled, and a gutter ran down the centre towards a drain. It appeared that Katsaros butchered much of his own fresh meat and fish. For convenience, the preparation area would be near the kitchen, so there must be an adjoining door out of her line of sight. She entered the room, moving along the central aisle, feet placed either side of the gutter, down which ran a stream of water. The floor was damp and slippery, as if recently hosed, and the air so chilly she could see her breath. Fresh spatters of blood marked the otherwise pristine route.

Turning to the right, she found another set of porthole doors. Beyond them was a vestibule. On the opposite side of a counter she spotted the dining area. Most of the lights had been doused, but there were other points of light that reflected off the huge windows that formed the prow of the Greek's boat. Past them she caught fleeting movement. People were in the dining area, using the pools of darkness to prowl through, while checking outside. They were probably searching for a clear way out past the imagined cordon of police officers. Tess thought she heard sobbing.

In the next instant the sound was drowned by a commotion from somewhere to her left. She pushed through the doors, keeping low so she didn't alert those in the seating area, and duck-walked along the vestibule. Pots and pans crashed. Voices hollered and cursed. A door slammed. A gun popped, but it was distant, the sound hollow. It might even have been Alex shooting outside.

She bobbed up to check through another porthole window, and at last found the kitchen. It was in disarray. Pans, pots, utensils all lay scattered on the floor amid squashed and splattered food. A frantic scuffle had occurred, and only moments before judging by the lazy swinging of a door across the kitchen. Tess checked behind. Nobody had come to investigate the commotion, already fully aware of what was going on and choosing to stay out of it.

Tess pushed inside the kitchen. Footprints and smears of trampled food, overturned equipment, a door hanging open on a refrigerator, all suggested the route the fight had taken. It was as if someone had tossed a hand grenade into the kitchen, there was so much disruption. Her gaze snapped to a meat cleaver. There was blood on the wicked steel blade. The battle had been furious, then.

More evidence presented in the form of a seated body. It was wedged in the doorway of a storage closet. A man. His legs splayed either side of a dented steel bucket, his hands in his lap, head drooping on his motionless chest. The front of his shirt was sodden with blood, from where his throat had been opened. This was the work not of Sower's mutilator, but of her friend. A qualm went through her. But she didn't turn away in revulsion.

If she had, she might've spotted Jacky Torrance prowling up behind her, before he reached for the bloodied meat cleaver and aimed it at her neck.

THIRTY-SEVEN

History repeating.

The last time a crazed knifeman attacked her, she'd almost lost a hand. She'd definitely lost a fiancé and a career, and an innocent clerk had lost his life. And all because fear and indecision made her freeze a fraction too long before she had used her gun. The same could be said now, because she froze again, and her arm never managed to get close to deflecting the killing blow. But that was all for the best. She froze, only because she'd caught Torrance's dim reflection in the brushed-steel door, halting her instinct to turn and face her attacker. If she had done, the meat cleaver would've found the soft skin of her throat and that would have been the end of Teresa Grey.

Coming out of her initial jolt of terror, she sprawled. The cleaver whipped through the space vacated by her skull and slammed into the doorframe. She scrambled for her life, kicking and pushing, her heels against the thigh of the dead man, and she launched herself out from under Jacky Torrance as he wrenched the blade loose with a snarl of rage. She rolled on her back, and as he came at her for a second cut, she booted his knee out from under him. Torrance fell on the corpse, his legs entangling with it. He fought to free himself, then stood, but already Tess had squirmed away. She was crushed up against a cabinet, the Uzi digging painfully in her side, staring as he aimed the cleaver at her. Her right hand was wedged under her thigh, and she couldn't move in time to avoid another cut.

'We should've taken you into the swamp and gutted you instead!' Torrance spat. In hindsight, Crawford Wynne was killed for nothing. What could Wynne say now that could prove troublesome for Sower, when the maniac had already damned himself? Torrance had apparently come to the same conclusion, and wanted to direct his frustration on a deserving target.

'You should have stayed in Louisiana,' Tess countered, giving him something to think about while she relaxed her leg, freeing her arm. 'You came back here for this? To be part of a psychopath's last desperate attempt at notoriety? Look at you, Jacky! Is it worth dying for Albert *fucking* Sower?'

Torrance blinked. He looked down, following the nod she'd aimed at his torso. His shirt was bright red, sopping wet. Alex had hit him with those opening rounds. He pressed his left palm against the hole in his chest, grimacing as if noticing the horrific wound for the first time. He lifted his hand, inspecting it. 'I'm not dying,' he said, but he was unsure. Something wormed behind his features, a shiver of understanding. Now conscious of his mortality and how fleeting it had become, his face darkened, as he raged against the inevitable. 'You did this to me! You shot me! But I'm not the one who's going to die. You are!'

With a howl he lurched at her, the cleaver rising high overhead as he built momentum for a savage chop.

Tess didn't try to escape. Calmly she drew the revolver from under her thigh. 'Don't do it, Jacky!'

Torrance saw the gun and realized how wrong he was. But what could he do? He brought down the cleaver in a whooshing arc. Tess shot him in the forehead. His head snapped back, and his last breath was expelled heavenward, though Tess doubted he'd be welcomed there. Torrance's knees folded, and he collapsed down on his butt before flopping sideways. The meat cleaver clattered harmlessly against the tiles.

She couldn't lower the gun. Her forearm was seized tight, the flexor muscles employed to pull the trigger contracting so violently that she experienced physical pain. In the next instant she began to shake, and then it was the exact opposite. Her arm went numb, nerveless, and it flopped by her side. A moan escaped her, a brittle sound of regret. It would be a long time before she'd be able to shake the image of Torrance's brains exploding from the back of his skull. No! God damn it! He deserved exactly what he'd got. No remorse, no regret, she told herself. You're alive, Tess, and if that bastard had his way it would've been your brains on the floor.

Get up!

Get up, because Po needs you.

She forced herself to stand. She also forced herself to look at the damage she'd done to Torrance. Her arm hung uselessly at her side. No, it was psychology at play. Her arm was fine, and it could support the weight of the revolver. To prove the point, she brought up the gun. It was such a simple task. The adrenalin flooding her body caused the only trembling she was aware of now.

As a child, she'd been in her grandfather's workshop, watching him as he stripped down an outboard motor. He stood, wiping fuel from a spark plug with a rag. Spotting a spider crawling on the bench towards her, she'd shrieked and jumped a foot in the air. Smiling, her grandfather had walked over, held out his finger and allowed the harmless arachnid to climb aboard. He'd offered the spider to Tess to pet, and she'd almost curled up and died on the spot. 'Tess,' he'd said in that wise way he had, 'there's only one way I know of getting past fear. If you're afraid of what's waiting in the cave, walk inside and laugh in its face.' Hell, her grandfather's aversion therapy had been right. She should've shot a murderous bastard in the forehead months ago! That thought almost made her laugh, but she fought against the impulse. If she began laughing, she might not be able to stop.

Instead she moved away, adjusting the Uzi on its sling so it didn't bump annoyingly against her ribs. It was only as she stepped over the man with the slashed throat, pushing through the door he'd blocked, that she realized that something had changed.

Everything had fallen silent.

It was probably a result of her shooting Torrance. The noise exploding from within the building, and perhaps even his yelling beforehand, had told the others that another of their enemies had gained entrance to the Macedon. She imagined them taking cover, waiting to ambush her, or anyone else stupid enough to go back through the way she'd come. Thankfully there was nobody lurking in the corridor she had entered. The lights were off, but there was enough of a glow from a fire-exit sign to see by. She passed the door, noting a plastic security tag on the push bar hadn't been disturbed. No one had left via that route. She paused at the end of the passage, with two choices of direction. One went to the right, back towards the dining area, and the other allowed entry through a door to a set of stairs. The stairwell was positioned oddly, and she could only assume it gave access to space above the jutting prow of the building. Going up there might be tantamount to suicide, because hemming herself in the confined stairwell would give even a poor shot a sitting target. She was about to turn away, but a smear of blood on the doorframe changed her mind. Earlier she'd decided that the blood couldn't have been Po's, but now? She'd found neither hide nor hair of her friend, and by the relative silence in the kitchen and dining areas she doubted he was in either location. She pressed the door open with her fingertips, poked her head into the stairwell. From above came the thump and rumble of feet. Tess went up.

The stairs ended on a short triangular landing. At the narrowest point small windows allowed a view across Smuggler's Cove. Tess got a sense of the surging ocean outside, but there was time for nothing else. She rapidly moved around the landing and found another set of doors. Out of sight and reach of the public, they were cheap and flimsy. One carried a brand-new hole, where it appeared somebody had kicked their way through. Po, she assumed, chasing someone. His quarry had to be Welshy, because she hadn't come across the man yet, dead or alive. After Po broke the neck of the man outside, had he then pursued Welshy, and the man had sought escape on the upper floor? There had to be another way down, probably at the far end of the building. She contemplated whether to go on, because the earlier ruckus had dissipated. Had the fight returned to the ground floor? Yes, she was probably wasting time up here.

A screech tore through the upper floor.

It wasn't the scream of a man. Not of pain or anger, or even fury. It was the voice of a woman, one teetering on the edge of insanity.

Emma Clancy!

It could be nobody else.

Tess had given up on finding Emma alive, and she'd been

wrong to do so. This was the woman Tess had wondered about, if she were in cahoots with Sower, using and manipulating her, but the soul-wrenching scream proved all her suspicions were not only unfounded but also ridiculous. Emma wasn't an enemy; she was Tess's boss, and her brother's lover and now, more than anything, to be saved.

Without pause, Tess plunged through the broken door, and into a dimly lit attic space, which was almost the length of the building. The huge room had been used primarily for storage, and defunct fridges and freezer units made geometric shapes down one side. Spare tables and chairs were stacked along the opposite wall. Boxed items and sundry equipment had been left in random piles, some of them blocking a view of the entire attic. But she could see movement, and the commotion of earlier resumed: thuds, bumps, and rattles. And Emma Clancy screamed again. The breath caught in Tess's throat, and it took a moment to shake off the fresh feeling of ineptitude that assailed her. *Cave. Enter. Laugh.* She rushed forward, holding her revolver before her, but any insane laughter was wedged beneath the lump in her throat.

Her feet drummed on the floorboards, then made a skidding, rasping noise as she stumbled to a halt, seeking a viable target.

Two figures writhed in combat, too closely wrapped up in their private battle to offer her a clear shot. One of them was Po, his black clothing now making him distinct alongside the second man, who was bizarrely dressed in a yellow slicker, and bright orange waterproof trousers and gumboots. The second man was dark-complexioned, with short, wavy black hair, flecked grey at the temples. His face was lumpy with scars – *no good would come from looking into that face*, it had once been described. Tess had never seen him before, had never viewed a photo of him, but instinctively knew who he was.

Albert Sower's killer. Sower's *mutilator*.

He was the one responsible for dismembering Sower's enemies, the one who'd abducted them, who'd tortured and then violated their corpses. He was the one who'd decapitated Crawford Wynne, displayed his headless corpse like a gutted fish, gelded him, and stitched his genitals inside his mouth. He was a monster, and he was trying his hardest to kill Po.

Po was trying his best to kill him too.

Tess had witnessed fights before – too many to count – but she'd seen nothing like this outside of a choreographed battle royal. Both men were evenly matched in skill, and to Tess's horror, evenly matched in weaponry. Both stabbed and cut with their respective blades, even as they kicked and punched, elbowed and head-butted. How could anyone withstand such maltreatment to the body? Any one of those strikes was enough to put anyone to sleep, and yet they shrugged them off and came back for more. Their knives whipped in and out, and blood dripped and spattered from their gouged arms and legs.

The fight took them from one side of the attic to the other, then back again. They went to the floor, but fought back to standing. Tess was caught, both awestruck and horrified by the extremes of violence. Only when the two staggered over a third figure, and Emma Clancy squalled in terror did Tess snap out of her trance.

Clancy was dressed in panties, but that was all. Her body was bloodied from what looked like a thousand small cuts, and her hair was tacky and adhered to her face, and some crimson-stained strands were stuck in the corner of her open mouth. Her eyes rolled wildly, and even when her gaze swept over Tess, there was no sense of recognition, only terror. The strong, intelligent, self-confident woman . . . reduced to a mewling child by Sower's killer.

Tess rushed towards her, even as Po slammed an elbow into the killer's chest and drove him back from his prey. The two combatants spilled towards the wall where the tables were stacked. They crashed among them, and the grunts and thuds told Tess their fight had taken a different direction now. She grabbed for Clancy's arm, to haul her out of harm's way. Clancy howled, snatching her arm out of Tess's grip. The investigator, now reduced to a wounded thing, wrapped her arms over her head and cried.

Tess felt the rush of air behind her.

The killer's slicker coat slapped rubbery and wet against her arm. Tess croaked, and threw herself out of his grasp, going down on top of Clancy. Clancy screeched, writhing wildly to be free of this fresh torment. Tess rolled off her, trying to bring around the gun. The fight had moved on. Briefly she watched as Po kicked at the legs of the man, and then had to swerve aside to avoid the thrust of the other's blade. The knife caught in Po's jacket, yanking it open, before Po stabbed at the killer's neck and missed by a hair's breadth. Then they were a series of juddering shadows in the corner of her eye as Tess again grabbed for Clancy.

'Emma! Emma! Listen to me. It's Tess. I'm here to help.'

Clancy's fingernails went for her face.

Tess backhanded the assault away.

'Aw, hell,' she snapped, and with no recourse, she snagged a handful of Clancy's bloody hair and hauled the woman to her feet. She shook Clancy's head savagely. 'I said listen to me! Emma. Do you understand? It's me! Tess Grey. I'm going to get you out of here!'

For extra measure, she gave Clancy another brain-rattling yank on her hair. 'Listen! Alex is waiting for you downstairs. Do you want to see Alex or not?'

Clancy's eyes were rimmed with blood, but for the first time there was a glimmer of awareness in them. She mewled, but now there was a different tone. Hope?

'It's me. Tess! Do you recognize me, Emma?'

'Oh God . . . Tess?'

'Yes. You have to come with me. Now. C'mon, Alex is waiting.' Tess took Clancy's arm in hers, determined to lead her out. Clancy wouldn't move. She tried to dig her bare heels into the floor. But Tess knew why.

Kenneth Jones – Welshy – loomed directly in front of them. The first time Tess laid eyes on him at the airport in New Orleans, he'd presented as clean cut, almost handsome with his blond hair and smooth features. Now he was a mess. His hair stood in ratty tufts, and his clothing was ripped and soiled. Worst of all, his face was slashed to the bone, a wet rag of skin hanging from his left jaw, displaying the bloody teeth inside. He champed his jaws in fury, and fresh blood pulsed down his neck, joining the sodden pool he'd already lost. He was seriously wounded, but very much alive. He must feel terrible, but it served to fuel his anger. He jammed the barrel of a gun to Tess's forehead.

'Drop the gun, you goddamn bitch,' he snarled. 'Or I'll blow your brains all over the floor.'

Tess felt her mouth open, but no words would come. Beside her, Clancy pressed tightly to her body, burying her face in Tess's shoulder. Tess slipped her left arm around her, even as she held her revolver out to one side, and let it drop with a clatter to the boards.

'Kick it away,' Welshy ordered.

Tess toed the revolver out of reach.

'That's better,' Welshy said. 'Now get over there.' He waved his gun at the stacked tables, now knocked awry. His eyes scrunched as he checked beyond his captives, weighing the odds on the outcome of the fight raging behind them. 'We're going to wait this out. Doesn't matter who wins; if it's your man, I'm going to blow his fucking teeth out for what he did to me.' He tapped his gun barrel against the cut in his face, then scowled at his stupidity.

So Welshy's dishevelled state was courtesy of Po? Tess's only regret was that Po hadn't finished Welshy off before engaging the killer in mortal combat. Never mind. It was down to her, and it was one task she wouldn't shirk from.

'You don't even get to look at *my man* the wrong way,' Tess snarled.

'Who's going to stop me? You?' Welshy laughed, and he couldn't resist a gloating look in Po's direction. His attention was off her, and that was all Tess needed.

In one move she thrust Clancy aside with her hip, even as she hauled up the Uzi that had been concealed by the woman's naked body. There was no need to charge the weapon, or to turn off any safety catches or anything else, because the gunner had seen to all those inconveniences before Alex shot him dead. Tess was already pulling the trigger as the gun swept up, and the blistering rounds tore splinters from the floor in one instant, flesh from bones the next. Welshy performed a strange disjointed jig, before the force of the bullets ripping him apart carried him off balance and threw him flat on his back. He was dead before his skull whacked the floorboards with resounding finality.

Ignoring the dead man, Tess looked for Clancy. She

was huddled a few feet away. Safe from harm. Tess swept around.

Fifteen feet away, Po and the killer had spilled apart.

They were almost as shocked by the thunderous roar of the machine gun as Welshy had been in the instant before he died. They stood, aware of the other, but watching Tess. Po had his left hand on his chest, stemming a deep cut, and another slash wept blood under his left eye. He offered the tiniest nod of appreciation at her handiwork, before shifting his attention to the killer.

The man was eyeing Tess with the strangest of expressions. It wasn't hatred, surprise, or even respect at what she'd achieved. The look was one that sent a trickle down her spine, worming and oily. She aimed the Uzi directly at his chest.

'Drop the knife, you sick son of a bitch!'

The killer shook his head, and an amused smile crept over his lumpy features. He pointed the knife at her. 'I watched you after leading you to Crawford Wynne, and was tempted to take you then,' he said, his voice heavily accented. 'I wanted to take you deeper into the swamp with me. I would have stripped the hide from your body, hollowed out your skull and left it for the snakes to nest in.'

Po didn't move. But he was coiled taut, ready in an instant.

'You didn't.' Tess returned the killer's smile. 'You couldn't, because my friend would've stopped you, the way he stopped you hurting Emma. You're not going to get another chance at either of us now.'

'I'm not?'

'Move an inch and you get what Welshy did.' She jabbed the muzzle of the Uzi at him for emphasis.

'Aah, *Welshy*. He has served me well, and I had such high hopes for him. Such a shame about my friend.'

'Was he your friend, though? You do know that he called you a greaseball behind your back?' Tess waited for a reaction, but got none. 'Where are you from? You're Bolivian, right? Like Alberto Suarez?'

The killer didn't reply. He didn't have to.

'Who is Sower to you?' Tess demanded.

'The man who once saved me.' His free hand touched his

scarred face, and Tess wondered if he'd been on the receiving end of similar torture to the one he'd been performing on Emma. 'I swore my life to Alberto, and any other lives he claimed. But Alberto's had all he will from me. Now it's my time to take back what is mine.'

'If he's had all he's getting from you, why do his bidding like this now?'

'I don't do Alberto's bidding. I've repaid the debt I owed my brother.' His face tightened in resolve. 'Now I do what I choose.'

'But in doing so, you choose to do exactly as he says? I get it. So basically you're as crazy as he is?' Tess waited a beat. 'That's good: it means you can keep each other company when you're incarcerated in the same insane asylum.'

'Alberto is behind bars, yes, but I won't be caged.'

'You will. Don't you hear that?'

From below them there came a chorus of commands, shouted orders, and the crash and thud of a dynamic entry by the responding ESU tactical team. Tess even thought she could pinpoint Alex's voice as he called for her and Emma with equal desperation.

'You're finished, asshole,' Tess told the killer.

'I told you. You have Alberto and can keep him. But I won't be caged.' He eyed her as if she was a prize on a shelf. 'It's *my* time again and I'll take what's *mine*!'

He sprang towards her, lifting his knife, as though inviting suicide by her hand.

No. His reckless attack was for another reason. He wanted a live hostage, and who better than Tess? The bastard had noted that the Uzi had locked open, the magazine now empty.

His blade was inches from her when Po crashed bodily into the killer and knocked him sideways. Again the two men spilled apart, and when Po stood it was to shield Tess with his body. His hands were empty, curled into fists.

The killer also stood. He still held his slick blade firmly in hand.

Po's knife handle jutted from the front of his yellow coat. Before, the rain slicker had been covered in stringy wet rivulets of gore, but now a fresh river flowed down it and dripped to

the floor at his feet. The killer gave a grunt, and pressed his
fingers to the handle of the knife as if to pluck it out. He
allowed his hand to drop away, then lifted his other hand and
inspected his blade. He nodded in a last-ditch decision, then
rose up, emitting a defiant shriek, and again launched himself
at them.

The crack of a gun broke his war scream.

The killer crashed down, his face smacking down at Po's
feet. Po stepped back to avoid the splash of brain matter leaking
from the hole in the back of the killer's skull.

Beyond them, Emma Clancy still aimed Tess's dropped
revolver at the corpse, and the look on her face was expectancy,
as if the mutilator would rise again like the unstoppable crea-
ture from a horror movie. She shuddered, the barrel wavering.
Tess reached slowly and placed her hand on the barrel, meeting
Emma's tortured gaze.

'He was going to take *everything I want* from me,' she
croaked.

'He's finished,' Tess assured her. 'You're safe now, Emma.
It's over.'

Emma's eyelids slid shut, and Tess took the gun gently from
her. Then Emma fell against her, and held on. Tess returned
the hug.

Behind them Po grunted something, and Tess turned to
check on him. He sat down heavily on the floor, his long legs
splayed. His turquoise gaze had dimmed from the familiar
twinkle. He squeezed out a smile, but then his head drooped
and he looked at where his hands were cupped over his belly.
His hands were now ingrained with blood, and Tess's heart
hitched in her chest when she saw more bubble out from
between his fingers.

'Oh no,' she moaned, and pulled from Emma's embrace.

Po slumped on his side. His right hand flopped alongside
him, and cupped in his palm was a pool of his blood. Tess
lunged for him, dropping the gun, and going down on her
knees. She ignored the dull pain in her knees; it was nothing
to the sharp jab of despair jolting through her. Any niggling
doubt she'd ever entertained about where his loyalties lay
dissipated in a flash: he'd taken the stab meant for her and in

that instant she understood how deeply he cared for her, and she did for him. 'Po? Po!' She grasped at him, pulling his torso over her bent knees, both hands cupping his face.

'Got me good . . .' Po's voice was thin. She felt the strength go out of him, his weight sinking down over her thighs as she tried to prop him up. His lids slid shut, his bottom lip hanging low.

'No, no, no.' Tess scrabbled at his clothing, tugging at his shirt, then ripping it away to disclose a wound in his abdomen. Like the cuts on his face and chest it didn't look too severe, being less than an inch wide, but that was the surface damage only: his innards could be sliced open. Blood pulsed out of him. He'd traded stab for stab with the killer to save her, and paid dearly for it. Emma had come over to them, but she was dazed by everything that had occurred and stood numbly, her pale face framed by her unruly blood-matted hair.

'Emma! Emma! Do something for God's sake!' Tess yelled. 'Go downstairs and find Alex. Fetch a paramedic. Now! Go before Po dies!'

Emma blinked down at them, and her mouth dropped open. She looked down at her body, as if aware of her nakedness for the first time in an age. Her skin was nicked and sliced, covered in drying gore, and vivid bruises covered her arms and thighs. She was hurt, but not dying. It was as if she abruptly became aware that she had *survived*. And yet her saviour might not. She nodded hard, and then turned. She screamed for Alex as she ran down the stairs.

'Po! Stay with me,' Tess urged, shaking him with one hand while she pressed down on his wound with the other. 'Don't you dare die on me. Help's coming. Stay awake! C'mon. Let me see those beautiful twinkly eyes again.'

His eyes opened a slither, and she caught a flash of turquoise, as if looking briefly into a deep pool of tropical water. They twinkled. Tess made a noise that was part joy, part relief, and she folded over him, holding him tightly.

'If you . . . keep squeezing me so hard . . . you're going to have every last drop of blood outta me,' Po croaked.

Tess reared up from him. Her eyebrows almost touched her hairline. Po looked at her for a drawn-out moment before his mouth made a little quirk at one corner. He winked, but it was an effort. Despite his blasé attitude to his mortality, he was seriously injured. But apparently his death wasn't imminent.

'Oh, thank God. I thought you'd died on me,' Tess whispered.

'Nah. That crazy man knifed me good, but not as good as I got him. I plan on sticking around a while yet.'

'If we don't stop this bleeding—'

Po laid a hand over hers on his wound. But it was to knit his fingers with hers. 'I can spare a pint or two,' he said. 'Don't worry, help's coming. In the meantime, you can tell me how beautiful my twinkly eyes are again.'

'Oh! So you heard that?'

'I heard.'

'Well, what can I say? They *are* beautiful.'

He didn't reply, just placed his other hand on the back of her head and pulled her down to meet his lips.

THIRTY-EIGHT

Emma Clancy had regained her composure by the time Tess visited her temporary office in a civic building on Cumberland Avenue, not more than half a mile from her apartment. But then it had been almost two months since the events at the Macedon. Emma again exuded an air of confidence, strength, and surety, and dressed in a pristine trouser suit, her hair sleekly styled once more, she looked like a woman who could take anything on the chin and come back fighting. Tess suspected it was a veneer, because what Emma had gone through was enough to permanently disturb anybody. It transpired that after Sower's group had snatched her, she'd been held prisoner in the confines of the Macedon until the return of the mutilator. As Tess suspected, Emma was never without her cell phone and one of her captors had emailed her office, purporting to be her, giving her superior an excuse to divert any search for her while they planned their next move.

Richard Jackson had been accepting bribes from Sower, but his final payment for assisting in Emma's abduction had been paid in flames. Her captors – among them Vasilis Katsaros – had proved to be thuggish bullies and molesters, but they were kittens compared to the monster that'd arrived to reap payment on his brother's behalf. Once Hector, the elder brother, had ruled their Bolivian empire, until he was almost killed by a rival outfit, and Albert had stepped in, not only to save his life, but to take the business reins with both hands while Hector recovered from his wounds. Having sworn a pledge of honour, to serve the man to whom he owed his life, Hector Suarez had taken a position below him, but one to which he was ideally suited. He enforced the strict rules and regulations of the family criminal empire and doled out punishment when and where necessary.

After Alberto had relocated his enterprise to Maine, Hector had continued to ply his trade to the highest bidders in Bolivia, but it was inevitable he'd travel north when learning of his brother's arrest and detention. From his cell, by word of mouth of intermediaries, Sower had directed his brother at his enemies, or those perceived to be potential witnesses. But when the finger was pointed at Emma Clancy was it purely hatred that drove both men to attack the one they deemed their prime nemesis or something more? With Hector dead, they'd never know for certain, though it had been intimated that Hector was planning a coup that would return him to his original position of power. The burning of Emma's office was simply a convenient start, and a precursor to worse to come: Hector intended making an unforgettable spectacle of Clancy. He'd begun his work, cutting and nipping, delighting in her debasement, and he planned to make her torment last.

Enter Nicolas Villere and latterly Teresa Grey.

Tess had heard the story from Po, though he'd delivered his tale without any hint of bravado or histrionics. When the opportunity arose, he'd moved to gain entry to the Macedon, still hoping to find Emma Clancy alive. A man had tried to stop him, and the fool made the mistake of shooting at Po. He'd no option but stop him, and yes, it had to be with finality. He denied deliberately snapping the man's neck, but also added that he wasn't responsible for the way the clumsy fool fell on his head. Kenneth 'Welshy' Jones was Po's conduit to Clancy, and yes, he'd taken a little persuading to admit the investigator was being held in the food-preparation area behind the restaurant. Stupidly Welshy had attempted to stop Po attempting a rescue, and Po had shown him the error of his ways. Leaving the man in a state of unconsciousness, bleeding from a nasty cut to his lip, Po had gone in search of the prisoner. By then the bullets were flying, and things had grown deadly. He'd cut the throat of the fool who tried to intervene when he found Hector dragging his naked captive for the stairs. After a mop handle was proven an ineffective weapon, the idiot tried to brain Po with a steel bucket he'd been using to sluice away Clancy's spilled blood, so cutting his throat with an available meat cleaver had been an act of self-defence. Giving chase to Hector, he'd kicked open the door in time to find the murderer with his knife to Clancy's throat in the dusty attic. It was his duty to free the woman from her abuser, wasn't it? Tess knew what had transpired after that, and there were images captured during those events that plagued her dreams for nights afterwards, but not all of them were disturbing.

Discounting Albert Sower, the key players were dead, or incarcerated awaiting trial. Hector Suarez, John 'Jacky' Torrance, and Kenneth 'Welshy' Jones had all been identified as the abductors and murderers of both Crawford Wynne and Officer Mitchel Delaney, and the extra charges of conspiracy to murder – and the kidnapping and assault of Emma Clancy – were added to the roll call of accusations damning Albert Sower. With his organization broken, his chief mutilator slain, and the testimonies of four witnesses in the shape of Tess, Po, Alex, and Emma, Sower was relegated to making empty threats from his cell.

Officer Alex Grey had been hailed as a hero, though out of sight and hearing of the media, he'd been on the receiving end of a dressing down from his superiors and warned that any further breech of protocol would be severely dealt with – but the only adulation he cared for was that shown him by Emma. Officially Tess and Po's vigilantism had suffered a similar berating, but it was leavened with handshakes and congratulations away from the media circus. Their actions were rash and illegal, but nobody was prepared to hold anything against them after risking their lives to save an abducted woman from murder and bringing down Sower's empire in the process. Police in Louisiana had made some noise about their activities in the south, but when all came to all, they'd helped clear up the murders of the Cottonmouth Motorcycle Club members slain at their clubhouse, and Crawford Wynne. It helped when the survivor of the massacre came forward and identified Torrance, Jones, and Hector Suarez as the men responsible for the killings. They'd also assisted in shutting down Rutterman Logistics, when Tess presented the evidence of the transponder device, directly tying the company to Albert Sower's murderous henchmen and their activities in Louisiana. A search warrant turned up further evidence that the transportation company acted as a portal through which Sower was bringing narcotics, firearms, and illegal immigrants into the country. It proved an incredible coup for the local PD, not to mention the wider law-enforcement community where the ATF, FBI, and even Customs all took a slice of the praise pie. No charges were raised against either Tess or Po under the circumstances, and – again off the record – they were congratulated for their exemplary work.

On a rare visit back to her old stomping ground at the Cumberland County Sheriff's Office, Tess received a slow clap from her past colleagues. It was even suggested that she'd been missed and would be welcomed back to duty at a heartbeat. 'No thanks,' she'd told them. 'I have a new job.'

And that was her reason for visiting Emma Clancy's office now.

'Hi. Take a seat.' Emma offered a comfortable chair across the desk from her.

The first time she'd been in Clancy's presence, seated across from her in her office, Tess had been ashamed of her scars and the wrong impression they might present. Now she didn't care a bit, and actually sat with her hands in her lap, the right cupped in the left with her scar proudly displayed. Emma Clancy had her own scars now, though she'd made an attempt at covering those still visible on her face and hands with makeup. Tess felt she should encourage the woman to wear her survivor scars as badges of honour, but it was too soon for Emma to accept that distinction. For now they'd remain reminders of the horrifying ordeal she'd gone through. Guiltily, Tess thought it might be for the best. It helped her when it came to negotiating the terms of her employment. Emma must feel that she owed Tess more than a career, and probably her life. But to be fair, Tess owed Emma as much. It was Emma who'd pushed the Uzi into Tess's hand when Welshy had them cornered and at his mercy, of which he had none, and it was Emma who'd put a bullet in the brain of Hector Suarez when he'd launched himself at her and Po. Injured as he was from their previous clash of blades, Po might have stopped him, or he might not, so Tess felt she owed Emma his life too.

But this wasn't about who owed who.

It was about mutual respect, and there was plenty of that between both women now. Perhaps when she'd been seeking a trustworthy investigator, Alex had initially placed the suggestion in Emma's mind, but Tess had proved that the recommendation was solid.

'You've considered my offer?' Emma asked.

'I've given it a lot of thought.'

'But it's not to your satisfaction.' Emma looked crestfallen. It wasn't an image she was comfortable with, and she squirmed in her seat, forcing a smile of acceptance on her face. 'As you know, I'm trying to rebuild this agency's reputation and need people I can trust. I was hoping to engage your services on a permanent basis. Tess, if the terms don't suit your needs, tell me and we can renegotiate.'

'The terms are fine,' Tess said. In fact she was more than happy with the remuneration and benefits package she'd been offered to work for the newly promoted Emma's office – they exceeded her expectations in many respects. But she was uncomfortable about the job's official status, feeling it would hamstring her methods, forcing too much accountability on her. 'But I would prefer to be a free spirit.'

'You wish to remain self-employed?' Emma lit up. 'That isn't a problem, Tess. What exactly are you suggesting as an alternative?'

'That you employ me as a private consultant to your office.'

Emma jumped at the offer. 'I'll have Monica redraft the terms and . . . there's something wrong?'

'No. It's just that my services come as a dual package.'

'Sorry? Can you explain?'

'Po.'

'Nicolas Villere?'

'We've agreed to work together,' Tess said. 'But Po has a past that might come back to negatively influence the outcome of some cases. You know how criminal defence teams work; they look for anything that can throw doubt on the value of evidence. They could point out that Po's an unreliable witness, or has a personal agenda, considering that he was a convicted murderer.'

'There's nothing I can do to clear his name. After what he did for me, I would love to, but it's beyond my influence to have him pardoned, Tess.'

Tess chuckled. 'That's not what I'm asking. No. All I want

is an agreement that Po's involvement is kept off the books. He's my partner, but he must remain a *silent* partner.'

Emma grinned: she clearly understood that concept, although her relationship with Alex was now fully in the open since her divorce had been finalized. 'I'm sure that can be arranged. We can engage you, and leave the running of your private business to you. Who you employ – or don't for that matter – is down to you. But of course, I also understand what you're saying. The remuneration package must be large enough to accommodate both of you.'

Tess shrugged. 'That's about it.'

Emma thought a moment, but really there was no argument. She stood up, reached across the table, and offered her hand. 'Deal?'

Tess accepted her hand. She held on to Emma. 'There's one other thing.'

'Oh?'

'I can't start immediately. I need a fortnight's grace before starting.'

'Of course, take whatever time you need to set up,' said Emma. 'Just drop Monica a line and let her know the revised contract date.'

Beyond signing contracts there was little Tess needed to do to launch her consultancy business. The time she'd requested was for personal reasons.

'Po still has some healing to do,' she explained. He'd undergone surgery on the wound to his abdomen, with successful results, though she knew he was still pained by his injuries and might be for a while yet.

'Then he deserves some well-earned time off to recover, and a gentle hand to nurse him better.' She smiled and her officiousness slipped some more as she leaned forward conspiratorially. 'I trust you and Alex have that in common. I'm not sure I'd've recovered as quickly without him.'

Tess grinned, then squeezed Emma's hand.

'Glad to have you aboard, both of you,' Emma said, and with another smile, she sat back in her chair, shooing Tess away. 'Now go tell Po the good news, and give him a kiss from me, will you.'

Tess left the office and found Po waiting for her in the parking lot. He leaned one elbow on the open window of his Ford Mustang; he touched the gas pedal and the muscle car gave a throaty cough. 'Everything good?'

'Everything,' Tess said, and he offered a subtle nod.

'You still up for this?'

'How could I turn down a road trip?' Tess slid on to the passenger seat.

Her luggage was already packed in the trunk, alongside Po's. It was a long way to Louisiana, but they'd agreed to share the driving. Po had promised a different trip this time, and she was looking forward to sampling the delights of the Old French Quarter, the Garden District and Bourbon Street, of New Orleans. He wished to show her the city as her guide instead of her guard. Po had also suggested a tour of his old stomping ground in New Iberia. His enthusiasm for returning to his homeland had altered since first they met; it was reinvigorated, and not only to catch up with old friends like Pinky Leclerc. She knew there were *others* he wished to catch up with, and if it happened then so be it. Tess wondered if he still carried a blade pushed down his boot, but barely felt any aversion to the idea. Sometimes you just have to walk into the cave, she reminded herself. And if Po wanted to laugh in the faces of the Chatards, then she'd be right beside him, laughing just as hard.

She leaned across and bussed him on the cheek.

'That's from Clancy,' she said.

'I think I'm going to like our new boss,' he smiled.

'Well, before you grow too fond of her, don't forget who the *actual* boss is.' She kissed him long and hard on the mouth. 'That one's from me.'

Little outward emotion was writ on his face, but Po's eyes sparkled, expressing everything she needed to know.

'Let's do this,' Tess said breathlessly, and Po peeled out with a squeal of rubber.

THANKS

'd like to extend my eternal gratitude to Luigi Bonomi, Alison Bonomi, Samantha Bulos, Nicholas Blake, Lily Childs, Susan Harding and Denise Hilton, for all their valued help, guidance, and expert opinions, and to Kate Lyall Grant and Severn House Publishers for setting Tess and Po loose on the world. Thank you, one and all.